"YOU'RE HERE ABOU[...]

"Yes, I am," Nate repli[...] the same fate as Gene Rich[...] to come here and investigate the matter."

"Whatever that boy suffered from, he doesn't deserve to be part of some *X-Files* freak show—"

"Dr. Thurlow," Nate said.

"I've heard enough tripe about spontaneous human combustion—"

"*Dr. Thurlow!*"

"What?"

"Did you hear those words pass my lips? Do you think the CDC is busy investigating claims of the paranormal?" Nate asked. "What we have here is a demonstrable pattern of events that points toward something much more real, immediate, and dangerous. You did the autopsy, correct?"

Thurlow nodded.

"Shall I tell you what you found? Combustion so complete that it interferes with DNA analysis. Involvement of 100% of the body's soft tissue including the bone marrow. No sign of chemical contamination or accelerants. The path of damage is reversed. The most complete damage is within the core of the body. You've run every possible chemical analysis, but there's nothing to find."

The doctor shook his head. "It was as if his core body temperature increased two thousand degrees in a second or two."

"We have fifteen cases with exactly the same signs. . . ."

Be sure to read all of Steven Krane's
acclaimed novels from DAW:

STRANGER INSIDE
THE OMEGA GAME
TEEK

STRANGER INSIDE

STEVEN KRANE

DAW BOOKS, INC.
DONALD A. WOLLHEIM, FOUNDER
375 Hudson Street, New York, NY 10014
ELIZABETH R. WOLLHEIM
SHEILA E. GILBERT
PUBLISHERS
www.dawbooks.com

First Printing, February 2003
1   2   3   4   5   6   7   8   9

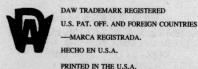

DAW TRADEMARK REGISTERED

U.S. PAT. OFF. AND FOREIGN COUNTRIES

—MARCA REGISTRADA.

HECHO EN U.S.A.

PRINTED IN THE U.S.A.

This book is dedicated to Anthony Peck, the first in a long line of people without whose inspiration this would never have been written.

1

JIMMY didn't know how the fight started.

He'd been standing in front of his locker and he remembered watching that asshole Frank Bradley pass by. In Jimmy's mind there was an abrupt cut from that directly to the sound of his skull hitting the locker. He didn't have time to shake the painful ringing out of his ears before he felt Frank's fist slamming into his gut.

Frank must be having a bad day.

Jimmy felt his back slam into the locker behind him. Copper breath blew from his puffed cheeks as Frank punched his side, above the kidney. Frank's other hand pressed against Jimmy's face, holding him back and obstructing his vision. Frank's hand smelled of sweat and grease.

Jimmy heard a crowd around them, though he could only catch glimpses of the semicircle of students. None of the faces were familiar, though Jimmy wondered exactly who he was looking for. He'd only been here two months—

Another jab in the region of his kidney brought the thought to an abrupt end.

He brought his arms in close to fend off Frank's fist, which kept pounding. Frank didn't seem to notice or care.

Frank was throwing wild punches, with little attention to where he connected.

Fuck, Jimmy thought. *The bastard isn't going to let up this time.*

In desperation, Jimmy brought his foot down, heel first, as hard as he could along the inside of Frank's leg. The hand over his face dropped away as Frank stumbled slightly. Frank's fist still connected for a fourth—or was it a fifth?—time, but the momentum was gone. It bounced off of Jimmy's shoulder.

Jimmy didn't stop to reason out what he was doing; he just launched himself at Frank. Frank wasn't any older than Jimmy, but he was a hell of a lot bigger. Fifty pounds heavier and about four inches taller. None of it was fat.

Fortunately for Jimmy, Frank was off-balance. All his weight was on the near leg, the one that Jimmy hadn't stomped. So, when Jimmy's shoulder hit Frank's solar plexus, the bigger kid toppled backward into the ring of students surrounding them. Out of his peripheral vision, Jimmy saw a couple of kids fall on their asses.

Jimmy knew that he was going to be seriously stomped when Frank got his breath back. He had to stop this fight now.

He balled up his fist and did the only thing he could to keep Frank down. He punched the bastard as hard as he could, in the groin.

Frank howled.

Jimmy scrambled away, tried to stand up, and fell back into the lockers, sliding down to land on his ass.

His face felt wet. He reached up to his cheek, afraid that he might have been crying in front of everyone. He was somewhat surprised when his hand came away covered with blood.

He stared at the slick redness on his hand in bewildered fascination. Frank was doubled over and throwing up, and the circle of spectators was backing away from both of them.

I'm bleeding, Jimmy thought, *how the hell did that happen?*

"The new kid . . ." Jimmy heard someone whisper. They meant him. ". . . he did time in prison. Bit someone's ear off."

Fucking moron, that was Mike Tyson. Besides, Juvenile Hall shouldn't count if no one ever pressed any charges.

"Did you see him go after Frank like that?" Someone else, a girl, out of Jimmy's immediate line of sight.

". . . out of control . . ."

Jimmy shook his head and kept staring at his bloody hand. Frank had jumped him. That's how it happened.

Frank's vomit gave off an acid reek.

Frank had grabbed him and shoved him into the locker. Frank had ground his hand into Jimmy's face. Frank had started it.

". . . nut case . . ."

Why am I bleeding?

"What the *hell* is going on here?" Jimmy heard the voice of a teacher over the sounds of the milling crowd. Coach Miller by the sound of it. The guy was five feet of sour gristle, and everyone called him "Miller Lite" behind his back. Everyone except the football team, and the wrestling team . . .

Frank, of course, was on both.

Jimmy, of course, was not.

Miller pushed and cursed his way through the surrounding students, opening a way for himself and a squad of hall monitors.

When he made his way to the center of the circle, he stopped cursing. His normally swarthy complexion had turned the color of bread dough. His lips pressed so hard together that Jimmy thought it looked as if his jaw might crack.

Jimmy imagined that he found it upsetting, seeing Frank, their first-string quarterback, clutching himself and lying in a pool of vomit.

"What. Happened. Here?" Coach Miller's voice was as sharp and as hard as a guillotine blade.

"H–he—" Jimmy began.

"No." Miller snapped, chopping the unspoken words out of the air. He jabbed a finger at someone in the crowd. The blond freshman Miller singled out winced as if impaled. "You."

"S–sir?"

"What. Happened."

"It was a fight."

"Thank you, Mr. Genius." Miller snarled. He whipped around to target another unfortunate witness. "You," he said to a black senior who had been trying to look cool and uninvolved.

"It's like he said something and he just wigged out."

"Who 'wigged out'?" Miller said, the voice a few degrees colder.

Jimmy closed his eyes because he didn't want to see who the black kid pointed to.

If Frank started this, why don't I remember?

"Get up," said Coach Miller. "Both of you get up *now*."

Jimmy opened his eyes. He could feel his heart racing now, something he hadn't even noticed during the fight. The blood dripping from his head felt cold when it landed on his arms. He felt dizzy and short of breath, but somehow he made it to his feet.

"No, you don't," Coach Miller yelled over the crowd at someone Jimmy couldn't see. There were now several hall monitors and one of the high school's security guards on the scene. From somewhere came the crackle of dialogue on a walkie-talkie.

The security guard, unlike the hall monitors, wore a uniform. Jimmy didn't know the guy's name. The students called him "Spam," and Jimmy didn't know if it was for the guy's greasy complexion, or if it was a dig at him not being quite a pork product. Probably the latter, since the more smart-assed of the student body took to singing the theme from *COPS* when he passed in the halls.

Even now, with his chest tightening from fear and his head spinning with the confusion of what had just happened, the theme ran through Jimmy's head . . .

Bad boys, bad boys, whacha going do . . .

In spite of his disorientation, or perhaps because of it, the sight of the ruddy-faced security guard poured into a uniform a size too small almost made Jimmy burst out laughing.

The amusement wasn't mutual.

"Everyone in this room," Spam called out. "I want every student in the sound of my voice in this classroom now!"

Jimmy took a step forward, but Spam held up a sweaty hand with little sausage fingers. He shook his head no—and Jimmy stifled a giggle because the guy's neck tried to remain stationary when his head moved. Jimmy fell back against the locker, relieved.

His classmates filed past him, into the empty classroom Spam had indicated. Every single one of them seemed to stop a moment to stare at Jimmy.

Spam took charge. "You two," he indicated two of the group of hall monitors and pointed up and down the hall with the antenna of his walkie-talkie. "Keep people out of here. We got blood and puke all over the place, and I don't want anyone through here before it's cleaned up." He pointed to a third hall monitor. "Go in that class and get everyone's ID. If someone don't got it, get their name and have the office call their folks. I want a confirmed list of every witness to this mess." He looked into Jimmy's eyes. "And someone get the goddamn nurse down here."

The gloves made it sink in.

The hall monitors had put on latex gloves before they would touch him. They held his upper arms, half to steady him, half to restrain him. The custodians who came to clean the mess wore long green rubber aprons and heavy rubber gloves that reached to their elbows. Even the nurse, when she washed Jimmy's scalp, wore a mask and latex gloves.

It was as if the hallway had suddenly become a plague zone.

Jimmy knew he was in deep shit. He was just now realizing how deep. Once the disorientation and confusion ebbed what was left was a fatalistic view of his future. A quadriplegic on the railroad tracks.

Anyone else, it would be less stark. If it wasn't Jimmy. If it wasn't Frank . . .

Jimmy had no illusions. The faculty here didn't love him, and the administration loved him even less. A foster kid, bad enough. A foster kid from the city, with a history of "problems." That was the kiss of death as far as any benefit of the doubt went.

Never mind if the "problems" weren't Jimmy's doing. If someone got in his face, he got in their face right back. If you took shit from *anyone,* it was painting a target on your face saying, "Kick this."

Jimmy had been in dozens of fights.

This was the first one *here.*

Jimmy had thought things had changed. He had told everyone that things had changed. They hadn't.

The vice principal, a cadaverous man with eyes the color of dirty, half-melted snow and the unfortunate name of Cummings, came down to the north wing about twenty minutes after the incident. Jimmy saw him talk to Coach Miller and Spam. Cummings nodded and looked grave—which didn't say much because the man only had one expression.

Vice Principal Cummings stayed well outside the plague zone and waited while the nurse cleaned Jimmy off. When the blood was mostly gone, Spam put a latex-covered hand on Jimmy's shoulder and maneuvered him toward the vice principal.

"What happened here, son?" Cummings asked. His voice was less obviously stressed than either Spam's or Coach Miller's. That seemed to have more to do with a lack of any emotion than any potential sympathy.

How the hell do I answer that? I don't remember what happened.

"Frank said something. The next thing I know he was shoving my face in a locker."

Cummings nodded and looked grave. "Is that what happened?"

"Yes." It took every ounce of control Jimmy had to keep the uncertainty out of his voice.

Again the eternal grave nod. "Things would go better if you tell me the whole story."

Jimmy spread his hands. He tried to say something, but

the words got all tangled up in his throat and all that came out was a choking stutter.

Cummings' expression didn't change when he said, "I should advise you that this school has a zero tolerance policy. The police have been called. The officers will take you both home and take your statements in the presence of your pare—guardians."

Cummings was such a cold SOB that for a few moments Jimmy thought he made the slip on purpose. But when he saw him walk away and talk to Frank he decided that Cummings was the kind of guy who couldn't take pleasure in anything, even rubbing Jimmy's nose in his family's history.

Jimmy's current family consisted of a couple in their fifties, the Carswells. They lived in a neighborhood that wasn't quite upper class. As foster parents, they were better than most, but, to Jimmy, it seemed that they had taken him on to patch a hole in their lives that was long past patching.

The Carswells lived in a split-level that had been built in the mid-sixties, and their house was filled with furnishings out of the mid-seventies. Above a gas fireplace, on a false brick wall in a room otherwise covered in aging paneling, there were pictures of dozens—and to Jimmy it sometimes seemed like hundreds—of kids. There were eight-by-ten glossies in dull silver frames, yellowing Polaroids held up by Scotch tape, graduation pictures in their original cardboard frames. None of them were the Carswells' own children. They didn't have any.

Ma and Pa Carswell were kind enough, but their words often felt so smooth and well worn that Jimmy couldn't sense any sincerity behind them. Their hopes for him, their desire to see him do well in school, even their concern about

his nightmares, all had the warmth and depth of a semiconscious reflex.

He wondered how many kids ever got driven home to
chez Carswell in the back of a squad car.

His uniformed escort was named Chuck, and kept trying
to engage him in conversation. "That was a nasty knock you
took.

"I saw the other guy, he was twice your size.

"You know, I understand the crap they can dish out in
high school . . ."

Jimmy kept his responses just the polite side of ignoring
the guy completely. He knew better than to believe that the
cop was his friend. It was a cop trick, trying to gain your
trust so they could stick it to you. Jimmy had got burned before that way—

When they pulled around the circle in front of the Carswells' house, Jimmy hadn't spoken more than five words to
the guy.

He wondered what Frank Bradley was going through at
this moment. Was his dad threatening, or saying "attaboy?"
Was Mrs. Bradley hysterical over her boy being brought
home by the police, or did she refuse to believe that such a
thing could involve her little angel? Jimmy had never met
Frank's mother, nor did he ever have the pleasure of knowing his own, but somehow he could imagine perfectly the
words coming from her lips. "No, Officer, there must be
some mistake."

This was the first time he had ever been in any trouble on
the Carswells' watch, but Jimmy knew that he wasn't going
to see that kind of reaction from his current disposable parents.

The school had called the Carswells ahead of time, so
both Mr. and Mrs. were waiting by the front door as the of-

ficer let Jimmy out of the rear of the patrol car. He wondered if Mr. Carswell appreciated getting out of work early.

Then he wondered what it was Mr. Carswell did for a living.

Mr. Carswell was shaking his head, as if having some deep-seated suspicion confirmed. Mrs. Carswell walked up to him and looked into his eyes, as if searching for something he'd left at school. "Are you all right?"

What a stupid question.

"I'm okay."

"What happened?" The question was directed at the cop, not to him. At least she wasn't wearing latex gloves.

"Fight at school, madam. Him and another kid got pretty busted up. With your permission, I need to take a statement from him." The cop nodded toward Jimmy.

Mrs. Carswell looked into his eyes again, and not finding what she was looking for, looked back at the cop. "Of course."

Jimmy found himself willing the Carswells to show some anger. He wanted them to be mad. No, he wanted them to be furious. He wanted them to threaten him, to scream at the cop. He wanted red faces and burst blood vessels. He wanted swearing and stomping. Anything besides this bizarre detachment, as if he was just a jug of milk that went bad in the fridge.

The Carswells led the cop, and the cop led him, into the living room where they all sat down. His guardians sat, impassive and watching, as the cop deconstructed his story.

"You said Frank Bradley was walking past you and you exchanged words."

"Uh-huh."

"What words were those?"

"I don't know, I don't remember." Jimmy stuttered and

felt his throat closing up. His palms were slick on his jeans, and when he looked down at his thighs, he almost expected to be bleeding again.

Just sweat.

"The next thing you know he was pushing you into a locker."

Jimmy nodded, still looking at his jeans. There were still spots of blood on them.

"Just before that, what did you say to him?"

"I don't know." The words hurt his throat.

"Why did he slam you into the locker?"

"I don't know."

"Have you had any problems with Frank Bradley before this?"

"I told you what happened!" Jimmy pounded his fists into his thighs in frustration. The silence his protest left in the living room made him realize, slowly, how loud he had spoken. He looked up and finally saw an emotion in Mrs. Carswell's face . . .

Fear.

Jimmy ran from the darkness with the slow deliberation that only happens in dreams. He ran naked through the halls of Euclid Heights High School, in one part of his mind knowing that this was a nightmare, in another part convinced that the danger was real. His feet slipped on the linoleum floors, sliding on a slick of his own blood.

He bled from wounds that peppered his body, his flesh torn by something invisible that was trying to eat its way inside of him, the Thing that lived in the ink-black shadow that followed him.

He couldn't turn around to face it, because it always stayed behind him, approaching from a direction Jimmy couldn't point to. He couldn't see the Thing, but he could feel it. It was a rasping on the back of his neck, a sick twisting inside his inner ear, a liquid whisper, the feeling of something reaching for him and not quite grasping hold.

The Thing wanted Jimmy. Wanted him with a dark lust that transcended Jimmy's wounded flesh. What the Thing wanted was worse than pain, worse than rape, worse than death, worse than anything that Jimmy had ever had the power to imagine.

Running, he slipped in his blood again and fell into a locker. His face smashed into the metal with more force than Frank could ever manage. He could feel the bones of his skull give way as the Thing grabbed for him again.

He could almost feel its grasp inside his brain.

Jimmy sat bolt upright, the sheets clinging to his naked chest, and he sucked in breath after breath. His upper body trembled as a deep chill set his muscles on autopilot. For several long minutes Jimmy had to will the muscles in his arms, jaw, and shoulder to stop trembling.

He could still feel the fear, and he was angry at himself for it. *I am not a wuss,* he told himself over and over. *I am not scared of no fucking boogeyman. I'm seventeen years old. People have waved guns at me without making me piss on myself.*

Still, his heart raced, breath came fast and heavy, and his shoulders kept trembling under slick palms.

After several minutes of muttering to himself and rocking back and forth he calmed down enough to realize the Thing's final gift to him.

"Oh, fuck me." Jimmy spoke slowly as he realized that he remembered how the fight with Frank Bradley had gone.

Frank's having a bad day, yeah. Needs to take the new

kid down a peg to feel better about himself. Jimmy barely notices him, at first.

It's the laughing that gets his attention. God knows why, but he turns away from his locker, half full backpack in his hand. "What's so funny?" Jimmy asks.

Frank elbows his fellow jock in the ribs. "It's a joke, pip-squeak, none of your fucking business."

Jimmy steps forward. "Must be pretty funny."

"You want to hear it?" Frank says. "Okay. Define mass confusion."

Jimmy doesn't say anything.

Frank's jock friend edges away from him after looking at Jimmy's expression.

Frank goes on, oblivious. "It's called Father's Day at Jimmy's house."

Students surround them, talking away, unaware until Jimmy speaks that anything is wrong. But what Jimmy says leaves the halls silent except for Frank's dumbfounded question. "What did you say?"

"I said," Jimmy speaks, hefting his backpack. "Take that back you dickless, pea-brained, steroid-sniffing sorry excuse for a left testicle."

"You want me to fuck you up?"

"You know, Frank, it's probably best if you keep fucking the rest of the football team—when you're not giving them nickel blow jobs."

Frank might have laughed it off if they'd been alone. He can't do that here. Somewhere, back in the circle of students that already is forming around them, someone sniggers.

"I don't need to take that from no pansy-ass special-ed kid."

"No," Jimmy says. "I bet you like your asses big and manly."

"You little shit—" Frank preps to take a swing at Jimmy. Jimmy preempts it. He swings the backpack, half full of text-books, and clobbers Frank in the side of the head with it.

"Shit," Jimmy whispered to himself. It *was* him. He had lost control and laid into Frank first. No wonder the witnesses said he just went nuts.

He had.

2

CLAYBORN'S Diner was a small out-of-the-way place off a badly-paved state road, about four miles north of a tiny Pennsylvania coal-mining town called Creighton Falls. The exterior was neon and milky chrome. The inside was linoleum and red vinyl around the counter in front, and the back was an anachronistic addition of dark paneling and ceiling fans. Half a dozen booths clustered around the edges of the room while the center portion was taken up by a pair of pool tables. The windowless walls of the rear room were decorated by framed black-and-white photographs spanning the last century and a quarter. The pictures that weren't of the local farms and surrounding countryside were portraits of police and firemen.

Nathan Adriano sat to one side of a large corner booth that lived under a triptych of prohibition-era pictures, pride of place given to a signed picture of Elliot Ness.

"So, Benny, why'd you give up on Pittsburgh?" The speaker was Kevin Stickling, a deputy sheriff for Abooksigun County. He was sandy-haired and a class of thin that stopped just short of making onlookers worry about his health. He was addressing Nate, who had introduced himself as Benny Jacobs, an ex-paramedic from Pittsburgh.

"The city just got to me," Nate said, taking a pull on his beer. "The last straw was having my car stolen twice."

There were a few appreciative chuckles from around the table.

"Twice," Nate continued, with the aid of a dramatic pause, "from the same lot, three months apart."

"God's telling you *something*," said Greg, another deputy. He was older than Kevin, shadows darkening the hollows of his face. Gray stubble showing on the edge of his jaw where the light hit it.

"Yeah," Kevin said, "like, 'Don't park there.' "

"You see," said the last deputy, a guy named Tony, the best looking and smartest of the trio of lawmen. "That's why I don't work in the city anymore." He pulled his own beer over and looked in the suds. "So much crap like that, you don't have the time to deal with it."

"I know," Nate said. "Since they didn't catch the guy red-handed, I was pretty much S.O.L."

"Collect the insurance and move on," Kevin said, "best you can do."

Nate gave them his most ironic chuckle. "That worked the first time. But my rates got jacked so high that the second time around I only had liability."

"Ouch," Kevin said.

"So what're you doing now?" Tony asked.

Nate shrugged. "Looking for work. Unfortunately, it's kind of hard finding openings where I *want* to work."

Tony nodded in sympathy. "When I decided to move out of the city, it took me three years to find this job. Trust me, though, it's worth it."

"I keep telling myself that," Nate said. "I guess I'm lucky," he nodded at Tony's left hand. "No wife, no kids. When I made my decision, I just typed up a résumé, gave notice, and tossed a suitcase in car number three—" Nate paused.

That was a slip.

There was a chance that one of these guys might have noticed Nate's rental car out front. It was too new for the story he was spinning, and the tags were from the wrong county.

Fortunately, none of them seemed to make the connection.

Nate quickly came up with a background story to hold in reserve, about Benny's number three junker having major mechanical problems on the Pennsylvania Turnpike and the sweet little loaner they gave him as they replaced three out of four brake drums.

Tony didn't notice Nate's internal regrouping. He had set down his drink and was twisting the ring on his left hand. "Yeah, makes it easier, doesn't it?"

There were semi-warning glances from the other two deputies. Nate actually was grateful for the obvious discomfort his random comment generated. It didn't matter if Tony was divorced, widowed, or deeply into an unhappy marriage, it gave Nate a fulcrum on which he could lever the conversation.

Nate took a deep swig of his beer and orchestrated his change in subject with calculated awkwardness. "What I miss, though—" Nate said, "is people to talk to about it all. I mean, it's not a job you can talk much about in mixed company."

"Yeah?" Greg said, seeming anxious to move away from the subject of wives and children.

"Doctors don't have anything on us when it comes to bizarre bullshit happening." Nate made a show of chuckling to himself, "Well, the week before I left there was this one call—"

"Do tell," Kevin said.

"Okay," Nate said, "Remember, *you* asked me." He looked at the other two deputies. Satisfied that there was a glimmering of curiosity in their eyes, he said, "Now you all remember your mother saying, 'Don't make a face like that, it might get stuck that way'?"

They nodded at Nate. He knew he had them hooked.

Nate continued, setting down his beer. "I'm sure that you've heard about guys who get drunk and do something stupid like putting a cue ball in their mouth?" Nate reached up and tapped the back of his teeth with a finger. "The curvature of your teeth and jaw means that, when we're talking relatively round objects, you can stick a larger object *in* than you can pull *out*." Nate laughed and shook his head, taking a pull on his beer. "You have to think of the most embarrassing and repulsive consequence of that fact."

Nate let them think for a moment.

"Now there's this 911 call my last week. Someone calls and leaves the phone off the hook. The dispatcher tries to get information but there isn't anything but the sound of some sort of commotion, and someone panting. Everyone hates those kind of calls, because you have no clue. Could be some old guy keeled over in the can with a broken hip, could be some freak on PCP waving a machete, could be some six year old's idea of a joke . . ."

"Always bad when you don't know what you're walking into." Tony said. He'd stopped fondling his ring.

"So they send a squad, and about five minutes later they call for an ambulance—no details, they just sent for an ambulance."

"Christ," Kevin said.

Nate nodded. "You imagine all sorts of crap when that happens. Now, I've seen some sick shit, but I did *not* imagine what was actually waiting at the end of that call." He leaned back and looked over all of them. "We have a suburban ranch house, and it's about ten at night. Lights are on in the place, but every curtain is drawn. There's this huge picture window, and you can't see inside because of the drapes. There's a BMW with a baby seat sitting in the driveway, and the patrol car is sitting next to it."

"You didn't see the guys who responded to the call?" Greg asked.

Nate shook his head, "And you can imagine what's going through our minds when we get out. I mean, I've got friends who've been shot at. One guy trying to take care of the wife at a domestic got hit by a chair when the husband got loose—"

"So this was a domestic?" Kevin asked.

"No, and we didn't have any officers down." Nate took a pull on his beer. "Now the front door was locked and deadbolted, but one of the cops must've heard us because someone shouted, 'Back here,' from the rear of the house." Nate took a dramatic pause. "That's when the dog started barking. Now this ain't no chihuahua bark. This is a great big 'fuck-you' bark."

Tony was shaking his head. "I do not like big dogs on a call."

Nate nodded. "It scared the shit out of me. I'm thinking some monster dog mauled someone. I'm thinking that one of us is going to be next."

"So you go around back?" Kevin said.

"There's a gate hanging open next to the garage. We walk down this gravel path while this dog is going nuts with the barking. I'm sweating cause I don't know what the hell I'm going to do if the guy I'm here for is hemorrhaging or something and has this attack dog hovering over him. I mean, if the guy needs immediate assistance—" Nate shook his head.

"That's a bad situation," Tony said.

"Yeah, I mean, walking down that path I'm imagining all sorts of nightmare scenarios. I heard about one guy, devoted to his dog, he falls down the stairs and cracks his neck. The medics have to get to him or the poor bastard's going to die, but the dog won't let them. It thinks it's protecting him— Cops have had to shoot animals in that situation. I didn't want to see that."

"So, you go around back," Kevin prompted.

"So, I go around back. We have this backyard surrounded by a seven-foot privacy fence. I see a water dish the size of a manhole cover. There's an expensive looking kid's play set in the back. And there are two cops standing in the light from a set of French doors. They don't look particularly worried, but they don't even look in our direction. They just have half-shocked, half-amused expressions on their faces. The dog, which must be in the house, is barking a blue streak, and occasionally giving one of these nasty, low-throated growls, but the cops are just shaking their heads."

"So what's the call?" Kevin asked.

"They wave us over, the one guy saying, 'You won't believe this.' We go over next to the cops and look in the French doors."

"And?" Kevin prodded.

"The dog's going nuts barking at us. It's this fucking huge Great Dane, head's about even with my chest, it seems. He's barking and, drooling, and growling, and baring his teeth. And, well, I can't blame him, he had good reason to." Nate sipped his beer.

"Yeah?" Kevin was shaking his head, waiting for the punch line.

"The dog's owner—a nice respectable banker type. Wife and kid off somewhere. He was alone and, apparently, had more than his share of sick little fantasies he was aching to try when his family was away."

"Oh, Christ," Kevin said, "You don't mean—"

Nate nodded, "The reason this dog was going apeshit, in my opinion, wasn't that he had four of us gawking at him. The boy was upset because he had about two hundred fifty pounds of naked banking executive locked onto his dick."

Chorus of groans.

Nate sipped his beer and knew that, for the evening, he was a member of the fraternity. At least paramedic Benny Jacobs was. Nate described the call to animal control, and about tranquilizing the dog. To add to Benny's bona fides, Nate elaborated on various medical details about the exec's broken jaw and canine anatomy.

When Nate was done, there was a long pause. Then Kevin shook his head, said, "Wow," and drained his beer. Tony looked a little thoughtful. "So what happened to that guy?"

Nate shrugged. "I didn't follow it past the morning DJ shows. I think the city pressed animal cruelty charges against him, but I don't know what came of that."

"Was the dog all right?" Greg asked.

"Full recovery," Nate nodded. "No thanks to his owner."

"Well," Kevin said, after finishing his beer, "I don't have anything quite that perverted, but there's this one idiot I pulled over once—"

"Do tell," Nate said.

It was two hours and three rounds later when the subject of the war stories had turned from the stupid to the morbid. Nate regaled the cops with the obligatory "strange smell" story. Like the Great Dane tale, Nate had stolen it from a

small paramedic listserv that, since Nate wasn't a paramedic, he shouldn't have been able to subscribe to. Like
many other such restrictions, Nate had found it easy to slip
his way around it. The fact his stories hadn't yet graduated
to the rank of urban legend helped the verisimilitude of
Nate's current alter ego.

And that alter ego, after a few hours of effort, bore the
fruit Nate was searching for.

"Well," Kevin said. "This is one place I think we got the
city boy beat." He turned to Greg and said, "You want to tell
him about our body? You found it."

Greg looked down into his beer. "I didn't find him. I was
just the first to respond to the call." He looked up at Nate.
"Have you heard about Ted Mackenzie?"

"No," Nate lied effortlessly.

3

"YOU all better buy me another round, because I'm going to need it," Greg finished off his beer. "I want J.D. straight."

He turned back toward Nate. "You got to know, from your work, that it's a sorry day when a kid dies. This one has got to be the sorriest of them all."

Greg had known Ted Mackenzie. It was that kind of town, small enough so that local law enforcement knew every resident teenager at least by reputation. Ted was quiet, bookish, and Greg would most often see him walking the short path between the school and the library. Lanky kid with incredibly intelligent eyes. He saw a lot more, Greg thought, than most other kids his age. He unquestionably *knew* more. He'd been bumped through a couple of grades, and somehow avoided fights with his older classmates.

The thing was, as Ted got older, he got quieter. The last few months of his life, everyone was concerned. A normally quiet kid, he was now almost mute. Normally bookish, he now seemed to spend most all his time with the printed page. If you waved at him, or said, "Hi," you were lucky to be acknowledged. Ask him a direct question, you'd get a "yes" or "no" answer.

Greg, the teachers, his pastor, his parents, everyone knew that these were warning signs. But no one was sure what they warned. There was no sign of Ted damaging himself, threatening himself or others, and there were no signs of anyone hurting Ted. So there was little anyone could do. Everyone involved had the same conversation with him, "If there're any problems, *anything,* we're here for you . . ."

Greg included.

Of course, getting normal teenagers to open up about their problems takes a degree in psychology and a lot more time than it turned out Ted had.

When Greg got the call, he had no idea it had anything to do with Ted. It was late at night and he got a call about an explosion at a radio tower about ten miles north of Creighton Falls. Greg BS'ed with the dispatcher for the fifteen minutes it took him to drive down there. It was a clear night, with a full moon, and Greg had the windows down to let the odor of the autumn mulch roll in from the hill-wrinkled countryside around him.

"What I got on the call is a white flash—"

"Uh-huh, you said *explosion.*"

"No, *I* didn't. Mr. Howard Perkins said 'explosion.' I'm just telling you what got called in."

"You think he was drinking at all?"

"Do you want the details or not?"

"Go ahead."

"Mr. Howard Perkins was asleep on his porch when this flash woke him up—"

"Yeah, you're sure he wasn't asleep when he called you?"

"Greg—"

"He *is* eighty years old."

"—the flash woke him up. White, no sound. It was centered on the old radio tower."

"Yeah," Greg looked around. The environment wasn't dry enough around here for brushfires to be a common occurrence, yet it was a worry. "Did he say anything about smoke or flames?"

"No, but I alerted the station house, just in case."

Greg nodded, though they both knew that if there *was* a major brushfire it would be beyond the capabilities of the local volunteer department.

"It was probably a freak lighting flash, Greg."

"More likely, it's Howie's cataracts acting up."

Greg turned the patrol car up a gravel pathway that led to the radio tower. The tower itself belonged to a local radio station that didn't exist anymore. It had vanished, leaving bullshit talk show feeds from New York.

Nowadays, Greg had to listen to Garth and Hank on an old tape deck he kept on the passenger seat when he was out patrolling. Right now the tape deck was playing "Boot-scoot Boogie," but he'd turned down the sound to take the call and it was now at a low volume that was at odds with the song. Greg could hear the gravel crunching under the tires even with it playing.

He turned the car around the first switchback up the hill and lost sight of the main road behind the trees. The wind through the open windows seemed to drop the temperature ten degrees and he felt very much alone.

"You still there?" he called on the radio.

"Coming through loud and clear."

Greg didn't realize exactly how much he had tensed until he felt the relief at hearing the dispatcher. Of course, he wasn't going to lose contact; the tower was dead, so there wasn't any interference, and he was driving up toward the best site for radio reception in the whole county.

"Anyone else call in about this?" Greg said, to disguise his unease. "Fire, smoke, strange lights?"

"Nah, been quiet. This was only the second call all night."

"What was the other call?"

"The Mackenzie kid, out past curfew. His mom got worried and called us."

"Richard?" Greg asked, thinking of the older brother.

"No, Ted."

"Ted? That's not like him."

"That's why his mom's worried. Don't worry, I got Kevin driving around looking. He'll scare him up."

"Uh-huh." Greg negotiated another pair of switchbacks. If he stuck his head out of the driver's side and looked up, he could make out the silhouette of the radio tower. The beacons were still flashing for low-flying aircraft.

Most of them . . .

"Hey," Greg said over the radio. "Howie may not be hallucinating. Looking up, I think I see one of the lights out on the tower."

"Maybe he saw one of the lights burning out."

Greg nodded and pulled his head back into the vehicle. "That's what I was thinking. I'm still going to check it out, if something damaged the tower—it's hovering over a busy stretch of road."

"Okay—" Pause. "I got Kevin, you want an update?"

"That's all right. I'll radio in once I see what's going on up here." Greg hung up the mike and pulled the patrol car to a stop in front of the gate to the property.

The tower was surrounded by a fifteen-foot-high chain-link fence topped by a quarter circle of barbed wire arcing over potential intruders. The gate was locked and emblazoned with "No Trespassing" and "Private Property" signs. The gate was held shut by a heavy-duty padlock and chain. Greg was about to start hunting for the key box that code specified should be here for emergency personnel, when he looked more closely at the gate.

The lower left corner of the gate, just within the beam of his headlights, had been cut and rolled back. The gap was wide enough to pass a human being.

Greg picked up the mike and tried to call in a B&E. There wasn't an answer. The dispatcher was either talking to Kevin or sitting on the john. He called in twice more and then said, "Fuck it," and grabbed his Mag-Lite.

If he had ever been a big-city cop like Tony, he probably wouldn't have gone out on his own. But this wasn't New York, and any backup was about twenty minutes away anyway. Everyone knew where he was, and the vandals around these parts weren't armed and dangerous.

He still released the snap on his holster as he got out of the patrol car.

Some teenagers probably thought this was a great place to drink and shoot off fireworks.

He walked up the gravel path to the gate and shone his Mag-Lite down at the scene of the break-in. The chain-link had been methodically snipped for about four feet up and three feet to the right. The cut was recent, and the severed steel wire glittered in the light, the near-chromed finish in stark contrast to the dull gray of the fence's weathered surface.

On the ground, next to the hole, rested a pair of heavy-duty wire cutters. *What the . . . ?*

Greg knelt next to the tool without touching it. As if to emphasize itself, the blades were dusted by tiny curls of metal shavings that glittered the same steel-chrome as the cut fence. *Not thieves, not vandals.* Neither would leave their tools behind like this. Either he was looking for someone incredibly stupid, or he was looking for someone who decided that they didn't care what evidence the police might find.

Oh, shit!

Greg ran back to the patrol car and started yelling into the radio, "Are you there—*answer me, damn it!*"

Greg was about to slam the mike down in disgust when the dispatcher answered, "Yes—"

"Ted Mackenzie, what did Kevin find out about Ted Mackenzie?"

"Come again?"

"The missing kid, Ted."

"Oh, nothing's turned up yet."

Greg dropped the mike, feeling something awful welling up in his stomach. He had known that Ted seemed to be working out some serious problems. He prayed to God that those problems weren't as serious as he had begun to think.

Greg ran back to the gate, while the radio cracked behind him. "What are you doing? Are you there, over?"

Greg bent down and pushed himself through the gap cut in the fence. He had to crawl on hands and knees, holding his flashlight by the shaft so that the gravel dug into the knuckles of his left hand.

Greg stood up on the other side of the gate and shone his flashlight down the path in front of him. There was still one more switchback in front of him before he'd be in sight of the tower's base.

For a moment he was afraid to move. His fear at what he'd find drove him through that gate, and now that same fear rooted him to the spot.

He did not want to find Ted's corpse. He did not want to see what a plunge from a five-hundred-foot tower would do to his body. Greg did not want to be the one to tell Ted's parents that their son had ended his own life.

You don't know, he told himself.

"I don't want to know," he answered himself.

The paralysis only lasted a moment, because worse than his fears was the possibility that Ted might have made the attempt, and might not have succeeded. In that case, there was going to be a desperate window where the kid would need first aid.

Greg ran around the corner of the switchback toward the tower. The flashlight picked out a rough pile of clothes once he rounded the corner, and the sight froze him so quickly that his momentum almost toppled him face-first into the gravel path.

The beam of his Mag-Lite shook as he pointed it at the ragged pile by the side of the road. He held his breath until he saw that the pile was just that. Clothes. Nothing else. No mangled body.

"What the?"

Greg walked a few steps closer and looked down. Nothing extraordinary, just jeans, a T-shirt, jockey shorts, socks, a pair of sneakers . . .

They could be Ted's clothes. But if they were, he had stripped completely naked. For a few short moments, Greg felt some relief. Well, of course he'd start acting odd if he fell in lust with some pretty young thing. After all, what was the most popular reason for breaking curfew?

The thought, while a happy one, did not hold back the dread for long. Greg shone the light up and down both sides of the path in front of the tower and there was no sign of any matching clothing from the other party to such a tryst. And that helped Greg's fear turn to sexual predators and other such monsters.

He slowly drew his revolver out and called, *"Ted! Ted Mackenzie!"*

No response. But Greg caught a whiff of something distant burning. He shone his light all around until he saw a footprint by the side of the road. He held his light on it, trying to make sense of it.

A bare foot, largish size, 11 or 12, had sunk into a muddy rut by the side of the road. The rut ran for about a dozen feet, and in that rut were half a dozen strides—and no other footprints.

An unhurried stride for a lanky teenager, showing no sign of pursuit. There was even one spot where his feet had left their imprint together, as if he'd stood still facing the tower. Greg halted next to the place where the barefoot person had stopped. He looked up where the barefoot person must have looked up.

The radio tower was directly in front of him, bisecting the sky. The blinded warning light was about three quarters up and was facing him. A lumpy shadow stood out in the superstructure about five feet above the burned out light. It didn't move.

"Shit."

Greg pointed his light up at the tower, but there wasn't any way the light could reach and allow him to make out any details.

He holstered his gun and ran to the base of the radio tower. Its four legs laid out a concrete square about thirty feet on a side. The pylon nearest him had a ladder bolted on the inside, leading up to a narrow cagelike tube.

Greg looked up and suddenly felt like the back of his throat was sliding down through the pit of his stomach, dragging most of his insides with it. He shook his head and aimed the light up into the framework of the tower. *"Ted?"*

There wasn't even an echo for an answer. Just a dead flat silence that sucked the moisture from his mouth.

There was no way he could see up, the body of the radio tower was backlit by the four super-bright halogen lamps that still worked. It was like trying to stare into someone's headlights and read their license plate.

He shone the Mag-Lite down at the base of the ladder and saw what he was afraid he would see. A half dozen muddy footprints marked the concrete by the base of the ladder.

Greg shoved the Mag-Lite into his belt and pulled on a pair of gloves.

I can do this, he told himself as he hauled himself up onto the ladder. The first ten feet wasn't a problem, the footing was solid, the treads of the ladder were flat and textured so his feet had good purchase.

Then he reached the cage.

In the daylight he might have felt different, but in the dark, with the ladder around him invisible except where the warning lights cut through the crazy erector-set shadows, the presence of metal surrounding him tightened the skin across his chest.

He knew he should feel safer; the cage around him would most likely prevent a fatal fall if he lost his grip. He couldn't convince his body. He pulled himself up rung after rung, and with each foot he gained, his pulse increased. When he had reached fifty feet, he was climbing with his eyes closed, sucking gasps of air though his mouth, and his palms were so damp inside his gloves that he felt they might slide out with each rung.

"Ted!" he called up at the invisible shadows. *"This is Deputy Greg Templeton. Don't move. I'm coming up to help*

you." It took a supreme effort of will to keep himself from gasping as he shouted.

Please, Lord God, Let us both live through this.

It felt as if the metal surrounding him had wrapped itself around his chest. He lost all sense of up or down, as if he had been cast into free fall. Each time he let one hand go to grip the next rung, panic tore into him. All he could think about was the terror of falling, and of the darkness.

"*Hold on!*" he shouted, face pressed so hard against the metal that he tasted rust. "*Don't panic. I'm going to get you through this.*"

Nothing but distant silence.

Greg kept moving, inch after inch, rung after rung. Two thoughts drove him on. The first was that Ted Mackenzie, or someone else who was seriously disturbed, had shed his clothes and climbed nearly to the top of the radio tower. If the warning light had exploded, or a freak lightning bolt struck the tower, the person needed help. He could be unconscious.

The second thing that drove him was the certainty that if he stopped moving, he would remain frozen there until morning.

Greg tasted rust on his tongue. His breath seared his mouth, blood throbbed in his ears. His skin slid inside his clothes on bearings of sweat.

And he smelled something burning.

It was a crusty ozone smell, slightly chemical, like an overheated transformer. Something had blown up. Howie hadn't been hallucinating.

Greg forced his eyes open. He was facing ahead, through a set of rungs in the ladder, and the only thing he saw was sky. His breath caught, and his grip slipped, slamming his back into the cage that enclosed him from behind. Greg stared wide-eyed at the stars in front of him, hyperventilating and barely feeling a pain that would leave four-foot-long vertical bruises across his back.

"Our Father. Who Art. In Heaven." Greg spoke between gasps. He reached up and felt for a rung he could barely see. His foot almost slipped out from under him as he pulled himself back upright.

Greg looked down. He could see the tree line, and the headlights of his patrol car picking out a slice of road no bigger than his thumb.

He pulled himself up one rung. Then another. He forced his gaze upward. There was a platform up there, near the burned out warning light. Something shadowed slumped on it, or above it.

He was almost to the blind light. The smell was stronger now, and it was clear that the light had exploded. The rungs crunched under his gloves, covered in a dust that had to be powdered glass.

He kept staring up, he could breathe better, focus on the person who was unmoving above him. He could almost see a human shape now that he had most of the light below him. It was still cut with incomprehensible shadows, but there was a head, possibly an outstretched arm.

The platform wrapped the tower just above the remains of the shattered light. The ladder fed through a hole in the floor of the platform, and Greg pulled himself through into an open space where the only barrier between him and the sky was a thigh-high abbreviated railing.

Greg stumbled carefully out onto the platform. His feet crunched on the metal grate that was the only thing between him and three hundred feet of nothing. He pulled out his Mag-Lite and switched it on. The first thing he saw was the grate he stood on, a dusty gray under his feet. The burned smell was nearly overpowering.

He turned slowly, trying to keep his balance. The wind picked up, and tiny motes danced in the shaking beam of the Mag-Lite. It was a bizarre sight, almost as if it was snowing.

Not snow.

A fine black-gray ash coated every surface around him. The wind blew it around him in swirls, covering his arms and jacket in it even before Greg had realized what it was.

Then he raised the beam to the tower itself, where a shadowed human form was cradled by a junction in two girders.

Deliver us from evil.

Ted's face was gone. Whatever holocaust had torn through Ted Mackenzie's body had left him without a face. Even the bones of the skull seemed caved in and shrunken, pitted and gray like the ash swirling around him.

The body had fallen from higher up, to curl in a fetal position at the junction of two girders about three feet above Greg's head. The twisted burned skull had been facing Greg, as if waiting.

The flesh of the body was black and cracking, pieces had already fallen away to reveal gray ash and bone underneath. Greg could see ribs and finger bones; a third of one hand was missing completely.

Greg tasted soot on his tongue. He gagged and dropped the Mag-Lite. He fell to his knees and between shuddering, retching gasps and through watering eyes, he saw his flashlight tumble the two hundred feet to the ground, bouncing off of girders and winking out as it struck the ground.

He stayed there for what seemed like hours.

"I was afraid," Greg said to Nate in a deathly quiet booth in Clayborn's Diner. He looked at the shot in his hand and downed it. "I was afraid that if I stood up, I might touch him."

Nate let the silence stretch to what he thought was a significant level. "So it was Ted?"

Greg nodded. "It took them a long time to come up with a positive ID. No one has come up with an explanation of what happened."

"You said the light exploded . . ." Nate said, only because they expected it of him.

Greg shook his head. "That's what I thought, but no. It overheated and shorted out. Anyway, Ted was burned all the way through. Nothing I've seen ever did that to a person, and I've seen guys run foul of high-tension lines."

Nate shook his head and looked at Kevin, "Well, you're right. That beats anything I've got."

4

"FORENSIC Data Associates, Nathan Adriano speaking." Nate barked into his cell phone as he hunched over his laptop computer. The shades on the motel room were drawn, so the only light in the room was dirty yellow sunlight that leaked in from outside.

"Nate, thank God, we need to go over your testimony in the Blankenship case."

"Tony?" Nate groaned.

The man on the phone, Anthony Gabriele, was a federal prosecutor who was in a small Minnesota college town that had the unenviable distinction of having been home to the largest child-porn server to ever have been placed on the Internet. They had hired Forensic Data Associates because no one there, not the police, not the lawyers, and certainly not Anthony Gabriele, had a clue what a server was. Tony barely knew what the Internet was. Tony was only on the case because it was high profile, and he had seniority in the region.

The upside; that Nate was getting hefty consulting fees for no-brainer work that basically amounted to explaining server logs and file sharing to a jury.

The downside; Tony really didn't understand his own

case, and needed way more reassurance and handholding than Nate had time to provide.

"Yes," Tony said, "I need to go over some things with you before you go on the stand."

"There's nothing to go over. The case is airtight."

"But—"

"Look, Tony, we've gone over my testimony. You have a transcript. If his lawyer lets it go to trial, the man's a moron. If you haven't convinced him to plead, I'll be back up there to help you with questions for jury selection—"

"Please, just a moment, then—"

Nate sighed.

Two billable hours later, Nate was off the phone.

He set down the cell phone and looked at the glowing screen. Before him, in notes, memos, and scraps of data, Theodore Mackenzie was taking form. Shaking off the call from his professional life, Nate returned to entering all the information he had gathered last night in Clayborn's Diner.

Nate stopped being CEO and sole employee of Forensic Data Associates, and returned to his effort to find out who Theodore Mackenzie was. Who he was, and what he had in common with fifteen other kids.

Ted had been fourteen years old. Bright, inquisitive, active in a host of school activities, a voracious reader, no serious illnesses—a relative was quoted in an article in the *Abooksigun County Dispatch,* that the boy was never sick a day in his life. All those facts were hits on the template Nate had spent the last five years developing. That, and a death by fire, had been enough for Nate to fly in from California to investigate things in person.

His interview with the cops last night confirmed it for him.

On the desk next to the computer was that three-week-old copy of the *Abooksigun County Dispatch,* and a pile of more recent printouts copied from the Internet.

The highlighted copy of the *Dispatch* was folded over to the story about the sensational death of Ted Mackenzie. The article was a page and a half long, and that was without any details about the tragic event itself. Nate supposed that the editor of the *Dispatch* was a man untouched by the tabloid impulse to glorify the bizarre aspects of the case.

When he was finished making notes from last night's activities, he reached for the paper and ran his finger down the side of the article, until he found the next person he wanted to check out.

Nathan Adriano stood in the office of Doctor William Thurlow.

Dr. Thurlow was a GP working out of St. Bartholomew, Abooksigun County's only hospital and home to a Level III Trauma Center that serviced most of the surrounding rural counties. Dr. Thurlow was also the duly elected coroner for Abooksigun County, running uncontested for the seat for the past two decades. Dr. Thurlow's signature was on Theodore Mackenzie's death certificate.

Nate looked around the office while he waited. It was a small space, cramped for someone who was both a doctor and an elected county official. So cramped that Nate suspected that there was another office somewhere, for the doctor's duties as coroner. As it was, it was a good thing that his office door opened out. There was a small carpeted space flanked by a desk, two filing cabinets, and a chrome-vinyl chair that was twin to those in the lobby waiting room. Bookshelves pressed the desk in from two sides, piled high with neat stacks of medical journals and reference books.

On a thin table behind the desk sat a fax machine, a coffeemaker and an oversized laser printer. The wall above that table was crowded by a bulletin board covered in memos, photographs, and a few crayon scribbles that must have been drawn by the doctor's grandchildren.

Nate looked for a medical degree and it took a while for him to find it, framed and sitting on top of one of the bookshelves.

There were basically two types of doctors. The first responded best to appeals to their professionalism and expertise, the second responded best by invoking the needs of their clients. Nate had expected that the holder of a political office would be the former, but experience showed that the former tended to have every degree possible on prominent display. The former would also probably insist on a larger office.

"Dr. Wingate?" someone asked from behind him. Wingate was the alias Nate had used at the reception desk.

Nate turned around to see Dr. Thurlow. The man was older than the pictures that Nate had been able to obtain, but he was still the same man. An imposingly large man who resembled a white George Foreman with a gray beard.

"Thank you for seeing me on such short notice," Nate held out his hand and the doctor shook it. Nate glanced at the open door and said, "Can we speak in private?"

Dr. Thurlow nodded and pulled the door shut behind him and maneuvered around to the other side of his desk. It seemed near miraculous to Nate that such a large man could fit in such a small space. He motioned to Nate to sit down, and Nate eased himself into the chrome-vinyl chair.

"So," Dr. Thurlow said, stroking his beard, "What exactly does the CDC want to talk to me about?"

Dr. Wingate was an employee for the Centers for Disease

Control. The man whose name Nate was using was an actual field officer for the agency, and Nate had been able to present a quite official-looking business card to the receptionist. They had been easy enough to obtain, once Nate tracked down where they were being printed.

Nate opened his briefcase and extracted a file. "I'm going to show you some files that have bearing on a recent case of yours. Before I do, I want you to understand that all of this is classified."

Dr. Thurlow held up a hand. "Why is it classified?"

Nate laid a folder on the desk. He kept his hand on it as he said, "Panic, primarily. So far, a very limited number of people have died. We're dealing with some very grave suspicions, and right or wrong, if the nature of the speculation leaked to the general public there would be an order of magnitude more damage."

"Grave? How?"

"Doctor, I came a long way to speak to you in person. I really want your help. But I can't tell you anything unless you agree what we talk about doesn't leave this room."

"I know, but can you appreciate my position? If what you have there," Dr. Thurlow nodded toward the folder "has anything to do with any of my patients, I can't give you that kind of promise."

"What if I promise you that this will have no effect on anyone you're treating?"

"You just said this has bearing on a recent case of mine."

"As an elected servant of the county."

There was a pause for a beat before the doctor said, "Oh."

"I'm sorry if I caught you off guard, I know you aren't wearing your coroner hat right now . . ."

"No that's all right. I'd still like you to tell me, 'Grave? How?' "

Nate made a show of thinking it over, even though he had already scripted an answer in his head.

"Take a hypothetical situation," Nate said, "assume for a moment that it leaked out that a government agency was seriously investigating an organized group that was intentionally infecting people with AIDS?"

The doctor leaned back, "Are you saying—"

"I'm not saying anything. It isn't the case, but I want you to come to grips with the kind of issue we're dealing with."

"Okay, show me the files."

The files Nate showed Dr. Thurlow were only half fraud. The data, the photographs, the detailed case histories, all were genuine. The only phony part of it all was the paper it was printed on. The files were presented with the CDC's letterhead, on the CDC's forms, all the way down to phony CDC file numbers. If the Centers for Disease Control had ever had anything to do with any of these cases, they had done so with even more secrecy than Nate pretended they were using.

The files themselves had been generated over a few weeks on several different software packages, with an additional few days of folding, rubbing, and adding the occasional handwritten note or highlighted passage. The information in those files represented nearly five years' worth of work.

Nate was gratified to see how respectfully the doctor took the folders. He picked up the top one, which, since it was the oldest case, had the most stains, creases, and hand notations.

He opened it and Nate watched him glance at the freshman high school picture of Gene Aaron Richardson. Clipped under it was a notarized copy of the death certificate. Nate watched his eyes move as he read the page until he was gazing at the bottom few lines.

Nate knew what the doctor was looking at; he had the lines memorized.

Cause of Death—Shock/Blood Loss, Due to/as a result of—3rd degree burns over 100% of body. Manner of death— could not be determined.

"*Could not be determined,*" meaning that no one had any idea if it was homicide, suicide, or some bizarre accident.

The doctor flipped past the death certificate and started reading the notes from the police report on the next page. There wasn't all that much to it, mainly because there hadn't been much to the police investigation. Popular fiction to the contrary, cops don't cut their teeth on enigmas. Most urban police departments have too many cases with actual suspects to expend effort on ambiguity. Nate knew that all too well.

Dr. Thurlow read aloud quietly.

"Body was found on roof of the Skyline Avenue Wal-Mart at seven-thirty in the morning by Elmer Vance, a maintenance man, after stock people complained that something smelled burned . . . was unsure, at first, what the object was . . . no sign of forced entry. External security camera footage show the victim, identified as Gene Aaron Richardson, scaling the west wall—opposite the parking lot—at 1:35 A.M. Clothing was found fifteen feet away from the body, next to an air-conditioning duct. Tar on the roof was melted in a circle roughly five feet in diameter centered on the body. Paint on a nearby fire door showed blistering . . . skin charred completely black, body curled into fetal position, bones on the face, hands, feet visible . . . No sign of accelerant or ignition source—"

The doctor looked up from the page. His face was ashen. "You're here about Ted Mackenzie."

"Yes, I am."

The doctor shook the folder. "What *is* this?"

"Theodore Mackenzie suffered the same fate as Gene Richardson. Or close enough that I had to come here and investigate the matter."

He dropped the folder on the desk. The doctor's hand was still shaking as it clenched into a fist. "Whatever that boy suffered from, he doesn't deserve to be part of some *X-Files* freak show—" The fist came down on Gene's folder.

"Dr. Thurlow," Nate said.

"I've heard enough tripe about spontaneous human combustion—"

"Dr. Thurlow!"

"What?"

"Did you hear those words pass my lips?"

The doctor paused. Nate knew some of what was passing through the doctor's mind. Dr. Thurlow lived in a nice, tidy rational world. He was a man who couldn't abide the existence of anything outside that world. But he'd seen past the edge of his own reality, enough to shake his faith. Drawing attention to the crack in Dr. Thurlow's reality was like poking a wounded animal with a stick.

But Nate knew what he was doing, he was ready with a Band-Aid; another fiction that would allow the doctor to believe what he'd seen and retain his faith in the rational nature of the world.

"Do you think the CDC is busy investigating claims of the paranormal?" Nate asked. "What we have here is a demonstrable pattern of events that points toward something much more real, immediate, and dangerous."

"What—"

"You did the autopsy, correct?"

He nodded.

"Shall I tell you what you found?" Nate waited a beat and then reached over and flipped the page on the folder between them, revealing the autopsy notes for Gene Richardson. Nate didn't even look at it. "Combustion so complete that it interferes with DNA analysis. Involvement of 100% of the body's soft tissue, including the bone marrow. The organic matter in the bone, the pulp of the teeth all show charring. No sign of chemical contamination, or accelerants. The path of damage is reversed, the most complete damage is within the thorax, the core of the body, where you can't even distinguish the remains of the major organs. You've run every possible chemical analysis on selected bits of the body, but there's nothing to find."

The doctor shook his head and rubbed his forehead with the tips of his finger. "It was as if his core body temperature increased two thousand degrees in a second or two."

"We have fifteen cases with exactly the same signs," Nate told him.

"What is it?" the doctor asked.

"We aren't sure, yet. But we do know that this isn't a freak occurrence, and we know it isn't supernatural."

"How?"

"Fifteen kids, all of them exactly the same age when they died. All of them show similar psychological profiles. All of them grow distant in the months before this happens. Every one picks out an isolated spot, takes off their clothes, and—" Nate waved at the stack of files.

"And what?"

"The patterns connecting these cases are too strong to be anything but conscious design . . ."

"Pardon?"

"I told you that there was grave speculation about these cases."

There was a long silence. Then Dr. Thurlow closed the file in front of him and placed it back on the stack. "What is it?"

"Assume, for the moment, a foreign power has discovered the ultimate in chemical explosives. A substance that is almost completely inert and benign, until a catalyst is introduced to it, at which point it burns with incredible ferocity."

"Are you saying that some spies killed—"

Nate held up his hand. "What if this compound was rather simple chemically. Simple enough that it only took a little genetic prodding to convince a bacteria to excrete it. A bacteria that can live quite comfortably in the human gut."

Dr. Thurlow shook his head. "I can't believe this."

"It's a theory," Nate said, "but it's one that fits the facts we have. I need to see Ted Mackenzie's records, as many of them as you have access to."

"Why would anyone—"

"They need to test it. They need to test the delivery system, the life span of the bacteria. They need to know if the buildup of the chemical in the human body causes obvious side effects . . ."

"Good Lord."

"Help me, Doctor. All I really care about is stopping this from happening again." That one statement, excepting the facts about the case histories themselves, was the first truth that Nate had spoken to Dr. Thurlow.

The doctor nodded, "Of course I'll help you, Dr. Wingate."

5

ULYSSES Boyden sat in a near-empty office in a building about two miles away from the main Agency campus in Langley. The only furniture in the office was a desk and a pair of chairs. The walls were white, and the carpet a speckled blue. The smell of paint hung in the air even though they had finished the remodeling over a month ago.

On the monitor facing him, Boyden ran through a digital movie over and over. Occasionally he would pause the movie, catching a frame or two, but mostly he let the movie loop. A little date-time stamp on the video told him that it had been recorded two months ago.

The scene was a white room that could have been the twin of this office except for the lack of windows. A cot sat against one wall, and a television sat on a low table opposite it. An open door showed a small slice of a bathroom. The room was dark, details picked out in the grainy green of light amplification. The time-stamp said it was one in the morning.

A fourteen-year-old girl sat on the edge of the cot.

She very calmly removed her pajamas and folded them, placing them on the foot of the bed. Then, just as she had done the five nights prior to this video, she tried the door to the outside hall. Just as in those five prior times, she found it locked.

This tape was different, though. Instead of being satisfied and returning to bed as she had done before, she walked into the bathroom. There was a short count, ten seconds by the timer, then the screen was wiped clean by a white flash that overwhelmed the light-enhancing video equipment.

The screen changed from greenish-white to gray-white to orange-white while the camera switched modes to regain the picture. The flash faded, and there was enough light for the camera to film in normal color. The light was coming from a large fire in the bathroom. Smoke rolled across the ceiling and the sprinklers were going. Flames lapped around the doorframe of the bathroom, and what could be seen of the tiles were blackened and cracked.

Then the video looped.

A thirty-second clip that Boyden played over and over, trying to discern something in the girl. He was looking for some sign of self-knowledge, some human emotion acknowledging her fate. However, watching the tape, he couldn't help feeling that what he was seeing was something alien, machinelike.

She knew, Boyden thought. *They all know . . .*

The video was interrupted by a dialogue box flashing a network message across his monitor screen. *"They're ready for you in the conference room."*

Boyden sighed and shut down the PC.

He walked into the room located in the geometric center of the fifth floor. The walls were soundproofed and RF-shielded. Even the electrical wiring ran through filters to keep it from piggybacking a signal. It was an appropriate place to discuss a security breach.

Boyden shut the door behind him and sat at the conference table facing the three-man security team of Department Blue. "Please tell me that it's not as bad as I think it is."

The first to answer was Jared French, the network guy. He was the youngest man in the room, had a blond buzz cut and wore anachronistic horn-rim glasses. "He was in charge of getting our data across into the new servers. I'm afraid he had access to pretty much everything we have."

Boyden shook his head. "How could an outsider have that kind of clearance?"

Kyle Chapman was the man in charge of personnel. He was gray-haired and had a reputation as a recruiter that long preceded his work at Department Blue. "He wasn't some consultant we found off of the street. He had a stellar record at the Pentagon, there wasn't one speck on his record. He was a career man, and if it wasn't for his medical situation—"

"Aren't we supposed to have annual psych and physical screenings?"

Kyle sighed. "That was the problem. He never was, strictly, an Agency employee. He was DoD, regular Army. But, he was the only man with the expertise *and* the security clearance we needed."

"We couldn't have hired him ourselves?"

"He wouldn't have taken the job if it meant giving up his army commission—"

"So we were relying on the Pentagon to monitor his mental and physical health?" Boyden rubbed his temples and said. "I have to brief the Director on this tomorrow. I would like to tell him some good news, something that won't be used as ammunition against this department."

"The lapse was on the DoD side," Kyle asserted. "They

should have caught it earlier. They certainly should have no-
tified us what his medical leave was for."

"Somehow, I doubt that will provide us much cover."

"It is not as bad as it could have been," said Cato Sullivan, the last of the security triad. His title was security director, and he ran a small army of agents that covered
security issues both internal and external to the department.
His people had been the ones to find the breach.

Lieutenant Samuel Flavian, one of Department Blue's
computer personnel, had died last week. He had been on
medical leave for a month, and his death was from natural
causes.

What Sullivan's people had discovered was that Lt. Flavian's death was due to a tumor in his brain that had been
growing undetected for at least two years and probably
longer. It had also been rendering him mentally unstable to
an increasing degree. For whatever reason, the folks at the
Pentagon did not pass along the information that their lieutenant had become a security risk. Sullivan's team didn't
even know what the medical issue was until after Flavian's
death.

A sweep of Flavian's quarters revealed a nightmare of
classified documents pilfered over a period of at least twelve
months, if not longer. Everything from analytical reports to
case histories. Piles of it.

Even so, Sullivan told him that it could have been worse.

Boyden asked him, "How?"

"We've been backtracking all his contacts, checking his
finances, his Internet activity. No exchanges of money seem
to have happened, and he does not appear to have knowingly
contacted agents of any foreign government. He hasn't
placed any classified material into the public domain, possibly out of fear of being discovered. He did initiate contact

with several reporters, but by that point he was suffering from obvious paranoid delusions and most of the journalists he talked to did not follow anything up with him."

"Most?"

Sullivan nodded. "We've confirmed that he had a face-to-face meeting with one freelance reporter named Abby Springfield. We haven't determined what information, if any, was passed along."

"That's not very reassuring."

"We're containing any damage," Sullivan said.

Boyden nodded. "And I hope you have a team on this Springfield woman. I want to know where she goes, who she sees, what she eats for breakfast."

"We're on it," Sullivan said.

Boyden picked up a phone by his chair. The line only went to one location in the building, it wasn't even connected to the secure phone network, much less an outside line. "Send the rest of them in," he told the secretary at the other end of the hard line.

The security team rose to leave and Boyden waved them all to sit back down. "We're going to go over the Theodore Mackenzie event, and there's an issue I want you all to sit in on."

The issue's name happened to be Nathan Adriano.

6

THE day after the fight, the administration of Euclid Heights High School, in its wisdom, decided to suspend Jimmy for ten days. Jimmy was certain that a lot of people on the faculty, including his guidance counselor, wanted to expel him. In Jimmy's opinion, that would have been just fine. He would prefer spending the rest of his life having nothing to do with Euclid Heights High. He would have been quite happy to spend the rest of his seventeenth year free of scholastic obligations. It was just eight months before he'd be able to control his own life, free of the county and their parents of the week.

Of course, Frank had fucked everything up.

The school administration had discretion to dish out punishment pretty much at whim. What they couldn't do was dish out different punishments to two kids who were caught breaking the same rules at the same time in the same incident. They couldn't expel Jimmy, or issue criminal charges against him, without doing the same thing to Frank.

Of course they didn't want to do that to one of their jocks.

The irony was so thick that Jimmy wished the administration had expelled both of them, just so he could see the look on Coach Miller's face. Two weeks' suspension turned out to be the biggest stick they were willing to whack Frank's pretty face with.

Even so, the equality stopped there. At 11:00 A.M., Jimmy had been called to the principal's office. They told him the verdict and had him unceremoniously escorted out of the building by Spam and his cohorts. They didn't even give him the chance to empty out his locker.

Spam took some obvious pleasure in saying, "If you step foot on school property before two weeks, we're going to get you for trespassing." Then they left him on the sidewalk.

Jimmy didn't doubt they would.

Fortunately—or unfortunately—Mr. Carswell was at work with the car, so Jimmy had the luxury of being able to walk home. He wasn't in a great hurry. He didn't want to deal with his foster parents of the moment. So, instead, he went to the McDonald's across the street, bought a Happy Meal, and sat by the window where he could stare at the brick pile that was his current nemesis.

From his vantage he could see that, lip service aside, he and Frank were not getting the same treatment. The jock, who'd been through the principal's office within about fifteen minutes of Jimmy, was sitting on the front steps yucking it up with a bunch of the steroid contingent. He had a full duffel at his feet, and had obviously been not only to his school locker, but to his gym locker as well.

"Spam ain't charging you with trespassing," Jimmy muttered from around a greasy french fry.

Jimmy was sitting in the booth, watching Frank hold court, when a squeaky voice interrupted his thoughts.

"I'm g–going to have to ask you to leave."

Jimmy turned slowly, another french fry halfway to his mouth. "Say what?" he asked.

The person addressing him was one of the paper-hat

brigade. He was skinny, sweaty, and had a red pockmarked face. "We don't serve students here during school hours."

"Christ on a stick."

"It's p–policy. You have to leave."

Jimmy shook his head and pointed the fry at the kid. "You sold me the fucking Happy Meal, and I'm going to eat it. *Here.*"

"Sir," the kid's voice dropped to a stage whisper, *"the manager—"*

"The manager," Jimmy said, raising his voice in response, "can kiss my skinny white ass." Jimmy felt an eerie sense of déjà vu as the conversations at the surrounding tables died. He was the center of attention again, and his stomach churned with a sick mixture of fear and exhilaration.

A man with a gut as wide as the whole booth walked over behind Jimmy's adversary. He wore a sweat-stained shirt two sizes too tight, a tie three inches too short, and a little gold name tag that said he was Charlie, the manager. "Is there a problem here?"

Jimmy gave him his widest shit-eating grin. "Yes, Charlie, there is." He picked up a fry and pointed to the smocked, acne-riddled peon who was trying to fade behind the manager's girth. "One of your employees is giving me a hard time."

"Young man, we have a policy here. We don't serve underage kids here during the day."

"Now that's funny," Jimmy said, "'cause I'd be willing to bet that the pizza-faced mamma's boy trying to crawl up your ass ain't old enough to buy a beer."

Charlie's face turned an interesting shade of pink. Somehow, his voice didn't change tone. *Must be all those people skills that got him to the top of his profession.* "If you're going to cause a disturbance, we're going to have to call the police."

"Charlie, believe me, there are more disturbing things in this life—" He picked the hamburger out of his Happy Meal and saluted Charlie with it. "The things they put in these burgers, for instance." He took a bite and looked around at the other customers. "Come on, people, don't look so shocked. Haven't you all been on the Internet? You're lucky if something for ninety-nine cents even *touched* a cow."

A meaty hand grabbed him by the front of his shirt and Jimmy gagged up the bite of hamburger he'd been eating.

"Now," Charlie said, "you're going to leave, you little bastard."

Jimmy spit the remains of the hamburger in Charlie's face. "Fuck you, you McNazi."

Charlie let go, and backed up. Jimmy slipped to the ground, his ass sliding in a spilled mixture of Coke and fries. *Christ, what the hell am I trying to do?*

Charlie rushed forward, but about five of his own employees grabbed his arms to restrain him. Three customers were standing up, whether to intervene or run, Jimmy couldn't tell. It was sinking in that he'd better get the fuck out of here.

He pushed himself up. "Maybe I *should* leave," he nodded sagely at the other customers while backing away. "I'm afraid you've lost a customer, Charlie. Your service sucks." As he reached the door, he said, "And the head clown's going to hear about it."

There was some muttered response, but Jimmy was already on the sidewalk and couldn't make out what Charlie said.

*   *   *

Carlos' Cosmic Comic Shoppe was about a mile down the street from Euclid Heights High School, the next suburb over toward Cleveland proper. It usually took Jimmy about half an hour to walk there after school, but today he took his time. Not only did his suspension mean he was out four hours early from school, he needed the time to calm down after the confrontation with Ronald McDonald's storm troopers.

He also wanted time to consider what to do about his pants before he showed up for work. The seat of his jeans was sticking to his ass. The sun's heat was turning the wet spot where he'd sat down in the puddle of Coke into a tacky mess.

Jimmy reached Coventry two hours early for work, so he had time to deal with the issue. On the south end of the street was a little mall of concrete planters and restaurant storefronts. One of those storefronts was a coffee shop where some of the more tolerable refugees from Heights High hung out after hours, a place that was far enough from the high school not to have any draconian policies about serving anyone under eighteen.

He slipped in, ignoring the multiply-pierced guy tending the counter, and headed for the door with the Day-Glo tempera mural of Jimmi Hendrix on the door. He closed himself into the john, made sure the door was locked, and stripped off his jeans and started filling the sink.

In the back of his head some semirational voice was telling him that not only had he already had enough time to walk home and change before work, but he *still* had two hours. Instead, he was standing in the cramped bathroom of the Coventry Arabica in his stocking feet, washing Coca-Cola from the seat of his jeans.

It wasn't until he saw the half-crushed French fry lodge in the drain that he started laughing. . . .

The upside of the Arabica's bathroom was that he could lock the door. The downside was that there wasn't a hot-air hand dryer. He had to blot his jeans as dry as he could with a handful of paper towels, which left the seat of his jeans covered in paper lint.

At least his ass wouldn't stick to anything now.

When he pulled on his damp jeans and put his shoes back on, he realized that his socks were wet now.

Turning into a perfect day.

On his way out, he purchased an overpriced Danish and a hazelnut coffee from the human pincushion because he didn't want to seem like a complete asshole, and because he was still hungry after having half his lunch end up on Charlie, the floor, and the seat of his pants.

He walked slowly down Coventry, sipping his caffeine and looking in windows. He was still getting used to the place, having discovered it shortly after moving to Euclid Heights. Until this point, the business districts that he had experience with had consisted of liquor stores, hair salons, and battered old convenience stores that made most their money off of lottery tickets. For food, you'd have a KFC or a Rally's, drive through only, please.

On Coventry, in the space of two blocks, there were about a dozen restaurants, and not a drive-through in the lot. The other stores ranged from an antique store to a place where you could buy a ceramic statue of your cat. There was a futon place and a shop selling Chinese herbal medicine and tai-chi classes. There were three bookstores if you didn't count Carlos', Mac's Backs, a used bookstore, Delphic Books, the New Age bookstore, and Revolution Books, the unrepentant Communist bookstore. There was a co-op grocery store, and a record store that carried vinyl.

In addition, it was just weird to see storefronts whose windows weren't hidden by rolling steel shutters five minutes after closing. Not only that, you could actually see in the windows. It wasn't until they moved Jimmy out of the city that he realized that you could do more with a storefront window than hang up advertising.

He circled the two blocks twice, until the coffee was gone. He was wired on caffeine, and he was only an hour early.

Carlos' Cosmic Comic Shoppe sat in a building all by itself, next to a huge Medic drugstore. The little building was wrapped in a psychedelic mural that, from pictures Jimmy had seen, hadn't changed since the place opened in 1968. One wall was dominated by a typically bottom-heavy Robert Crumb fantasy woman, combat-booted, leather skirt, riding crop, twice life-size overlooking a precipice where a herd of eyeballs with arms and legs were stampeding into a canyon.

Reggie Carlos, the store's owner, claimed that Crumb actually came and helped paint the mural. Jimmy thought that Reggie hoped the story would impress his customers. It seemed unlikely that it did, since the bulk of the clientele here were *X-Men* fans with no memory past the DC-Marvel buyout, and who wouldn't know Crumb from Kirby.

Jimmy pushed his way into the store, and Reggie was sitting behind the register reading a vintage copy of the *National Lampoon*. Despite the fact he wore a white button-down shirt, Jimmy thought he still looked like a hippie. There was just something about his face that called out for tie-dye and a peace sign. The Grateful Dead belting through "Keep Truckin'" helped, as did the matted and framed Peter Maxx posters high up on the wall.

Reggie looked up when the door opened. At the moment—about half an hour before school let out, they were the only two here. Jimmy's work schedule normally started right before the afternoon rush.

"Got out of school early."

"Uh-huh," Reggie said. "What happened?" Reggie was fond of saying he had an excellent bullshit detector. Though Jimmy figured that it would take someone with an A+ in oblivious to miss how stressed out he was right now.

Jimmy wrestled with himself over what to tell Reggie. In the end, Jimmy decided he owed the guy the truth. Reggie had cut him slack to spare, not to mention hiring him in the first place—after quite a few places took a pass on him.

"I got handed a two-week suspension."

Reggie whistled and shook his head. "Why'd they do that?"

"The star quarterback on the football team took a swing at me," Jimmy shrugged. "I swung back."

Reggie arched an eyebrow and looked over the tops of his glasses at Jimmy. "You don't look too worse for wear."

Jimmy's hand reflexively touched his forehead where Frank had split his face open. Had it only been twenty-four hours? It felt longer. "I really looked a mess after the fight." *All the blood, dripping from his face. The nurse with her latex gloves. The custodians coming in dressed like the EPA cleaning a toxic chemical spill.* "I heal quickly." There should be something to mark the event. Hell, Frank had a bruise or two. Jimmy knew, though, if it wasn't for all the witnesses, no one would believe Frank had touched him.

"Why'd he swing at you?"

What business is it of yours, you geriatric burnout?

Jimmy bit down the words before they'd fully materialized. Reggie was a friend, as much a friend as any ten assholes at Heights. He couldn't go off on him like that. Jimmy could feel the pulse racing in his neck as he realized what he had almost said. "Do we need to talk about this?" Jimmy asked instead.

"Okay," Reggie said, holding up his hand, "I'm just a little concerned. Thanks for telling me, anyway." He bent back over his *National Lampoon*.

The silence stretched for a long time. Finally, Jimmy couldn't stand it any more.

"I called him a 'dickless, pea-brained, steroid-sniffing sorry excuse for a left testicle.'"

Reggie looked up from his magazine. "A *what?*"

"'Dickless, pea-brained, steroid-sniffing sorry excuse for a left testicle.'"

Reggie stiffled a grin. "And you're surprised he took a swing at you?"

"In retrospect—no."

Reggie held it back half a beat, then he started laughing.

"Left testicle," he wheezed out, shaking his head.

7

REGGIE was good enough to let Jimmy clock in early, and since the afternoon rush hadn't started yet, he sent him back to do sorting and inventory. That was fine with Jimmy. Since Reggie didn't like dealing with superhero comics, he really had no idea what he had in the basement. So he never really had any idea how much—or little—work Jimmy did when he was down there.

The rickety narrow staircase was a portal into another universe—and that universe had a god whose brain exploded in a flurry of four-color newsprint. The air smelled of cardboard and old paper, and the small space was crammed floor-to-ceiling with gray metal shelving units that held cardboard boxes of everything from *Action Comics* to *Mad Magazine*. The walls were hidden by piles of boxes, and here and there the aisles were blocked by a stack that wouldn't fit on the shelves.

The only clear spot of the basement was a small area, half under the stairs, lit by one of those funky curlicue fluorescent tubes that Reggie had screwed into a fifty-year-old porcelain light socket. Nestled under the steps was a beat-up metal desk painted a chipped institutional green, a wooden desk chair that was missing all four casters, and a smaller metal shelf that held mailers, office supplies, and a postage meter.

Sitting on the desk, like a visitor from some uncluttered post-millennial future was a two gigahertz Dell server attached to a cable modem. According to Reggie, that server was nearly eighty percent of Carlos' Cosmic Comic Shoppe. Reggie's main job, in fact, was watching over the server and filling orders over the Internet. According to Reggie, the sales he got in the actual comic store only did slightly better than pay for the space and his employees.

However, since the store had only been computerized for a little over a year, Reggie still had decades worth of inventory that wasn't in his on-line database. So Jimmy's job was to take down a box from the uncataloged shelves, key the stats on the box's contents, and file the magazines on the single shelf of cataloged and sorted material.

In Jimmy's opinion, that was going to take another two decades or so. Especially since, whenever he got to do inventory, there wouldn't be a box that he sorted through that wouldn't have stuff he needed to read in it.

This time was no different. The first box he chose to key in had a cache of old *Spider-Man* comic books from the late seventies and early eighties, before Marvel got into all the bullshit with alien symbiotes and Parker clones.

It never fails. When they change the uniform, they fuck things up.

It happened to Batman, for a blessedly brief time, and—God almighty—what they did to Superman was a fucking sin. The downfall for Spider-Man was when they gave him this gosh-neato black suit replacing his red and blue duds—of course, when enough readers cried bloody murder, they took the alien suit off of good old Peter Parker and turned it into a super villain.

Jimmy didn't like any of the current DC-Marvel stuff because of crap like that. He preferred less mainstream comics, especially *Spawn*. The only stuff with the old standbys that he read were either old issues, like the ones he was reading now, or graphic novels that weren't tied to the soap-opera format that the regular comic books had to adhere to.

Jimmy had the ratty cardboard box at his feet as he sat down in the office chair. He would methodically pick out a comic book, flip through it—supposedly to determine its condition but actually to read the issue—place it in a plastic bag from a stack by the computer, slip a sheet of white acid-free cardboard inside the sleeve behind the comic, key the information into Reggie's database, and place the book in a clean white box on the cataloged shelf.

What kept Reggie from catching on was the fact that Jimmy could read fast. It was a skill he kept very much to himself. It was the key thing that gave him free time in school; he could usually kill off a whole week's worth of reading during a slow period in class and he could spend the rest of the time sketching out his own comic books.

Even with reading the whole issue, his average time from box to shelf was under five minutes. Quick enough that, when Reggie called him upstairs to man the register for the afternoon rush, he had emptied half the *Spider-Man* collection.

Reggie's operation was so slick that, as Jimmy climbed the stairs, the database had already looked up a sale price from a comprehensive database and posted the comic books on-line. Reggie used half a dozen auction services as well as his own web site and domain, and it was quite likely that in forty-eight hours any one of the comics that Jimmy had read would be on the other side of the world.

Jimmy was glad for the time he had spent in the basement. He had needed the time to zone out and relax, otherwise he'd have been in no shape to man the register. Ten minutes into it, he was too busy to think. Between three-thirty and five-thirty the shop was swamped with customers, so many so that it was hard to believe that this was the less profitable end of the business.

The youngest kids were first, from the elementary school down the street, nine out of ten of them buying *Pokémon* cards with sticky, crumpled dollar bills and handfuls of pennies. Then came the junior high kids who either bought superhero mags or tried to shoplift. The high schoolers were the last to show up. They bought more of the graphic novels and role-playing stuff.

This was the part of the job that felt like work. He served a line of customers that started at three-thirty or four, and didn't let up until sometime after five. It gave him some understanding of why he never saw a convenience store clerk who didn't look pissed at something.

While Jimmy ran the register, Reggie played house detective, watching for kids lifting stuff. He averaged about two attempts a night, even with his rather obvious presence looming over the displays.

It was nearing five, and the store was emptying out, when the inevitable happened. He had just rung up three books, all wrestling mags that he never realized Reggie carried. He was staring at the leather face of Mankind, dominating the cover of one of the garish magazines when he asked, "Will that be all?"

A familiar voice whispered, "No, I want to know how much it would cost to have you eat shit and fucking die."

Jimmy looked up and saw Frank's face glaring at him. This was the first good look he'd got at the guy since the fight. There was a purple knot on his face under the right eye. Jimmy had landed at least one solid punch. Jimmy's hand went automatically to the place where his scalp had torn open. Not even a scar.

Jimmy responded without thinking. "You can't afford it, you'll have to hire someone else for your little perverted whack-off fetishes."

Frank leaned over the table. "I bet you think you're funny."

Jimmy knew that prodding this son of a bitch had "bad move" written all over it. He couldn't help himself. "No, Frank. But I think you're hilarious."

There was something in Frank's eyes that told Jimmy he had pushed the guy too far. It was the glassy gaze of someone who didn't give a shit anymore. Jimmy knew the look; he had cultivated it himself to gain some breathing room in the war zones he'd spent most of his school days in.

"Laugh, you monkey-assed bitch. See how easy it'll be with a tube down that smart-ass throat of yours." Frank reached over and grabbed the magazines. "We know you, ain't no fucking way anyone won't believe you had it coming." Frank walked away from the counter.

Jimmy waited a moment and cleared his throat. "You going to pay for those?"

Frank turned around, said, "Fuck you!" and threw them at Jimmy. He missed, and the magazines hit the counter with a thwap. The bastard was long gone before Reggie reached the door. Reggie stepped out and came back a few minutes later with a shrug.

"What was that about?"

"That was the left testicle," Jimmy told him.

"What a shithead." Reggie picked up the damaged magazines and looked at them. "I carry this crap?"

*　　*　　*

Jimmy worked through closing, which on a weeknight was nine o'clock. He managed the register all that time, but after about six, things were slow enough for him to grab a notebook and doodle. The notebook was an older one that he'd left at the store, the stuff he *had* been working on was in his locker at school. That annoyed the hell out of him, but there was nothing much he could do about it. There wasn't anyone going to the circles of Hades called Euclid Heights High School that he trusted enough to give the combination to his locker, and—thanks to Spam's little warning—Jimmy wasn't going to step on school property to liberate his notebooks himself.

So instead, he used the blank half of the old notebook to start a new story line between Cain and Baphomet. Of all the characters that he'd created in his doodling, those were the two he liked the most.

Cain Jimmy liked because he had been the first superhero he'd come up with who wasn't all-powerful. When he'd first tried his hand at his own comics, three or four years ago, he'd come up with all these characters with all these neat powers—gravity manipulation, energy manipulation, *reality* manipulation—and every time he tried to build a story around these characters, it ended up so much crap. Present hero, present problem, hero solves problem, hero *might* break sweat. It wasn't until much later that Jimmy came to the realization that a good hero was more than a neat costume and a laundry list of all-powerful mutant/technological/alien/cosmic abilities.

It wasn't until Cain that he realized that a good *story* was one where none of the hero's superpowers helped him at all. It was the villain who should have all the cards, the all-powerful abilities. If no one else, the villain should be able to hurt the hero, and in the worst possible way.

So Jimmy had come up with Cain and his demonic arch-villain Baphomet, and the pair had just seemed to click. Jimmy had been writing exclusively about those two for the past six months, and—unlike with the Justice League's assortment of cardboard heroes and villains he'd come up with before—he actually had to *think* of how Cain was going to foil one of Baphomet's plans. Each time it was getting harder, because each time Baphomet was learning more about Cain's strengths and weaknesses.

It was time, Jimmy thought, for Baphomet to attack Cain directly.

He became so engrossed with what he was writing that closing time came and went without his notice. It wasn't until the phone rang that he looked up and saw the clock next to the register reading ten-thirty.

He picked up the phone before it rolled over to voice mail. "Carlos' Cosmic Comic Shoppe—"

He wasn't surprised when he heard Mrs. Carswell's voice. "Thank God, you were supposed to be home an hour ago."

Jimmy swallowed. "I stayed late at work." *How the hell could I lose time like that?*

"I'm sending John to get you."

No, Mr. Carswell is the last thing I need right now. "You don't need to do that, I was just closing up."

"But—"

"Look, I'll see you both in about fifteen minutes. I gotta go."

"Jimmy—"

When Jimmy hung up the phone, he realized his hand was shaking.

I have to go back. I have to face them, don't I?

He picked up his notebook and started shutting off lights

and closing up the store. *When I'm eighteen, I'll be out of school. On my own, I could get Reggie to hire me full-time. Enough for an apartment.*

It was going to be the longest nine months of his life.

Interlude One: THE MARK OF CAIN

PAGE: 1 [FOUR PANELS]

Panel 1: EXT. EUCLID HTS. HIGH SCHOOL—MIDDAY
We see the school from above, as if in a traffic copter. In fact, the shadow of the helicopter is visible centered on the central courtyard of the school. Traffic barriers are visible, as are a fleet of cop cars.

Panel 2: INT. HELICOPTER
Facing the AV geek manning the video. School's reflected in the lens.
CREWCUT type with headphones and mike is leaning over him to look out.

CREWCUT

"We are entering hour five of the standoff now. Police have cordoned off two blocks surrounding Euclid Heights High. Hostage negotiators have been called in—"

Panel 3: VIEW UP WALL FROM COURTYARD
Main entrance with view of the front doors and clock tower. The helicopter is in the sky above. Three or four SWAT guys, all in black, are rapelling down the face of the building.

CREWCUT

(Cont. from prior panel)

"—Wait, something is happening. I see movement. The police are moving in—"

SFX

(Snaking along bottom of panel)

SSSSSSSSssssssssssssssssssss

Panel 4: HELICOPTER'S VIEW OF SCHOOL
A massive explosion rolls out from the wall where the SWAT team was. Windows are blown out.

SFX

(Large-looking type, but in the distance w/smoke, etc.)

KAAAABOOOM

CREWCUT

(Large word balloon, tiny script.)

"Shit."

PAGE 2: [SPLASH PAGE]

STREET-LEVEL VIEW OF SCHOOL
We're looking from behind CAIN's silhouette. He is on the corner of an intersection just across from the school. Glass is raining down all around, and cops are ducking behind patrol cars. Cain is the only one standing. Smoke is obscuring most of the visible sky.

TITLE

Sow the Wind . . .

CAPTION

"Somebody, someday, has got to tell me why I still watch the news."

PAGE 3: [FIVE PANELS]

Panel 1: LONG SHOT ANGLED TOWARD CAIN

CAIN is staring over his black sunglasses at the destruction caused by the explosion. He is wearing his signature black trench coat, and fingerless gloves. He has shoulder-length black hair that's blowing behind him from the force of the explosion.

CAPTION

"I know his name. I know why he's doing this."

Panel 2: MID SHOT CENTERED ON CAIN
Cain's walking across the street now. He's passing the cop cars, but in the chaos, the cops aren't paying attention to him.

CAPTION

"Jerry Smith. He is, or was, a sophomore here. Stereotype outsider, few friends or none. Known by the faculty here mostly as a disruptive influence."

Panel 3: CLOSE-UP, CAIN FROM KNEES DOWN
Black boots in foreground, crunching on glass as he walks. Past Cain's feet, we see a cop, butt on the ground, back to a patrol car. The cop is watching Cain pass by.

CAPTION

"Disruptive because he was just too good a target for the 'cool' kids not to hassle. To taunt. To beat."

Panel 4: OVERHEAD, COP AND CAIN
The cop is shaking, leveling his weapon at Cain, staring into Cain's eyes.

COP

"Y-you can't . . ."

CAPTION

"Yeah. I know who he is, and why he's doing this."

Panel 5: OVERHEAD, COP
The cop has lowered his gun, and the expression on his face is one of pure terror.

COP

"No, no, no . . ."

CAPTION

"It doesn't make my job any easier."

8

JIMMY stood in front of the Carswells' house feeling the bottom drop out of his stomach. He suffered the discontinuity of memory that always told him something bad had happened. He stood in the shadow just at the edge of a streetlight, as if he'd been reluctant to step into the light . . .

. . . as if he'd been standing here for quite some time.

The lights in the Carswells' house were off, as well as the lights on most of the houses on this street. Jimmy shook off the disorientation and took a step across the street, looking down at his watch to see how late he was. . . .

That's when he saw the blood.

His watch was gone, and his hand was covered with a brown crust that had to be blood. Jimmy stared at the back of his hand as if it were some alien creature.

"Holy shit," he whispered.

He looked down at himself and he was a mess. His jeans were torn in half a dozen places and his shirt was stained with grass, mud, and blood. In his left hand he held the notebook he had taken home from *The Cosmic Comic Shoppe.* He gripped it so tightly that his knuckles were white under the bloodstains.

Jimmy slowly released his grip and looked at what was left of the notebook. He felt an ache inside him, an ache he knew was rage that burned so bright and hot it had only left a hole for him to feel inside himself.

All the pages had come free of the binding. Half were water-stained, and a few had footprints on them. Two of the pages had been (*deliberately*) crumpled and torn. He saw fingerprints on them bigger than any of his (*ground under his heel*).

Who had done this? Who had (*felt cartilage give way beneath his fist*) . . .

Jimmy ran for the house. All he wanted was to escape the darkness that was drawing in around him. All he wanted was to escape the memory of (*the taste of his own blood as his lip splits open*) . . .

He slammed though the door as if Baphomet himself was at his heels and he heard Mr. Carswell snort awake and call out, *"James!"*

Jimmy was running, and he locked himself in the bathroom before Mr. Carswell had come fully conscious. Jimmy had already stepped fully clothed into the shower when Mr. Carswell pounded on the bathroom door. "James, do you have any idea what time it is, young man?"

. . . (*watchband snapping off as his fist connects with someone's face*) . . .

"Didn't mean to wake you, Mr. Carswell." In his own ears, Jimmy's voice sounds like a terrified eight-year-old. "I took a shortcut and got lost."

"It's one in the morning."

"I'm sorry." Christ, his voice was cracking. It was only just now that it sunk in that he was standing in the shower, fully clothed, water going full blast. Water was already pulling his clothing down, and a soup of mud, grass, and blood was already swirling around the drain.

"We have to talk, son."

About what, old man? What the fuck do you think you can say to make this better, make it go away?

"Jimmy?"

"Yes?" He drew his fingers through wet, knotted hair, pulling free the clots embedded in it.

"Are you all right in there?"

Am I all right anywhere?

"I'm fine."

There was a hesitation.

Is the door locked? God, don't let him come in here and see me like this. Don't let him ask what happened . . .

"We're going to talk tomorrow."

"Yes, sir," Jimmy answered.

Mr. Carswell grunted, and after a moment, Jimmy heard him walk away from the door. Jimmy's shoulders slumped and he collapsed against the tile. His knees slowly gave way, and he slid down into the tub.

"What's happening?" he whispered.

(*Jimmy.*)

He peeled his clothing off, sticking it in a sloppy pile in the corner of the tub opposite the drain. His muscles tensed when the cold water sprayed against his naked skin, but he didn't reach to adjust the faucet.

(*Remember me, Jimmy?*)

For a long time, Jimmy sat naked under the cold spray, hugging his knees and rocking back and forth. The water rinsed the dirt, the mud, and the blood off of him, and Jimmy wished that the water would reach inside him and clean the tar-black stains he felt inside, wash away the tatters of memory that tugged at him.

(*Still think you're funny, bitch?*)

Jimmy hugged his legs tighter pressing his forehead into his knees. He didn't want to know. He wanted the memory to stay lost. He wanted to lose even the knowledge that the memory was missing.

It wouldn't let go of him. Inside his mind's eye, he saw an image of Frank's face taunting him.

(*What've we got here, bitch?*)

In the black part of himself that held the memory he knew that something bad had happened. Something worse than the fight at school. Much worse . . .

Hours later, Jimmy was lying in his bed, wide awake, naked, trying not to remember the blood.

But the blackness that had taken the memory insisted on giving it back to him . . .

(*"Jimmy!"*)

He winced at the voice, as if it was in the bedroom with him.

(*"Remember me, Jimmy?"*

Dark residential street, halfway between the comic store and the Carswells' house. Frank's voice echoes out of the darkness, sourceless and disembodied. Jimmy doesn't want to stop walking. Doesn't want to acknowledge the asshole's presence, as if to acknowledge him would give Frank power over him.)

Jimmy shivered and pulled the covers around himself. They didn't help. The chill had nothing to do with the air around him.

(*"Still think you're funny, bitch?"*

Jimmy slows down. He walks next to a wooded lot and ahead of him on the sidewalk he can see a human silhouette blocking his path. Jimmy glances behind him, and sees two more approaching from behind. He turns back and there Frank is, standing inches in front of him, forcing Jimmy to stop to avoid plowing into his chest.

Jimmy clutches his notebook tighter.)

"Please," Jimmy whispered to his own memory. To himself.

(*Arms grab him from behind, dragging him into the wooded lot. Frank is laughing, the bruises on his face twisted and surreal under the mercury glare of the street lamps.*

"Thought a fucker like you was going to get away with your shit?"

Jimmy shakes his head, and one of the guys on his arms says, "He don't got much to say, do he, Frank?"

Jimmy wants to object. He wants to tell this asshole what a small-dicked wimp he is that he needs to get two of his butt-buddies to hold him down so he won't get his pansy-ass hurt. He wants to say it, but his mouth isn't working. Too dry.

He still clutches the notebook.)

Jimmy could sense what was about to happen, even before he remembered it. He curled up under the covers, rolling into a ball as if making himself a smaller target might help the blows glance off of him.

(*"What've we got here, bitch?"*

Jimmy's mouth is no longer dry. It's salty and tastes of his own blood. His vision is dizzy and slightly blurred, and he can feel long warm areas where Frank's fists have fallen. His notebook has fallen from his grasp.

Frank bends down to pick it up.

Words finally come.

"Don't," Jimmy says, spitting up a bloody glob of phlegm.

"It speaks," says one of the golems holding him down.

"What did you say?" Frank asks.

"You don't want to do that . . ."

Frank shakes his head, unaware that the voice warning him no longer belongs to Jimmy.)

The memory twisted itself, the mind's eye vision removed from himself. He relived the event from a point a few feet from behind where Frank stood. He was a bodiless point of view, feeling nothing, locked away from what the memory-Jimmy was thinking, or feeling. It was as if the rage that had been building had completely displaced him so that (*the Jimmything hasn't moved. Frank is, as he was before, oblivious, wrapped in his own petty anger. The two others, similar jock types, hold the Jimmything back as Frank thumbs through the notebook with dirty hands. Pencil smears under thick, sweaty fingers already dotted with the Jimmything's blood.*

Frank sees something in the notebook and tears out a page. The Jimmything's muscles tense, and the two golems laugh and look down at the small creature they have trapped between them.

"What the fuck is this?" Frank shouts. The golems are surprised at his intensity. Frank is quite pissed. Losing it. Face red. Eyes wide. Spit flying as he shouts, shaking the page in front of the Jimmything. "What the fuck is this?" He literally screams a few inches from the Jimmything's face.

The golems see the page and their smiles widen.

The Jimmything is very quiet. It whispers through a split lip, but the voice is dry as a crematorium ash. "That is Stone Cold Steve Austin, the wrestler . . ." The Jimmything raises its face to stare into Frank's eyes, barely an inch from his own. "He's fucking you up the ass and you like it."

Frank lets lose with an inarticulate bellow and takes the notebook and smashes it across the Jimmything's face. The spine of the notebook tears as Frank hits the Jimmything

again and again with it. The golems let go and back up, star-
tled by the ferocity of the attack. Pages fly everywhere.

The Jimmything falls to its knees, and Frank throws the
remains of the notebook away. Frank rolls his sleeves up,
his expression lethal. "You think you're funny. So fucking
funny . . ."

Golem one looks uncertain and takes a step forward.
"Frank—"

"Bad idea," says the Jimmything as its fist comes up to
connect with the patella of Frank's knee. The fist doesn't
come straight on, but at an angle, the uppercut digging
knuckles up under the lower edge of the kneecap.

Golem one, realizing that the Jimmything isn't inert any
longer, turns toward it and reaches down. The Jimmything
grabs the uppercut fist in his opposite hand, and pushes his
forearm back to plow the elbow into the golem's kidney.

Frank's knee gives way underneath him and the golem
doubles over as the Jimmything stands. It looks toward the
other golem who stands, not quite realizing what has hap-
pened.

The Jimmything speaks. "You don't get it, do you?"

Frank tries to push himself up, and the Jimmything's heel
comes down on Frank's outstretched hand, grinding it into
the gravelly soil. "FUCK!" Frank yells.

The Jimmything whips its head around as the remaining
golem starts a lumbering run to tackle him. The Jimmything
steps aside, pivoting on Frank's hand—this time eliciting a
scream from the pinned jock. The golem misses, and as he
does, the Jimmything brings its fist up into the golem's face
hard enough to crush the nose and send the watch flying
from its wrist.

The golem rolls to the side like a wounded bear, skidding
shoulder-first into the ground. He doesn't move after that.

Frank is crying now, sobbing like a baby.

"Yeah, Frank," says the Jimmything, "I think I'm fucking hilarious." *He twists his foot for good measure. The bones haven't broken yet, but the flesh has split and blood soaks into the soil, making it glisten.*

"Do you get it now?" *the Jimmything asks the golem who has taken the kidney blow. This one freezes at the sound of the Jimmything's voice. The stink of fresh piss hangs in the air.*

"Do you GET IT?" *says the Jimmything.*

The golem opens his mouth, but nothing comes out of it.

"Let me explain the joke," *says the Jimmything.* "This fucking pansy asshole," *he prods the crying Frank with his foot.* "Lefty here. Yesterday, he got his ass whipped but good. And, today, this pathetic piss-stained Neanderthal THREATENS ME." *The Jimmything shakes his head.* "That's comedy."

Frank grabs for the Jimmything's leg, and the Jimmything drops down on him, one knee falling on the back of his neck, pushing Frank's face into the dirt.

"You're crazy," *says the golem as it gets to its feet.*

"Well, aren't you swift?"

"Get off of him." *The golem takes a step forward.*

The Jimmything reaches under Frank's face and does something that elicits a painful bellow. Frank's back arches and tries to buck it off, but the Jimmything is firmly planted, straddling Frank's neck now.

"How does it feel to have someone's life in your hands?" *the Jimmything says to the golem.* "One more step and something permanent is going to happen."

The golem pauses. "You ain't going to kill him."

"Boy, you are quick on the uptake today," *the Jimmy-*

thing says. "You read my mind. It'll be a lot more amusing if the gloryhole here has to play football without any eyes."

The Jimmything repositions his hands and Frank starts screaming and shaking, "No, damn it, NO! GET HIM OFF OF ME!" The warm odor of shit wafts up from Frank's prone form.

"Your call," the Jimmything says.

The golem stops moving.

"GET HIM OFF! GET HIM OFF!"

"Good move," says the Jimmything. "Now pick it up."

"What?" The golem looks dumbfounded a moment and glances at his ex-partner, who is still lying on the ground, unconscious.

"THE FUCKING NOTEBOOK, YOU MORON!" the Jimmything cries, its voice breaking for the first time. Even Frank stops moving at the outburst.

The golem looks down at the pages scattered around the clearing.

"Miss one page," the Jimmything whispers in the silence, "and you better know where to pick up a guide dog.")

Jimmy didn't sleep. He curled up and sank into the memory as if it were a black stagnant ocean. The blackness filled his eyes and ears, and slid down his throat. Like his dream, the blackness claimed him.

But he wasn't dreaming, so he couldn't wake up.

9

THE next morning the police came.

Their arrival didn't surprise Jimmy. He had run the memory though his head dozens of times. If the episode had been less severe, Jimmy could see the trio's macho circuit overloading at telling the cops they'd been beaten up. But Frank had crapped his pants and one of them had been left stone-cold unconscious.

Not to mention these were middle class suburban teenagers who did not actually believe the police were the enemy. If Frank hadn't called 911 on Jimmy, it was almost certain his mom did.

Jimmy knew when the cops arrived because he heard the knock on the door, and shortly afterward he heard Mr. Carswell saying, *"Jesus Christ."*

Jimmy didn't move. He stayed curled up in himself in the darkness under the covers. He wanted nothing more at that moment than to dissolve, curl tighter and tighter until he shrank away into the darkness. Right now, the dark was less frightening than what he knew was coming.

Under the covers, he screwed his eyes shut and pressed his fists into his temples. He heard the march of footsteps up to his room, and he heard the door slam open.

"You need to explain yourself, young man." Mr. Carswell's voice seemed distant and muffled. Jimmy's head was packed in cotton that throbbed in time to his pulse. He pulled himself even tighter under the blanket.

"James, I know you're awake. *Answer me.*" There was something cold and dry in Mr. Carswell's voice that reminded Jimmy of what he had become last night. Jimmy didn't respond. He couldn't form a coherent sentence if he wanted to.

The blankets tore away with a sudden rush of cold air. His skin, naked and damp with night sweat, contracted and broke out in gooseflesh. The muscles in his upper body and his jaw began vibrating on their own.

"I want you to explain this to me—"

Jimmy rolled and sat up on the edge of the bed away from Mr. Carswell. His foot squished and he looked down at a soggy pair of jeans. A puddle of brownish-gray water welled up from the saturated fabric.

Jimmy hugged himself against the sudden cold, blinking against the light that flooded the room. "Explain what?" he whispered.

"You damn well know what," Mr. Carswell said, his voice raising in timbre. He sounded as if he was on the edge. Inside Jimmy there was a small perverse impulse to push the man, taunt him so the dam would finally burst and there would be an end to the agonizing anticipation.

Jimmy kept his mouth shut.

"I'm talking to you, James—" His hand grabbed Jimmy's shoulder, and he felt the hot breath of the creature that had taken over last night.

"Mr. Carswell?" A mature voice, calm, used to being listened to. Jimmy turned and saw Chuck, the cop who'd taken him home from school an aeon or two ago.

The grip on Jimmy's shoulder tightened as Mr. Carswell turned to look at the cop.

"I'm afraid he's going to have to come with me."

"You have to let me talk with the boy." The anger was gone from the man's voice. It carried a pleading undertone that Jimmy wasn't sure anyone else was aware of.

Chuck nodded. "Yes, I do. But not here. Not until we process him."

"Can I get dressed first?" Jimmy asked.

Mr. Carswell let go of Jimmy's shoulder. He looked old now, and lost. "What happened?" he asked.

"I don't know." Jimmy said. It was only half a lie.

The cop wouldn't let him dress alone. God only knew, he might hide a bazooka in his socks, or a pound of cocaine in the crack of his ass. It was humiliating.

"You're arresting me?" Jimmy asked.

Chuck nodded.

"What for?"

"Assault, aggravated menacing, conspiracy to commit various felonies."

Jimmy stopped, his pants mid-leg. "What are you talking about?"

"Son, I don't have the details. I'm just serving the warrant."

Jimmy shook his head. "Who the fuck am I conspiring with?"

"Would you please finish getting dressed?" There was little of the fake warmth in Chuck that Jimmy had seen when the guy escorted him back from school. In fact, it was beginning to sink in that the officer's right hand had not left the butt of his side arm since Jimmy had started dressing.

No, he wouldn't shoot me . . .

"And why the fuck wouldn't he?" Jimmy whispered to himself.

"What?"

"Nothing." Jimmy muttered and finished pulling some random clothes on. When he was done, Chuck said, "Come over here and give me your arms."

Jimmy knew what was happening, but when the cold metal of the cuffs snapped across his wrists he still winced. "Do you have to—"

"You have the right to remain silent . . ."

This time there wasn't any attempt at chitchat while Chuck drove him down to the police station. The last Jimmy saw of the Carswells, they were standing on their front stoop watching the police car pull away, and Mrs. Carswell had her face buried in Mr. Carswell's shoulder.

Jimmy leaned back and tried to feel something beyond a shocked numbness. But, at this point, all he could muster was a small appreciation for the fact that Chuck had cuffed his hands in front of him. If he'd cuffed his hands behind him, there'd be no way for Jimmy to lean back in the seat.

The charges Chuck had mentioned still bounced around his brain. The only one that made sense to him was the assault charge, and even then he'd been defending himself. But conspiracy? And Jimmy didn't even know what aggravated menacing *was*.

A drone from Cuyahoga County Family Services was waiting at the station for them. This one was new, which wasn't a big surprise. County social workers had a higher turnover rate than your average Wal-Mart. Jimmy rarely had seen the same social worker more than six months in a row. The new one was too much the burnout to put on the phony smile and feign some concern for Jimmy.

While the cops hustled Jimmy through the process, fingerprints, photographs, emptying his nearly empty pockets, the county guy followed along, giving most of his attention to a cell phone that seemed grafted to his ear.

"Jesus Christ," Jimmy overheard the guy while they rolled his fingers across a glass plate slick with ink. "If they can't fax the proper form, they can't come to us for money . . ."

". . . and how is this my problem?"

". . . I *know* that, but I handle how many cases a day?"

". . . And what makes you think I have any idea what this kid's social is?"

". . . I'm a caseworker, not a database."

They finally took him to an interview room and closed the door on him and the county guy, who was still babbling on the phone.

"Look," he said, "it's not my fault someone forgot to enter him in the system, fix it. I've got to go, I have a thing to deal with here." He snapped the phone shut without so much as a "Bye," or a "See ya later."

Jimmy swore that the man's eyes were dead. He was looking into the face of a corpse.

"What the hell were you doing?" he asked.

Jimmy was at a loss for words. "Sir," he said, trying to force himself into the proper mode of interaction. "I really don't know what's going on."

The guy rubbed his temples. "Son, I'm supposed to help you. I can't do that if you bullshit me."

Jimmy just shook his head.

The man pulled out a chair and sat down across the table from him. "Here's what we have, Jimmy. I got handed your file at eight this morning. I've already talked to the prosecutor for Euclid Heights, and he handed me a list of charges that do not look good. They look pretty damn awful, in fact—"

"What are they saying I did?"

"Now I want to keep you out of the justice system. I've seen your history, and you don't belong there."

Jimmy nodded. "Thanks, but can you tell me—"

"I don't have a lot of options, but there's a county program that can keep you out of jail and keep you from having a felony conviction on your record. I just have to convince a judge you're eligible." He looked at Jimmy with those dead eyes. "You're willing to be part of this program?"

Jimmy was still trying to gather his wits about him. He wasn't even sure what the guy was offering him. "Yes, I mean if it's a choice between that and jail, but what is—"

The man stood up and smiled. "Good, I think you're making the right decision. We'll make sure you have the help you need. Now I have to talk to the judge again. Maybe we can fast-track this thing so that you're not stuck in a cell—"

Jimmy stood, and he realized that the cuffs were still on his wrists. "Wait, tell me—"

The county guy was already stepping though the open door. He was reaching for the cell phone as he said, "Look, I have to run, but call me if you have a question."

"But—" Jimmy sputtered and edged around the table, to be stopped by a cop at the door of the interview room. "—who the hell are you?" His voice dropped to a whisper because of the certainty that something bad was going to happen.

10

"DAMN, damn, damn . . ."

Nate hunched over the keyboard on his notebook computer. The light was dim, and the table was slightly too tall for his wrists. There were the beginning twinges warning of the unnatural angle of his wrists, but there weren't any alternatives in the motel room, and nothing to prop up his chair. Typing on the bed would be even worse, and he couldn't type on his lap without throwing his neck out of whack.

"Damn," he muttered again.

He had the headache that always came with lack of sleep. He had been in Pennsylvania for a total of sixty-four and a half hours. In that time he had got, at best, ten hours of sleep, and half of that was only a semi-drowse he'd caught in the fragments between hitting the streets and hitting the computer.

He stood up and stretched his hands hard enough for the knuckles to pop. The knuckles were swollen, the backs mapped by heavy blue veins. His hands seemed older than he was.

He shook his head as he walked to a small bag on the end table next to the bed. He *was* older. The fact crept up on him at times like this, when he was alone and feeling the myriad aches that had infested his body over the years.

He reached in the bag and took out a small bottle of Relafen and chased one of the white oval pills with a cup of stale coffee left over from breakfast. His gut protested, and, in response, Nate drank the rest of the ice-cold coffee. Once his stomach was beaten into submission, he sat back down at the keyboard.

Five years older, said an angry voice in the back of Nate's skull. *Five years older and not one day wiser.*

Doing this so long, it really seemed he should know *more.*

But, as always, he had reached the point where it was patently clear that he had nothing new to add to the database other than another corpse that fit the pattern. There should be more, but there wasn't. He had gathered details from pastors, family, friends, doctors, police, funeral directors. He had transcribed about fifty pages of notes so far, accumulated about five hundred pages of documents, and none of them told him the two things he needed to know.

How?

Why?

Nate stared at the screen, unsure exactly what he had been doing. His eyes were blurring.

"I got to get some sleep," he muttered. It was no use pounding his head against this. If there was something to find in all the data on Ted Mackenzie, he was likely to miss it while he was half-asleep.

Besides, time was no longer a factor. He had hit all the bases he needed to hit in Creighton Falls without anyone catching on to him. The rumors might be circulating now about the reporter, or the medic, the doctor, the health inspector . . . but that really didn't matter anymore. Nate had what he had come for, and it was the nature of information that no one could take it back even if they decided he'd cheated.

Nate collapsed on the hard motel bed and listened to muscles creak and bones pop. He felt the tentative aches of arthritis beginning in his knees and his shoulders. He hoped he'd taken the Relafen in time to head off the worst of it.

Sleep dug its claws in behind his eyes. The penultimate thought to cross his conscious mind, *What are you doing with your life?*

The answer was: *The only thing I can do.*

Nate opened his eyes after a dreamless sleep. Morning sunlight streamed across his face from the gap in the heavy green drapes. Dust motes hung frozen in the beam as if afraid of the light. His stomach churned acid from old coffee and possibly the Relafen. He opened his mouth slowly, letting his pasty tongue peel away from the roof of his mouth.

His brain was no longer trying to push itself through a fog of exhaustion, but his joints felt as if they'd been lined with sandpaper and his back felt as if it was on the verge of being locked in a permanent cramp.

Can't sprawl out like that, Nate thought, though it probably had more to do with the cheap motel bed than how he lay in it. For some bizarre reason he didn't want to consider the fact that he might not be able to get a good night's sleep in a cheap motel bed anymore.

He got up slowly, wincing every time a muscle tensed, threatening to cramp. Fortunately, while there were false alarms from his shoulders all the way down to the arch of his left foot, nothing seized up on him.

He looked at the end table and saw the clock radio read

7:10 A.M. He had slept over twelve hours. He shook his head. No wonder his body felt like hell. Can't stay in one position that long without consequences.

He picked up his cell phone and checked for messages. Two from Tony, one other consulting client, and a number that he didn't recognize.

That was the one he listened to first.

A woman's voice. "Mr. Adriano, I would like to talk to you. If you would, please meet me for lunch at 1:00 P.M. this Friday at the Eat-And-Park off the Pennsylvania Turnpike exit 237. I have access to information regarding a matter of long-standing interest to you."

If this was a consulting job, it was the most bizarre one he had heard of. His work might be fighting the bad guys, but he still wasn't a character in a private eye novel. His clients were almost exclusively lawyers and law enforcement personnel.

If it wasn't about a consulting gig, there was only one other thing it could be about. That made Nate nervous. He had spent five years keeping his personal investigations separate from his job.

He did that for two reasons . . .

First, the past five years had given him more cause than most to believe in shadowy conspiracies manipulating events. The kids themselves were indirect evidence of *something* of that nature. Though Nate suspected that if the malignant force behind the deaths was a human agency, they would have neutralized Nate a long time ago.

Second, it would be a bad career move if some defense attorney were to cross-examine him and bring up his strange idea of a hobby. The truth was, everyone he contacted straight-on about these kids considered him a nut. The only ones who didn't were nuts themselves. Not a great credibility builder.

Nate repeated the message, listening carefully for any clues to what it meant.

The voice was middle American with studied diction. The woman said, "Eat-*And*-Park" not "Eat-*N*-Park," which was the restaurant's actual name, or "Eaton Park," which was what the natives called it.

She was being coy, which likely meant that she *was* one of the conspiracy/UFO/Fortean/New Age misfits who rattled across his path from time to time.

Nate was wearing his public face again as he walked into the Eat-N-Park off the Turnpike. He arrived thirty minutes early, and had the waitress seat him at the booth he chose by the window. It was in the corner, so his seat was backed to a wall and he could see most of the restaurant to his left, and most of the parking lot to his right. His rental car sat in the space directly opposite his chosen booth.

Nate ordered coffee and waited.

Outside, in the parking lot, Nate watched as a young woman got out of a yellow late-model VW Beetle. She wasn't the only one to move about the parking lot since he'd arrived, but Nate felt certain that this was his anonymous caller. The VW had been parked there since he'd pulled in, so the woman had been sitting for nearly fifteen minutes in her parked vehicle.

Seeing if I came alone?

Nate sipped his coffee and shook his head as he watched her walk toward the entrance. Her youth didn't bode well for the possibilities of this meeting. The nuts tended to be young. *Early twenties,* Nate thought, *almost in the same category as the kids.*

She strode forward with square shoulders and a righteous posture that made him think of Jane Fonda, post-*Barbarella* and pre-*Workout*. She had long black hair that contrasted with a navy-blue suit. Her hair belonged with a peasant blouse.

Nate's suspicions were confirmed when the woman in question walked up to his booth and said, "Mr. Adriano?"

You know damn well who I am. Don't you?

"Miss?" Nate asked, looking into the woman's eyes. He could tell that there was an element of role-playing about her right now. He was good at sensing that after doing so much of it himself. The suit wasn't her, and neither were the thick black-framed glasses that hid brown eyes that were a little too narrow for her features.

She slid into the booth across from Nate without answering him. "I am glad you came," she said. "You are a difficult man to track down."

"Not difficult enough, apparently." Nate reached into his pocket and took out a small cassette tape recorder. He hit the record button and gauged her reaction. "What's your name, and why am I here?"

"My name is Abby Springfield," she told him. "I'm a reporter, and I have possession of something that I can only show two people I know of in the whole world."

She looked up at him. "And the other one is dead."

11

A REPORTER. Nate rubbed the side of his head. That would be fine if she was here because of something to do with Forensic Data Associates. His consulting business didn't *need* media exposure—he served a client base so small and cliquish that he only needed a little human networking and word of mouth to get clients—but the occasional story about his work in criminal investigation and as a prosecution expert witness didn't hurt. A news story might not give him clients, but it did tend to enhance his credibility with the clients he did have, especially the elected ones who didn't know a BIOS from a bit map.

What worried Nate was the context. She was not talking or acting like a reporter interested in that part of his life. She spoke as if there were men in black ready to spring out of the woodwork.

"What paper do you work for, Ms. Springfield?"

"I've published in *The Washington Post, The New York Times* . . ."

"You're a freelancer." She didn't answer him, just gave him a slightly downcast look, as if he had uncovered a dirty little secret. Jane Fonda, right out of *The China Syndrome*.

She was here about the kids, he was sure. That put Nate in a quandary. As much as he wanted—*needed*—to find some reason for the deaths he was investigating; as much as he knew that the normal channels of medical, legal, and forensic investigation broke down when attempting to explain what happened; as much as he suspected that someone was suppressing information about these deaths; as much of the last five years as he had expended on this, he did not want his name publicly attached to something that was held in the same regard as UFOs, psychic channeling, and the Loch Ness Monster. Tie that albatross around his neck and he would be useless in the face of any decent cross-examination, and there would go half his income.

"I'm sorry I've wasted this much of your time," Nate said. He reached over and picked up the tape recorder and shut it off. "How many years out of school are you? Two, three at the most? Do you think you're the first to discover this story?"

"What do you mean?"

Nate leaned forward. "This subject, and worse, the circumstantial thread tying the cases together, is what a Mr. Charles Fort called a 'damned thing.' "

Abby nodded and brushed a stray hair from her cheek. "I know."

"It's too far outside the common definition of reason to be taken seriously."

"I know." She reached out and touched his hand, where he'd been taking away the tape recorder. "Put that back, and turn it on."

It was strange, but her touch unnerved him. He withdrew his hand, leaving the tape recorder on the table. She glanced down at it and turned it on herself.

"I apologize for being so transparent," she said, once the machine started running again. "But I do not want to write a story about supernatural fires, spontaneous combustion, demonic possession, or whatever is actually behind all of this. I am a journalist. I deal with facts. And I am not even certain I believe it myself."

Nate was taken aback by the way she suddenly diverged from his initial impression. Not only did she not belong in the nut camp, she was establishing herself as a staunch member of the skeptic brigade. The same people who kept most of what he investigated on his own time out of print in the first place.

"Why are you here, then?" Nate asked, finally interested.

"What *I* want is *your* story. Nathan Adriano, expert witness for the government, high-paid consultant to the FBI and local law enforcement. Founder of Forensic Data Associates, which makes a seven-figure annual profit. By all accounts, he should be a millionaire. But his home address is a one-room studio apartment, which doubles as corporate HQ. He has no real personal assets aside from cash, and he has spent several years of his life chasing an explanation for a series of deaths that most reasonable people would consider a chain of freak accidents." She looked into Nate's eyes, and there seemed to be less innocence there than he had first thought. "You are the story. I know a dozen editors who might slam the door on me if I presented a story on your kids, but who would eat out of my hand if I handed them an exclusive interview and a bio."

Nate was silent for a few long minutes. The waitress came and Nate ordered something just to make her go away.

"No," Nate said finally, "I can't do that."

"You want this story in print," Abby said.

"What makes you think that?" Nate said. "I'm doing this for my own reasons. Reasons that do not need to be paraded in front of my clients. I don't need some fluff piece of reporting making me look like some New Age wacko."

"Are you?" she asked.

Nate stood up and took his tape recorder. The whole idea was making him angry. "I think I'd better go." She reached out and touched his arm. He angrily shook it off.

"What happens when you find out?" Abby asked.

Nate had slid halfway out of the booth. He turned and looked at her. "What?"

"This private research of yours. Will it remain secret forever?"

Nate stopped moving.

"If you uncover proof of what is happening, will it simply be to satisfy your own curiosity?"

"I want to stop it."

"Would you, if it cost your credibility as an expert witness?"

"You're offering me that?" Nate shook his head.

"I may be," she said. "Why don't you stay for lunch and find out?"

Apparently, Nate wasn't the only person investigating what was happening to these kids. Abby showed him a thin jewel case with an unlabeled CD inside.

She told him it was research data going back over a hundred years. She said it was given to her by a man who, like Nate, wanted to stop what was happening. A man who was dead now.

She called the man Sam. Sam had been a career soldier who had worked in Washington D.C. most of his life. He had been a computer expert, and had skills that could probably earn him ten times as much as a civilian. A sense of duty had kept him in the army—at least that was what he had told Abby.

For years before Abby met him, he had been a database

analyst in the Pentagon. He had security clearance to, in his words, "mess with every computer the army had—and a few the army didn't."

One of the latter was a small mainframe in Langley with a legacy operating system that dated from the early sixties. The hardware was going, and the Agency needed someone to port over the old databases to a modern server. Several gigs worth of data with complicated interrelationships that had to be moved to a new operating system, reedited for Y2K compliance, and checked for integrity about five different ways.

The mainframe belonged to something called Department Blue. Sam found out very little about it, other than the fact that it seemed to have more than its fair share of doctors on the payroll.

Sam wasn't told what the data was for, and he didn't ask, but in transferring the data he had to become intimately familiar with the material. Probably more familiar than the people using it.

It became clear to Sam that Department Blue, to some degree, was conducting domestic espionage. That put Sam in an ethical bind. While he had a duty to notify someone, he was also bound by his security clearance. Sam was enough of a realist to know that just about anyone he'd inform who was cleared to see this data must have already signed off on it. And, illegal or not, if he leaked any of the data, he would be guilty of several felonies himself. Perhaps even treason.

So Sam did his job and tried not to see more than he wanted to.

Unfortunately, Sam was not one able to wear intentional blinders. Every day he would work on the translation, and every day he would see another piece of the puzzle—the demographics, the birth date vs. the death date. The abstracts of newspaper articles, medical records, police blotters . . .

He also overheard cryptic discussions while he walked down the corridors of Department Blue. Doctors would talk of "Symptomatic cases," "Possible clients," and "Post-mortem confirmation."

He even heard one doctor refer to a "flameout."

It wasn't long before Sam understood exactly what Department Blue was investigating. It took a while before Sam believed it. By then, Sam was researching on his own, going through newspaper clippings for the names of kids he saw crawl by his computer screen during the day.

Initially, Sam was afraid that the "flameouts" themselves were some black government project. Eventually, his side research led him to the conclusion that Department Blue was only investigating the phenomenon, by authority of an executive order signed by LBJ.

Despite his fears, Sam continued working on Department Blue's computer systems. The project was endless. Sam went though most days in a depressive fog, fighting back what he thought were stress headaches. What he knew ate at him, but he couldn't risk his commission. Especially after he understood that, whatever the phenomenon was, it wasn't being caused by Department Blue. Which would make any such sacrifice on his part particularly pointless.

Still, the stress and the guilt began affecting his behavior. At least that's what he told himself when confronted with mood swings and sudden rages. You couldn't work on an illegal black project for long and keep a sense of honor. What had been a duty became first a job, then a trial.

He began thinking seriously about early retirement.

On many levels he didn't want to, but he learned more about Department Blue. These kids, the ones who were dying, represented a national security threat. While Sam was certain that the *cause* of death was the unknown that scared the doctors around him, the talk always seemed as if the children themselves were the threat.

Doctors always did that, depersonalized people, like the bastard at the hospital who didn't take his headaches seriously. That guy would tell his nurse something like, "Give the migraine in five this Imitrex script and get him out of here."

His thinking became muddled and less clear over time. Worst of all were the headaches.

Sam realized two things at about the same time.

The first realization was that his doctor was seriously mistaken.

The second realization was that Department Blue was doing more than passively investigating.

The data that Sam was sifting through contained more than what could be gathered simply from the existing record. There were clinical notes, medical records, autopsy records written by Agency doctors. Somewhere, Department Blue had a test facility where they had isolated more than one of these kids.

That fact began preying on his mind. Kids that were somehow programmed to die, spending the last few weeks of their lives in the custody of some government facility. A facility run by scientists who seemed more interested in studying the phenomenon than preventing it, something they didn't seem able or willing to do.

"By the time I heard from him, he was on disability leave, an inoperable tumor the size of a fist growing inside his skull. He said that the doctors detected it too late, and gave him three weeks to live if the radiation didn't work."

She placed the CD on the table. "That's when he gave me this. I was the last on a long list," Abby said. "His story, combined with his state of mind at the time, made very few reporters willing to talk to him—"

"You're saying he came across as a nut."

"He was subject to some paranoid fantasies. As I said, I'm not wholly convinced myself." Abby looked down at the CD. "I had nothing to lose by talking to him. This was a gesture of good faith that he didn't live long enough to follow up on."

"So what's on the CD?"

"From what he told me, 'an image of part of a data transformation series.' I think it was burned as part of a diagnostic procedure and was supposed to be destroyed afterward."

"He just walked out with it?"

"From what he said, he gathered all manner of sensitive data. He was obsessed."

"It's hard to believe."

"What is?" Abby asked. The ironic note in her voice was so subtle that it might have been unconscious on her part. Nate, however, was continually aware of how bizarre the universe he lived in could be. He *had* to believe in at least three impossible things before breakfast. The axis on which his world currently spun was an impossibility.

His current thought, however, was on a matter much more mundane. "How does someone walk out of a top secret facility run by the CIA, carrying a disk of classified information?"

Abby smiled. Something more than amusement there. "You are better off asking why it doesn't happen more often. The physical security of this nation's secrets relies primarily on trust. Sam had the clearance, so he was not suspect. And, since he passed none of the information on to anyone before this," she tapped the case of the CD, "he never became suspect. How do you think Mr. Aldrich Ames did so much damage?"

"So why are you here with me, if you have that?"

Abby shook her head. "What good does this do for me? It's a huge mass of tables of dates, places, names, statistics that I don't even know how to read. I want a story."

"So you've said."

"Exclusive rights, interview, book, everything. In return, you get the data."

"You're asking a lot," Nate said.

"I don't think so," Abby said, "Especially since, if you don't take my offer, you don't know what you are investigating."

"You're saying another kid died somewhere?"

"No," Abby said, "one of your kids *survived.*"

12

THEY had a lawyer from County Family Services there when they questioned him. The guy was pretty useless except he managed to keep the cops off Jimmy's back for not answering any questions. That was good, because for a lot of them he didn't really know the answers.

More than once the detectives would say, "You're not fooling us, we know what's going on here."

More than once Jimmy responded, "That's good, I wish you'd tell me."

They kept him on ice for something, Jimmy didn't know why. They kept him in a holding cell rather than shipping him off to Juvenile Detention like Jimmy expected them to. That was all right with Jimmy; he had no wish to revisit that particular hellhole. He had already been through that doorway once, and that time they'd never charged him with anything. He had to sleep on the common floor with a hundred or so hardcore bastards, most of whom wanted to stick a knife or a dick in you, and half didn't particularly care which.

The worst part of it, aside from the waiting, was a meeting with the county lawyer and the anonymous social worker with the cell phone. It was in the same interview room where the detectives asked all the questions. The place had a bad fluorescent tube that buzzed insistently in the background, and the faint smell of piss followed Jimmy from the holding cell.

Jimmy knew it was going to be bad when the cops left him alone with the two county guys. For some reason the pair made him so uneasy that he had the bizarre impulse to ask for a cop in here.

The lawyer extended a stubby-fingered hand and gestured toward the metal stool on the opposite side of the table. He was a head and a half shorter than the social worker, and reminded Jimmy of a mad scientist's assistant. "Take a seat, Jimmy."

Yes, Igor.

He looked over at the social worker. He was just folding his phone to put it away. *It's alive.* Jimmy couldn't get over the man's corpselike first impression.

"Jimmy," said Igor, "we need to ask you a few questions. Now this is in confidence. None of this leaves this room."

Uh-huh.

Jimmy shrugged because he didn't know what to say. This guy pretended to be *his* Lawyer, but the asshole worked for the county. The county that seemed to have taken over the mommy/daddy role since he'd been escorted from the Carswells'. *You'd think they would have come to visit once.*

Igor patted his brow and Jimmy saw that he was sweating badly. The collar of his powder-blue shirt was dark where the top cut into his fleshy neck. "We have a preliminary hearing before the judge in three days," he nodded over at the Frankenstein Monster, "Dr. Schuster here has done a lot to get us that expedited hearing. With his diagnostic assessment, it seems you're a good candidate for the TRACE Program Dr. Schuster explained to you about—"

What diagnostic assessment? What explanation—

Jimmy seriously began to worry about whether he had suffered some blank time with these county people and couldn't remember what they had told him. "Sir, what exactly is TRACE?"

"Oh—" Igor began, but the Frankenstein Monster beat him to the punch. "It stands for Treatment, Responsive Action, Caring Environment is what I think he was asking. It is a positive alternative to juvenile incarceration, with a limited number of slots with matched federal and state dollars."

"Yes, indeed. Dr. Schuster assures me that you'd want to take advantage of it."

Jimmy nodded slowly, watching the dead eyes on the Frankenstein monster. He didn't seem to react at all; his face kept the same even pallor. Jimmy wondered if this guy freaked Igor out, too, because Igor seemed nervous around him.

Maybe, the dark void behind his brain echoed, *he's afraid of me.*

"I believe his quote was, 'If those are my options . . .' Right?"

Jimmy said, "Yes, but—"

"You were saying?" interrupted Monster, prompting the lawyer to streamroller over Jimmy's next question.

"Yes," continued the lawyer, as if Jimmy had asked the question. "What we need is your point of view on what happened, on what you think it was you did."

"I'm not even clear on what I'm being accused of."

"Don't worry about the specific charges," Igor said, "That's all a legal muddle. I just want to know a few facts in your own words."

"Okay, I guess. But I want to know why—"

"Good," said Monster. He pushed over a few xeroxed

sheets of paper. Jimmy looked at them and in a wave of disorientation saw Cain's face looking up at him.

"W-w-w—" Jimmy couldn't get the word to form. Someone had broken into his locker, pawed though his notebooks. Why the hell would anyone do that? Those were *his!* No one had any fucking right to look at them, much less take them. The muscles on Jimmy's upper arms vibrated. He held on to the edge of the metal table as if loosening his grip would allow the growing rage inside him to throw him against the wall.

"Where did you get these?" asked the cold voice of the Jimmything.

Fuck No. Not Now.

"From the Euclid Heights Prosecutor," said Igor. "While they admit self-defense as far as Mr. Frank Bradley is concerned—their own witnesses state that he attacked you before you struck him—this is the prosecution's main charge."

From behind his own eyes Jimmy felt his brows knit.

What?

"What?"

"Did you write these cartoons, Jimmy?" asked the monster. "Are they all yours?"

"They *are* mine," said the Jimmything, "and I want them back."

Igor shook his head. "They're in evidence against you."

"Evidence of what?"

Monster spoke. "Evidence of menacing, conspiracy—"

"They're fucking comic books!" The chair clattered behind him as he stood. He still held the edge of the table, muscles taut as cables. He felt something warm on his face, and had a coppery taste in his mouth.

Igor and his Monster—no, make that Monster and his Igor—both stared at him. Igor looked as if he was about to crap his pants. Monster nodded and said, "I know, Jimmy. But they weren't just cartoons to Frank Bradley, were they?"

"It was none of his business," Jimmy whispered.

"It was his likeness." Monster leaned slightly forward, still out of reach, though. He tossed Jimmy a handkerchief. "Take care of that."

Jimmy looked down and saw a dime-sized drop of blood on the table. As he looked, another one joined it. He stared at it a long time before he realized that the blood was coming from his face.

A fucking nosebleed?

He grabbed the handkerchief and saw his shirtfront spattered with it. The rage inside him seemed to have subsided for a moment, as if it leaked out with the blood.

Jimmy held the handkerchief to his nose and said, "Ny nookth. They're ny nookth."

"Do you understand what you were illustrating, Jimmy?" Igor asked.

"Do you thing I'm thupid?"

"There are very graphic scenes of violence, occult beliefs—" Igor kept saying.

"Thath againth the law?"

"—and you show a disturbing portrayal of an attack on your own high school."

"Tho?"

Monster shook his head. "You use the likenesses of teachers and students, the setting, in a violent scenario that is seen as a graphic threat by both the Euclid Heights High School Administration and the Euclid Heights City Prosecutor."

"Thug you. Ith a thugging thory."

Igor said. "You have a picture of the vice principal's head on a spike."

"Poetic lithenth."

They were both looking at him as if he was some alien creature. Jimmy figured that he must have returned the favor. He wiped off his nose, and when he felt sure the nose-bleed wasn't going to repeat itself, he said, "Okay guys, I get the fact that I'm here because I lost it on Frank. The bastard jumped me, tore up a few weeks' worth of work. That pissed me off, and I whaled on him. Okay, I got that. You cannot tell me that I'm here talking to you two nimrods because of something I *wrote*."

They kept staring at him.

"No, this ain't happening." He shook his head and grabbed one of the xerox copies. Fresh crimson spattered Cain's monochrome face. "This," Jimmy held up the page, "it ain't real. It didn't happen. It's not going to happen. It's a dogfight between an immortal and a fucking demon, for crying out loud. What, do they think I have a temple to Baphomet in my bedroom?"

"They see a potential for violence—" Monster began.

"Christ, watch TV sometime."

"They see these images as an explicit threat, Jimmy." Igor said. "Because of violent incidents in the past, they take these threats seriously."

"What the hell happened to the First Amendment?"

"It doesn't cover this," Igor said.

The paper slipped from Jimmy's fingers. He shook his head in bewilderment. "No, wait. You didn't just say—"

"Threats, menacing, incitements to panic are not protected speech," Igor said.

"That's it," Jimmy said. "I want another fucking lawyer."

"I think you should calm down," Monster said. "You have a lot of anger that we need to deal with, but we're going to get you help."

"I don't need help," Jimmy shouted. He balled his hands into fists. "I need a lawyer who understands the difference between a comic book and a ransom note."

Igor looked across at Monster. Monster nodded, as if they had some prearranged signal. "Jimmy," Igor said, "we've looked at the case they have. A judge or a jury looking at what you've written. It will be seen as a threat. At the very least it will be seen as a deliberate attempt to produce panic—"

"How? Did I tell someone to break into my locker and steal my work?"

"Frank's reaction to your portrayal of him can be used to show intent—"

"His intent to be a fucking asshole."

"—And if we can get the judge to agree to enroll you in this program, we can avoid bringing any of this into court."

Jimmy paced on the far side of the room, as distant from Igor and Monster as he could get. "I don't believe this shit. I didn't do anything wrong. You're supposed to be a lawyer, you should *know* that."

"Jimmy," Igor said, "we're trying to get the best outcome for you."

"Bullshit." Jimmy said, looking at Igor's little round face and stubby fingers.

"I think we're done here," said Monster. "We'll get you into a place where they can help you."

"What the fuck do you mean by that?" Jimmy shouted. "What the hell is this TRACE bullshit, anyway?"

Igor and Monster were moving toward the door. Jimmy shook his head and walked up to them. He grabbed Igor's arm. "Answer my goddamn question. What the hell *is* this?"

Igor actually looked as if he was about to hyperventilate at Jimmy's touch, and Monster took Jimmy's wrist and removed his hand. "It's a funding program for residential treatment. Treatment you need, Jimmy."

Before Monster had finished his sentence, a set of cops had entered the room and were holding Jimmy by the shoulders. Igor and Monster slipped out of the room, Igor striding twice as fast as his pale companion.

"What kind of treatment?" Jimmy shouted after them.

No answer.

13

JIMMY felt the world had spun completely out of control. He couldn't put his finger on exactly when things had gone loopy, but it had passed beyond the limits of an already insane system.

He'd had to sit for six hours in a packed waiting room for his hearing before the juvenile court judge. It was a white-walled room with uncomfortable plastic seats bolted to the floor. A nasty looking cop sat at a desk next to a metal detector that led toward the courtroom.

Around Jimmy sat all the local juvenile cases, and kids waited with their parents, or their grandmothers, a lot of them dressed in ill-fitting suits that obviously didn't belong to them. Jimmy was marked by the fact that he wore the same clothes he'd been arrested in, and there wasn't even a fake parent accompanying him. He got Monster.

Here, at least, Monster had to give up his cell phone to the troll manning the desk. At first Jimmy thought that was a good thing. Unfortunately, that meant Monster had no one else to talk to. Jimmy tried to fake being asleep, but he could only do that for so long.

"Now you don't have to say anything in there," he'd say.

I don't have to say anything out here either.

"The lawyers are going to do the talking. I think everyone has agreed that we can get you into the program—"

Shut up. Just fucking shut up.

Everyone around him was fucking nuts. Little Igor had told him that the only charge these people had was around the *comic book.* Jimmy knew enough to realize that there was no way anyone could make that kind of charge stick. While Monster droned on, Jimmy planned things out in his mind.

He would ask to talk to the judge, and request a new lawyer. Someone who wasn't on the county payroll. Hell, the ACLU should be all over this like Frank on a porn video. He'd fight the charge, then he'd get someone to sue the bastards for putting him in jail for something he wrote.

Where the fuck were they living, anyway, China?

Planning it out like that kept the hot kernel of rage from blowing up inside him.

Then came the hearing. They pulled him out into the courtroom, even as the judge was dismissing the previous case. Jimmy had the feeling of being on a conveyor belt.

"City of Euclid Heights vs. James Allan Somerset," someone said. Hearing his full name made it seem as if they were talking about someone else. The judge shuffled some papers as Monster escorted Jimmy to the front of the courtroom. "I understand that counsel has come to a mutual agreement?"

Igor was in front and stood, "Yes, your honor, we have."

"No contest to the charges," the judge read, "and Mr. Somerset will enroll for a year in a residential treatment program—"

"Just wait a fucking minute—" Jimmy said.

Igor turned toward Jimmy as if he had just started waving a gun.

The judge sighed and lowered the papers in front of him.

"—I didn't agree to any of this. This county ass-wipe agreed to it all for me. I don't want to cop to any fucking plea when I didn't do anything wrong." Monster grabbed his arm.

The prosecutor guy cleared his throat and the judge leaned forward and said, "That's enough."

"I just wrote a fucking comic book." Jimmy said, trying to shake free of Monster. Somehow this wasn't going as eloquently as he'd planned.

"*Enough.* One more profane outburst and you'll be facing a contempt charge, young man."

"But—" Jimmy pulled himself free and was suddenly looking at the chest of a very large uniform filled with about two hundred and eighty pounds of nasty.

"Bailiff," the judge said. "Please escort the defendant to the bench."

A large meaty hand clamped down on Jimmy's shoulder, and he found himself being pulled in front of the judge. The judge leaned toward Jimmy, while pushing the microphone away. "I don't have time for this. Now, are you requesting new counsel?"

"I just wrote—"

"I've seen what you wrote, and it's appalling. That's not my question. Do you want the court to appoint you new counsel?"

"Hell, yes! I don't want someone who'll fold. I want to *fight* this thing."

The judge nodded. "I am certain you do. Do you understand what that means, son?"

Jimmy opened his mouth, then closed it again. It was as if his tank had run dry. Slowly he managed to say, "I have a right to think. I have a right to write down what I think. They shouldn't have this kind of power . . ."

"What it means," the judge told him, "is that this will go to trial. If it does, you will lose this deal your current attorney worked out for you. You will get a public defender who's more overworked and less qualified than the man who is representing you now. And, unless someone posts bond for you, you spend the duration waiting in the juvenile lockup."

"I thought you were supposed to be impartial."

"Those are facts, young man. I've seen too many kids with wasted lives walk through here. This deal offers you an opportunity to salvage yours. Whether you committed a criminal act or not, if someone's offering you a hand out of the criminal justice system, take it or you're a fool."

The judge sat up and adjusted the microphone. "Bailiff, please escort the defendant back to his seat."

Jimmy was manhandled next to Igor and Monster. Igor looked severely flustered. Monster just looked as if he had gas.

"Now that we have dispensed with the drama," the judge said, "I am going to ask the defendant to rise."

Jimmy got unsteadily to his feet from the seat where the bailiff had shoved him.

The judge looked at him squarely and asked, "Do you understand the nature of the plea counsel has presented?"

Jimmy looked around. He felt alone and adrift. There wasn't a familiar face to look at, no one to offer support, advice, comfort. He realized that he was upset that the Carswells weren't here. *Why Jimbo,* said an evil voice in his head, *they knew you were spoiled goods. Good riddance to bad garbage and all that.*

"Mr. Somerset?" the judge added.

"Yes, I do," Jimmy said.

"And it is your wish that the court accept the plea entered by counsel?"

What the fuck do I do? Jimmy realized he was shaking, and he felt on the verge of blacking out again. He could feel the Jimmything pressing at the surface of his mind, and God help him if that broke out. He couldn't go nuts here like he did with Frank. People had *guns* here.

Jimmy almost choked on the word. "Yes . . ."

"Good," the judge said. "The plea is entered and we remand you to the custody . . ."

Jimmy didn't hear the rest of it. He had a sudden brief awareness of his cheek pressing into the grimy carpet, and of a view of the underside of Igor's table, before he lost consciousness completely.

Something dreamed, or thought, or imagined . . .

The Jimmything stands on a black rock high above a cracked, blasted plain. The land—dry, wrinkled and cracked—stretches off in all directions, unbroken except for pinnacles of rock that break the surface. The rocks are jagged as broken glass.

An impossibly large sky looms above everything, ink-black and starless. The sun hangs blood-red, filling half the black sky, blazing down with sterilizing intensity.

Jimmy knows he is looking at hell. He can feel the pull of the darkness trying to envelop his soul. He turns to see the direction he has come from.

A tiny, cool, white light.

Jimmy reaches for it and feels the blackness tearing at him. Shadow claws dig gobbets out of his flesh. Jimmy fights it, pulling toward the other familiar light. He hears whispers at the edge of comprehensibility.

A face appears in front of him, a sad-looking woman that Jimmy recognizes as his mother. He's seen photographs of her.

Snakes of darkness are slipping into wounds on his back, his chest, arms, legs. It tries to fill his mouth as he calls out, "Help me, *please*."

The sad-eyed woman shakes her head and turns away.

No! Jimmy tries to say, but he can't speak anymore. He falls away from the light, spinning into the darkness. It consumes him as he falls, so there's nothing left to strike the cracked, sterile ground.

Jimmy woke, his skin clammy from sweat, brain hot from already fading visions. He tensed, expecting some nightmare vision to come again, but nothing pulsed out of the walls, and the sky outside the louvered window stayed an ordinary shade of blue.

Jimmy stared at the window for a long time. The normalcy of it was disorienting after the dream-visions. After a while he turned his head to see where he was.

Acoustical tile, darkened fluorescent lights, a track that bent in a broad U above him, curtain hanging from it to his left. His gaze landed on a device hanging from the wall. It took a while for his brain to make sense of what he was seeing. A blood pressure thing, all curling black tubes, bladders and a Velcro cuff. Jimmy closed his eyes because it reminded him of the thing from his dreams.

Hospital.

What happened?

No answer. Not even a hint of a memory. Not even a memory-shaped hole so he could tell anything was missing. He remembered the courtroom and his collapse, so he turned back toward the window to look for bars.

No bars.

Okay, did I hallucinate the whole thing? Igor, Monster, Judge?

He looked down at himself and saw a tube going into the back of his hand. He raised his hand and looked at the tape holding the thing in place. *They're injecting stuff into me.*

He looked up and saw the bag hanging from a rack above his head.

"This is fucked up," he whispered. His mouth was dry and pasty, as if he'd been asleep for months.

"Jimmy," said an unfamiliar voice.

Jimmy jerked and looked down at the foot of the bed. A man was standing there. He hadn't been there before. Jimmy also realized that the light from the window had changed and the light fixtures were lit now.

Oh, shit. Did I just black out and not even realize it?

The man at the foot of the bed wore a charcoal-gray suit, a powder-blue shirt, and a black tie with some sort of geometric pattern in the weave. The tie changed from cubes to triangles when the guy shifted his weight. Jimmy didn't like looking at it, so he shifted his gaze up to meet the guy's face.

Young-looking guy, jet-black hair, smoky eyes that matched his jacket. Jimmy thought he looked like an upscale used car salesman, one from a Lexus dealership.

"Jimmy?" he repeated. His voice sounded as if it was coming from down a well. Then Jimmy had a shift of perspective and realized he was the one down the well. Everything had pulled back, out of his reach, even his hands felt as if they were somewhere on the other side of the room.

"What?" Jimmy said. His mouth felt full of cotton.

"I'm Dr. Altroy, I don't think you remember the last two times I was here."

Jimmy nodded, craning his neck to see the doctor.

Altroy saw him bend his neck and reached around for a box that dangled from the edge of the bed. "Here, you can adjust this to be more comfortable." He put the box in Jimmy's hand—his left one, the one without the tube running into it.

Jimmy stared at the box for a second or two. For a few weird moments he was convinced that the controls weren't labeled in any coherent language. Then he felt another perspective shift and realized that he was just looking at the words "up" and "down."

Jimmy found the button for the upper half of the bed and stabbed his thumb at it. The bed ground out a mechanical whir, and his head and upper body began tilting upward. He was glad he did this rather than attempt sitting up, because with the change in orientation came a nauseating wave of vertigo.

"Are you up to talking for a few minutes, Jimmy?"

When the vertigo passed, Jimmy looked around again. From his new perspective it seemed almost a different room. He could see the other bed, empty at the moment. A pair of doors off to his left, one open wide enough to show a slice of toilet. There was a rolling tray, and a TV bolted to the wall above Dr. Altroy's head.

"Where am I?"

"The Cleveland Clinic," replied Dr. Altroy.

"What happened?"

"You fainted." He looked down at Jimmy. "I understand you were under a lot of stress. When was the last time you ate or drank anything?"

Jimmy shrugged. "I don't know."

"According to the examination you were severely dehydrated, and had nothing solid in your stomach. Your body ran out of fuel and started to shut down."

Jimmy shook his head, "No, that ain't right. I know they fed me in detention. I remember, the food sucked . . ."

"Well, from the state you were in when you came through the emergency room, you hadn't eaten or drunk anything for at least six days."

"No, that can't be right. There was this slop on Wednesday—"

"Jimmy, you collapsed from dehydration and lack of food. Whether you realize it or not, you were depriving yourself of food and water." Dr. Altroy took a chair and pulled it up next to the bed and sat down. "Do you remember being hungry at all? Thirsty?"

Jimmy shook his head. All he could remember feeling in his gut was the burning rage at what was going on around him. He had to be wrong, though. Jimmy knew he was too stressed to eat a day or two before the hearing, but he could clearly remember eating before that. He remembered potatoes the consistency of lumpy paste, and mixed canned vegetables that stained the bleached-white potatoes green at the edges. Then there was the slab of mystery meat in brown gravy that looked like the runs it wanted to give you.

Fuck, though, he *ate* the shit.

Yeah, but how many meals are in there that you don't *remember?*

"I had other things on my mind," Jimmy said.

Dr. Altroy nodded. "Do you think that was all? How did you feel about the meals they served you?"

"I told you, the food sucked."

"What's your favorite food, Jimmy?"

"Huh?"

"I'm just curious," he said. "I don't think either of us want this to happen again. You said the food they gave you 'sucked,' I just want to know what food you think doesn't 'suck.' " He even pulled out a notebook.

Jimmy shrugged. "Hey if you're going to get me something to eat— Start with a pizza. Deep dish, double cheese, and whatever meat you can fling on the thing, pepperoni, sausage, ground beef—speaking of hamburger, I could really go for a bacon cheeseburger. Or one of those cheddar melts you can get at Arby's, got to have curly fries with that. Taco Bell is cool, too."

Jimmy closed his eyes and realized he really was hungry, ravenous in fact. Even the damn jail food was looking good in retrospect. Memory or not, it felt as if he hadn't eaten in months.

"You seem to eat a lot of fast food," Altroy said.

Jimmy shrugged. "Who doesn't?"

"What do you eat when you're at home?"

Home? That's funny. "Whatever's around, I guess." Jimmy looked at the doctor and said, "Look, you went and made me hungry. You think you can get them to send up something? Anything?"

Dr. Altroy nodded and put his notebook away. "I'll go check with Dr. Husam to see if you're ready for solid food."

Jimmy watched him stand and asked, "What, aren't you my doctor? Don't you know?"

Dr. Altroy smiled and shook his head. "No, I am your doctor, but I'm not an internist. I'm a psychologist."

Shit . . . "I'm not crazy!" Jimmy blurted.

"No one is saying that. I'm just here to help you."

"I don't need that kind of help."

Dr. Altroy nodded. "That's fine, Jimmy. But the court's enrolled you in the TRACE program for twelve months, and it's sort of my job to talk to the kids."

"This whole thing is fucked up." Jimmy threw his head

back on the pillow. "I'm only here because the county bastards caved in. I shouldn't have even been arrested for what they charged me with, much less enrolled in some fucking tracing program. Who the hell are you, Big Brother?"

"I work for a nonprofit, privately funded, children's welfare agency, it's called Trinity House."

"Great, I'm happy for you."

"We'll talk again, when you're feeling better."

"Yeah, right."

Dr. Altroy smiled and shrugged. "Well, *I'll* talk. You don't have to if you don't want to." He walked out the door and left Jimmy alone in the room.

This is wonderful. Fucking wonderful.

Trinity House sounded like a Catholic fraternity to Jimmy. He didn't want any part of it, but he didn't seem to have much choice.

After a few minutes, an orderly came up with a tray of food, and Jimmy forgot about everything except how hungry he was.

14

DR. Farid Husam did not like Dr. Schuster, not since he had first laid eyes on the man. It was more than the fact that Dr. Schuster ignored the posted signs forbidding cell phone use in the hospital. It was more than the sheer impoliteness of his guest—rattling off instructions to some country bureaucrat in Dr. Husam's office while Dr. Husam, one of the senior staff in this hospital, waited patiently for him.

It was the fact that the man seemed to be crass arrogance personified, as if all the worst personality traits of Dr. Husam's adopted country had been distilled into one individual.

After what seemed an excruciatingly long time, Dr. Schuster browbeat his phone into submission and flipped it shut. "Sorry," he told Dr. Husam in a tone that said that he wasn't. "Now where were we?"

"My patient, Mr. Somerset."

Dr. Schuster nodded, as if he really had to be reminded why he was here. "Doctor, my understanding is that James Somerset recovered fully from his faint. I'm having trouble understanding why you are giving us grief about discharging him."

Dr. Husam frowned. "Doctor," he said, forcing unwilling

politeness into the word, "Mr. Somerset may have no overt symptoms, but I do not believe he is recovered."

"He fainted from dehydration. That's your own diagnosis."

"Dehydration is a symptom, Dr. Schuster, not a disease. The boy has shown very abnormal test results. Liver, kidney, and brain function all showed elevated activity. There are worrisome concentrations of heavy metals in his blood. His metabolism is working at an abnormally high rate. I need to keep him here for observation."

Dr. Schuster nodded. "I am certain you are a competent doctor." The words rolled off the man's lips like a vile insult. "But my agency has custody of Mr. Somerset, and we're responsible for his care. I have a mandate from three federal and state agencies as well as an order by a judge to put this child in a residential treatment program."

"He needs to receive care here."

"He can't, Doctor. You are not his primary doctor—"

Dr. Husam closed his fist. "I beg your pardon—" He willed himself calm. "But, respectfully, the county assigned Mr. Somerset a primary doctor on the West Side who has never even *seen* him. Much less—"

"You are not responsible for him," Dr. Schuster said. "And, unless you give me a signed affidavit that he has some definitive condition that cannot be safely monitored by the clinical staff at Trinity House, I want him discharged today."

Dr. Husam stood. "This is not some political game."

Dr. Schuster stood as well. "I do not like what you are implying."

"Think of his welfare for a moment. He's not just a news story—"

"Dr. Husam."

"Something to be swept under the rug—"

"Dr. Husam."

Silence. The air felt hot and dry, and Dr. Husam was mortified over losing his temper.

"Dr. Husam." Dr. Schuster spoke as if explaining things to a child. "Be quiet and listen to me for a moment. First, the county child welfare budget does not have bottomless funding. Every dime we spend has to be answered for, and that includes reasonable justification for any and all tests being run. I've had James Somerset's PCP review the test results you are concerned about. None of them are outside the normal range."

The other doctor was a fool. One of these things alone might not be an issue, but all of them, together . . .

"Second, both a court order and the state program we got him into have solid enrollment windows. So today he's going to Trinity, or he's going to jail."

Dr. Schuster leaned forward and laid his index finger on Dr. Husam's chest, "Third, I've been in charge of Family Services in this county for five years. In that time I've managed to double the mental health services we give these kids while dealing with a twenty-five percent funding drop. I've doubled the adoption rate out of our foster care program. I've cut the number of kids going into the juvenile justice system by a third, and I took on this case myself because I didn't want to see one of our kids lost in the rat's nest of our court system. So don't give me any bullshit about how I don't care about these kids."

Dr. Schuster straightened up and walked to the door. "You are releasing Mr. Somerset today unless you commit to some sort of diagnosis."

Dr. Husam shook his head in frustration. "That is the point. Without more tests I cannot tell what is the matter."

"Doctor, I am walking downstairs to file the paperwork. Please do not make this an issue. I've already talked to the hospital administration, and if I need to, I can have another doctor sign Mr. Somerset out."

Dr. Husam frowned. "Do so, then. I will not be a willing party in having him leave this hospital."

Dr. Schuster shook his head and closed the door behind him, leaving Dr. Husam alone in his office. He sat down slowly. How could any doctor look at James Somerset's test results and say the boy was fine to leave the hospital? The doctor approving that must have no sons.

What could he do? Dr. Schuster was right. The county had control of the child. All Dr. Husam could do was voice his opinion to the child's custodian. He had little legal right to interfere unless there was some immediate physical danger, and Dr. Husam couldn't say that there was. Dr. Husam could only say that there was something deeply wrong with James Somerset's biochemistry.

He should just wash his hands of the case. He had already composed a memo objecting to the discharge, that was all conscience should demand of him. He couldn't be responsible for people who were no longer under his own care.

But he was a doctor, not a bureaucrat.

Dr. Husam fished around on his desk until he found the business card that the doctor from Trinity had left.

Altroy.

The man wasn't a physician, but he would be the lead contact for James Somerset's care while he was at Trinity. They had talked briefly, mostly about Dr. Altroy's concerns that Mr. Somerset's collapse had been the result of an eating disorder or some such.

Conversely, Dr. Husam was more convinced than ever

that the faint had been the result of some undiagnosed disease.

He picked up the card.

No one would object if a senior staff member decided to volunteer his consulting services to a local nonprofit agency, would they?

Dr. Husam picked up the phone.

15

NATE had made a deal with the devil.
      He kept telling himself that it was worth it. Her data,
what he'd been able to look at, was legitimate. He was able
to confirm her background. He had found feature articles by
her in *Village Voice* and *Rolling Stone*. She came out of
Berkeley in California, and wrote about corporate and government wrongdoing, police brutality, CIA drug-running,
Enron payoffs . . .

Nate didn't know how he liked being a story. But the
"survivor" she suggested was out there was the holy grail as
far as this phenomenon went; a kid that matched the pattern,
but had somehow managed to avoid his or her fate.

According to Abby's source, Department Blue believed
that there was just such a child out there. Some statistical
gap in the pattern of deaths that led them to posit a hypothetical "survivor" to fill the gaps in their tables.

They even had a code name for the kid, "Golden."

She sat cross-legged on a twin bed in Nate's motel room
while Nate hunched over a desk with his laptop open, staring at raw dumps from the CD that she had given him. He
still wasn't quite sure what format the data was actually in.

He worked, and she asked him questions.

"How did this start?" was the first, inevitable question. "You were a cop once?"

Nate chuckled, tapping at the keyboard, trying another database driver to look at the files on the disk. "I worked for the LAPD—civil service exam and everything, paid out of the same budget—but I wasn't really a cop. I worked in the IS Department as a database analyst. That was seven years ago." *Time flies when you're having fun.*

Nathan Adriano had once been a different person. He had gone to school at UCLA and had come out with a degree in computer science just at the lowest ebb of the LAPD's popularity. In retrospect it was simply a geeky obliviousness that allowed him to take a Y2K remediation job for a department bearing the twin crosses of O. J. Simpson and Rodney King. His white friends from UCLA thought he was crazy, his black friends thought he was now some sort of fascist.

However, once he was hired, high turnover and bad press made him rise quickly to the number two position in the IS Department. He wasn't paid nearly the salary the folks in Silicon Valley were making, but by the same token, if he worked somewhere else, he would still be a nameless troll somewhere in the data mines. Where he was, he had charge of several city-wide networks and databases that held critical files for everyone from the Municipal Court and the DA's office, to the cops typing in license tags in their patrol cars.

For ten years he was an anonymous but crucial part of law enforcement in Los Angeles. At least that's what Nate told people who asked him what he did. He rarely got deeper than that, since very few people could be as interested as he was in the minutiae of table design and the details of smoothly operating heterogeneous data structures.

That was why Deborah Nielsen caught his attention. She actually allowed him to use the words "client-server" in a sentence without yawning or letting her eyes glaze over.

Deborah was an attractive, raven-haired cop working dispatch in South Central. Nate saw her at a Christmas party and something about her caught his attention.

He was standing by a long buffet table talking to his boss, who had been talking to the police chief, who had been talking to the mayor about some completely irrelevant detail that might save some secretaries five seconds of data entry time and was so pressing that they thought that he should get on to it now . . .

"Do you know who that is?" Nate interrupted his boss.

Nate's boss must have seen the whole train of thought he'd been expounding as the executive bullshit it was, because it was with audible relief that he asked, "Who *who* is?"

Nate motioned his drink in the direction of the dark-haired beauty standing by the multicultural Kwanzaa/Christmas/Hanukkah gift table.

Nate's boss shrugged. "I don't know. Looks kind of familiar."

Nate finished his drink and said, "I guess I'll have to ask her, then."

"When are we going to finish this conversation?"

"I'll e-mail you." Nate walked toward the woman, wondering what exactly was driving him. He really wasn't a people person. If he wasn't talking to someone about his own area of expertise he'd usually get tongue-tied and trip all over his own thoughts. For some reason, though, he found himself standing next to an attractive young police officer saying one of the ultimate singles lines, "Can you tell me why you look so familiar?"

It fell out of his mouth before he realized exactly what he was saying. He was instantly mortified.

He was also confused when she turned to him, still smiling, and said, "Deborah Nielsen. You probably saw the story on the news."

He thanked God he didn't blurt out, *"What story?"* Now it was sinking in that, old lines aside, she *did* look familiar to him. The name began clicking gears in his mind. Then it hit.

"Oh." Nate nodded, as if it was what had brought him down in the first place, "You saved that kid."

She nodded.

Deborah had been a twenty-four-hour sensation. In the days of the riots and Mark Fuhrman she had been one of the few recognizable heroes that wore a badge in LA. She had earned that fame during one of the ubiquitous high-speed pursuits on the Los Angeles freeway system. Ironically, it was a chase that she didn't participate in, or had even been aware of. She was on foot walking past a string of storefronts, when a bank robbery suspect in a black Trans Am blew out of an exit and onto the surface roads going 110 mph.

Deborah saw the Trans Am, and the police flashers, and immediately ran for the intersection the Trans Am was barreling toward. People in the crosswalk were already scattering, and the next three seconds were one of the more horrible incidents caught on tape by an LA traffic helicopter.

Nate remembered the details now.

The first second, the camera zooming in on the panicked people running for the safety at the edge of the street. A child in a red-and-white striped shirt falls, shoved aside or tripping over someone's feet. The Trans Am barreling in toward the intersection, swerving with little or no control.

The second second, someone in an LAPD uniform runs into frame, scooping up the fallen child. For the brief moment, as Deborah holds the child up, it is almost believable that the two of them might make it to safety.

The final second, and the car hits. The man behind the wheel is swerving maniacally to avoid them, but the rear fender collides with Deborah from behind. Her body sails forward with the impact, landing fifteen or twenty feet away. The Trans Am jumps the curb and plows into a liquor store window while the camera zooms in on the fallen cop.

The uniformed figure isn't moving. And for a few long moments, neither is the figure in her arms. Then, as if it had all been some thrill ride, the child gets up, just as the pursuit cars skid to a stop.

Nate wondered what it had been like for her, having to watch that tape on the news, over and over, in slow motion while she recovered.

"I'm sorry I didn't realize sooner," Nate said.

Deborah smiled. "Don't be. I don't like being well-known for being a half-step too slow." She took a step forward, and Nate could see a pronounced limp. "So what do you do here? I don't think I've ever seen you."

"Just another cog in the LAPD machine."

"What division?"

"Administration."

"Ah." She smiled.

"What does that mean? 'Ah'?"

"Nothing," she gave him an innocent smile.

"No, it wasn't nothing. That was a knowing 'ah.' You meant something by it."

She shook her head and smiled. "You're certainly paranoid enough. What exactly do you administer?"

"The main data warehouse, a handful of servers," Nate shrugged. "Just a little IS troll."

"We have a data warehouse?"

"Well it's just in the implementation stages. The fact is that we have years' worth of computerized data with no easy means of analysis. So the current hot project is to gather all this old information from the legacy systems—"

For some reason, Deborah remained interested in his conversation past that point. At first, Nate thought he'd found a fellow computer geek, but it was obvious from her questions that it was completely virgin territory for her.

She was the first person who'd shown an interest in what he did who didn't have a professional obligation to do so. About three hours later, after he concluded his explanation of OLAP data cubes and the concept of multidimensional database tables, she said, "I think we're going to have to pick up this conversation later."

"I'm finally boring you," Nate said.

Deborah laughed. "Nate, look around. I think the janitors want us to go."

Nate looked around and saw she was right. The party was pretty much gone. Nothing but garbage bags full of red-and-green paper plates were left. Nate shook his head and said "Whoa. I guess I lost track of time."

"You must love what you do."

"Yeah, I guess I ramble on about it when someone gives me a chance—" Nate stopped when he felt a hand on his arm.

"No, don't apologize. Please." She lowered her hand and looked off to the door. There was a deep sadness in her eyes

now. "Being able to do what you love—*need*—to do, that is
a gift from God."

They parted friends that first time, and it wasn't until several months later, when they were more than friends, that he
understood Deborah well enough to know what she had
been telling him.

Deborah's claim to fame, her heroism, had taken away
her first love. She had been born to be a cop, from her father's father. Since she was six, it was the only thing she had
ever wanted to do. She had been lucky enough to be born at
the birth of the women's movement, so her mother didn't
stifle that desire. The happiest days of her life had been
walking the streets behind a badge, and the riots, Rodney
King, and the public reaction to the police didn't change
that. She wanted to protect the good people from the bad
people.

The kid in the intersection would be the last good person
she would ever save directly. The accident tore up her back
and her leg. She was no longer physically capable of being,
in her words, a "real" cop anymore. She was eligible for disability, but she had insisted that the department take her
back in some capacity, and with a shortage of good images
in blue to go around, the department was happy to take her
back—at a desk job. So Deborah worked dispatch and the
911 line in South Central, about the highest stress job you
could have in the LAPD without having to dodge bullets.

Psychologically, though, Deborah was still a mess. She
couldn't stand not being on the beat, and in every social situation she was in, someone, somehow, would bring up Deborah's selfless heroism. She would have to grit her teeth and
take it, when she wanted to scream at them that she lay
awake nights wishing she had never seen the Trans Am.

Nate had been attracted to her because she was the first

person who had expressed interest in what he did. She was interested in him because he was the first person not to express interest in what she had done.

The cruelest part, Nate felt, was the guilt. It was something she didn't admit to anyone, even to him when she cried herself half to sleep on his shoulder. Sometimes, in the dark, when she thought he was asleep, Nate could hear her whisper to herself.

"Why can't I stop?" she would repeat, over and over again. If Nate ever stirred or spoke, she would lapse into silence. If he tried to comfort her, she would deny she'd said anything.

"Why can't I stop?" she whispered into his shoulder. "Why can't I stop wishing him dead?"

Nate was groggy, but he heard every word. He wanted to reach out for her, but he knew if he moved she would shrink away. Nate couldn't stand that, the implied mistrust. He remained still, letting her talk to his unmoving form as if he was participating in some bizarre act of faux necrophilia.

"Every night," she whispered, her breath hot on his shoulder. "I wish it never happened. It cost too much." She rolled away to lie next to him on the bed. He could feel her thigh on his. Nate could feel where the smooth skin became lumpy and hard, where the surgeons did what they could to reconstruct her knee. In his mind he could map the scars, the ones wrapping her leg, engulfing the patella, digging concave grooves through the muscle of her calf. Then there were the long ones on her back, where they fused three vertebrae together.

Many people had told her that she was lucky to be alive. Somehow the woman lying next to him didn't see it that way. "It should have killed me," she told the darkness. "If I had to be a goddamn hero, I should have finished the job. Heroes don't survive."

Abby leaned forward as Nate paused. "Is something the matter?"

"You haven't asked me." Nate said.

"Asked you what?"

"Anything," Nate said. "You got me babbling, and you haven't asked me a single question."

"That's not right," Abby said. There was a notebook next to her on the bed, and she flipped most of the pages over to one side. "Yes, here. Two questions, 'How did this start?' and 'Weren't you a cop, once?' "

"That was what, two hours ago?"

Abby shrugged. "I told you, I wanted your story."

"Yeah," Nate said. "I see."

Don't interrupt the mark when he's talking. It was one of the hardest lessons to learn when you were digging for information; an ill-placed question could do more to shut off lines of communication than just about anything else. You got the guy to relax and open up, especially when he was talking about himself—everyone's favorite subject—you got an order of magnitude more information than you'd have uncovered by interrogating him.

Abby had hit him just the way he would have. One or two nudges in the general direction and let the mental needle find a worn memory groove and let the thing play out.

I'm overanalyzing. Nate rubbed his temple. *She was just listening. Her job, remember?*

"Are you feeling all right?"

For some reason, he was aware of her diction again. The way she fully spoke "all right" as two separate words. "I'm fine," he said. "I just need some sleep."

Abby nodded and closed her notebook. "We can pick up this conversation later."

Nate stared at her, letting the words bounce around his brain. Was she consciously echoing Deborah? Was it unconscious? Did he even mention her words that first night?

Too many questions. He had lived too long with too many questions. He was incapable of seeing anything at face value. He only saw masks over masks over masks over nothing at all.

"Why can't I stop?" he whispered to himself.

If Abby heard him, she pretended not to.

16

THE CD was a tough nut to crack. As Sam had told Abby, it wasn't the end product. It was a backup of some intermediate step in transferring a much larger database. Not only that, it was a differential backup, which meant all he had here were the *changes* that were made to the target data warehouse. This was good and it was bad.

The good part was that, since this was simply an intermediate stage of the data that had never been intended to be archived, there wasn't any encryption. The data itself was in a fairly standard format, so after a few hours of tinkering, Nate could actually read what was on the CD.

The bad news was there was no clue as to what it all meant. Encryption or not, the data was still encoded with alphanumeric strings that only made sense to some 1970s-era CIA programmer. Something like "W03" could mean anything and the only initial clue was the fact that a three-digit code like that could handle up to 2600 separate values—if it held to the Alpha-Number-Number format.

Another complication was the fact that he didn't have a schema for the tables involved. The column names weren't descriptive or helpful, just five-character labels like "0023B," "0001S."

It was about eight in the morning when Abby knocked on

Nate's door. He stretched, yawned, and walked over and opened the door for her. She looked annoyingly fresh for the hour of the day, and the sunlight was painful. She held up the "do-not-disturb" tag and glanced over to the desk where he had set up his laptop.

"You've been up all night with that?"

He nodded, yawning, then went back to the laptop, finished typing the last few commands in his latest query, and clicked the run key. His mouse cursor obediently turned into an hourglass as the machine began processing his request.

"What are you doing?" she asked as she came in.

"Trying to make sense of this CD of yours."

"I thought you said you could read it now."

"Yeah," Nate nodded as he slipped back into his chair. "That's just the first step in this battle."

"I don't understand you."

"I can read the data. That doesn't mean I know what it means. I've found half a dozen separate table structures, a hundred tables or parts of tables, a quarter million records. And almost all of the fields are written in coded entries that sacrifice readability for storage space. No schema, no comprehensible field names, no translation lists. I don't even know what *kind* of data is stored on these tables. As luck would have it, there aren't even any memo fields on this disk, no plaintext at all."

"You make it sound impossible." She walked over to join him.

Attractive woman, Nate found himself thinking. "No," he said, stifling another yawn, "Just very difficult. You'd be surprised how often companies find themselves in the same position, having legacy databases with little or no documentation and the people who know how to maintain them retire, quit, or get laid off. This might be more cryptic, but it's not impossible."

She bent over to look at the screen. Nate felt her left breast pressing into his shoulder, but he didn't move—as if to do so would acknowledge the contact.

"What are you doing now?"

"Looking for foreign keys."

The pressure on his shoulder withdrew as she backed up slightly. "Foreign keys?" she asked.

"In a well-constructed relational database," Nate saw her eyes start to glaze over and changed his explanation. "Like at the LAPD, there's a master record of officers in the system. Each officer has one record with an employee ID that's unique, a 'primary key.' We also have a master table of every suspect that's been arrested with a suspect ID that's unique. When you look at the arrest table, there's a single record for every arrest, and there're fields for the primary arresting officer, and the guy being arrested. Those fields contain the identifiers for the two master tables. Those two fields are 'foreign keys' for that table."

"Oh, I think I see."

"The idea is to conserve space. You have cops involved in thousands of arrests, suspects involved in almost as many. Multiply that by thousands of officers and suspects, and think of just how much space would be wasted if you only duplicated their *names* in every arrest record."

"I see that. But what is it you are doing here?"

"I wrote a query asking my database software to filter through all the tables on the CD looking for a few different things. I want to see any fields that don't duplicate values within the table they're contained in; those are potential primary keys. Then it's going to sift through all the other tables and look for fields that seem to mach the data in the 'primary key' candidates of other tables."

"It seems to be taking a long time."

"It will. The query has to identify a 'primary key' and then it has to scan through every value in every other field in every other table to find any matches. Then it has to do it again."

"If it will be thinking for a while, why don't you join me for breakfast?"

"More third degree?"

"Or an omelet. Your choice."

Nate looked over his shoulder at her. *Is she hitting on me?* Nate found himself thinking. *Why?*

Abby pulled him away from the hourglass on his screen and bought him an omelet at the motel diner. She also took out pen and paper again.

She let him finish most of his breakfast before she asked, "What happened to Deborah?"

Nate lowered his fork and shook his head. "She couldn't have children, you know. Because of the accident. A lot of internal damage that didn't show. I think it's why we never got married. It tore her up more than the job, I think."

"She wanted children?"

"She wanted someone to protect." Nate finished off his omelet. "That's why you and I are here. Why she isn't."

"Are you sitting down, Nate?" the voice on the other side of the phone had said. Nate knew the voice on the other end, his name was Dennis something-or-other. Dennis was a mutual friend of Deborah and himself. More Deborah's.

"What is it?" Nate asked. He was standing before a workstation that, up until three minutes ago, had been the center of his universe. The connection to the LAPD's server was blithely blinking on, returning records even though Nate was ignoring it now.

"Are you sitting down?" Dennis repeated.

Nate shook his head. He didn't like this at all. Dennis was a Homicide detective. "Yes, goddammit," Nate lied. "What is it?"

"It's Deborah . . ."

With those two words, Nate lost most of his perception of the outside world. There was some sense of distant talking in his ear, and there were shapes and colors in his field of vision, but none of it made sense. His body had been cut adrift from its sense of place, and even the thoughts inside his head seemed too distant to be comprehensible.

With a great effort, Nate was able to form the words, "Please. Repeat. That."

Only a few words seemed comprehensible at the time.

". . . last night . . ."

". . . found in her apartment . . ."

". . . single gunshot . . ."

". . . nothing anyone could . . ."

Nate dropped the phone and walked out of his office leaving Dennis talking and the workstation displaying the server's response to his query.

The police were still at her apartment when Nate arrived. No one was blocking the door, so Nate walked in, ignoring the plastic police-tape barrier. It tore free of the wall and wrapped around his left leg. It made a rustling sound as he walked.

There were a couple of uniformed police here, a guy from the forensic lab, another guy with a camera, and two detectives, one of whom Nate recognized as Dennis. The forensic guy was bent over Deborah's couch, stretching a string back from a hole in the wall that was almost invisible within a red stain so dark it was nearly black.

The flash on the camera went off, momentarily blinding Nate. When he blinked the room back into visibility, everyone except the cameraman was looking in his direction.

Dennis said, "Oh, shit."

The other detective said, "Who the hell is that? This is a crime scene. Please get back outside—"

"Who the hell did this?" Nate whispered.

"Hernandez," the detective said to one of the uniformed cops, "Get this asshole out of here."

"Wait—" Dennis began.

"Who did this?" Nate's vision was blurring, and his throat felt hoarse and bloody.

"Jesus Christ—" said the guy from forensics.

"He knows Deborah," Dennis said.

"Who—" Nate tried to ask them again, but his voice wouldn't work. The question broke into a series of painful coughs. His face was warm and he felt his knees almost give way as he felt Dennis grab his arm.

"Get him out of here," repeated the other detective.

Dennis pulled him out into the hallway and whispered at him harshly, "I thought you knew better than this."

Nate shook his head. He couldn't look Dennis in the eye. *"I need to know what happened!"*

"Get a fucking grip," Dennis took his shoulders. "Look in my face and suck up some control."

Nate looked up into Dennis' face, and what he saw there almost mirrored his own.

"You can't lose it like this. Take a deep breath and stop yelling."

"But . . ."

"Don't say anything," Dennis said. "Just breathe."

Nate tried to do as Dennis asked. His breath came in ragged gasps.

Dennis let his grip go. Nate looked down and he felt a hand on his chin. Dennis lifted his face up until Nate could see Dennis pointing at his own eye. "Look at me. Listen to me. Deborah shot herself."

Nate tried to shake his head. "N—"

Dennis' hand clamped tightly on his chin, not allowing him a word or gesture. "No, Nate. Breathe. Look. Listen. Sometime last night, Deborah Nielsen put on her dress blues, put her service revolver in her mouth, and pulled the trigger. She left a note. No forced entry. No ambiguous ballistics. Powder burns on her hands. One shell casing, which we recovered. She did it herself."

Nate shook his head. This time Dennis let him.

"This is no place for you. Go home."

"I just—"

"Go *home*."

Nate went home.

He didn't return to work. Not that week. Not the following week. The week afterward he took a leave of absence, though by then he was fairly sure that he wasn't going back. In those three weeks he did three things;

First, he followed Dennis' advice and got a grip on himself. Reacting emotionally wasn't going to achieve anything on his part.

Second, he attended Deborah's funeral. He managed it without any embarrassing displays. Enough so that Dennis watched him during the eulogy as if he was a different person.

The third thing he did was to start his first investigation. Unlike the police, who took suicide as an answer, Nate treated it as the question it was. He needed to know *why*.

*   *   *

Nate paused. The coffee was cold, and the runny remains of the omelet had congealed on his plate. He wiped his mouth and said, "I think that query should be done by now."

Abby nodded, looking at him.

"You're waiting for the connection, aren't you?"

"This is your story, I just want to write it."

Nate nodded. Soft sell when she could gain more that way. "Her suicide note said, 'I couldn't save him.'"

"Who? The child from the chase? When the auto hit her?"

"That was the obvious assumption. Though the kid was alive and well in Oakland. Even made it to the funeral."

"Who, then?"

"You should know. You have the same list that I do."

"One of these kids—"

"—fourteen year old, burned alive. Nothing left but ashes." Nate ran his hand through his hair, and felt it shaking. He pressed his palm into his scalp to make it stop. "She had the mother instinct bad. Since the LAPD wouldn't let her go out and protect people anymore, she went out of her way to do it on her own time. She did foster care and volunteer work, helping as many kids as she could. Licensed and everything. I really was oblivious as she became more and more obsessed . . ."

"What happened?"

"It was a boy she was mentoring. Mother in her twenties, father missing in action, living in the worst part of town—a place where the gang bangers don't go out at night alone. Deborah was helping this kid out, at home and at school— had a lot invested in him." Nate shook his head. "She picked the wrong kid. Not because of where he came from, who his parents were, who he hung with, or what drugs he took. He was wrong because someone, some*thing,* made the kid a time bomb."

Nate didn't know, at first, how badly Deborah had been affected by the kid's death. She cried on his shoulder, like she had every night, but she didn't open up to him. She kept it in the same place she kept her nightmares about the Trans Am that had stolen so much of her life.

Somehow, she had slipped herself into the investigation. She was still a cop, and she had friends in the department who would let her see what was happening. Nate never found out exactly what she had seen, or had been involved with. But he knew the official story.

"With the help of a lazy coroner, the charred body came in, and because the victim was black, and from a bad neighborhood, it got 'drug-related' written up all over it. They found traces of cocaine and a pieces of a burned crack pipe on the corpse. Never mind that the body was found in a playground littered with that crap."

"How could they believe it was drug-related? The burning is so complete . . ."

Nate shook his head. "All you need is one man looking for the easy answer, willing to sign a piece of paper."

Back then, Nate was convinced that Deborah had struck out on her own. The kid's death wasn't normal, and the police investigation was perfunctory. She would have kept looking into it.

Nate had suspected that she found something that someone didn't want her to know.

"I spent the first two years of this—building my consulting business, tracking down these kids—convinced I would find the people who had 'really' killed her." Nate shook his head. "If she found something in three weeks, I should have found it. The fact is, if her suicide was staged, the same people should have finished me off a long time ago."

"So you don't think—"

"I loved her, but she was borderline when we met. Psychologically, she was getting worse every day. I just didn't want to think she would leave me like that. Denial, pure and simple."

"Then why are you still doing this?"

"You can find out a lot in two years. Kids are dying. That should be enough." He stood up. "Let's get back to the room and see what that query turned up."

17

THEY kept Jimmy in the hospital for another two days for "observation." It didn't make much sense to Jimmy; he felt fine. However, he wasn't in any position to bargain. He could tell he had some special status just from the way the nurses and orderlies acted around him. They wouldn't look him in the eye, and they edged out of his room as soon as they had finished whatever they'd been doing.

The window didn't have any bars on it, but it didn't open. It was triple-thick glass that Jimmy probably couldn't break if he tried. There was the front door. He wasn't strapped in, and the door was unlocked. He had thought seriously of just walking out in the middle of the night, at least until he discovered that they hadn't left any of his clothes. Jimmy didn't have any desire to go streaking through the nighttime Cleveland streets in a hospital nightgown. Too fucking embarrassing.

He ran through a list of scenarios in his mind, and while all of them would be workable on the page, he didn't see any of them working as well in the real world. Cain would walk out of this place without blinking. Jimmy knew that *he* would run into a nurse, an orderly, a janitor, or a security guard—none of whom would believe any of the plausible explanations of why he was walking the halls at that particular hour.

He had to face it. He was fucked, but he wasn't as fucked as he would be if he walked into a cop's arms this time.

So for two days Jimmy watched TV and tried not to think about head doctors, treatment programs, or his missing notebooks. After about the eighth hour of television, he was reduced to watching gall bladder operations on the surgery channel. Hell, Jimmy decided, must be something like this—a clean little room you can't leave, where you can be bored waiting for eternity to end.

When a guy from Trinity House came with a duffel bag of the clothes he had left at the Carswells', Jimmy was ready to go. Unlike the cop, this guy let him have some privacy to dress. He hovered outside while Jimmy pulled on a black Ramones T-shirt and a ragged pair of jeans.

"You're a gift from God," Jimmy told him through the door. "You know that? I was going out of my nut here."

"Ready?"

"Yep," Jimmy zipped the duffel shut and shouldered it. He meant it. He didn't really care where they were going, as long as it was away from here.

The guy opened the door for him and Jimmy walked out. The man was about six feet tall, wore a dark green polo shirt and Dockers. He wore an ID tag on a thin nylon cord around his neck. Jimmy noticed a small plastic breakaway clasp about halfway up the left side of the cord. The ID read "Trinity House" and had a cute little graphic of a dove next to the name.

"Gordon Pag-ni-kow-ski," Jimmy read off the ID.

"Pagnokowski," he corrected, letting the door shut behind them. "I work at the cottage where you'll be staying."

"Uh-huh."

"Van's this way," he said, swinging his arm wide and indicating the direction down the corridor. Jimmy also noticed another man with a similar name tag, sitting in a chair next to the door they had just come out of. This guy was built like a linebacker, shaved bald with a single diamond stud in his left earlobe. He wore a white button-down shirt that blazed against his dark skin. He wore the sleeves rolled up to biceps the size of Jimmy's thighs.

"Jimmy," Gordon said, "This is Marid Sharps."

"Uh-huh," Jimmy said.

"Pleased to meet you," Marid said.

"Marid's a nurse in our partial hospitalization program."

Jimmy looked at Marid, unsure if he had heard Gordon correctly. A nurse? Marid grinned at Jimmy, and the expression was disconcerting. Not that there was an ounce of intimidation or ill-will in the expression. It was just the expression itself seemed incongruous, like an "I ♥ My Cat" bumper sticker on an M1 Abrams main battle tank.

"You're a nurse?" Jimmy couldn't help saying.

"A good one, too," Gordon said. "He'd spent what, three years?"

"Five," Marid said.

"Five years in a Level I Trauma Center before we got him."

"Oh," Jimmy said. He didn't know exactly what that meant, but he had seen *ER*. Jimmy started down the corridor, but out of the corner of his eye he caught Marid shaking his head.

Jimmy stopped and turned around. Marid rolled out a wheelchair that had been parked by the wall next to him. "You get to be chauffeured out of here."

"You're kidding. I didn't break my leg or anything."

"The hospital gets upset if their patients just walk out,"

Marid said. "You're still their responsibility until we sign you out."

Jimmy sighed, looked at Gordon, and when he didn't say different, he handed Gordon his duffel bag and sat down in the wheelchair.

It turned out to be a good thing to have his own rolling seat, because it took nearly two hours for Starsky and Hutch to sign him out. Apparently, there had been a shift change since the pair had fetched him, and the new receptionist didn't know a damn thing about nobody checking out no county kid. Of course, half the required paperwork had disappeared with the prior receptionist.

Jimmy heard the woman at the desk say, "No. Excuse *me*. This is not *my* problem. All I know is what *you* need to sign that boy out. No, sir, I *am* the supervisor. Please come back with the proper documentation."

Jimmy sat in his mobile chair while Gordon, the Starsky half, tried his best to shuffle through the bureaucracy. Being parented by the county, Jimmy was used to waiting for people to shuffle papers. He spent the time rolling the wheelchair in circles. The Hutch half, Nurse Marid, only intervened to keep him from popping a wheelie, which, Jimmy reflected, was probably within his rights.

Jimmy rolled around in tight circles in the lobby off of the reception desk, alternately watching the corridors back into the hospital, and looking out the long windows at the parking lot. It was raining, the sky a slate gray. The parking lot shone a glistening black, the reflections in the asphalt shattered by intermittent showers. The world outside looked like a T-shirt that had been washed once too often. By comparison, the hospital waiting room was vibrant and cheerful.

There was another person in a wheelchair, facing the

windows at the other end of the lobby. He was probably one of the oldest men Jimmy had ever seen. Ancient skin wrapped his too-thin arms and hands, and his spotted scalp held only a few wisps of bone-white hair. Most of his face was covered by a plastic mask with tubes running back to a green cylinder that rode on the back of his wheelchair. The man looked through the windows with an uncomprehending stare, as if he might just as well be watching a game show, a cardiac arrest, or a blank wall. Nothing in those eyes. Holes that revealed only absence, the insides corroded by an acid darkness . . .

Jimmy had to force his hands to cooperate in moving the wheelchair to face the outside again. When the chair turned, he slowly unclenched his hands. They ached as if he had just punched a wall . . .

I'm not crazy.

Jimmy stared out at the rippling asphalt.

I'm not crazy. I only have bad dreams.

Jimmy asked where Trinity House was, and Gordon told him an address that didn't mean anything. So Jimmy watched out the window of the SUV as they rolled east, away from downtown.

Jimmy pictured that they were heading toward something like the Juvenile Detention Center. Some overcrowded institutional building set in the middle of a city block or two's worth of urban blight. As they rolled up Cedar Road, the environment gave Jimmy little cause to revise his opinion. They passed boarded-up storefronts, burned-out buildings, a few nasty-looking vacant lots—

"It started out as a Catholic mission and orphanage during the Civil War," Gordon was saying, relating some sort of civics lesson about Trinity House. "It was pretty much an orphanage through World War II."

Jimmy tuned the guy out as he watched the winos, the addicts, and the dealers huddling in the doorways, staring at the vehicle with the same empty eyes he'd seen in the relic in the waiting room. They stared at the SUV, not even as a tiger would stare at its prey. There was no passion, not even hunger, just the mechanical stare a furnace might give a lump of coal.

When they pulled past University Circle and started to climb into the suburbs, Jimmy was relieved. It was disorienting how quickly the character of the neighborhood changed. At the foot of Cedar Hill it was all traffic, buses, institutional buildings, concrete, and graffiti.

When they crested the hill—barely a quarter mile, if that—they were already into deep suburbia as far as Jimmy was concerned. There were trees, lawns, houses set back down wooded side streets, apartment buildings that weren't just free of graffiti, but looked as if they'd been painted and landscaped within Jimmy's lifetime. The storefronts they passed were more than wino shelters, and he couldn't see a single boarded-up window.

They weren't in Cleveland anymore.

Jimmy wanted to ask where they were headed, but they'd probably told him already and he didn't want to let on that he hadn't been paying attention.

Gray water rippled across the windshield as they rolled past the storefronts and into the suburbs. The street split into a wide boulevard as they passed briefly through Euclid Heights and into Shaker.

The houses kept getting bigger.

Jimmy stared at the mansions through the rain. Jimmy had never been up this way, and he had only seen places this

big on television. On either side of the divided street rose
Tudor houses with leaded windows wide and tall enough to
admit a city bus. There was a Victorian with a six-car garage
the size of the Carswells' whole house.

They passed a building that seemed to be a transplanted
Roman bathhouse complete with marble fountain. Even the
drab colonials, boxlike as they were, were of an overpowering size—larger than some of the apartment buildings
Jimmy had lived in.

Even the cars passing them seemed to know what neighborhood they were in. Jimmy saw a Lexus, a BMW, a Mer-
cedes, a Jaguar, a Lincoln . . .

They had passed through an invisible membrane into an
alternate universe. *The kids living in these houses, if there
are any,* Jimmy thought, *would never have a lawyer who'd
settle for the crappy deal I got.*

They reached the place before Jimmy realized it. The
SUV suddenly turned into the driveway of what he'd passed
off as another in a long series of walled estates. As they
passed the entry, the only identification of the place was a
tarnished green brass plaque that gave the address and read
"Trinity House."

The place was clearly institutional now that Jimmy focused on it. There was a long parking lot in front of a cluster of low brick buildings. The buildings were 1920s
architecture with sloped slate roofs and peaked gothic windows. Some of the outbuildings looked newer, but tried to
match the older structures in feel.

"Looks like a college campus," Jimmy whispered.

"Most of the buildings were built about the same time as
John Carroll," Gordon's voice intruded on Jimmy's reality.
"The Jesuit University down the road. Same architect."

"Uh-huh," Jimmy said. He was just noticing one detail

that was unlike a college campus. Two neighboring structures flanked a parklike area of green space that had a single picnic table sitting in the center of it. The rectangular park was flanked on two sides by two-story brick buildings, the other two opposite sides were walled off by a twenty-foot-tall chain-link fence.

The only way in or out of the area was a door set in one of the buildings. The windows facing the courtyard were subtly barred by chain-link that had been painted brown so it almost blended into the brick.

"Uh-huh," Jimmy said again, as the SUV drove around a circular drive toward the rear of the "campus."

Welcome to Trinity, Jimmy thought.

18

DR. Altroy still looked like a used car salesman. He wore the same charcoal-gray suit, this time with a blood-red tie. He sat at a round table in a small meeting room on the first floor of one of the residential cottages. Jimmy walked in, tentatively.

Dr. Altroy smiled at him. "So how are you doing?"

"It's still raining," Jimmy said. He didn't know why.

"Have a seat," the doctor waved at one of the half dozen chairs that ringed the table.

Jimmy debated standing, just to be contrary, but he decided the gesture would be pointless. He was still trying to figure out what the hell was supposed to be going on here.

The door was closing behind him, and he could hear someone laughing down the hall. Jimmy tensed. The laugh made him uncomfortable; it wasn't *healthy*.

"Is something bothering you right now?"

"What do you think?" Jimmy asked. "What the hell isn't bothering me?"

"Why don't you tell me about it?"

"Tell you about it?" Jimmy swung his arm to indicate the area beyond where the door had just closed. "I'm locked in with a freak show. Half the kids out there are strung out because they're aren't getting their drugs, the other half are strung out because of the drugs you're giving them. There's a kid out there talking back to the fucking TV, and it isn't even *on*."

"You're feeling uncomfortable here."

"Aren't you Captain Obvious."

Dr. Altroy nodded and scribbled something on a pad in front of him. "At least you haven't lost your appetite over this."

"Huh?"

"You haven't forgotten to eat," the doctor said. "That's an improvement."

"If you say so." Jimmy folded his arms and leaned back in the chair. He looked at the room. Square, whitewashed, with only the single door to the hall. The walls were blank except for a washed-out Thomas Kinkade print of a gazebo and a couple of posters, one advocating adoption, the other spouting some bullshit about United Way donations.

The circular table was off-center in the room, so the wall to the left of the door, behind the doctor, could accommodate a low bookshelf. The shelves held dog-eared coloring books, and several abused-looking board games. Jimmy saw Candyland, Chutes and Ladders, chess, Yahtzee . . .

On top of the shelf was a pile of paper and one of those old boxes that held sixty-four Crayola crayons. Crayons were scattered across the paper, some worn to nubs, others broken in half. The wall behind the shelf was marked by a few scrawls.

"Christ," Jimmy muttered, "why am I here?"

"I believe you know," said Doctor Altroy. "You're smart—"

"This place is for children," Jimmy waved at the bookcase. "I don't belong here."

"You don't see yourself as a child?"

"I'm seventeen years old."

"I see." Dr. Altroy looked down at his notes. "We are a child services agency, we serve clients from infancy through early adulthood. You're here because you *are* a juvenile, and the program you're covered by assigned you here. We serve as many teenagers as preschoolers here."

"Uh-huh."

"So can we talk for a bit?"

Jimmy looked at Doctor Altroy, *If you're asking,* he thought, *why don't you leave me the fuck alone?* Like it actually *was* his choice. Sure he probably could leave, but then what? He was stuck here for a year, and if he managed to slip out before that—well the fuckers who put him here probably wouldn't repeat the mistake. When they caught up with him, he'd be shoved somewhere worse, where the nutcases didn't have televisions—on or off—to distract them.

"It's your dime," Jimmy said. *Well, the county's dime.*

"How did you feel about Euclid Heights High School?"

Jimmy shook his head. "How do you *think* I feel?"

"I think you had some unpleasant episodes there."

"'Unpleasant episodes?' Did that come out of a manual somewhere? The entire fucking building and everything within a city block radius is an 'unpleasant episode.' The place is a cesspool filled with Neanderthals and dime-store Fascists."

The doctor nodded. "I understand you had difficulties there."

Jimmy slapped his hand on the table. "Are you *trying* to bait me?" His other hand had curled into a fist on his lap. The skin on his gut was as tight as a drum, and muscles all the way down on his body ached as they tensed.

"No, I'm not," Dr. Altroy said. "If you're not comfortable talking about this now, we can—"

"No." Jimmy shook his head. Under the table his fist slammed into his thigh, which resonated like a frozen slab of meat. *I am in control.* "Look, you have no idea what kind of hell I went through there."

"Jimmy, neither of us knows. My job is to help both of us understand it."

"Believe me, I understand."

Dr. Altroy paused a bit before he went on. "Do you know Frank Bradley very well?"

Jimmy shrugged. "Just another jock with the brain of a sea slug."

"You didn't like him."

"I could care less about him. The fucker jumped *me.* He's the one with the issues, why don't you have *him* here?"

Dr. Altroy looked down at the notes he was making, and said very evenly, "You haven't seen him since the night he jumped you, have you?"

"No," Jimmy shook his head. He slowly unclenched his fist. "I suppose I would have if my county lawyer didn't plead me into this place."

"His knee will heal," Dr. Altroy said. He looked up from his notes. "He won't play football again, but he'll be able to walk without assistance."

It wasn't his legs now. Jimmy's body felt as if all of it had become a lump of frozen inert meat. "He jumped me," Jimmy said, "it was self-defense—"

"I wasn't questioning that, Jimmy." The doctor tapped a stack of manila file folders that were resting on the table in front of him. "I have all the court documents. Affidavits from Frank Bradley and his two friends. Their intent was clearly, in the words of one of them, 'to beat the living shit' out of you."

For some reason, hearing the words out of Doctor Altroy's mouth made him feel smaller, colder, and more alone.

"You regret what happened, don't you?"

Fuck no, the bastard deserved it—

Even as the words filled his head, another part of his brain—a part that was now very scared—was thinking that Frank Bradley did not deserve it. Jimmy knew that something inside himself had mercilessly baited the homophobic jock to the breaking point, just so the Jimmything could pounce.

Jimmy's eyes burned, and he kept his face lowered so the doctor wouldn't see the tears. "Christ, what do you think? You think I wanted to do that?"

"You didn't have a choice," the doctor said.

Jimmy nodded vigorously. "Yeah. The guy didn't give me a chance."

"He just kept after you until you couldn't control what happened."

"Yeah, he . . ." Jimmy's voice trailed off. Inside he was thinking, *Oh, shit. What did I just admit to?* Dr. Altroy was making a note and Jimmy wanted desperately to see what he was writing.

After a moment Dr. Altroy looked up and asked, "Were you going to add anything?"

"No, sorry."

"Can we talk about your artwork?"

Jimmy sighed and folded his arms. "Whatever you want."

"Do you have problems with discussing it?"

"My problem is with shitheads who can't distinguish a comic book from a Unabomber's Manifesto."

"You're referring to the school administrators—"

"Who broke into my fucking locker, tore into my private

papers, then shit a brick 'cause they can't separate fiction from reality. If I had a half decent lawyer, a half decent judge . . ." Jimmy shook his head. "Come on, are you going to tell me I'm wrong? I have a *right* to draw whatever I want."

Dr. Altroy nodded. "I understand your argument. But I've seen your work in the court documents. There is an old free speech counterargument that there's no right to shout 'fire' in a crowded theater."

"Doctor," Jimmy said. "This stuff was *mine*. I didn't show it to anyone. They *stole* it and decided that I had to be put away because it scared them."

"I'm not saying they're right. But they hold an understandable position."

" 'Aggravated menacing?' How the hell can I 'menace' anyone if I don't show anyone what I'm supposed to be menacing them with?"

The doctor leaned back and folded his hands. "Jimmy, do you understand other people's reaction to your work?"

"Huh?"

"You didn't show your work to anyone, you said. Why was that?"

"Why should I? It's none of their business."

Dr. Altroy shook his head and Jimmy again got the impression of someone just a little too slick to be trusted. "That's not what I was asking," he said, giving Jimmy the used car salesman voice. "I wasn't questioning your right to keep things private. What I wanted to know was why you crafted a rather polished piece of art, and chose not to share it with anyone."

"You lost me, Doc." Even as he said it, some small part of Jimmy's ego was grabbing hold of Doc Altroy's comment for dear life. The word *polished* resonated in his skull.

"Art, any type of art, is a form of communication. Judging from what I've seen of your work—from the court records alone, you understand—you have some ambition to be a comic book artist—"

"Writer," Jimmy said, without thinking.

The doctor made a note on his pad. Jimmy felt uncomfortable. Admitting to his own ambition was an invitation to ridicule. That, he could stand, but the ridicule would ignite the anger, and the anger—

He shouldn't think about the anger.

"Have you tried to get any of your work, art or writing, published?"

Jimmy laughed. "Oh, come on. Who the hell would *publish* me. The first time someone sees my notebooks, they call the police."

Dr. Altroy looked up. "That was the *second* time."

"No, it—" Jimmy caught himself. "You mean Frank."

The doctor nodded.

There was a long silence.

"Why did you draw that picture of Frank Bradley?"

"I— I— Fuck, tell me the bastard didn't deserve it."

"Deserve what?"

"To be made fun of. Popping his homophobic oh-so-superior jock bubble." Jimmy rubbed his face. "I should have had him being fucked by *himself,* but the bastard wouldn't have gotten it."

More notes. "Jimmy, did you intend for Frank to see that drawing?"

"Fuck, no," Jimmy shook his head. "I knew how it would set him off. You think I wanted that?"

"Then why would it matter if he 'got it' or not?"

"You're twisting my words?"

"I just want to understand what you're saying."

Jimmy looked up and stared into the doctor's eyes. "Doc? Have you ever been pissed off? Totally, royally, completely pissed off at anyone?" He gripped the material of his pants leg, above the thigh, and started making a fist. The denim cut into his leg, and his hand shook, but he couldn't stop. "You don't have any fucking idea what poor old Frank Bradley was like. Lording it over his minions and passing out judgment like Heights High was some banana republic and he was the generalissimo with the biggest dick. Can you go through that and not express your disgust some way? It's as hopeless as deciding you'll never take another shit 'cause you don't like the smell."

Jimmy's leg had fallen asleep.

"I think that's enough," the doctor said.

Jimmy stood up. The chair fell backward and he limped slightly as his hand untangled from his pants. "What? You set up this damn meeting and then when I decide to be fucking honest you— Christ, you're a hypocrite."

The doctor stood as well. He was very good at looking unflappable. "Please calm down. It just happens that our time is up. I'm glad you're ready to continue our talk, but I do have another client waiting for me."

Jimmy stood there with his jaw hanging open, his face turning several shades of stupid.

"Let's have another session in a couple of days. Give you a chance to be acclimated. Perhaps you can decide on something *you* would like to talk about."

"Yeah, sure."

The doctor led Jimmy outside the meeting room, Jimmy followed meekly, trying to understand what had happened, and who had won.

19

WELCOME to Trinity.

In the four days since he had come here the only question he had come up with for Dr. Altroy's next meeting was, "When the fuck am I getting out of here?"

The answer was, sixty days of residential treatment followed by eight to ten months of what they called "transitional living" but sounded more like house arrest without the ankle bracelet.

Jimmy had withdrawn as far back as he could, because the other kids here scared the shit out of him. If they'd locked him up in juvenile hall, at least he'd understand the general population. Not here. There wasn't a common rulebook, written or unwritten.

There was tutoring for about half the day, which wasn't that bad. Jimmy didn't have to deal with the other inmates, and trying to catch up with schoolwork kept him from thinking about where he was.

There were a couple of hours that he had free, which he could spend in a large gym area, but he dealt with the time by hiding out in the small room they gave him.

However, that wasn't a very workable solution. The problem was they wouldn't accommodate him by bringing meals. And while he could shut the door on the rest of the place, going to the bathroom and taking showers were still an issue.

Then, of course, between the classes and his "free" time, were four hours of therapy, which was nonnegotiable. While he could spend his own time behind his door, and no one made any explicit threats, he had heard stories . . .

Someone worse off in the mental resources department than Jimmy was had barricaded himself in his room and had started shitting and pissing on everything. Apparently, the kid now resided elsewhere, but the guy had made a lasting impression on the staff.

So, while no one explicitly described the consequences of refusing to attend his therapy sessions, hearing about that kid placed Jimmy in a cooperative mood. He did not want to be shipped off to where the mad defecator had gone. Jimmy had no desire to meet the denizens of *that* place.

Jimmy's first group session was supposed to be about anger management.

He knew it was going to be bad when he saw who was running the class; a blonde in a flower-print dress that looked like it belonged in a documentary on the seventies. She was smiling and Jimmy couldn't picture her ever being pissed at anything. Jimmy looked at the other five kids seated around the room, and wondered why she hadn't been eaten alive.

"Before we get started," she said, "since we have a new participant, I think we should introduce ourselves. My name is Grace Fujimara. I'm here to help you deal with some of your emotions, and I'm glad to see you all here. If we could go around and have you introduce yourselves to each other?" She walked back to stand by the corner of the room so Jimmy couldn't keep his eyes on her.

What the hell is she doing with a name like Fujimara?

The first kid to speak was one of the most intimidating. He wore sweatpants, combat boots, and a black T-shirt that had the sleeves torn off. His arms were more muscular than Frank's had been, and they were scarred by homemade tattoos, black words that bit into brown skin. The words were mostly names, followed by the initials "R.I.P."

He looked like he could chew off Mike Tyson's ear, and he was younger than Jimmy was. "I'm Dion," he said. He looked at Jimmy when he said it, so there'd be no mistake who the new guy actually was.

The kid next to Dion was a contrast. He was short, thin, and had long dirty-brown hair that hung in his face. He looked like he might only be ten or twelve. He stared at the ground between his feet, and kept his hands solidly planted on his knees. "Eric," he told the carpet.

The next one in the circle was a girl who folded her arms across her chest and glared at the rest of the room as if it all was some insult directed at her. "Lorraine," she said, her mouth half smile and half sneer. Jimmy noticed that she had a long scar that started behind her left ear and trailed down her neck to hide under her collar.

Charlie was a guy who was bigger than Dion, a mountain of heavyset flesh topped with a crew cut. He should have been named "Moose." He wore steel-toed work boots, stained denim jeans, and a blue work-shirt.

The last one in line was another girl. Her body language seemed normal, and she struck Jimmy as rather pretty. However, there was something disturbing in the way she spoke her name, "Salina." As if she wasn't talking to Jimmy, but to someone slightly to the left and behind him.

Jimmy was silent for a moment before he realized that the baton had been passed to him, and everyone, except the kid with the long hair—Eric—was looking in his direction.

"Oh," he said. "I'm Jimmy. Hi." He made a feeble wave at the rest of the motley band he found himself with.

This is where the world puts you, Jimmy. You're one of the misfits, one of the rejects.

"Does anyone want to say a little bit more about themselves?" Their fearless leader paused for a response and was greeted by a thundering silence. She seemed to have expected it. "Well, there will be time for all of you to get to know each other."

Great.

"We are here to learn the most effective ways to deal with our anger." She seemed to be talking directly to Jimmy right now. "It's a skill, like learning to drive, like learning to read. Does anyone here remember what the most important part of that skill is?"

There was a silence that extended for a long time. In his own head he came up with his own answer, *know when to duck*.

He wasn't surprised when he found out that wasn't quite the answer that Mrs. Fujimara was looking for. After an agonizingly uncomfortable period of quiet, Eric mumbled something like, "Know when you are."

"Yes," Mrs. Fujimara responded. "That is the first and most important skill. We need to know *when* we are angry. We need to cultivate an awareness of how our surroundings affect us." She looked in his direction, and Jimmy was made aware of the fact he was chuckling to himself. To his relief, she didn't do the typical teacher thing of singling him out—

Mr. Somerset seems to have noticed something amusing. *Care to share your wisdom with the rest of the class?*

Jimmy stifled himself, though he thought it was pretty damn amusing. Hell, it was the most ridiculous thing he had ever heard. He had no idea about the damaged goods around him, but Jimmy was pretty fucking aware of when he was angry . . .

"—stages leading up to a confrontation." She had gone on without Jimmy. "If you are aware of the way you're reacting before that happens, then you can make the decision to remove yourself from the problem. You can choose how you deal with it." She was walking around them, and Jimmy felt uncomfortable. Suddenly he was sure that she saw inside him, saw the blackouts, the rages, the darkness that seemed to well up inside him until he was someone else . . .

"Who has had to deal with their anger since our last meeting?"

Who's had to deal with my anger? Can I give you a list?

"Does anyone want to start?" she asked. Jimmy didn't like the quiet. It made him aware of the sweat on his palms, and on the back of his neck. He felt his pulse in the side of his neck, in his temples, and his breath felt hot.

To his surprise, it was Salina, the girl with the distant gaze, who spoke first. Jimmy was thankful because it took the focus of the room off of him.

"I talked to my mother," she said.

There was a pause long enough to allow an elaboration that remained unspoken. Mrs. Fujimara pushed things along, "What happened when you talked to your mother?"

"I got mad."

Jimmy had trouble picturing it. There was no emotion in Salina's voice. None. Jimmy's homeroom teacher called out attendance with more passion.

"Why did you get mad?" asked Mrs. Fujimara.

Salina was looking off in a direction that faced no one else in the room. Her profile was stark and pale, her eyes the gray of slate after a rainstorm. "She always makes me mad," she said. There was still no heat in her voice, no break in the marble facade, the only sign that there was any content at all in her words was that she closed her eyes when she spoke. "She always has to be right. I'm here and she still has to be right."

"How did—"

"Lay off of her," said Charlie, the big guy with the crew cut. "You want me to tell you when *I'm* angry?"

"Charlie, we're here to help each other."

"No right to badger her like that. You know why her mom—"

"It's all right," Salina said. She opened her eyes. "You were going to ask me how I dealt with it, weren't you, Mrs. Fujimara?"

"Yes, Salina."

"You'd be proud of me. I didn't throw the phone. I didn't hit anything. I just said, 'Mom, I can't talk to you about that anymore.'"

"That's very good—"

"I hung up on her," Salina said flatly. "I've never hung up on her before."

"You felt that was the only way you could control the situation?"

Salina nodded. For once, looking at her, Jimmy felt a connection to someone here. He didn't know why, but something about Salina pulled some string of empathy, even when the dark voice inside him was saying, *Fuck she's got to complain about, at least she* has *a mother.*

"Why you got to push on her like that?" Charlie said. "You supposed to be helping us here. Why you all got to do things like that? It ain't right."

Jimmy heard something scraping on the carpet, a repeated thumping noise. He looked past Charlie and saw Eric rocking back and forth in his chair. The kid didn't look up, just back and forth, back and forth.

"Everyone has issues to deal with here, Charlie. We have to acknowledge a problem before it can be solved. We can't change behavior patterns if we don't—"

"It is fucking *sadistic*." Charlie stood up and his chair fell backward. "You *know* what she's gone through. No call to push on her like that. No call at all."

Jimmy tried to shrink as far away from the epicenter of this outburst as he could without drawing attention to himself. Mrs. Fujimara held her ground, like some sort of oblivious flower child in the path of an onrushing National Guard tank. Eric seemed to be rocking himself into some sort of catatonic state.

Dion, on the opposite end of the semicircle of chairs, was grinning widely. It looked as if nothing would please him more than to see Charlie smash something.

Lorraine looked up at Charlie and said, "Boy, you better sit your ass back down." She folded her arms and Jimmy heard her gum snap. "Some of us here are trying to *learn* something."

"Charlie," said Mrs. Fujimara. "Please pick your chair back up."

She didn't move, didn't raise her voice, but Jimmy could feel the tension in the air. He felt what held this room in check. Behind the words was the force of something that no one here wanted to test, and Jimmy saw that demonstrated by the way Charlie stood a moment, shook his head as if trying to clear water from his eyes, then slowly bent down to pick up his chair.

Eric stopped rocking.

"Little angry there," Charlie muttered.

Dion gave a silent clap that wasn't in Mrs. Fujimara's

line of sight, but Jimmy wouldn't have been surprised if she was aware of it.

"You're doing better," said Mrs. Fujimara. Jimmy didn't want to see worse. Charlie looked as if he could tackle a brick wall into submission. "Does anyone else have something they want to share?"

"Other than Charlie is a royal fuckup?" Dion chuckled.

Charlie took a deep breath, and formed fists, but he closed his eyes and unclenched his hands as he exhaled. "Don't say that," Charlie said quietly.

"Say what—" Dion started.

"That is inappropriate behavior," Mrs. Fujimara said.

"Whoa, sorry, Teach," Dion said, "I'm cool."

"Any further verbal attacks and you will not be allowed to continue in group session."

"No problem. I'm one chilled-out motherfucker." He smiled and pursed his lips at Charlie. "Just playing with you, dude."

"Do you have anything to contribute?" Mrs. Fujimara asked.

"Yeah, sure. I got pissed at the tuna salad on Monday. Man, that shit was nasty. Any of you had it? Should've been called toe jam salad—"

"Thank you, Dion."

"—fucker smelled like feet."

"Thank you," Mrs. Fujimara repeated.

She went on to Lorraine.

Lorraine talked about going out on a supervised shopping trip with some kids from her cottage and how one of the managers of one of these mall stores came down and accused her of lifting some stuff and how her escort from Trinity didn't believe her when she said the guy was full of shit and how even though she didn't have anything on her the

manager was saying she must have ditched it somewhere
because there's all this fucking crap missing and how it had
to be the kids and not just the fucking kids but this specific
kid must have been stealing and obviously this dude has
some fucking racist bug up his ass and how her own supervisor who's been in sight of her the whole damn time is taking her aside and asking her where she hid the fucking
clothes and it goes on like that until they're about to call the
cops and fuck up the rest of her life when one of the cashiers
finally gets the manager's attention and tells him the stuff
that's missing from the rack is in the changing room thank
you very much and the bastards don't even apologize . . .

She basically didn't shut up for about fifteen minutes.
Jimmy was out of breath just listening to her. After her
monologue, Eric's halting speech was a relief. At least the
guy gave you space to think between words. Sometimes
even within a word.

"Watching the TV, have the radio on. Someone comes
and change it. They don't ask." He still spoke to the floor.
Jimmy wondered what his face looked like.

"How did you react the last time that happened?" Mrs.
Fujimara asked.

"Try to say something." He shook his head. "Just sit
there."

Christ, of course no one's listening to you.

Mrs. Fujimara nodded and asked Eric if his reaction had
helped make him feel any better. He admitted that it didn't.
She asked if anyone had any suggestions on how to deal
with the situation to help Eric. That brought a flood of suggestions.

"Whatever you do," came a voice Jimmy barely recognized, "don't write your feelings down." It wasn't until
everyone was looking at him that Jimmy realized that he

was the one who spoke. His voice was hoarse and tasted of blood, as if he'd been screaming. He rubbed his temples with damp fingers, trying to push his pulse back into his head.

"Why not?" someone asked.

Not-quite-Jimmy chuckled. "Never give them a chance to find a piece of paper with what you think written on it. They'll nail your ass to the wall."

"Why do you say that?" Mrs. Fujimara asked.

Jimmy looked her in the face. "*Come on.* You mean you don't know why I'm here?" He looked around at the others. "You guys want to know? I put some poor jock numbnut into the hospital and that shit doesn't even rate a mention. They haul me in and put me away because I *drew* something that scared them. A fucking picture."

"How have you been reacting to that?" she asked.

"Huh?"

"How have you been dealing with—"

"Give it a rest already," Jimmy said. "We're not talking about someone being inconsiderate or pushy or stupid. These people took away a year of my life because they didn't like something I *wrote*. I have a fucking right to be pissed off."

"You give it a rest." Charlie had turned toward him. "No call to interrupt Eric like that—"

"What are you," Jimmy asked, "the politeness police?"

"Don't come and start saying you got it worse than anyone else," Charlie told him. "You're wrong."

"And what's your story, big boy?"

The room fell silent. After a long pause where Charlie looked uncomfortable, Lorraine spoke up. "Don't you go asking things like that. It ain't none of your business if he don't want to talk about it."

"I was raped," came a voice next to Jimmy. He turned to
see Salina talking. This time she was actually looking at him
with those slate-gray eyes. Her voice was still level, her face
almost expressionless, but still, something in that gaze deflated whatever it was that had been building up inside
Jimmy.

"My father raped me. From when I was six until I was too
old to interest him anymore." She turned away from him and
looked back to the nowhere she'd been looking at before.
"Mom insists I'm lying about it. It never happened."

Jimmy felt himself in a bit of free fall. He really hadn't
thought of *why* anyone else might be here. Thirty seconds
ago he had been convinced he'd cornered the market on injustice.

Apparently, there was enough evil in the world to go
around.

He looked around at the rest of them, and said something
he'd rarely, if ever, said to anyone before.

"Sorry."

Mrs. Fujimara took that as a cue to start steering the
group again. "Now, Jimmy. No one said you don't have a
right to feel anger. What we're talking about here is how you
act in response to that emotion. How you come to that emotion in the first place . . ."

Throughout the rest of the session, Jimmy kept looking at
Salina. *How could anyone . . .*

No one answered him.

Interlude Two: ENTER THE DEMON

PAGE 6: [FOUR PANELS]

Panel 1: INT. HALLWAY EUCLID HTS. HIGH SCHOOL
The hallway here is empty, lit by emergency lights and what sunlight reaches through the abandoned class-rooms. CAIN is kneeling over a body that's lying face-down in a pool of blood.

CAIN

"Jerry, you shouldn't have listened to him."

Panel 2: CLOSE-UP OF CAIN TOUCHING BODY
The body has suffered multiple gunshot wounds to the chest, plus, a *coup de grâce* to the back of the head. The blood reflects sunlight from a nearby window. CAIN's fingers are tracing a pentagram that has been carved in the flesh of the corpse's back. The fingers of his glove smears the blood.

CAIN

"Children, you bastard. They're only children."

CAPTION

"At times I feel I'm centuries beyond feeling anything. Times I feel that nothing that Old Nick can do can catch me off guard."

Panel 3: CLOSE-UP OF CAIN'S PROFILE
CAIN is grimacing, almost in pain. The pentagram is re-flected in his sunglasses.

CAPTION

"*Of course, he has this thing for proving me wrong.*"

Panel 4: MID SHOT OF CAIN
CAIN is turning away from us and the body, to face down the corridor where the shadows are the deepest.

SFX

(Small type on bottom of panel)

C-CLICK

PAGE 7: [TWO PANELS, JAGGED DIAGONAL DIVISION]

Panel 1: CLOSE UP OF SHOTGUN
Flames and smoke come from a sawed-off double-barrel shotgun as it fires.

SFX

BA-BOOM

Panel 2: FULL SHOT OF CAIN
CAIN is blown up and back by the shotgun blast. The left side of his trench coat is rippling behind him, the edge tattered by the shotgun. Blood is flying backward, toward the observer.

PAGE 8: [FIVE PANELS]

Panel 1: LONG SHOT OF CAIN
CAIN's body is spread out next to the corpse with the pentagram. His blood is mixing with the other's. His left arm is stretched out toward us, his sunglasses slightly beyond his reach.

CAPTION

"He wants to hurt me."

Panel 2: MID SHOT OF CAIN
The same as the previous panel, but closer, and the arm
is closer to the sunglasses.

CAPTION

"Not being shot—though that's painful
enough."

Panel 3: CLOSE-UP OF HAND
The gloved hand grabs the sunglasses in a fist.

CAIN

"Ugh."

CAPTION

"He just wants to show me that He owns the
kid now."

Panel 4: CLOSE-UP OF CAIN'S HAND
Same as prior panel, but the fist clenches, shattering the
sunglasses.

CAIN

"Arrrgh."

CAPTION

"He wants to show me that it's too late."

Panel 5: MID SHOT OF CAIN
He's pushing himself up from the ground, blood drip-

ping from a massive wound in his gut. Ambiguous
pieces of himself are hanging from the hole, their shadows half-spilling on the ground.

CAIN

"Jerry!"

CAPTION

"He wants to show me *He's* won."

PAGE 9: [SPLASH PAGE]

MID SHOT, FACING CAIN
The wound is already closing. Blood streaks the skin
that's visible behind tears in his clothing. He's standing
upright, facing the direction the shotgun blast had come
from. We can see the same thing now that the cop did.
His eyes are lost in shadow, leaving black holes in a
skull-like face. Death personified, he's calling after the
gunman . . .

CAIN

"Jerry!"

CAPTION

"I was never very good at taking a hint."

20

"LBJ once said, about J. Edgar Hoover, that he would rather have him inside the tent pissing out—"

"I understand." Director Oberst tapped the eraser end of a pencil on his desk, next to the phone, as he looked at Agent Boyden. "I don't think you do."

"The man has shown expertise that we happen to need badly."

"This is not the time," Director Oberst said. "You've got your share of Homeland Security money, a much needed upgrading. Please don't push your luck."

Ulysses Boyden frowned. "Sir, all due respect, but I don't know what I am supposed to be doing, then. I have brand-new state-of-the-art database servers, and I don't have the authority to recruit people who know how to use them?"

"Flavian is fresh in people's minds." The pencil stopped tapping. "You should remember how sensitive Department Blue is. Any information leak would be potentially disastrous to the Agency, to the Intelligence Community as a whole. You can't even assure us that situation has been contained."

"We have both Abby Springfield and Nathan Adriano under surveillance."

"And you think you can undo the damage by recruiting him?"

"For six years he—"

"I've seen the file. I saw it the first time you suggested this. The answer is still no. More so since this journalist is involved with him."

"With a fraction of the data we had access to, he—"

Oberst shook his head. "Adriano is too high profile, and already too publicly identified with the issue. I wasn't ready to approve it before Flavian, I am certainly not going to approve it now."

"Sir, what if he finds out why this is happening?"

Director Oberst shook his head. "You have too much faith in him. But if he does, and somehow gets the truth published, all the better that it is not made public by us."

Cato Sullivan, security director for Department Blue, was waiting for him when Agent Boyden walked into his antiseptically empty office. Boyden grunted as he walked around the chair where Sullivan sat.

"I was thinking," Sullivan said, "you need some plants in here."

"Yeah," Boyden replied absently, tossing his overcoat on the chair next to Sullivan.

"He said no."

"He said no." Boyden sat behind the desk. "Which shouldn't surprise me, should it?"

"Can I show you a few things?"

Boyden looked up. "Is it bad news?"

"That depends on your perspective." Sullivan took two folders and placed them on Boyden's desk. Boyden took up the first folder, marked "secret" in bold red letters, and opened it.

"This is from the NSA." Boyden looked at Sullivan over the top of the folder.

Sullivan smiled. "Some inter-agency cooperation. Outside our own little world, our own SIGINT capability is practically nil."

Boyden flipped through a few pages and asked, "What am I looking at?"

"Cell phone transmissions, transcripts, locations. The important thing is who is calling whom. The callee is a gentleman named Ling Pak, a businessman from Hong Kong who has been suspected of financing and overseeing various extragovernmental operations for the Chinese government."

"The caller?"

"Abigail Springfield. The last one is just a couple of days after Flavian's death."

"Christ."

"The last anyone has a record of Pak's whereabouts was his arrival at the Toronto airport, two days after that."

Boyden shook his head and looked at the other folder. He placed his hand on it, but he looked at Sullivan. "Tell me," he said.

Abby Springfield had not come to her current subject recently, or suddenly. A careful study of her movements showed her appearing at the same sites as Nathan Adriano. This, despite the fact that she never produced a word in print about the burning children.

Unlike in Mr. Adriano's case, there was no obvious financial support for her movements. Someone else was paying for her investigations.

Perhaps more importantly, she had a personal connection to all of this. When she was six years old, her big brother walked into a vacant lot and combusted.

"How come we didn't know this immediately?" Boyden said.

"No one checked."

"Good lord. So what happens? She goes to Berkeley and they approach her—"

Sullivan nodded. "She may not even know who she's working for."

"You said it depends on your perspective. Well, from my perspective, it looks like bad news across the board."

"Consider it, though. How else does anyone get backing in this business? What better wake-up call for Oberst and the folks with the purse strings?"

Boyden nodded. Sullivan had a point. Department Blue had always been supported with a reluctance. The new offices and servers were just a few scraps from a major funding boost to the Agency in general. However, if he had something concrete to point to and say, *"This is a clear and present threat . . ."*

"Do you want us to bring her in?" Sullivan asked.

After a few moments of consideration, Boyden said, "No."

"Can I ask why?"

Boyden set down the folders and slid them back to Sullivan. "Because they are using Mr. Adriano in precisely the manner I wanted to. Which means they expect him to discover something. I want to see what he discovers as well. Keep on top of both of them."

"Yes, sir."

21

AFTER a few days at the motel, Nate had developed a working schema for the tables on Abby's CD. He still couldn't identify most of the fields, but he had found birth dates, death dates, social security numbers, and a few coded ID fields that linked the tables together. Most importantly, he now had enough hooks into the alien tables that he could compare information from them to the information in his own databases.

Abby did her best to appear fascinated by what he was doing. At least she kept asking questions about it.

"See that field," Nate would say, pointing to one of the cryptic columns on the spreadsheetlike display. The data in it was a three-character alphanumeric code. "Looks like gibberish, right?"

Abby would nod.

"Okay, but since we have the socials for all the kids on this CD, and I have maybe a quarter of those kids in my own database—we filter for the ones I have a full dossier on, then we link the tables together, sort on that field, and see if we have any correspondences . . ."

The simple and fairly straightforward query finished within a minute or so, and since Nate was redoing it for the sake of demonstration, the corresponding columns were al-

ready next to each other. One held the cryptic code, the other
held the city, state, and county fields from his own database.
And the places where the kids died.

"*Voilà!*" Nate said. With the unknown social security
numbers filtered out of the table, the screen was left showing a near one-to-one relationship between the code and the
place where the kids died. "XN9, we have Boston, Massa-
chusetts. G5C, we have Kansas City, Missouri."

"And how did you discover this?"

"No shortcuts, just simple inspection. They've given
every county in the United States a unique three-character
identifier. The good news is that once I do this for this column the translation is—ninety percent of the time—going to
carry over into all the fields that contain this kind of information. There are fields for county of birth, county of last
residence, and a few other fields with this encoding that I
haven't identified yet."

"You are impressive, Nathan."

"Nate. And I've been doing this a long time."

His laptop beeped at him.

"What's that?" she asked.

Nate turned around and looked at what was being shown
on the screen. He had been running a query in the background to find other fields that bore some relation to geography. He had loosened the criteria a bit to allow near
matches and relationships that weren't exact or strictly one-
to-one, so there was a predictable mess of garbage. However, there were two columns that looked almost
comprehensible.

"Nate—"

Nate held up his hand and said, "Shhh."

The two columns were numeric fields, decimals carried
to a consistent six digits of precision. They lined up against

the county code of the kids' deaths. The groupings were in a narrow range for the counties he had identified. One column stayed between the mid twenties up to slightly less than fifty. The other column roamed much more broadly, from the upper sixties to a hundred twenty-five. Both ranges were positive, though the field was signed. He could see a number of entries with numbers outside the range, even negative values, but all outside the selection of counties he had already identified.

"What have you found?"

"I'm not sure," Nate said, scrolling around the result set and looking at the raw numbers. Out of a sense of perversity, he scrolled down to Los Angeles County. Four kids in the database had deaths recorded there over a span of about forty years. That was the greatest concentration in any one of the geographic codes, even the ones that he had yet to identify.

The numbers in the two new columns were very close, but not exact matches.

"Wait a minute here . . ." Nate stared at the figures.

For Deborah's kid—what Nate thought of as the "first" one even though, timewise, he was one of the more recent in the database on Abby's CD—the first number was +33.9275, the second was +118.2772. The other numbers were similar, varying from 33.1 to 33.9 and from 118.26 to 118.29.

After a moment of staring, Nate slapped his forehead. "Of course."

"Of course what?"

To confirm his suspicion, he ordered the table by the larger of the two columns. Just as he suspected, the locations suddenly sprang into order east to west, Los Angeles County being near, but not at, the bottom.

Nate smiled. "I've just cracked the geography of everything in this database." He tapped the screen, at the two columns. "Those are decimal-encoded longitude and latitude. A good map, and I'll have every one of these codes down."

He started typing.

She asked him if he had ever seen one of the kids.

He had.

The first time, the thing Nate had been surprised by was the smell. He had expected the cool air, and the quiet so heavy that it forced you to whisper. He had expected the alien whitewash of the fluorescent light fixtures. He had expected the cold white tile.

The *smell* of the morgue, that's what caught him off guard.

It wasn't an intense odor. It was possible to miss it under the heavier scent of hospital disinfectant. However, even if he hadn't noticed, something visceral in his reptilian hindbrain would have recognized it. Not quite rotten fruit, not quite spoiled milk, the floral hint of decay slipped in under his guard to start twisting his abdomen in a painful knot.

"Thank you for accommodating me," Nate said, wiping the sweat off his face. This was the first time he had gone so far with this kind of deception. But it was also the first time he had caught up with one of the kids before the body was in the ground.

"Happy to do so, Agent Whitman. Anything to help the Bureau, especially if you can clear up this kid's death."

Does he notice me sweating? Nate's heart was racing, and the skin on his face was clammy under his handkerchief. He wanted to put his hand down, but the sweat was drenching him, sliding down his neck, sticking his shirt to his back like a sheet of ice. He was still digesting the fact that the Samson County Coroner had accepted his FBI ID, which had been created with an old copy of PhotoShop and a discount inkjet printer just six hours ago.

"I'm surprised you got here as fast as you did."

Nate nodded. "We've been watching for this kind of event. They're using a chemical that doesn't leave the signature of a normal accelerant—"

"I'll say." He pushed the swinging door open and walked into the examining area.

Nate followed, steeling himself.

"This kid," the pathologist said, "from all outward signs looks as if he burned inside out."

Nate stopped in the doorway.

He knew he had come quickly. He was building up a private little network though his consulting business, law enforcement people quietly keeping an eye out for these cases. He had arrived here before the news media got the story.

He had shown up in the coroner's office half an hour ago—with his bogus ID and his more bogus story—and the coroner had the pathologist on duty come to escort him down.

He didn't realize how quickly he'd arrived.

"The combustion of this body is amazing, I've never seen anything like this . . ."

The corpse was on the examination table. Operating lights washed it in light so that it seemed the most solid thing in the room. The flesh had turned black and pulled so tight that it cracked, showing the blacker flesh inside. The body had curled into itself, showing a back where the spine and ribs were now visible. The face was a charred skull with a fallen jaw.

The pathologist pulled back on a shoulder, and the whole

thing moved as a unit, as if all the joints had fused together. There was a hideous rattle as the paper-light body rolled toward the doctor and away from Nate. As if there was something inside it. As if something was *nesting* in there.

"You can see right here, where I opened him up. There's nothing in there, just ash. Any normal fire would have to burn for hours—"

There was an electronic beeping. The pathologist turned and looked to the wall, where the phone was ringing. "Hold on a minute, Agent Whitman."

Nate stared at what had once been human flesh. The black surface of the skin on the back of the body's right hand reflected the light, as if it was slightly greasy. It was spiderwebbed with cracks where the surface had pulled apart enough to see the black-gray bones of the hand.

The third finger was marred and pitted worse than the others. The remnants of something pebbled and sooty, with a hint of metallic reflection. *A ring,* Nate thought, *In the picture the coroner showed me, he was wearing a ring . . .*

Remembering that photo, and seeing the melted remnants of the friendship ring, forced his mind to make the connection between the human being, and the pile of ash on the examination table.

Nate was hyperventilating.

I shouldn't be here. No one should have to see this . . .

His back pressed into the doorframe behind him.

"Yes, yes. Oh? *Really . . .*" The pathologist looked in Nate's direction. Nate couldn't see his expression because of the glare from the operating lights. "We will be *right* up."

Nate heard him hang up the phone. "There's another Bureau agent upstairs. He wants to talk to you, *Agent* Whitman."

Nate wasn't listening. He was already turning, his stomach five steps out the door before he stumbled through it. He was running down the hall before the pathologist seemed to realize what was happening.

"Agent Whitman?"

The words echoed behind Nate as he slammed through the doorway to the fire stairs. He was up a flight and through the emergency exit before he threw up. He had to stop, leaning against a car in the parking lot, as the exit swung shut behind him, and the fire klaxons started going off.

When he had expelled everything he had inside him, he resumed a stumbling run to his car, doubled over and heaving. He made it before the pathologist and a pair of security guards ran out the door.

"And they didn't catch up with you?"

"No. Even though I was using a half-assed ID, my own car, and left about a quart of evidence at the scene." Nate looked away from the laptop screen. He could still remember the smell, and it still made him a little queasy. "I wasn't a cop, but I *know* cops. What I described to you is a complete nuisance that anyone with any sense of priorities would put at the very bottom of the to-do list. If I had killed someone, there's a fifty-fifty chance that they would have had lab guys, a photographer, and a detective or two on the case in time enough to catch me before I got my shit together. Bluffing my way in to see a corpse and vomiting on a Honda Civic—that would only rate one uniformed cop who was being punished for something."

"What about the other FBI agent?"

Nate chuckled. "You know, I never asked that question myself until about six months later—when my investigation technique had got a little better. Special Agent Ulysses Boy-

den, FBI, apparently there about a gunshot victim in an un-
related bank robbery case."

"An interesting coincidence," she said.

"Yeah," Nate didn't like the way she said that.

Why am I talking to her?

A reporter stepped into his life and he couldn't shut up.
He was back at the Christmas party, and a young woman he
didn't know was genuinely interested in what he was doing
with his life.

*Is it that simple? Am I that hard up for some sort of af-
firmation?* He looked across at Abby, and realized that she
reminded him of Deborah.

22

"**O**H, my God," Nate said quietly.

The motel room was dark; the only light came from streetlights from the parking lot and the bluish glow of his laptop. Abby had gone home to her room hours ago. He had been unable to go to sleep, hadn't been able to since he had begun to map the data from Abby's CD. Now that he was able to interpret dates and geography, his search for pattern proceeded feverishly.

He found pattern.

Now that he had a sample of statistically significant size, he found that these deaths were more ordered than he had thought possible. The pattern he saw on the screen was so perfect that he had to rerun the queries just to make sure that he wasn't missing anything, or creating it out of a desire to see something.

In the six years and fifteen bodies—sixteen including Ted Mackenzie—that Nate had investigated, he had the sense that there was a clustering. He had found almost half of those kids in the first year, and most of the rest happened over a sixteen-month period about three years ago. Ted had been one of the first new cases in a while. Nate always suspected that pattern of deaths was not random, and they weren't distributed uniformly over time.

Nate had plotted the number of "events" from the CD on a time line, and confirmed his suspicions more than he ever could have suspected.

A red bar graph laid out the distribution on the screen. There were distinct spikes every three years, so precise that the bars almost traced out a perfect sine wave. Right now they were almost at the top of a new hump. The peaks and troughs were so uniform that Nate could even get the cycle's period defined as 1320 days, plus or minus five days.

What shook him was a fact that was a consequence of that cycle duration.

One of the central puzzles was the fact that all these kids were the same age when they died, give or take at most a month. That being the case, a plot of the kids' births would show the same sine-wave pattern. That wasn't surprising. It was, in fact, a tautology.

"Why didn't I see this before?"

The fact that left him sweaty and staring at the screen in disbelief was the fact that the birth cycle was out of phase by 270 days.

Nine months.

Put another way, if Nate added nine months to the kids' average age, he came up with an exact integral multiple of 1320 days—exact to three significant figures, anyway. So, at the same time one set of kids was burning, a future round of victims was being conceived. Once conceived, the kid would last exactly four cycles before the fire claimed him.

Looking at the glowing screen, Nate realized he was seeing the first hard evidence that, in some strange way, these children were predestined to burn. This was also the first evidence that there was a pattern that somebody could conceivably use to determine if a kid had "survived."

Department Blue's survivor.
Golden.

In the morning, light was streaming into the hotel room and Abby was sitting on the edge of the bed looking at him. He had let her in after about thirty seconds of knocking, and immediately sat back down at the computer, plotting geographic distributions of births and fatalities.

The patterns here were varied and maddening. He had one distribution map that shaded North America, darkening the color the more cases were born. While the map showed the expected concentrations around high population centers, it also showed a strange preference for latitude. The area of highest concentration was a band wrapping the country a little south of the Great Lakes, fading north and south.

When he plotted a graph simply on latitude, the distribution showed a pronounced bell curve.

"Have you been up all night?" Abby asked him.

"I found something," Nate said.

Another pattern, which he didn't understand. If he compensated for daylight savings time, kids would combust in a two-hour window during a given day, and that window seemed to progress earlier and earlier throughout the year. So while kids were burning in the middle of the night in January, they were burning midday in June.

"You can't constantly push yourself like this." Abby stood up and walked over to Nate. She stopped next to the chair and leaned on the back to look over his shoulder. He could feel one leg pressing against his upper thigh. "What is it you found?"

Nate nodded at the screen. "That's what I found." He was very aware of the weight of Abby's breast on his shoulder.

"What is it?" Her voice was a near whisper. He could feel her breath on his cheek.

Nate explained the correlations he had found.

Abby grabbed his shoulders and turned the chair away from the computer and toward the bed. "You do good work Nate, but you need to sleep."

"I'll sleep as soon as I figure out—"

"The whole thing? No, you'll drop from exhaustion."

Nate nodded and let her push him up and guide him toward the bed. She walked behind him, her whole body pressed up against his side. Through his clothes, he could feel the curve of her hip, the flat smoothness of her abdomen. The roundness of her breast and the hard pebble of her nipple pressed into his back about an inch under his shoulder blade.

Nate wanted to slip into bed now, before his current train of thought became embarrassingly visible.

She helped him slide into the unused bed and when he touched the mattress, the thought of sleep became more erotic than anything else. He looked up at her face and asked, "No third degree?"

"When you've rested."

Nate closed his eyes and nodded.

In half-slumber, Nate opened his eyes. He saw Deborah hunched over his computer, quietly typing away. His groggy mind accepted seeing his deceased ex-fiancée, and he was about to tell her to get away from his work and come back to bed, but he fell back to sleep.

Nate awoke after a long dreamless sleep and opened his eyes to see Abby watching him. He blinked a couple of times, getting himself oriented. As he sat up, his clothes stuck to him, despite the air-conditioning. "What time is it?"

"Six thirty," she told him.

Nate felt an awful wave of disorientation when he was unsure if she meant A.M. or P.M. He had to look out the window and decide if the slant of the sun was east or west. He rubbed his hands over his face. His skin was sticky with dried sweat and scratchy with a couple of days' growth of beard.

"I hung a 'do not disturb' sign on your door. It looked like you needed it."

"So," Nate asked, "how long have you been sitting there?"

"You were talking in your sleep," she said, as if it answered his question.

"I was, huh?"

Abby nodded. Unlike him, she was dressed in clean clothes and had recently showered. Her long hair shone brightly in what he'd decided was the evening light. The eyes watching him from behind her glasses looked a lot more alert than he felt.

"What was I saying?" he asked her. He found his gaze drifting to the side of her cheek, along her jaw, down to the hollow at the base of her neck, just visible at the V of her blouse. He turned his head before his stare became embarrassing.

"You were talking to Deborah."

Ouch.

"You were saying there wasn't any time left."

Nate nodded as he stood. He wasn't sure he wanted to pursue the question anymore. "Have you eaten yet?"

She didn't show any concern about the change in subject. "Not since lunch. I thought I would wait for you."

"You didn't have to do that."

"If I didn't, would you eat, or would you just sit down in front of your computer again?"

Nate turned and looked at her. She was looking up at him with an expression of concern. "You know, I've been doing this for years without a baby-sitter."

"How much of that work have you lost or had to redo because of fatigue?"

Nate was about to say something sharp about her journalistic objectivity, but he couldn't. The sincerity might have been there because he wanted to see it, but he still felt it. Instead he asked her, "Can you go and arrange dinner? I need to clean myself up."

Abby nodded. There was a half smile on her face that made Nate think of Deborah again . . .

He walked into the bathroom and shut the door.

It took him a long time to feel clean. It wasn't until he was shaved and out of the shower that he realized that his clothes were unwearable. They were damp from sweat and they stank. He sighed and kicked them into a corner. He had stayed here about five days longer than he had planned for, and he didn't know if he had a change of clothes left.

He wrapped a towel around his waist and stepped out into the room to look for something wearable. Abby was still there.

"I thought you were going to go and—"

The sun had set, the shades were drawn, and the only light in the room came from a single table lamp and the screen of the notebook on the desk by the window.

Abby sat in one of the two armchairs by the window. On a table between the armchairs sat a white cardboard box. "I ordered a pizza."

"I see."

She uncrossed her legs and stood up. "Do you feel better?"

"A lot."

Abby walked over to where he stood. She reached out and touched his arm. He almost flinched at the contact. No more than three fingers on a naked bicep, but his whole body seemed to shudder. "Wait," Nate whispered.

"Why?"

The pat answer came to his lips, he just wasn't ready after . . .

Abby's eyes answered his unspoken question. Six years was more than long enough. Much more.

Nate reached up and removed her glasses. Without any convenient place to put them, he tossed them on the bed. Her hand reached up and traced his jaw-line, free of stubble for the first time in a couple of days. She looked into his eyes as if searching for guidance.

Nate bent forward and touched his lips to hers.

Inside his head, alarm bells were going off. This woman was half his age. She was here pursuing her own agenda. He didn't know a damn thing about her.

She responded to him, her body collapsing against him and her mouth melting into his. Her hand found the edge of his towel and started drawing it away, slowly, from between the two of them. As the terrycloth rubbed against him, Nate's hand found the zipper at the back of her skirt, just above the curve of her ass.

Nate wondered at what point this particular bad idea had become inevitable. She maneuvered him toward the bed as she worked her way down his body. By the time she took him into her mouth, he had lost track of all his second thoughts.

23

DR. Farid Husam decided that he should have been vol-
unteering his time long ago. The on-site clinic was
woefully understaffed, and while Trinity House had a few
psychiatrists on its payroll, they didn't have a physician.
After the first three hours that Dr. Husam spent at the place,
it was clear that they could really use one. The campus had
three outpatient programs, a high school for the learning disabled, and four residential treatment buildings.

Somehow, the place had managed to run on a rotating
staff of half a dozen RNs. Just providing medications and
dealing with the special medical needs of disabled clients
was a full-time job. Add to that the kinds of injuries Dr.
Husam hadn't seen since he worked the emergency room,
and he knew how much he was needed.

He had seen a broken arm, a hand impaled with a pencil,
two severe allergic reactions, and one halfhearted suicide attempt in the two days before he got to see James Allan Somerset again.

Dr. Husam walked into the one cramped examining room
and shut the door behind him. James sat on the edge of the
bed, watching him. He was a little small for his age, but to
all outward appearances, he was perfectly healthy.

He extended his hand to James and said, "My name is Dr. Husam."

"Uh-huh." James did not take his hand. He looked at Dr. Husam with unconcealed suspicion. "What you want from me?"

"I saw you in the hospital. This is just a follow-up examination."

"Yeah, I'm fine. I peed in your cup, and I gave up some blood to the vampire with the needle." James rubbed the lower part of his right arm. "You want me to blow my nose on something?"

Dr. Husam pulled out a pen and looked down at the chart. Nothing extraordinary; a slight temperature, somewhat elevated blood pressure, somewhat elevated pulse. Still, he found it troubling on the heels of James' unusual lab results. It was as if the boy was suffering from an infection that he didn't know how to test for. "I don't need any more samples from you. I just want to ask you some questions."

James sighed and asked, "Is that all anyone knows how to do here?"

Dr. Husam gave him a disarming smile. "We've been having some difficulty finding your medical records—"

"I ain't surprised."

"Oh?"

"Never saw any doctors before this month."

"I find that hard to believe—"

"Oh, they gave me some vaccination shots when I was a kid. But that's it."

Dr. Husam noted that on his chart. "So you had never been hospitalized before your fainting episode?"

"Never even been to the emergency room."

"No allergies you know of?"

"Nope."

"Any illnesses lasting over a week?"

"Nope."

"Do you know anything about your family's medical history."

"I don't have a family, Doc."

There was nothing to James' medical history. If Dr. Husam was to believe him, James didn't have one. The lifestyle questions were a little more informative, even if they didn't illuminate the mystery of James' biochemistry.

No drug use. No smoking. Limited consumption of alcohol that amounted to one or two illicit beers a week before he'd fallen into the criminal justice system. When Dr. Husam asked if he was sexually active, he became defensive.

"What the fuck business of yours is that?"

"I have to ask you, as a doctor. It has as much bearing on your health as smoking, drinking, drug—"

"Okay, okay. No, I'm not."

Dr. Husam nodded. "Have you ever been—"

"Christ, now you're getting personal."

"As I said, it has a bearing—"

"Fine. No. I haven't. Next question."

After an hour examining James Allan Somerset, Dr. Husam was no wiser. He was, in fact, on the verge of giving up his misgivings. If there was anything wrong with James, it was completely asymptomatic. Dr. Husam had checked everything from neurological and motor function to James' lung capacity.

Everything was within normal limits—except in the places where Jimmy exceeded normal functioning. His lung capacity was about 150% of normal for someone his age and size. Eyesight slightly better than 20/20. When Dr. Husam had him hold out his arms to test any neurological weakness, it was like pushing down on the arms of a weight lifter.

When Dr. Husam asked about any number of symptoms ranging from unusual thirst to night sweats, James responded negatively to every question. The only sign that he experienced any unusual symptoms at all was a slight hesitation when Dr. Husam asked if he ever had trouble sleeping.

When Dr. Husam pressed him about it, James admitted to having an occasional bad dream.

"But that's not your department, Doc, is it?"

Dr. Husam admitted that, but wrote the note down on James' chart.

It was nine in the evening before Dr. Husam packed his briefcase to go home. It had been a long day. He had started his shift here at six, right after coming off of a ten-hour shift back at The Cleveland Clinic. He hadn't worked hours like this since he had been an intern.

"Dr. Husam?"

Dr. Husam turned to acknowledge the speaker. "Yes?"

Dr. Altroy was standing in the doorway. "I wanted to thank you for helping us with the kids here."

"Thank you for indulging an old man's paranoia."

"I don't think any of us cares why you're helping out. I just hope that you might consider making this a regular contribution . . ." He looked down at Dr. Husam's briefcase. "How is James?"

Dr. Husam sighed. "I don't know. Perhaps I'll see better with this second round of blood tests." He shook his head. "Maybe I am imagining things. He seems almost too healthy, to look at him."

Dr. Altroy nodded. "He's why I came, actually."

"Yes?"

"I got a message, since he's my patient, but I think it is for you. You were asking for medical records?"

"Yes, I was. James hasn't seen a doctor in several years, and the county is no help in finding any."

Dr. Altroy nodded. "Well, there is a message from a Dr. Singh at the Metro Health Medical Center—"

"Do you have his number?"

"Yes." Dr. Altroy took a slip of paper from his pocket. "Dr. Singh actually seemed quite anxious to talk to someone about James."

Dr. Husam took the paper. "Thank you."

"Forgive me if I hope your fears are unfounded."

Dr. Husam placed the phone number in his briefcase and closed the lid. "I hope so as well."

Perhaps Dr. Singh can enlighten me . . .

24

JIMMY couldn't get Salina out of his mind. The starkness of what she had said ate into his mind. So much so that, instead of retreating to his room for the short free period after his third group session, he followed half the group to the gym.

There were basically three options in the residential treatment during "unstructured" free time. You could lock yourself in your own room, Jimmy's preference up till now. You could hang out in one of the common rooms and watch consensus TV or dig around in their cabinets for board games missing their pieces, or books with torn and Crayolaed pages.

Last was a gymnasium built directly adjacent to the residence. This seemed the most popular choice for Jimmy's group. Twice before he'd seen Charlie, Lorraine, and Salina break off to go there after group. This time he followed them.

The gym was larger than Jimmy had expected. It accommodated a basketball court, a jogging track around the perimeter, and a small set of bleachers on one wall. At the moment, half the court held a three-on-three basketball game, while the other had a volleyball net set up. Flanking the bleachers were doors to boys' and girls' locker rooms and—presumably—showers.

Jimmy stood in the doorway, unsure of what he was doing. The folks from his group had already disappeared into their respective locker rooms. He was uncomfortably aware that he didn't have any gym clothes. They all would have been at Euclid Heights High.

Thinking about that pissed Jimmy off.

Jimmy sat down on the bottom bleacher and shook his head. He looked out at the kids playing ball out on the court and tried to fathom what had brought them here. How he fit.

Why am I here?

Why am I, period . . . ?

"So how are you doing?" Jimmy looked up and saw the familiar tall, lanky form of Gordon Pagnokowski. He wore the same photo ID, but he was clad in jeans and a white shirt today. He sat at the top of the bleachers.

Jimmy shrugged.

"Staying out of trouble?"

"Don't you think it's a little late for that question?"

Jimmy heard something off to his left and looked around to see Salina, in T-shirt and gym shorts, tying her shoelaces by the edge of the track. She tossed a towel on the lowest bench of the bleachers and stood up.

Jimmy opened his mouth to say something, but she had already started running away from him. Jimmy stood up and watched Salina jog around the end of the gym with the basketball game. She had long legs, and the way she moved showed that she used them a lot. Her gaze was fixed solidly ahead of her. She didn't look left or right, and if one of the basketball players had strayed into her path,

Jimmy wouldn't have been surprised if she'd run right into him.

She circled the course, coming back toward Jimmy. This time he managed to get "Salina . . ." out of his mouth before she had run past him.

Damn it.

Jimmy ran after her.

It wasn't as easy as it looked. She kept quite a pace, and Jimmy had to sprint to catch up with her.

"Hey. Salina." he called when he got within a few feet of her.

They ran around the basketball players. Jimmy was aware, in a sort of peripheral manner, that they had stopped playing. She didn't respond. Her long legs kept pumping, and her long hair, tied in a ponytail, bounced behind her.

"Hey," Jimmy repeated, between breaths.

She didn't turn her head or slow down. "What?"

Jimmy was so surprised at hearing her voice that he almost tripped over himself. "Can I talk. To you?"

"About what?" She didn't stop moving.

Jimmy paced her. He was breathing like a bellows, but his legs seemed to be moving better. *Please don't let me trip and look like an idiot.*

"I wanted. To apologize."

They circled again. Sweat was stinging Jimmy's eyes. He was beginning to realize that, at the very least, he should have taken off his jacket.

"Why? What did you do?" Still running.

Jimmy sprinted until he was even with her, running on the outside of the track. The basketball players were now staring at them. Jimmy saw them staring as he looked at Salina. "Sometimes I'm an idiot. It was my first group session and—"

He saw wetness on her cheek, and her eyes were closed. She shook her head and said, "Don't pity me."

"Huh? I was just saying—" Looking at her, Jimmy did not see the brick wall before he ran headlong into it. He must have been running at quite a clip, because the impact sent him sailing back about ten feet to land flat on his back.

There wasn't a wall there . . .

Jimmy shook his head and sat up in time to see the wall walking toward him.

Shit.

Jimmy spread his hands and said, "Hi, Charlie."

"You leave her alone."

Jimmy scooted back on his ass, using his legs to push away from the oncoming avalanche of Chuck. "Hey, remember group?"

Charlie bent down and grabbed the lapels of Jimmy's jacket and lifted him to his feet. "You got no reason to bother her—"

"We're supposed to think of options, defuse the situation . . ." His voice trailed off and he shook his head. He was swallowing hard on the growing anger that burned in his gut. The dark was crawling up inside of him.

Who the fuck is this guy? What makes him think this is his business?

Jimmy was hyperventilating and he felt his hands balling up into fists. He had lost himself and he could see the next few moments unfolding with the inevitability of a nightmare. The Jimmything was ready to tear into this guy like a lawnmower into an overripe pile of dog shit—

"Charlie. *No!*" A girl's voice. Salina. The one word carrying as much anger as Jimmy had balled up in his gut.

The spell was broken as suddenly as it had come. He stood there, slightly wobbly, as Charlie released his jacket.

It had felt like an eternity, but the whole episode was barely long enough for Salina and Gordon Pagnokowski to run up to him. Gordon was speaking into a walkie-talkie as he interposed himself between him and Charlie.

Charlie backed away a little dumbfounded.

"What's happening here—"

Somewhere inside himself, the Jimmything looked at Charlie and said, *"I own you, you bastard . . ."*

Jimmy unclenched his fists and, for once, thought carefully before he spoke. "It's okay. I wasn't looking where I was going. Ran straight into Charlie." Jimmy looked over at Charlie and got some faint amusement at the puzzled expression he saw there. "He was just helping me up."

Gordon looked down at Jimmy, as if he knew how much of the story was bullshit. "Are you hurt?"

Jimmy shook his head. "Just winded."

Gordon turned around and looked at Charlie and asked him, "What about you?"

"No, fine . . ."

"Is that pretty much what happened?"

Charlie rubbed his forehead and said, "Yeah, pretty much."

Gordon looked at Jimmy again and said, "Be more careful." Gordon walked back toward the bleachers. After he barked a few words into the walkie-talkie, Jimmy heard him mutter something about incident reports and how much he hated paperwork.

Jimmy started sucking air as if someone had just loosened a noose around his neck. He felt a little shaky, and decided that he didn't want to be in the gym anymore.

"Why do you do this, Charlie?" Salina was glaring at Charlie. This moose, who'd have no problem snapping

Frank in half, withered under her stare. "Why do you have to embarrass me like this?"

Charlie winced. Jimmy actually felt sorry for him. "I thought he was . . ."

"Don't. Just don't—" her voice was lowering to her normal, distant, tone. She turned to look at Jimmy and gasped, *"You're bleeding."*

"Huh?" Jimmy was caught off guard and looked down at himself. He seemed unhurt. But he watched as a small red sphere detached from his face and fell to make a dime-sized spot on his left sneaker. "Fhug, anotha nothbleed." Jimmy raised his hand and covered his nose. He looked up and said, "Ith noth hith fault. It juth happent thomtimeth."

Jimmy backed up and walked a little unsteadily to the bathroom, leaving Chuck and Salina to iron out their differences. He made sure to keep his back to Gordon. The last thing he wanted right now was to deal with more people in latex gloves.

When Jimmy came out of the bathroom, he heard a familiar voice call out, "So I hear the newbie came out to play."

In a sick, slow-motion repeat of what he'd felt when Charlie grabbed him, his gut tightened and freezing needles of tension rolled up his spine, pulling the muscles of his jaw tight as he turned around. His hands were already balling into fists as he faced Dion. "What?" Jimmy snapped.

Dion was a few feet down the corridor, leaning up against the doorframe of the cafeteria. He folded his arms so the tattoos on his left bicep were visible.

Dion was smiling, and his posture was so relaxed that

Jimmy's surge of adrenaline had nowhere to go. "You made an impression on Charlie."

Jimmy stood there and looked at Dion. He felt his face go expressionless.

While Jimmy stood there laboriously putting two and two together, Dion leaned forward, "You okay?"

"Huh?"

"You look a little green."

"Just a little tired . . ." Jimmy was more than a little tired. He felt dizzy and light-headed. It was as if the adrenaline surge that had just happened inside him had washed out the pilings that supported him. It was as if he had exploded into the action that had been threatening inside him, all that energy sapped from him even though he hadn't so much as moved.

He looked up at Dion briefly convinced that he had suffered another blackout, more missing time. Dion was still there, but he wasn't smiling, he wore a concerned expression that looked out of place. "Bad trip? Should I get the nurse?"

"Fuck, no."

Jimmy walked up and pushed by Dion, into the cafeteria. He had to lean over one of the tables and take a few deep breaths. He remembered how he felt in the courtroom, right before he fainted. Had he forgotten to eat?

But he *had* eaten breakfast . . .

"Just need something to eat," Jimmy said. His stomach felt hollow and flat. It felt as if energy was leaking out from every pore of his body. *What's happening to me?*

"I'll go see if they got any lunch left over. Sit down."

Jimmy slid into a seat and tried to focus his thoughts, but the supports of his mind seemed to be crumbling away with the supports of his body. Everything was falling into the black void that had opened inside himself . . .

Dion came back with a pair of foil-wrapped sandwiches and a can of Dr. Pepper. Jimmy muttered something that sounded like *"Thank you,"* and took one of the packages. His hands shook so badly that he almost took a bite without unwrapping it. He shoved it in his mouth as soon as he had peeled enough off of one corner. He still bit down on a piece of foil, but the metallic taste wasn't enough to stop him. Suddenly, getting the nourishment into his body was the ultimate priority. The moment he saw the food, smelled the lunch meat, tasted the slightly stale Wonder Bread and mayo, he was racked by a craving so painful that he almost passed out.

Sandwich one disappeared in five bites. Number two disappeared in three because his hands were steadier. He washed it down with the aluminum-tasting syrup from the Dr. Pepper can. He clutched the can with both hands as he drank.

The dizziness had gone away, and his hands were steady. He felt more normal now. Apparently, his body had some sense of irony, since *now* he actually felt hungry. It was as if the two chopped-ham sandwiches had fallen into the same black hole his insides were falling into, and had vanished into another universe.

He set down the Dr. Pepper can, still clutching it with both hands.

"I *had* breakfast," Jimmy whispered to himself. How could he be on the verge of starving himself? He was eating. He had been making a point, after what had happened, not to skip a meal . . .

"Do you need someone?"

Jimmy had forgotten about Dion. The guy was sitting

across from him, watching as if Jimmy was the geek act in a sideshow. Jimmy looked at the tinfoil scattered on the table between them and didn't blame him. It looked as if a wildcat had torn into the food.

Jimmy shook his head. "No. Thanks."

"You diabetic? Low blood sugar?"

Jimmy shook his head.

"Got a cousin like that. She needs to eat something, you better feed her. You all right now?"

Jimmy nodded. "Yeah." Jimmy looked down at the can. It felt strange, slick with his own sweat and condensation. His hands tingled against it, as if his fingers had fallen asleep.

Jimmy looked up from the can and stared at Dion. His first impression was off, he wore the same clothes, same tattoos, but the face looking at him wasn't the aggressive mask he'd been wearing in the group.

Younger than me.

Jimmy glanced down at the tattoos on his arm. Five names, dates, R.I.P. . . .

Dion caught him looking and held up the arm for him. "Friends," he said, "my brothers. Shows my respect."

"All dead?"

"Not all," Dion pointed to a name, unfaded, freshly cut into the skin. This one had an "RIP" but only a single date. Jimmy realized that it was Dion's name.

"Some fucking gang, huh? Hell, get three black kids together it's a gang to someone, right? All these guys, we were tight from grade school." He pointed at the first name. "Todd, he was ten. He was in his gram's house when the place torched. Wayne, thirteen, he lifted some videos from a Blockbuster, they sent him to Juvenile Hall and the assholes there had an accident trying to restrain him. Kenyon, no one knows what the fuck happened, just found his body on East 55th with a bullet in it. Dave, he was the oldest of us, smartest, too. Year ago he gets spinal-fucking-meningitis." Dion looked up from his arm. "Can you believe that shit?"

"Why did you put your name there?"

"Look at the odds. Think I'll make it to twenty-one?"

Jimmy didn't answer. He was thinking of the kids he knew in grade school. Few stuck out in his memory, and he wondered how many of them were dead now.

His hands felt sticky, so Jimmy peeled them off of the can and wiped them on his jeans.

"What the fuck!" Dion exclaimed.

Jimmy looked up at Dion who was staring at the can that sat on the table between them. "What?"

Dion reached over and picked up the can. He held it with his fingertips gripping the edge of the top, as if he was afraid of touching it. The names rippled on his arm as he lifted it and turned the can in the light. As the fluorescents reflected off the surface of the can, Jimmy saw what Dion was so struck by.

The surface of the can was *etched* by Jimmy's fingerprints. The paint had been eaten away in whorls and ridges mirroring the impressions of Jimmy's hands. At first, it looked as if the paint had peeled away, but when he looked more closely at the fingerprints, it seemed almost as if the metal underneath had been eaten away. The etchings gleamed as if they had been polished.

"What was on your hands?"

Jimmy glanced at his hands. There was no sign, no paint. Nothing. They weren't even sweaty anymore. He reflexively scrubbed his palms on his jeans.

He pushed the chair back with his feet and looked at his

jeans. He didn't see any residue there either. "Sweat," Jimmy said. "Just sweat."

Dion set the can down. "Yeah, sure. Just don't wipe off with any of my towels."

Jimmy stared at the can, the handprint shining on its side like evidence for a crime that wasn't completely of this world.

25

THE next day was art therapy. Ms. Fujimara took Jimmy's little sextet into a room with a few long tables and the instruction to draw "how they were feeling."

To Jimmy's mind, that was just asking for it. He picked up a stray pencil and a newsprint tablet, looked at the blank page, and for once found himself stymied.

What the hell?

It was crazy, but it had been so long since he had been given the freedom to draw that the creative well had gone dry. Jimmy closed his eyes and shook his head. This couldn't be happening.

He could almost hear Dr. Altroy's voice saying that his bad experiences with his art had given him a creative block. If that was the case, Jimmy was going to sue the pants off of somebody. He didn't want to face the rest of his life if he couldn't put something down on paper.

He looked around the room at his fellow cell mates to see how they were taking the latest therapy du jour.

Eric was hunched over a pad holding a big permanent marker in his left hand. He was drawing something that required thick, jagged black strokes. Dion and Lorraine were chatting in a corner, showing little concern for whatever they were doodling with a shared pack of felt-tip pens.

Charlie was using a box of crayons to color something he shielded from everyone's view with a beefy arm. Even Salina was drawing what looked to be a bouquet of black and white flowers with a ball-point pen.

Jimmy looked at the pen in his own hand. *I'm always doing everything in black ink, maybe I need a change.*

He set down the newsprint and looked around the table for something else to draw with. His gaze landed on a lonely box of broken pastels. "Why not?" he muttered to himself.

Okay, to hell with Cain et al. That's what they're expecting from you anyway. Let's surprise them . . .

It worked. As soon as he let Cain slip from his mind and picked up a pink-shaded fragment of pastel chalk, his hand started moving without him having to think about it. He covered the 11 by 17 newsprint with broad strokes of color, sketching out the outline of a face against a black-gray background before he really knew it was a portrait.

It was strange working with the pastels, with no hard lines, no stark boundaries between black and white. Everything was one color bleeding into the next . . .

"Boy, you are *good.*" A snap of gum let him know it was Lorraine.

Suddenly, Jimmy remembered where he was, and reflexively tried to hide the pad. Unlike his notebooks, the picture he had drawn was too big for one hand to hide.

"You should look at this, girl."

"Look," Jimmy said, defending himself in advance, "it's just a picture."

Salina stood up and walked around the table. It might have been his imagination, but Jimmy felt as if everyone, even Eric, was staring at him. He could feel blood rushing to his face.

Salina walked over and touched Jimmy's wrist, moving his hand away from in front of the drawing.

"I couldn't think of anything else to draw—" *Christ, man, you couldn't sound lamer if you tried.*

Salina looked into her own eyes on the page. Jimmy watched her fingers trace the cheek of the pastel image, not quite touching the paper. Sitting there, as his stomach sank, he saw every flaw, every asymmetry of the drawing as if it was spray painted on the side of the Terminal Tower. The picture was hideous.

"It's beautiful," she said.

Jimmy's mouth opened, but nothing came out. After a few moments of disorientation, he thrust the whole pad at her. "Here."

She backed up, "What?"

"It's yours, take it."

She looked at him and some of the distance seemed gone from her eyes. "Thank you."

"Sure," Jimmy said, still too flustered to manage a complete sentence.

After a few moments, Jimmy looked around and said, "What are you all looking at?" He grabbed another pad, a black marker, and helped Cain resume his fight against injustice.

That evening, Jimmy took a long, cold shower trying not to think about anything. He let the water run out over him and spiral down the drain. It didn't matter, the afternoon stuck with him like a tattoo. He turned off the water and leaned against the cold tile.

Let's not go there. You know she's as fucked up as you are. Maybe worse.

Jimmy heard something.

He scrambled to his feet, almost losing his balance. His skin peeled away from the tile and he had a brief flash-memory of the etched soda can.

He faced the door to the shower, and he could see a human shadow on the other side of the frosted glass.

There were three separate rooms with showers and another three half-baths on the first floor. They were shared, but they were supposed to give some measure of privacy. There were signs on the door to mark it occupied.

Jimmy pulled the shower door open and saw a kid standing there, freckled, sandy-haired, no more than thirteen years old, wearing an electric-blue Pokémon T-shirt. The youngest kid he'd seen locked up in here.

"Sorry," Jimmy said. "I'm using the shower."

Water rolled down his body, dripping from his nose, elbows, his dick. The kid stared at him. Jimmy didn't like the way that stare felt.

"Come on. Beat it. I'll be done in five minutes."

The kid didn't say anything. He just stared at Jimmy with a slight frown, his hands clenched into fists. The kid was biting his lower lip, and Jimmy thought he looked constipated.

Christ, not another one going to take a dump on the floor.

"Look, just let me dry off at least." Jimmy stepped out of the shower and reached for the kid's shoulder to maneuver him out the door to the bathroom.

When Jimmy put his hand on the kid's shoulder, the kid screamed—a wail that hurt Jimmy's ears and sounded as if he was trying to amputate the kid's pecker with a dull hacksaw. Jimmy let go immediately, but whatever demon had awakened wouldn't go back to sleep that easily.

Jimmy raised his hand, his head already rushing with all the molestation accusations that were going to be fired at

him. This bawling little kid was going to put him in jail.
"I'm sorry . . . Please shut up . . ."

Without warning, the kid sprang forward and bit down on
the meat of Jimmy's right hand.

"FUCK!"

Jimmy slipped backward on the tile floor, slamming into
the narrow space between the john and the shower. Spikes
of pain fired up his spine when his tailbone hit the tile. His
head bounced off the wall behind him with a stunning impact.

The kid got pulled in after him, attached to Jimmy's
hand. The kid folded over the toilet, holding on to Jimmy's
wrist with both hands while he shook his head like a dog.
The Pokémon shirt was going purple with Jimmy's blood.

After a stunned moment, Jimmy raised his left hand to try
to push the cannibal kid's face off of his hand. "Get off of
me."

Blood.

How the hell could there be that much blood in his hand?
Jimmy tried to push the kid off, but his hand just slid off the
kid's face, smearing more blood.

Someone was trying the door, and Jimmy called out,
"Get this fucking vampire off of me!"

Jimmy was no longer stunned. His mind had snapped
back into focus, cold and dark. There'd been no anticipation,
no adrenaline wave to ride into combat. The Jimmything
had been caught unawares. Only now, anger focused by the
pain of teeth grinding on bone, did it awake.

"Bad idea kid," it whispered.

It looked deep into the kid's eyes and its left hand
wrapped itself around the kid's face. This time, it didn't
push, didn't slide on the blood slick.

The kid's eyes widened above the edge of the Jimmything's hand as the Jimmything squeezed. The cartilage of the nose was the first thing to give under the Jimmything's palm. *"Getting hard to breathe, ain't it?"*

The door burst open and spilled four orderlies into the room. The Jimmything looked up at them and said, "You better get this fucking munchkin off of me."

It wasn't that hard for them, because in a couple of seconds, the kid had to gasp for air. When the kid's jaw lost its death grip, the Jimmything pushed, and the kid flew backward into one of the orderlies, spraying blood and spit everywhere.

One of the orderlies said, "Someone get a nurse up here."

Jimmy shook his head and flexed his left hand. His right was numb and tingling. He looked up at the kid who had bit him. A few seconds ago he'd been ready to *kill* the little shit.

The orderlies were restraining the kid, but he wasn't reacting to them. The kid kept staring at Jimmy. His eyes were circled and his nose was smashed against his face.

As Jimmy watched, he saw something that convinced him that he might actually be crazy. No one else seemed to notice it, as if it wasn't there, or never happened . . .

As the kid looked at Jimmy, standing frozen where the orderlies held him, several drops of blood rolled *up* the kid's face and disappeared into the wound of his broken nose.

The darkness isn't chasing him anymore. It doesn't need to. It swirls around him like some negative galaxy. Its tendrils drain into him, anchoring him to the center of the vortex. If Jimmy moves, takes a step in any direction, the darkness tears into the world around him, sucking chunks of reality into itself.

There are people on the fringes of Jimmy's vision, but when he tries to reach out to them, the blackness rips them apart and sucks them into itself. He can see Frank, and the kid who bit him, just before they are pulled into the darkness . . .

Jimmy *is* the darkness.

A small consolation for Jimmy was that they believed his explanation of events. Apparently, whatever the kid had said pretty much matched with what Jimmy thought had happened. If the kid had been sane enough to fabricate something himself, Jimmy could have been in a whole shitload of hurt.

Apparently the kid, Raymond, had serious issues. No one explained it to him, but Jimmy gathered from overheard conversations between the staff that Raymond was a serious abuse case. He had been beaten so often, and from infancy, that a normal human touch felt like an attack. Jimmy didn't know how the kid ended up in the bathroom, but he had wandered away from the more intensive part of the cottage—which seemed to concern everyone more than his attack on Jimmy.

Jimmy spent his night in a bed in Trinity's health clinic. Nurses with masks and latex gloves washed the blood off of him. Again, it made Jimmy feel as if he'd been contaminated. They washed out the bite wound with antibiotics and hydrogen peroxide. The wound didn't look half as bad as it had felt, they closed it with some butterfly dressings and wrapped the whole thing in gauze.

The dream had woken him up in the strange bed. It was four in the morning, according to the clock on the wall. The room around him was dark, lit only by a sliver of gray light that fell across the clock face, arrowed across the linoleum floor to the base of a door that was cracked open about an inch.

He was sweating, and his hand itched. Jimmy remembered the can of Dr. Pepper and felt that there was something wrong. Something deeply wrong.

He swung himself up to a seated position so he could hold up his left hand to the light. It was still wrapped in gauze. There was a tiny spot on the gauze, blood marking the bottom edge of the bite. Jimmy traced his finger along the arc where the wound was under the gauze. He could feel the bumps of the butterfly stitches where they held the wound together.

Jimmy found the edge of the gauze with his fingers, peeled tape away, and started unwrapping his hand. The gauze unraveled, spilling onto the crack of light on the linoleum under his hand.

The last of it fell away.

Jimmy flexed his hand, unsure exactly what he was seeing.

There was no bite. There wasn't even a scar. The edges of the butterfly stitches were brown-black with blood, but the skin beneath was unmarked, unstained.

Jimmy remembered the kid biting down on him. He remembered teeth grinding on bone. He remembered blood. Less than eight hours ago. Jimmy had always healed fast, but never *this* fast. It wasn't normal, and he didn't know how to explain it.

26

THE next day's therapy wasn't group, it was individual counseling. The weekly appointment with Dr. Altroy had been made before his incident with the cannibal kid from hell. Even so, Jimmy felt uncomfortable about the whole thing, as if he was on trial again.

It wasn't my fault . . .

If they hadn't pulled him off of you, you would have—

"Would have doesn't count," Jimmy whispered to himself. He flexed his left hand. He had rewrapped the gauze so no one saw that he didn't have any bite marks anymore. He had even managed to con the day nurse by telling her that he had woken early and the nurse on the prior shift had changed the dressing for him already.

He didn't know how long that particular deception would last. He was scheduled for yet another physical with Dr. Husam in two days. The doc would probably want to look at his hand.

Well, a miraculous healing over seventy-two hours would be a lot more credible than the same thing in less than eight.

Dr. Altroy met him in a different room this time, this one a little less juvenile. This place rated an actual desk and office chairs, though the surfaces were all bare.

"Hello, Jimmy," Dr. Altroy greeted him as if he had just decided to walk in off of the street. He stood and extended his hand in a gesture that could have been offering to shake, or just indicating one of the chairs on the other side of the too-clean desk.

Jimmy assumed it was the latter. He was self-conscious about touching anyone—anything—lately. Dr. Altroy nodded and sat down, and Jimmy got the feeling that his choice would make it into his file somewhere.

"How are you feeling today?"

Like a trapped lab rat. "Okay, Doctor."

"I heard about what happened between you and Raymond—"

"That wasn't my fault." Jimmy was already pissed at himself before he had finished his protest. Sure, it really wasn't, but getting defensive like that only made it look worse. He didn't need to be acting like he had something to hide.

"I know. He wasn't supposed to be there, and you couldn't know how he might react. Unfortunate, but it wasn't your fault." Dr. Altroy leaned back and said, "I just wanted to know what happened from your point of view."

"I've already gone over it with a bunch of other people."

The doctor nodded. "Is there anything else about what happened that you'd like to talk about?"

There's a loaded question.

Jimmy glanced at his hand and shook his head.

For a few long moments, Dr. Altroy looked as if he wasn't going to take no for an answer. However, after studying Jimmy, he apparently decided to strike off into other territory.

"Do you feel you're making progress?"

"Huh, progress in what?"

"Progress with the issues that brought you here?"

Jimmy shook his head. "Doc, let's not pretend I came here for some sort of help. I was *sent* here."

Dr. Altroy nodded. "Perhaps, but you don't think you have some problems you need to work out?"

"Apparently that's what the rest of the world thinks."

"What do you think?"

("Do you get it now?") "I think I wouldn't be here if Frank Bradley hadn't jumped me." *("Do you GET IT?")*

"That wasn't my question, was it?"

Jimmy sighed. "Damn it. It wasn't as if I was some crack addict knocking over liquor stores. I was holding down a job. I had a bank account. If it wasn't for Euclid Heights High School and the county, I would be one of those productive members of society they keep talking about."

"You don't think you should be here?"

"I think *Frank* should be here."

Dr. Altroy made a few notes. "You had shown an impressive change since you started living with the Carswells. I don't see any disruptive incidents for nearly seven months. You held a job over the summer—"

"Then they injected me into the general population."

"What?"

Jimmy sighed. "I know what you're looking at. The county moves me into the suburbs and I do great, don't I? They snuck me in at the end of the school year, so I was in some special remedial catch-up class at the end of last year—they even have a separate building for that crap. I didn't get dumped into Euclid Heights High until the start of this year—mmm, let me think, can this be a coincidence?"

Dr. Altroy jotted some more notes. "Do you like your job?"

Jimmy snorted. "You mean, *did* I like my job. You think I still have it after all this crap?"

"How did you feel about it?"

"Come on, it was a dream. That's what pisses me off most about all of this. I have this primo gig that probably could have paid for an apartment when the county cuts me loose . . . Now I'll be lucky to find a job at McDonald's."

"Part of the program you're in is helping you build that sort of independence. Job included."

"So you're going to get me my old job back?"

"We'll see. How much time did you spend working there?"

"As much as Reggie would give me. Four or five hours a day three days during the week, one eight-hour shift on the weekends."

"What did you like about it?"

Jimmy shrugged. "I like comic books."

"Do you mind talking about your comic books?"

"I guess not." He flexed his left hand again. *You're going to talk about them anyway.*

"Tell me about Cain."

Jimmy looked up from his hand and at the doctor. "If you read it, that's everything you need to know."

"I don't imagine it's everything. I just want to hear your description of the character. What do you have in your mind when you write?"

Jimmy thought of telling this guy to fuck off, but for some reason he liked having someone interested in his work, no matter what the reason. "He's a superhero," Jimmy said. "A crime fighter, like Batman, like Spider-Man."

"He's not typical."

Jimmy shook his head. "Who's more interesting, Superman or Batman?"

"You tell me."

"Come on. Superman is so clearly over the top, can you think of any fictional hero who's *more* powerful? He's invulnerable, he's the strongest thing on the planet, he flies, he can time travel, he has x-ray vision, heat vision—a whole laundry list of crap."

"So Superman is more interesting?"

Jimmy almost said something rude, but he realized that Dr. Altroy was being obtuse on purpose. That was okay . . .

"Not only that, but at least until recently, this guy has been good incarnate, so moral and righteous that he was practically a joke. But when it comes down to it, Superman only has weaknesses that are contrived." Jimmy shook his head. "Compare that to Batman. In the whole catalog of superherodom the guy is unique. He's *human.* He bleeds. He can be killed. He's a hero, but his motives are dark, and a lot closer to something the rest of us can relate to. You see, in a good Batman story, there's not just the possibility that the Joker might kill him, but the possibility that he might kill the Joker . . ."

Dr. Altroy nodded. "So you're saying that your character, Cain, is modeled more after Batman?"

"*More* after him. When I wanted to make my own hero, I knew what I didn't want to do. The guy had to be on a human scale. He couldn't be a hero just because he's such a good guy. He couldn't be overwhelmingly powerful— He had to be someone who would take a beating. He had to bleed . . ."

"He does that."

Jimmy smiled. "I also had to give him an adversary that's way more powerful than he is."

"So who is he, this hero you created?"

"Cain's immortal. He committed some great sin that

caused him to be cursed by God so he can never die. However grievously he's wounded, he'll recover. After a few thousand years he's decided to try and earn back God's favor by playing the hero."

"I don't know a lot about the genre," Dr. Altroy said, "but that seems unusual."

"Well, in the mainstream comics, they sort of ran out of original origins about twenty years ago. They invented the X-Men, and suddenly they said, 'oh, of course, they're all *mutants.*' Talk about your laundry list of interchangeable characters. The thing that comes closest to Cain is probably Spawn, and that's from a completely different angle. I was trying to be original."

"I think it may be, though like I said, you're more familiar with the genre than I am. Is he *the* Cain?"

"Well, I got the idea from the Wandering Jew, but I thought Cain was a better name. I'd like to leave that open in the story, but I have a strong suspicion that he is."

"Hmm." Dr. Altroy made a few long notes on a pad in front of him, and Jimmy was reminded that there were ulterior motives for his interest. Jimmy was suddenly uncomfortable with everything he had just said. Why should he be telling this guy anything? It was none of his fucking business.

Jimmy stopped talking and Dr. Altroy looked up, as if waiting for him to continue. When he didn't, Dr. Altroy asked, "What about Baphomet?"

"A demon," Jimmy shrugged.

Dr. Altroy tapped his pen against his pad. When Jimmy didn't elaborate, he asked, "Are you religious?"

"It's a comic book." Christ, what a load of BS. He couldn't escape it. Even this guy, who should know better, was trying to insist that it was some sort of warning sign. There's a fucking demon in it, so he had to be a Satanist.

"I know, Jimmy. But you're using religious and metaphysical themes of sin and redemption in your stories that are unusual in the form. The subject obviously interests you. I just was wondering what sort of beliefs you had. You don't have to go into it if you don't want to . . ."

Okay, you fucker, you really want to know? "I suppose you're a Christian?" Jimmy asked.

"That's a broad category."

Sure, don't *answer, you slick, superior piece of shit.* "Have you looked at the Bible?"

"I'm familiar with it."

"Then you know there's a really noticeable shift in tone from one half to the other?"

"You mean between the Old and New Testaments?" Jimmy nodded.

"I suppose you can characterize it that way."

"You're a head doctor. You have a patient that undergoes a sudden and unexplained shift in mood and personality, they have a problem, right?"

"That can be a symptom of some greater difficulty—"

"You think God's manic depressive?" Jimmy looked at Dr. Altroy and was gratified when the doctor didn't answer him immediately. "If you believe in the New Testament, you believe that God, the supreme omnipotent infallible deity, made this sudden unexplained transformation from the über-Fascist who asked Abraham to chop up his own son and plagued Job just to test his faith, to this warm and fuzzy beacon of eternal love that allowed his only son to be nailed to a stick so he could forgive all of us. Do you detect a slight change in attitude?"

"An argument could be—"

"From the beginning of time up to two thousand years ago, God's reaction to sinners has been pretty much consistent, don't you think? They're banished or they're slaughtered. He booted Adam and Eve. He booted Cain. He drowned everyone but Noah. He nuked Sodom and Gomorrah. He is generally someone you don't want to fuck with." Jimmy leaned forward. "Now, I want to ask you—given the psychological history of the subject in question—if this guy sends his only son among the heathen to do some missionary work and the dim fuckers kill the poor bastard, what do you think his most likely reaction would be?"

Jimmy held up a finger. "Choice A, 'Well, now that you killed my kid, I can offer all of you forgiveness.'"

He raised a second finger. "Choice B, 'To hell with the lot of you.'"

Dr. Altroy was quiet. He was good at hiding his reaction, but Jimmy thought he might have hit a nerve somewhere in there. "That is not what the New Testament says."

"No, but if you're an Apostle and your savior comes back from the dead and says, 'Dad told me that you all fucked up, so don't wait up, you're all going to hell.' You think that's what they'd write down? Can't found a religion on that."

"Do you feel that God's abandoned you?"

"Think about it. We had a pretty hands-on deity until about two thousand years ago. Set aside the lack of miracles and prophets, when was the last time He rained apocalyptic destruction on any sinners? You would think that—given the Jews are God's chosen people—that He'd consider Nazi Germany at least as bad as Pharaoh's bondage of the Hebrews. I'm not great on history, but was there even one plague? Any rivers of blood? Frogs? Locusts? Darkness?"

Dr. Altroy nodded and wrote in his notebook. If Jimmy

had shaken him, he had recovered quickly. "This is what you believe?"

Jimmy leaned back. He had blown most of his energy, and again he felt weak, shaken, and hungry. "It fits the facts." He had expected Dr. Altroy to argue with him. No, that wasn't quite right. He knew that the doctor wasn't going to engage in that sort of verbal sparring with him. He'd be a pretty shitty shrink if he got into arguments with his patients.

No, Jimmy had been *hoping* that he'd argue with him, at least come up with a good counterargument. He *wanted* someone with a rational point of view to explain to him why he was wrong.

That wasn't going to happen today.

"This is the basis for your stories? That God has abandoned us?"

Jimmy nodded, feeling adrift. The doctor kept asking questions, and Jimmy answered them without paying much attention. There didn't seem much point to any of them anymore.

Jimmy walked back to his room, purposeless and adrift. What the hell was the point of anything?

Passing through the common areas he heard a female voice call out quietly. "Jimmy."

He stopped, turned around, and saw Salina standing there. It took him a moment to gather a word together. "Hello."

She held out a piece of paper to him. When he didn't move, she said, "Take it, please."

Jimmy reached out and took the paper from her. It was folded in half. He unfolded it and saw a detailed line drawing of a single rose. Jimmy was impressed at the detail. The flower had gone just slightly past its bloom, and one of its petals was dangling, about to fall.

"I wanted to thank you. I'm not as good as you are. I can only draw flowers."

Jimmy shook his head. He didn't know what to say, though he could feel an embarrassing heat on his cheeks. "No, Salina, this is good. Really."

"You like it?"

"Yeah." He looked up from the rose. "No one's ever given me one of their drawings before."

"No one ever gave me one either. I have it taped up in my room now."

Jimmy reached out to touch her hand. "Thank you."

Suddenly, everything changed and Jimmy didn't know why. Salina flinched and pulled back, her eyes became distant, and her voice lost all of its color. "I have to go."

"Hey, wait . . ."

She turned around and said an abrupt, "Good-bye." She strode away from him, toward the girls' side of the residence. Jimmy stood there, holding the rose, dumbfounded.

He turned around and saw Charlie standing there.

"Oh, Jesus fuck. I was just talking to her."

"I know." This interaction also wasn't going as expected. "I just don't want her hurt, Jimmy. I care about her."

Jimmy shook his head. "I'm just trying to get to know her—are you her boyfriend or something?"

"No. Her brother."

Charlie took Jimmy aside and told him things. He told him, in a slow, halting way, of a little circle of hell called the Robb household. A hell whose principal demon was named Quincy Robb, a man whose size frightened Charlie. He ruled with his fists, his belt, and, occasionally, a baseball bat. Carol, his wife, had been beaten into submission and couldn't admit what Quincy was doing with Salina.

Charlie tried to protect her from him, and that's when he'd use the bat, or threaten to kill her. After years within this twisted knot of a family, he did end up saving her, by sucking up all the shame and going to the cops himself.

It didn't quite turn out the way he expected. Sure, the county removed them from the household. But the legal system . . .

Jimmy thought it had screwed him. What it had done to Charlie and Salina was horrifying.

Quincy Robb went to trial. His wife took the stand and called her children liars. A half dozen witnesses testified how Quincy was a family man who loved his children. Salina was too psychologically damaged, her doctors wouldn't let her take the stand.

All they had were medical records and Charlie's testimony. Charlie sat up there and did his halting best to say what it had been like. The defense lawyer tore him apart. By the end, the defense had the jury convinced that it was Charlie who was raping his sister and abusing his mother.

Quincy Robb walked away a free man, and his children ended up here.

"My God," Jimmy said.

"Be kind to her," Charlie told him. "She's the only family I have."

27

DR. Singh held up Dr. Husam's release form. Dr. Singh was a nationally recognized trauma surgeon. He sat behind a desk that was large and modern, a workstation sitting on an L-shaped extension, out of the way. Behind him was a view of the Cleveland skyline wrapped in red evening light.

For a long time, the doctor stared at the release.

"Thank you for seeing me," Dr. Husam told him again.

"You surprised me with this. It has been a long time since I've seen this name." He set down the form and looked at Dr. Husam. "He is your patient now?"

"I'm participating in his treatment."

Dr. Singh nodded, "And you are seeing some unusual test results, I suspect."

"Indeed, is there a history of it?" Perhaps now he might have an answer.

"There is a history. Quite a history in fact. I only treated him once, but I've remembered it ever since."

The original medical records had been archived long ago. Not only had Mr. Somerset fallen into the Medicaid system because he became a ward of the state, but he had not been hospitalized since. If it wasn't for Dr. Singh's memory, there

memory, there would be no sign he had *any* medical history.
The computer system had been upgraded twice since then,
so only Dr. Singh knew that there were records to pull out of
the archives.

Sixteen years ago, as a toddler, James Allan Somerset
came to the hospital as a victim of a gas explosion and house
fire. He was the only person to be pulled out of the building
alive, and his condition was so bad that the paramedics
didn't think he'd make it back to the hospital alive.

With a very young child, *any* burn is serious. The medics
had found James with third-degree burns over half his body.
He was in shock, most of his small blood volume had already seeped through the massive wounds. The paramedics
did the only thing they could, and started IVs and got the infant on an ambulance to the trauma center.

They drained two IV bags into James Somerset while the
ambulance raced back to the hospital. That wasn't unheard
of with a burn of this severity, though the amount was more
in line with an adult victim than a baby.

In the trauma center, where the doctors, including Dr.
Singh, worked to stabilize the child, James Alan Somerset
was officially listed as having second- and third-degree
burns over forty percent of the body. At the time it seemed
as if the paramedics slightly overestimated the severity of
the injury.

The call into the hospital had listed third-degree burns to
all the extremities, as well as substantial involvement of the
chest area. In the trauma center the chest was of minor concern, the major life-threatening issue the second- and third-
degree burns on the arms and legs.

It was easy for someone in the field to overestimate the
extent of a burn from a house fire, especially if the victim
was covered in soot and dirt. No one would have ever no-

ticed the discrepancy if it wasn't for the fact that James kept getting better.

Most of the fluid given to stabilize a burn victim is given in the first day, half in the first hour. An average-sized man with the burns James had in the trauma center would need about twelve or fourteen liters in the first day.

The infant James, with a body mass a tenth that size, took in that much and more. The little body was a bottomless sponge that absorbed everything they could give it.

And, miraculously, the burns receded. After the first day, while the trauma team was debating the best course of treatment, and deciding when the patient would be stable enough to cope with treatment, the burns now covered a little over thirty percent of the body, the damage was sliding down the tiny arms and legs as if trying to crawl away.

This was not easily dismissed.

It was easy for a trauma surgeon to believe a paramedic in the field might misstate the scope of a wound. It was a little less believable that a whole trauma team would make the same mistake *again*.

Of course, the alternative was just as unbelievable. James was healing. That was impossible. A human body couldn't heal a third-degree burn any more than it could regrow an amputated limb. That was the nature of the injury, the flesh wasn't injured, it was *destroyed,* burned away. The only way to deal with it was to harvest living tissue from another part of the body, and until then, keep the wound as sterile as possible.

The burns kept shrinking, despite this.

No one could account for it. The infant Somerset's medical record was a catalog of anomalies. White blood cell counts way above normal, dropping blood pressure, and continual fluid loss while showing no sign of internal bleeding or fluid seepage. Almost no passage of urine, but without any signs of kidney shutdown. Liver function all over the map.

"I'd never seen anything like that," Dr. Singh said. "I was one of about thirty consultants on that case, specialties ranging from urologists to neurologists. No one could form a consistent picture of what was happening. Every test, *every* one, showed abnormal results. Results that, if they happened to be found in a routine physical, would result in immediate hospitalization. But he recovered."

Baby Somerset's doctors found themselves in the uncomfortable position of being relegated to the role of tribal elders, with no idea what was wrong, or how to fix it. The only thing they could do was order more tests, more IVs, and watch.

As the burns receded completely, James Somerset's fluid intake returned to normal, and so did his insides. Within a couple of days, all the abnormal test results drifted back to within normal levels. Within two weeks from the trauma, there was no sign that James Allan Somerset had ever been seriously hurt.

"That was the first time I had ever seen anything I could describe as miraculous without any trace of hyperbole."

Dr. Husam struggled for a polite way to say it. "You understand my skepticism."

Dr. Singh nodded and stood up. He bent over and picked up a cardboard box and hefted it onto his desk. It landed with a thud and a small cloud of dust. "This came back from storage. These are the medical records."

"That entire box?"

Dr. Singh lifted the lid. Dr. Husam stood and looked into a box filled with yellowing pages, file folders, envelopes of x-rays. "Every test, every examination, over the course of a week." He rifled through until he found what he was looking for. "After it was clear what was happening, we took photographs of the progress . . ."

He opened the folder in front of him, showing a sheet of paper, with half a dozen Polaroids taped to it showing an infant's burned arm. In the first there were obvious third-degree burns up past the elbow.

In the final picture, the baby's arm was pink and fresh and unharmed.

Dr. Husam looked at the sequence of photographs for a long time.

It was late in the evening when Dr. Husam got the call on his pager. It was from the Health Clinic at Trinity. "Yes?"

"Dr. Husam?"

"Yes?"

"I'm glad I got you. My name's Marid Sharps, I work in the Health Clinic at Trinity House."

"Yes, I remember you. How can I help you?"

"I know you're interested in the test results of one of our clients, Jimmy Somerset?"

"Yes, has something happened to him?"

"No, not to him." Sharps paused for a few moments. "I found something pretty much by accident. Had a minor injury, with some blood. So we had to run some tests on this kid. Now I was going to wait until you showed up on Tuesday but this kid was just brought into the clinic—"

Dr. Husam brought the car to a stop on the shoulder so that he could concentrate on the phone call. "Forgive me, it's late and I do not think I'm following you."

"I'm sorry, Doctor. Yesterday I happened to see this kid's results, and they're the same as Jimmy's."

"What?"

"I'm not a doctor, and I can't tell you what it means, but this kid scored the same on every measure the two had in common. I pulled Jimmy's chart, just to be sure."

"That is interesting."

"Yes. More interesting because this kid's injury happened when he assaulted Jimmy Somerset."

"And there was blood, you said?"

"This kid took a bite out of Jimmy's hand. Jimmy was lucky to get away with just some stitches."

Dr. Husam nodded. This might be a break. If what Jimmy suffered from was communicable, it narrowed the field of what it could be. *A new virus, perhaps?*

"Doctor?"

"Oh," Dr. Husam came back from his thoughts. "Yes, this may be important. I'll see about coming in tomorrow morning to examine—"

"Doctor, this kid may not be here tomorrow."

"Pardon?"

"I'm calling you now because he just came in the door with a fever of 101, and if his temperature keeps going up, we're going to call an ambulance."

Dr. Husam pushed though the door to the clinic. For a moment it seemed as if something was wrong, as if he had walked into the wrong building. The reception area was abandoned, and nobody was in view. He stood there a moment.

The door to the examination room burst open. Dr. Husam was startled by the tall, bald figure of Marid Sharps. Sharps looked at him, and Dr. Husam saw the intense urgency of his stare.

Dr. Husam knew that gaze from every emergency room

he had ever worked in. Things were bad, critically bad, "Where is he?" Dr. Husam said. "What's his status?"

Sharps grabbed him. "He's back here. He came in coherent and feverish. But his temperature is still rising, and he's completely nonresponsive now."

"Ambulance?"

"Should have been here two minutes ago."

The child was laid out on a stretcher, bags of ice lining his body. Two assistants were holding him down while he thrashed in the midst of a seizure. His skin was flushed and dry.

Marid ran up and helped to hold the kid down.

Dr. Husam ran up and bent over the child, making sure that the airway was clear. "What's his temperature? His blood pressure?"

"106," someone called. "90 over 50. His pulse is going too fast and thready for me to count."

"You," Dr. Husam pointed at Sharps. "Get an IV, *now*. Someone get more ice. We have to get his temperature down."

Dr. Husam stood there, holding the child's head steady as his muscles tensed and vibrated. Dr. Husam was no longer an intern, and hope had long given way to realism. There was very little chance that he would see this child live. The fever was too great, the shock too severe. Holding his skin was like touching an engine running too hot.

Sharps came back with an IV bag and slid the needle into the child's arm.

Dr. Husam took the bag from Sharps, held it up, and started to squeeze. "Get another."

There was no way they were going to get his temperature down and his blood pressure up . . .

In the distance Dr. Husam heard sirens.

The child froze in the midst of the seizure, his muscles locking, back arched, eyes showing only whites. "I've lost his pulse," one of the others said.

"My God," Dr. Husam whispered, "what is James Somerset carrying?" He handed the IV bag to the person next to him and looked at Sharps, who was carrying another. "You do compressions, I'll breathe."

Dr. Husam started respiration for the child, even though he knew it would be hopeless. Touching his lips was like kissing a mummy. There was no moisture left in the tiny mouth.

Sharps started compressions while someone else replaced the IV.

"One thousand. Two thousand. Three thousand. Four thousand. Five thousand. Breathe."

Dr. Husam breathed for the child. It was like blowing into a desert. The siren was closer.

"One thousand. Two thousand. Three thousand. Four thous— Shit."

Dr. Husam did not see what Sharps was reacting to. He was staring into the child's face. For a moment, it was peaceful, angelic even. As if it was lit from some internal glow.

Dr. Husam had a half second to watch as that glow became hideously literal. The child's skin became translucent, spiderwebbed with veins shadowed by the half-opaque shadow of a skull that hid an internal fire as bright as burning phosphorus.

Then it was too bright to see anything.

Then came the burning.

28

THE alarm woke Jimmy up, a blaring klaxon so loud that it was as if a Mack truck was blowing all its horns inside his head. Jimmy looked across to the cheap clock radio the room came with, but the numbers were dark.

He sucked in a breath and started coughing.

Holy shit.

The air above his bed was wrapped in impenetrable smoke. He rolled off the bed and landed on the floor, where the atmosphere was somewhat breathable. He was completely awake now, panic shooting adrenaline straight to his hypothalamus.

Clad only in jockey shorts, he crawled toward where the door should be. The darkness in his room was complete, and every other breath gagged him with the smell of smoke. The only sound he could hear was the fire alarm.

He found the door and wasted fifteen seconds forgetting that the door opened in, not out.

Outside was another universe. There was enough light to see by here. At one end of the hall, toward the exit, were points of light shining through the smoke like streetlights through fog. The other end of the hall was lit with flickering orange. The klaxon nearest Jimmy died with an electronic pop.

That allowed him to hear the rustle of flames.

It also let him hear someone calling for help, back toward the flickering light. He was crawling in that direction before he realized what he was doing.

You're violating the first rule of fire safety—get yourself the fuck out!

Jimmy realized he just didn't give a shit.

The voice was weak, down the corridor, toward the flames. The smoke itched on his naked skin. His eyes watered. His nose felt as if he was trying to breathe through a bucket of tar. Jimmy crawled toward the voice, toward the flames. Inside his head, his pulse was throbbing. The fear was almost a rush. That, and probably the lack of oxygen, made him feel high, disconnected. As if he was watching from some dark place deep inside himself.

The carpet felt odd under his hands. Itchy and slightly tacky, as if it was breaking down in the heat. The air was already uncomfortably hot and filled with the smell of burning polyester and foam rubber. The smoke hugged the ceiling, rolling above him in thick black billows.

The voice stopped calling for help, and Jimmy cursed. "I'm almost there, damn it! Where are you?"

No answer.

Jimmy looked at the doors next to him, trying to figure out which one the voice had been coming from. The doors were all closed, except one that was hanging open a crack. Jimmy pushed on that one, and felt resistance against the door. He pushed it harder and heard a very weak groan.

"Oh, fuck. *Move it!*"

The person beyond the door either couldn't hear him or couldn't respond. Jimmy had to push the door open against the deadweight enough for him to slip inside the darkness beyond.

Jimmy felt around on the other side, and his hand found a shoulder up against the bottom of the door. It was a small kid, wearing pajamas. Still breathing. When Jimmy felt down by the kid's legs, he found why the kid had been trapped. The kid's left ankle was swollen to the size of a grapefruit, the skin inflated tight against the fabric of the pajama bottoms. Must have tripped in the dark.

Jimmy bent down, forehead to the carpet, and rolled the kid's body over his head and on to his shoulders. There was no reaction except some unconscious groaning.

Jimmy stood up with the kid on his shoulders. He was much lighter than Jimmy expected. He almost stood up too fast and fell over. He kicked the door open and stepped back out into the flickering light of the corridor. The rustle of the flames was closer now, and the radiant heat wrapped him like a bad sunburn. His head was cloaked in smoke now that he stood, and the exit felt way too far away for the kid on his shoulders, whose breathing was labored and irregular against his shoulder.

Jimmy headed for the cafeteria, which was only one more set of doors down the corridor. Unfortunately, that was toward the flames. Jimmy dashed for it anyway. There were windows to the outside there.

He ran toward the flickering heat and turned into a doorway to his right at what felt like the last moment. He draped the injured kid across one of the tables and stepped up to one of the cafeteria windows.

Even with the dim, smoke-hazed emergency lights, he could still see outside pretty well. About fifty yards away from the building was a crowd of people, the ones who'd got out in time. Their faces were lit orange. Shadows danced and whipped at the spectators from the trees, away from the building. Tendrils of darkness reaching toward them . . .

Half the building had to be engulfed.

Jimmy tried to open the window and discovered the major flaw in his escape plan. The big cafeteria windows weren't designed to open. They were thick, insulated glass in frames that were near flush with the wall. There wasn't even a place to get a grip on the frame, or a track to slide the window up, down, or sideways.

"Fuck, fuck, fuck!"

Jimmy grabbed at it, pushed it, tried to stick his fingers along the edge of the frame, but the bastard wasn't moving. The rage built up inside him with each attempt. When it crested, he balled his hand into a fist and slammed it into his reflection as if it was Frank, the fucking county lawyer, Dr. Altroy, and every other asshole that had ever fucked him over.

The impact sent daggers of pain down his forearm and flashed stars of color in front of his eyes. When his vision cleared, his reflection had been replaced by a hazy gray cloud of spider cracks, centered on the place where his forearm extended through the remains of the window.

"Holy shit." Jimmy whispered. At first glance he had thought he could have bounced a chair off this glass without scratching it. He withdrew his arm, and a two-foot-diameter section of window fell into the room in a shower of safety-glass chunks the width of his thumb.

Wind sucked in past him, through the hole.

Jimmy punched and kicked the remains of the window out of the way. Some of the spectators had seen him and were running up to the side of the building. He didn't get a chance to see who they were before he fed the kid in the pajamas down toward them.

In the light from the fire above, he saw the kid's face. It was Eric, from his group. Eric's face was covered in soot and blood, and it was a moment before Jimmy realized the blood wasn't Eric's. The arm that Jimmy had slammed through the window was streaked with blood, lacerations wrapping it like a net.

Once the folks below took Eric, Jimmy reached up and grabbed the window frame and raised his foot to vault outside to safety.

He hesitated.

The dark part inside himself was whispering. There were more people trapped in this building. The fire had hit too fast.

He looked out at the crowd and couldn't see Lorraine, Dion, Charlie . . .

Salina.

Jimmy let go of the window frame and turned around. Someone outside yelled at him, but Jimmy walked back into the smoke-filled cafeteria, his naked feet crunching on broken glass.

The air was thick, each breath felt like he was inhaling burning fiberglass. Still, Jimmy stayed upright because he couldn't waste time crawling around. His feet stuck to the carpeted floor, and he couldn't tell if it was because he was bleeding, or because the synthetic carpet was half-melted. He managed to speak, despite the smoke filling his lungs.

"Who's out there? Salina? Charlie? Dion?"

At first, nothing.

Jimmy headed toward the flames. Even though he was running, everything seemed to have slowed down. He pushed against the smoke as if it was a solid thing. The heat was a wind pushing against him. Flames licked the walls on either side, while ice-cold water sputtered from sprinkler heads above him.

The flames fought the water and seemed close to winning.

"Who's still in here? Lorraine?"

Coughing.

Distinct, hoarse, and very weak. Ahead of him, toward the door to the stairwell. Someone else, someone small, crying. Jimmy ran that way.

At the end of the hall by the fire stairs, there were no walls. The corridor snaked through a path of rolling sheets of fire, the path itself only kept clear by sputtering sprinklers. Now it was the carpet that stuck to his feet, sticking to his soles and pulling away from the floor. The closest smell of burning now was the smell of his own hair.

The fire door had been painted red, but the paint was blistered and black, the window was cracked and opaque with soot. Jimmy heard someone call out for help from the other side.

Jimmy didn't recognize the black twisted flesh that reached for the door. He knew it was his own hand, but it didn't seem part of him anymore. Something else was in control, and Jimmy was locked somewhere deep inside watching it play out in front of him.

The flesh of Jimmy's hand sizzled when he pushed open the fire door.

The scene in the stairwell was a vision from hell. The concrete tube lit by flickering orange from above, the air filled with smoke, mist and rain falling from sprinklers above. The air so gray black that Jimmy could only see the bodies lying on the landing in front of him. Two kids, unconscious. Then, as the middle distance resolved into something more than lumpy shadows, Jimmy saw more . . .

He had made it to the girls' residence, somehow. Six girls

were draped on the stairs, none moving. He saw Lorraine, facedown, overcome by the smoke.

He didn't see Salina.

Jimmy ran down the stairs, stepping past unconscious and semiconscious bodies. At the foot of the stairs Jimmy found two teenage girls, draped against the escape to the outside.

Somewhere inside himself, Jimmy knew that he should have been overcome by smoke as well. He should be dead . . .

The door was stuck against something outside. He pushed the crash bar, and the latch opened, but the door would only move a fraction of an inch.

Christ, come on, there are people trapped here.

Jimmy kept pushing, but the door wouldn't budge.

"Come on," Jimmy shouted at the thing, *"Move you bastard!"*

Jimmy slammed into the door with his shoulder and felt resistance on the other side.

"We don't have time for this!"

He slammed into the door again, and again met the same resistance.

"No, you fucker," Jimmy called out. He shouted out of a hoarse and bleeding throat. *"You don't quit now!"*

Jimmy spread his arms, as if to embrace the immobile door in front of him. "You want me. You fucking *want* me? You *have* me! Pull me in. Take me over. But first, you got to get me out the goddamn door!" For the first time, he willingly drew the Jimmything forward. He reached his mind into the dark, threw himself into it, let it engulf him.

The Jimmything fell against the door.

The Jimmything smiled.

Its shoulder slammed into the door again, and something

snapped. It could have been something in the door, or it could have been bone. At this point it didn't matter. It slammed again. Again. Again.

A large dent was in the blank face of the door, and a grinding noise came from the edge near the bottom. The Jimmything heard and felt the resistance.

It backed up and raised a foot to bring it out in a kick above the resisting part of the door. Its foot hit with a shuddering impact ten times worse than its fist striking the window. The blow splattered blood from the torn sole of its foot. But the door moved with a riflelike snap.

The fire door swung open with enough force to tear the hydraulic hinge free of the doorframe above him. The door slammed into the opposite wall.

A pile of bricks and half a broken window frame were swept out into a parking lot by the force of the door opening, debris that had fallen from the inferno above. The parking lot was free of spectators. Everyone else was in the courtyard on the other side of the building.

Oblivious fuckers.

The Jimmything started dragging out bodies.

Interlude Three: THE FACE OF EVIL

PAGE 11: [FOUR PANELS, WIDTH OF PAGE]

Panel 1: INT. HALLWAY EUCLID HTS. HIGH SCHOOL
We watch from above as Cain steps into the hallway
from the left, tattered trench coat trailing behind him.
Light carves the hallway into alternating strips of light,
and absolute blackness.

CAIN

"I'm not going to let you win, you bastard."

Panel 2: INT. HALLWAY EUCLID HTS. HIGH SCHOOL
Same scene, Cain is now halfway down the hall.

CAIN

"Do you hear me?"

Panel 3: INT. HALLWAY EUCLID HTS. HIGH SCHOOL
Cain has reached the end of the hall, and his hand is on
the handle of a door that is wrapped mostly in darkness.

BAPHOMET

(Slimy undulating word balloon from offscreen)

"My poor deluded friend . . ."

Panel 4: MID SHOT OF CAIN OPENING DOOR
Our point of view is near the floor of the room, looking
diagonally at Cain so the view of the door is twisted to
fill the long, narrow panel. Cain stands there dumbfounded at what he sees.

BAPHOMET

(Slimy undulating word balloon from offscreen)

". . . how can you win a battle . . ."

PAGE 12: [SPLASH PAGE]

Panel 1: INT. CLASSROOM EUCLID HTS. HIGH SCHOOL
We look at Cain from a corner of the classroom. The angle is still twisted so our view is almost ninety degrees off of vertical. A dozen students sit at desks, facing away from Cain, toward us. They've been tied to the chairs by their arms and necks, so they'd face the end of the room even after they died. Their eyes have been cut out, and their cheeks have been slashed to open their mouths into too-wide bloody smiles.

BAPHOMET

(Slimy undulating word balloon along bottom of page)

". . . that's been over for thousands of years?"

PAGE 13: [FOUR PANELS]

Panel 1: SMALL PANEL, CLOSE-UP OF CAIN'S REACTION
Cain's face is hard and blank, holding back powerful emotions. Most of it is shadowed, except for skull-like highlights around the jaw and cheekbones.

CAIN

"Are you doing this to frighten me?"

Panel 2: SMALL PANEL, OVERHEAD VIEW OF CLASSROOM
Cain stands in the doorway, facing the same direction as the dead students. Squatting on the desk at the end of the room is some*thing.* It isn't quite in the frame.

BAPHOMET

"Megalomaniac to the end, aren't you? As if my every move is orchestrated strictly for the benefit of your exiled soul. I construct what is before you because it amuses me."

Panel 3: SMALL PANEL, VIEW FROM BASE OF DESK, TOWARD CAIN
We look at Cain, past the twisted shadow cast by the thing on the desk. Cain is reaching behind him, into his trench coat.

CAIN

"Prince of liars to the end, yourself. Why manifest to me if I am so inconsequential to you?"

Panel 4: LARGE PANEL, VIEW OF THING ON DESK
Baphomet's manifestation had once been one of the teachers. The suit still clings onto its knobby, twisted form. Shreds of flesh hang off of the flayed skull, resembling bloody tentacles. One bright blue eye is seated in a fleshless socket. The lower jaw is unhinged, dropping its tongue to its chest. Its arms are naked and twisted with fresh scars that appear to have been stapled shut. Its legs have twisted to the side at an impossible angle that has it squatting with its feet pointing backward. It glistens with blood and plasma, and in one hand it holds what appears to be a human heart.

BAPHOMET

(Word balloon emerges from the hole behind its tongue)

"Perhaps I find your torments as sweet as those sitting before me. Perhaps more so, since you cannot die. Your soul may not be mine, but I can be satisfied with your disillusionment. The boy is mine, Cain, willingly and enthusiastically. Look upon his works."

PAGE 14: FIVE PANELS

Panel 1: VIEW OF DESK FROM JUST BEHIND CAIN'S RIGHT HAND
Cain is pulling something out from behind him. Just a shadow of it in this panel.

CAIN

"Sorry to disappoint you, but I don't think you have it quite right."

Panel 2: VIEW OF DESK FROM JUST BEHIND CAIN'S RIGHT HAND
A long, elaborately carved cane/staff unfolds in Cain's right hand. There is the glint of ivory, and gold, and gems, all along its length—except for a spot at the end, bare of any decoration. Much of the carving is Hebrew and Latin text.

SFX

Click.

BAPHOMET

"You would do well not to anger me. The fact you cannot die means you are capable of feeling more pain than any other creature on this planet."

Panel 3: CLOSE-UP OF CAIN'S FACE
Cain is wearing a determined expression.

CAIN

"If the kid was yours, well and truly, what interest would you have in appearing here to distract me?"

CAPTION

"I would be a liar if I said I wasn't terrified. I was confronted with something that predated me by an aeon or two. I didn't even know exactly what this thing was . . ."

Panel 4: OVERHEAD VIEW OF CLASSROOM
Cain and the *thing* are converging from opposite sides of the classroom. Cain is holding his staff in both hands, and the *thing* is skittering between the seated bodies like a deformed crab.

BAPHOMET

"I will drink deeply from you. I will take every agony you have to offer."

CAPTION

". . . just that the flesh it animated would be as unstoppable as my own . . ."

Panel 5:MID SHOT, CAIN AND THING
Cain and the thing collide. The *thing* forces its arm completely through Cain's abdomen. Its hand, black with blood and curled into the shape of a claw, has torn through the back of Cain's trench coat. Blood vomits from Cain's mouth and down his chin. He clutches the cane above him with both hands.

SFX

SLASH

CAPTION

". . . and the body, stronger."

PAGE 15: FOUR PANELS

Panel 1: CLOSE-UP OF CAIN'S FACE
The *thing's* other hand is clawing the flesh off the side of Cain's face. Its fingers dig deep grooves underneath which glisten the bones of Cain's skull.

CAPTION

"Physically, I didn't stand a chance of fending this thing off."

Panel 2: OVERHEAD VIEW OF FIGHT
Cain is pushed into a wall so hard that the plaster has buckled. He still holds the cane above him, both hands in an overhand grip.

SFX

SLAM

CAPTION

"I had placed my hope in a relic that I was uncertain would work."

Panel 3: CLOSE-UP OF CANE/STAFF
The bare wood tip of Cain's staff seems to glow slightly. Cain's hands grip it so tightly that his blood is running from between his fingers.

CAPTION

"The fact that the monastery that profited from selling me the reliquary succumbed to the black death within a week of the sale seemed, at the time, to speak to its authenticity."

Panel 4: CLOSE-UP OF CANE/STAFF STRIKING
The unadorned tip of the cane/staff strikes the center of the *thing's* back, opening up the flesh and spilling black, fetid blood. Steam rises from the wound.

SFX

THUD, sssssssssssssssssssssssss

CAPTION

"All I know is, it hasn't failed me yet."

PAGE 16: TWO PANELS

Panel 1: MID SHOT OF THING
It is bent over backward, the staff's tip pointing out of its chest. It bubbles from a dozen places, primarily the wound and the hole where the mouth should be.

SFX

KEEAHHKEEEEEEEEE

Panel 2: MID SHOT OF CAIN
Cain is torn up and bleeding. The wounds still fresh and open on his body. At his feet lies the remains of the *thing*, now only a mutilated corpse.

CAPTION

"Score one for my piece of the true cross."

29

CIA DIRECTOR Oberst did not look pleased. He strode into the secure conference room in the heart of Department Blue with the calculated movements of a powerful man going somewhere against his will. It was the first time that Boyden's boss had visited the new location. Boyden could tell by his expression that Oberst thought it was a waste of money.

Given the current effectiveness of the department, it probably was.

Boyden stood in front of a projector that was beaming data from his laptop on to a screen on the far side of the room. Oberst wasn't even looking at the screen. The Director's gaze was reserved for Boyden, and his watch.

"And what, exactly, is it that could not be done over a secure line?"

Boyden cleared his throat and looked down at his laptop. Two sheets of paper lay next to it, both made of a specially impregnated paper that prevented copying, faxing, and most forms of electronic transmission. "Two reasons, sir." He slid both pages toward Oberst's <u>side</u> of the table.

"First, you're going to have to sign one of those sheets of paper before you leave." Boyden looked up at his boss.

"Second, I'm old-fashioned enough to believe that a man should deliver his ultimatums in person."

Oberst frowned. "Are you trying to be insubordinate?"

"No, just honest. There are two forms there. The first is my resignation."

"And the other?"

"Is what I need authorization for, if I'm staying on in charge of this department."

Oberst pulled a pair of reading glasses out of his jacket and looked at the two pages without picking them up. After a second or two, he said, "You can't seriously think that I will approve this."

"Sir, I understand you don't think much of this department. It is a legacy from your predecessors—"

"Son, Department Blue is an embarrassment. It is tabloid intelligence gathering of the lowest order, and if it was up to me, I would shut this place down in a heartbeat. If it wasn't for two senators on the Intelligence Committee, we wouldn't be having this conversation at all."

"You don't have to tell me that, sir. I'm aware of that every day I am here."

"So why are we having this conversation?"

"Because you aren't reading our intelligence reports. Because if I'm not given the authority and resources to act, I do not want my fingerprints on the debacle that's coming."

"What are you talking about?"

"On your desk is this," Boyden gestured at the screen. "The latest event. Our satellites monitored the transmission originating in suburban Cleveland, Ohio." Boyden quickly paged the slides through the technical data about the transmission, and pictures of the fire damage, until the screen showed the picture and file of the victim.

"Raymond Germain," Boyden read off the screen. "The

state of the body was consistent with our previous events, but there are serious discrepancies. He's a statistical anomaly on just about every measure, as well as being the only victim who was not asymptomatic before the event itself. He suffered from a high fever and seizures before he combusted—"

"Your point is?"

"My point is, we've studied this for years, and we have solid evidence that all these kids, *all* these kids, were affected from birth. Except for Raymond Germain. Raymond Germain shows all the signs of being infected—"

"You're saying this is a disease?"

"I'm saying that we are facing the ultimate nightmare scenario with these kids. The possibility that this is communicable."

Oberst sucked in a breath. "Your doctors have continually assured us—"

"That we had no evidence of transmission. Now, sir, we *do*. We even have a possible vector." Boyden clicked a button on his laptop and the slide changed to a file on James Allan Somerset. "James Somerset is a young man that hits on every demographic criteria we've assembled to profile the victims, with the exception that he has lived three years longer than he should have. He was housed in the same facility as Raymond, and was *bitten* by the deceased."

"Bitten?"

Boyden nodded. "James fits the criteria for Golden. Down to his medical test results, which match tests we've run on the few children we've been able to study before combustion . . ."

Oberst sat quietly a moment, as if weighing several options. None appeared satisfactory to him. He studied the papers in front of him. "This is what you think you need to take control of the situation?"

"It's the minimum I need to *contain* it. James is already a news item. It is only a matter of time before the wrong people connect him to Raymond."

"Who?" Oberst asked.

Boyden tapped a key on his laptop, and the slide changed to the file describing Abby Springfield.

Cato Sullivan came in five minutes after the director left. Boyden looked up from his computer and said, "You should be in politics, I think your skills are being wasted here."

"We got it?"

Boyden slid the paper across the table to Sullivan. "We got it. Our pick of people from operations, transport, and a transportable secure biomedical lab—" Boyden shook his head. "Abby Springfield did us all a favor by providing a threat that our boss can understand."

"So what are we going to do, now that we can do something?"

"What're your people on the ground there telling you?"

"Somerset's not going anywhere. He was burned alive, pretty much. Even if he is the vector, and has the infection himself, our doctors estimate it will be weeks before he recovers completely."

"Okay, I want your people to secure a place for us to set up shop. Room for our doctors to work. Once we have a secure base, we're taking charge of him."

"*Our* doctors?"

"We're moving everything to Cleveland as soon as I get the logistics worked out."

Sullivan arched an eyebrow. "Are you sure about this? These aren't field agents we're talking about."

"I know. But if it turns out that he is a carrier for this, we have to get this kid contained. Besides, I saw Oberst's mood when he left here. He's behind us now, if only to avoid the embarrassment of having this department exposed. If it turns out we need field agents, we'll get them."

30

THINGS had changed.

Things had changed before he started sharing a bed with Abby. This excursion to investigate Ted Mackenzie had gone over a week longer than he had intended. He should be back now, working on half a dozen different projects . . .

She was pulling him deeper into something he had already been borderline obsessive about. It was a bad situation, and not just because of some taint this all might give to his credibility as an expert witness. This whole hunt he followed was self-destructive. He thought about these kids too much . . .

Who else did?

In a darkened motel room, sharing a double bed that forced Abby's naked body against his side, Nate's mind traveled long overgrown paths.

Tracing a hand across his chest, she asked him, "What are you thinking?"

Nate almost made a comment about the journalistic third degree, but somehow it seemed inappropriate in this situation. "I'm thinking that I am wasting my time. I'm thinking that I should walk away from this."

"You're close. It could end tomorrow if you, or anyone, finds the tie that joins these children together."

"I'm no closer than when I started. I just have more questions." Nate sat up, and shivered. "What makes you think I'm close?" he asked.

"Look at what you've done in the past few days—"

"All I've done is find more patterns, as inexplicable as the ones I've already found."

She placed a hand on Nate's back. "I think you'll find Golden. I'm sure of it."

"If he—or she—exists."

"Golden exists." There was such certainty in her voice that Nate wondered if she had a source of information beyond what she had given him already. He had a dark flash of paranoia. He wanted to grab her and insist she reveal what she wasn't telling him.

What he did do was get up so that her hand fell away.

"What are you doing?"

"Going online," Nate said, "to look for dead kids."

Nate logged on to his subscription service to run a periodical search over nearly all of the past month. It was something he did periodically, and was usually his first source about one of *his* kids. The string he typed in the command line of the system was familiar.

">\fa child[ren] fire|burn died|dea[th|d] unknown"

He gave the search a date range starting with his last search. The database obliged by chewing its way through the thousands of periodicals that it had consumed over the last month. With every tick of the clock, the database service charged Nate's account another few cents.

The lag had never bothered him before. But, unaccountably, he felt a sense of urgency. He sat naked in front of the laptop, the text-only telnet window on the screen motionless except for a blinking cursor, and it felt as if time was running out. He was in danger of losing a race he hadn't even known he'd been running.

Nate tapped the side of the notebook, leaning forward as if he could contribute to the momentum of the search.

After a few more moments, the results flashed across the screen:

">7,832 matches.

">_"

The cursor sat there, waiting for him to command the database. Nearly eight thousand hits. Normally, he'd add another parameter to the search to narrow it down. The engine on this database was fairly sophisticated, and he could define a search of arbitrary precision. But the same feeling that gave him a sense of urgency made him afraid that a narrower filter might exclude something important.

He started to browse the results . . .

". . . two children died in house fire today . . ."

". . . fiery car crash claims three teenagers . . ."

". . . burned infant, the surviving children have been placed into foster care . . ."

". . . trial in the arson death of two six-year-old . . ."

". . . resulted in no deaths, but an unknown amount of property damage . . ."

". . . probable cause was an unattended child playing with matches . . ."

". . . fought the blaze for five hours. Seventeen people were treated for smoke inhalation . . ."

". . . memorial held today for three children who died last week . . ."

Nate had paged past the header by a few lines before it struck him that there was something of interest in it. He backed up and reread the headline.

"*17 Year Old Saves Fellow Patients.*

"Early this morning a fire burned through one of the buildings on the campus of Trinity House, a local residential treatment facility for children and teenagers. The building housed thirty children ranging in age from twelve to seventeen. Firemen fought the blaze for five hours. Investigators confirm three deaths, including one resident whose name is being withheld pending notification of his family. Injuries include seventeen people who were treated for smoke inhalation, as well as two people being treated for severe burns.

"According to Gordon Pagnokowski, a child care worker at Trinity House who was present at the outset, one of those burn victims is a heroic patient who saved several residents from the blaze.

"'It happened too quickly,' said Mr. Pagnokowski, 'it was out of control within a few seconds of the alarms. We were outside, and the top floor was completely engulfed. We barely had time for a head count before he broke open the cafeteria window.'

"The seventeen-year-old resident of Trinity House, whose name is being withheld, broke open a quarter-inch-thick pane of safety glass to lower another child to safety. He then went back through the burning building where he forced open a fire exit blocked by fallen debris and dragged four fellow residents out to safety.

"Richard Fenniman, one of the first firefighters to reach the scene, said, 'I don't know how the kid did it. He managed to carry out four people, by himself, in about half a minute. I'm trained for this, and I couldn't manage that.'

"The seventeen-year-old hero was seriously injured in the fatal blaze. A Life-flight helicopter took him and Nurse Marid Sharps, the only other victim suffering severe burns, to the Metro Health Burn Center. Both were suffering burns over eighty percent of their bodies.

"All the deaths occurred in the Health Clinic adjoining the residence. In addition to the juvenile patient, fatalities included fifty-three year-old Dr. Farid Husam, internist from The Cleveland Clinic who was doing volunteer work at Trinity House, and twenty-two-year-old Debbie Gale, a child care worker who had been working in the Health Clinic. Sixteen residents and one firefighter were treated for smoke inhalation and released.

"The cause of the fire is unknown, but investigators report that it probably started in the examination room of the Health Clinic, where all three fatalities occurred and where Mr. Sharps had been working. Sources confirm that Mr. Sharps called 911 shortly before the fire started, requesting an ambulance for a resident. By the time the ambulance arrived, the building was already on fire. No one was able to confirm if the one residential fatality was the same child that Mr. Sharps called the ambulance for.

"Both Mr. Sharps and the seventeen year old are in critical but stable condition."

From the *Plain Dealer*, Cleveland, Ohio, two days ago.

Even without any further research, Nate was almost certain that this was one of his kids. It happened around the right time of day—according to his new pattern—and it involved a residential treatment facility. That was another pattern, the kids usually had shown some sort of mental disturbance before the event.

This showed something more, though.

Never before had he seen a case where one of these kids had been restrained or confined. God only knew what might happen if one of these children ignited in a confined space. Then, there was the fact that the nurse, Mr. Sharps, called

911 before the fire started. If this was one of Nate's kids, what kind of symptoms would he exhibit before igniting?

They were all in the examination room. All the fatalities.

If this was one of the kids, Marid Sharps would have seen it happen . . .

Nate forced down the euphoria and concentrated on getting more background information. Enough to justify pulling up stakes here and going to Cleveland . . .

In two hours, he was convinced.

Nate stood up and started getting dressed. Morning light was streaming into the hotel room. Abby was asleep in the bed, wrapped up in a sheet. He looked at her and realized that he could just walk out of here, end all of this . . .

Nate reached over and shook Abby's shoulder.

"What?" she mumbled.

"Wake up, we're flying to Cleveland. I'll explain on the way."

31

GORDON Pagnokowski shook his head and said, "You're from *The New York Times*?"

Nate nodded, smiling. He had chosen the alias for two very simple reasons. First, Abby was with him and he really didn't trust her to act like anything other than a reporter. Second, Gordon was a named source in every third article Nate had downloaded. Anyone that widely quoted had to be someone who couldn't *not* spill his guts to a journalist.

The three of them sat at a small hole-in-the-wall coffee shop in Shaker Heights, Ohio. They were about three miles from Trinity House itself, in one of the inner ring suburbs of Cleveland.

Gordon wore jeans and a purple polo shirt. There were pieces of gauze taped on one side of his neck and small scabs pockmarked that side of his face. His hair was shaved close and his hand would occasionally run along his scalp, as if searching for the missing hair.

Nate had seen his BMV photo, and Gordon used to have longer hair.

"We're considering doing a feature on the rescue." He used a little indirection, partly out of habit, partly because he believed a direct attack on the source of the fire might undercut his cover story.

"Yeah, it was incredible . . ." Gordon looked down into his coffee. "He shouldn't have been conscious, as badly burned as he was. Somehow, though, he managed to get that exit open and move four people out of the building. If you looked at them all today, you'd say they had to carry *him* out."

Nate nodded. "Let's talk about how that evening started . . ."

Gordon didn't use names, but that didn't bother Nate. He had other sources for that kind of information. Everything was okay up until about an hour after lights out. Then one of the kids in the intensive residence got sick.

Gordon explained the layout of the buildings. There were two "cottages" flanking the Health Clinic and the gymnasium. One was a boys' residence and the other was a girls' residence. There was a smaller, more intensive residential facility across a courtyard from them.

A twelve-year-old kid in intensive started getting real sick shortly after lights out. This was a kid who had a history of acting out violently, and at first the staff thought he was just having another episode of his violent temper. Then, when they got the kid restrained, they realized that there was a lot more wrong with the kid. Fever, hallucinations . . .

Two workers restrained the kid and took him to the clinic.

Nate asked Gordon if he worked in the intensive residence.

He didn't. He knew all of this because everyone in the residences was in radio contact. He never left the boys' residence until the fire alarms started going off.

No, he didn't know what started the fire.

He started again with the amazing feats of the teenage savior. He described the kid actually punching through a window, and how the layout of the buildings meant that he had to walk through the heart of the fire to get from the cafeteria to the exit where he saved those four girls.

He slipped once and called the boy by name.

Jimmy.

Nate noted it without comment and tried, subtly, to turn the interview back to the kid in the Health Clinic. Did he know any of the other victims.

He knew Marid Sharps, the nurse on duty. Good guy, didn't deserve what happened. Dr. Husam, Gordon knew slightly, he was treating the other kid and was donating his time to Trinity. Gordon had no idea why he was there that late, he was supposed to be there second shift, two days a week.

The kid who died, Gordon didn't know him at all . . .

Well, he *had* seen him before. A couple of days earlier he had wandered out of the intensive lockdown and walked into the boys' cottage . . .

"Ironic, when you think of it," Gordon said.

Nate nodded. He didn't know quite what to make of it. The kid he was here about was diverging from the established pattern, and not only in behavior. Not only was the kid involved in an assault before the event—on Jimmy, the other focal point of this fire—but the kid was too young. He was a year outside the widest window Nate had drawn to date, and that included the kids listed on Abby's CD.

Nate seriously wondered if he was on the right track.

Abby did well covering for him. While Nate looked at his notes, second-guessing, Abby kept at Gordon with question after question about Jimmy.

Abby was quiet on the drive back to the hotel room. That wasn't like her, she was usually badgering him with questions. Nate cast a few glances in the direction of the passenger seat, and she was scanning her notes from the meeting with Gordon. Unlike Nate, she didn't use a PDA, her notes were on paper. Scrawls that Nate couldn't interpret except for the occasional emphasized word.

One particularly emphasized word was *"Jimmy."*

"Thinking about the kid?" Nate asked her.

Her head snapped up as if Nate had just caught her at something. "Yes, I guess I was." She looked out the passenger window at the houses sliding by them. "You've heard a lot of stories like this, haven't you?"

"Not quite like this."

"I mean, the burning. The children burning . . . I cannot even imagine that."

Nate nodded. *Why is it I think that wasn't your current train of thought?* "Maybe you want to wait in the car, then. My next stop is going to be the autopsy records. The physical signs will tie this to the other kids, or not. The more I think about it, the more I think probably not."

"Probably," Abby looked down at her notes again. "How are you going to do that, you don't have a name . . ."

"Short side trip. Death certificates are public record, and I know the time of death, the age, and how the victim died. A name will take me less than fifteen minutes."

"You don't think this one is connected, though?"

"It doesn't really fit the pattern. Other than the time and the fire . . . I may have been too eager to find something."

"What will you do if this doesn't pan out?"

"I have a day job to get back to. I make my own hours, but this hunt is stretching me too thin." He looked over at Abby. She was closing her notebook and slipping it into her purse. What was on her mind was obvious from the fact she *wasn't* mentioning it.

"Jimmy?" Nate finally asked.

"What about him?"

"Quite a hero, huh?"

"I suppose so."

"Are you thinking of actually doing an article on the kid? It seems worth it."

Abby shook her head, "No."

"Amazing what people can do with the right motivation."

"Yes, it is . . ."

What is it, Abby?

The death certificate wasn't a problem, and Abby waited in the car as Nate went up to talk the coroner out of the autopsy records. He came out of the building carrying a manila envelope that held the details of the death of Raymond Germain, the twelve-year-old victim of the Trinity fire. Details that were way too familiar by now.

It wasn't a question that the kid had suffered the same event as the other kids that Nate was investigating. Also, after a talk with the pathologist, Nate had learned that the other two deaths in the fire were of a more conventional nature.

There wasn't any doubt in Nate's mind that the cause of the fire was the combustion of Raymond Germain. Which placed into doubt every single pattern that Nate had discovered up to this point—even those on the CD.

The question, *Now what?* ran through his brain as he walked across the parking lot to the waiting car.

Abby was gone.

"Abby?" Nate looked into the empty vehicle, then started looking around. He had left her in the car both in deference to her—in retrospect, sudden—squeamishness, as well as to prevent any problems with his well-oiled cover as a CDC investigator.

Nate placed his hand on the hood of the car and looked around. There wasn't really anywhere to go around here. A cluster of office buildings, multiple lanes of asphalt, a Rapid Transit stop up the street.

"Abby?" Nate called out at the top of his voice. No response.

He had a sinking feeling.

He opened the door to the car and tossed the autopsy results into the passenger seat. That's when he saw that not only were Abby's bags missing, but his own laptop as well.

A single sheet of note paper was folded and slipped under the visor on the driver's side. Nate pulled it out and read a single word in Abby's handwriting.

"Sorry."

"Motherfucker." Nate stood up and slammed his fist into the roof of the car. *"Abby! Where the hell are you?"*

He spun around, but there wasn't any response aside from two people on the far end of the parking lot, staring at him now.

"What do you think you're doing? Abby!"

He had been seriously duped. He looked over at the Rapid Transit stop. He remembered from his arrival that the train line there terminated at the airport. He had been inside for over an hour.

Abby could be at a counter, buying a ticket to anywhere, right now.

And the bitch had stolen his laptop.

Why?

Fuming, Nate slammed open the door to his hotel room carrying a brand new purchase from Comp USA. He suspected that the clerks there were still dizzy. He had managed to walk in, specify the model numbers, pick up his purchases, and walk out all in the space of twelve minutes. It was an extra three grand on his corporate Amex, but he was pissed, and unlike most of his avocation, replacing his laptop was a legitimate business expense.

He tore through the packaging and hooked up the machine, and while it was booting for the first time, Nate dug through his luggage for his backup CDs.

By eight in the evening, he was back in business.

Okay, what was it, Abby?

Everything she was doing had a hidden agenda behind it. She was hunting for something, and using him to do it. Nate didn't appreciate that.

You were too interested in Jimmy, weren't you?

Nate got on-line.

He returned to the periodical database and started with the article on the Trinity House fire. He read the article a few times over, this time studying the teenager savior rather than the cause of the fire.

". . . broke open a quarter-inch-thick pane of safety glass . . ."

". . . four people, by himself, in about half a minute . . ."

". . . burns covering eighty percent of his body . . ."

The unnamed Jimmy wasn't showing the pattern he had been looking for. However, he saw what could have piqued Abby's interest. What the article described, what Gordon had described earlier today, was as extraordinary as the cases Nate investigated.

At the flashing prompt, Nate typed ">\fa trinity house fire"

Less than a dozen articles. Four were reprints of the first article in the *Cleveland Plain Dealer* and elsewhere. Still, he read all of them. To his surprise, he found a few telling differences that formed a strange pattern.

Chronologically, the first read:

". . . burns covering ninety percent of his body . . . the seventeen year old is in critical condition."

The second, the one he'd read first:

". . . burns covering eighty percent of his body . . . in critical but stable condition."

The third:

". . . sixty percent of his body . . . in critical but stable condition . . ."

The fourth:

". . . forty-five percent of his body . . . in stable condition."

In each case, Jimmy's fellow victim, Marid Sharps, was unchanged.

Nate had seen his share of revisionist history in the press before. Most people would be appalled at how often the things printed in their local paper were just plain wrong. It wasn't particularly unusual for papers to revise facts on the fly, especially in a continuing story.

This, however, bordered on extraordinary. The seventeen year old in the story had radically improved between the first and last story, printed less than forty-eight hours apart. The other articles on the fire that mentioned the kid followed the same pattern. The ones printed just after the event mentioned, "life-threatening burns over most of his body," while those printed twelve hours later mentioned "serious burns," and a day or two later "recovering from burns over nearly half his body."

Early articles mentioned third-degree burns, while later articles only mentioned first- and second-degree burns . . .

These couldn't be random mistakes unless they all came

from the same source. And they were different enough in the details they covered to make that unlikely. The errors across these stories shouldn't all be in the same direction.

With ten stories, five bylines, eight different named sources, and thirty unnamed sources— If it was a mistake, *someone* should have got it correct right out of the gate. Then there was the way the hospital graded the kid's condition. The articles listed it upgrading as the kid's condition improved. If they had the initial condition wrong, that didn't make sense . . .

Unless the doctors were the ones correcting themselves.

Nate's avocation didn't give him great faith in the medical profession, but he thought that it would be hard to confuse third-degree burns over eighty or ninety percent of the body with first- and second-degree burns over less than half.

And it was impossible for anyone to heal that fast.

This was the diametric opposite of what he was supposed to be investigating. Burns spontaneously healing.

Nate stared at it, thinking about Abby, what she would be interested in. She had told him about "Golden," a seventeen-year-old kid who was supposedly a survivor of what these other kids were suffering.

Jimmy was seventeen . . .

Was this kid what you wanted me to find?

Nate needed to find out who this kid was.

Given an age and a first name, it wasn't that difficult.

The nature of Trinity House meant that most of the population had some brush with law enforcement as victims, wards of the court, or as juvenile offenders. That meant a paper trail. And while some of it was supposedly inaccessible to him, there was enough left out there for him to produce a profile.

From what he remembered of Gordon's interview, Nate knew that the kid was a new resident as well as the fact that the kid fell into the juvenile offender category.

A little research on Trinity House's programs gave Nate a list of ways this kid could have been admitted.

A search of news stories about juvenile court cases gave him a list of ten kids in the region who were the right age, and eligible for one of the programs that Trinity House participated in. Three of those kids were named something other than Jimmy or James, two more were female, one mentioned another treatment facility.

A little more digging gave him James Somerset.

With name in hand, Nate tried a hunch. Perhaps there were other fire-related stories involving Jimmy . . .

There were.

"House Fire Claims Five.

"A fatal gas explosion and fire woke up residents of Rocky River early this morning. Firefighters said that the new single-family home on Lakeside Avenue was engulfed when a spark ignited a gas leak. The resulting explosion was heard as far away as Public Square and smoke from the blaze was visible to morning rush hour commuters across four communities on the West Side.

"The residence belonged to Samuel and Margaret Somerset, their three children, and Helen James Kirkpatrick, mother to Mrs. Somerset. All were at home, asleep, when the explosion ripped through their house. The only survivor of the blast was the Somerset's infant son, who was lifeflighted to the Metro Health Medical Center in critical condition.

" 'It's amazing anyone survived at all,' said Lt. Edgar Wallace of the Rocky River Fire Department. 'The initial explosion tore off the roof and two walls and collapsed the second floor. The building was a total loss even before it started burning.'

"Damage was estimated at four hundred thousand dollars."

Nate stared at the screen and read aloud, *"It's amazing anyone survived at all."*

32

"THANK you for talking to me, Mrs. Carswell." Nate sat on the couch in the Carswells' living room. The atmosphere was stale and a little creepy. The furniture was frozen in time around 1977, and facing them from the mantel of the faux fireplace were photographs of dozens of children. Some were yellowed and cracked with age.

"I understand," said Mrs. Carswell. She was a plump, almost archetypal mother figure—except for the way her flesh sagged, as if she had been slightly deflated. "Jimmy was unusual. With all the children, we never had any of them—" She sucked in a breath.

"Would you prefer if your husband was here for this?" Nate said it because the person he was playing would have.

She shook her head. "No, he'd think it was a waste of time."

"It isn't," Nate said. "Detailed survey data will help us with future placements."

She nodded. "So what does the county want from us?"

Nate fell into his role as family services bureaucrat. He had taken less than two hours to fabricate the persona, but he knew people whose lifeblood was paperwork, and he knew how to carry off the precise blend of bored insensitivity and psychopathic concern for meaningless detail. Mrs. Carswell had never even asked to see his identification.

The fictitious outcomes survey was harder to manufacture. However, he had managed to cobble together an impressive set of questions from several state agency web sites as well as a copy of the MMPI.

The nice thing about the "survey" was that it prompted Mrs. Carswell into talking while the multiple-choice script kept Nate's half of the conversation to a minimum.

Jimmy was a troubled kid on a number of levels. The doctors labeled him as having "Borderline Personality Disorder." He had a real serious problem with authority and had spent almost all of his life in the custody of the county. Despite everything, he had been showing signs of improvement. His grades were showing improvement, and he had a job he liked.

Nate noted everything, all the psychological and social measures. Every question seemed heavier and heavier, as if he was itemizing the weight bearing down on this kid . . .

Nate left Mrs. Carswell feeling that James Somerset was the focus of some evil destiny that no one could quite fathom. The sense that Fate personified had marked him.

Una Morrison was a legal aide in the Euclid Heights prosecutor's office. His calculated run in with her was in the City Hall cafeteria where he was playing someone very like himself. He talked shop with her for an hour or so, and elicited a number of details relating to the plea bargain that had kept Jimmy out of jail.

Una thought that the comic books Jimmy had written were horrid—you wouldn't catch her children writing such nasty stuff, or listening to gangsta rap or wearing their pants round their ankles—but *she* thought her boss had gone over-board. If the kid fought the charge, he would have won.

"You think," Una said to him, "if this was some preppy white kid who had parents with deep pockets and lawyer friends—you think my boss would be backing the school board in that case?"

"Call me Reggie," said Jimmy's former employer.

Nate shook the man's hand. "Do you mind talking about Jimmy?"

"It depends who I'm talking to . . ."

"I'm just following up on some details for the court," Nate said.

The beefy security guard nodded. They stood outside the main office of Euclid Heights High School. From other interviews, Nate already knew that the kids called this guy "Spam." He tried not to let it show in his expression how apt he thought the nickname was. "Now, if you don't mind, can we go over the fight between James Somerset and Frank Bradley?"

Dr. Singh held up a release form. The document he was looking at was one of the dozens of general-purpose forms that Nate had digital copies of. Even though the form had signatures from "James Alan Somerset" and "Anthony Carswell," dated about three months in the past, it hadn't had a physical existence until Nate had faxed the image to Dr. Singh's office.

"Dr. Harris?" Dr. Singh asked.

"Yes?"

"What exactly is it you're researching?"

*   *   *

By the end of forty-eight hours, Nate had a better idea of who Jimmy Somerset was than he did about Nathan Adriano. Something was happening with this kid, and Nate didn't know what it was, but he knew everything else.

He knew the path Jimmy traveled, from his freakish survival as an infant, to his equally freakish survival of the fire at Trinity House. His survival in inadequate foster homes and less-than-adequate schools, and his self-destruction in what to all appearance was a much better environment.

He knew in detail the injuries suffered by Frank and his peers. Self-defense it might be, but the severity of the damage spoke of someone who was barely in control.

He knew that one of the fatalities of the Trinity fire, Dr. Husam, was there because of Jimmy. Because of test results that didn't make any medical sense.

He knew that Raymond Germain had bitten Jimmy before he burst into flame . . .

He typed notes about Jimmy's life into his new laptop, sitting up on the bed in his hotel room. Abby was looking for this kid, and he had an intimate connection to the kids Nate was looking at.

Looking at all the background data he had on the other kids, demographically, Jimmy fit right into the pattern. He followed the profile of a kid who should have burned out three years ago. Birth date, location, even his history of psychological problems.

What if it is a virus?

What if Jimmy is a carrier?

That's when someone kicked the door in.

Nate heard wood crack and splinter. He turned his head and saw half a dozen men running through the door of his motel room. They wore black uniforms and body armor, their heads covered by matte-black helmets, their faces hidden behind the reflections on Plexiglas face shields. Each carried an assault rifle with a flashlight mounted on the barrel.

"Don't Fucking Move!" shouted one who flanked the bed. The gunman swept the laptop off Nate's lap with the barrel and pinned him to the bed, jamming the rifle into his gut. Nate froze.

Two kicked in the closet and swept it with the barrels of their weapons. One bent and stuck his gun under the bed. The last two flanked the door to the bathroom while one from the closet, not finding anything, turned and kicked in the bathroom door.

"Who—" Nate began to say, the question vanishing in a puff of air as the barrel of the gun in his gut pressed into him, forcing the air from his lungs. They didn't need to tell him to shut up.

The guy who kicked in the door took point into the bathroom while the two flanking the door pointed their weapons into opposite corners of the room, one high, one low.

Nate distinctly heard someone say, "Clear." This was echoed from various points around the room, which seemed a lot smaller to Nate now.

The one who stormed into the bathroom came out with his gun lowered. He spoke into a headset that Nate could barely see under his helmet. "The area's secure."

The other men lowered their weapons, all except the guy who had his weapon trained on Nate.

"Yes, sir," continued the one by the bathroom. He looked up at Nate and said, "Pack him up and clear out."

The one holding the gun on Nate took a step back so a pair of his friends could get on either side of him. One patted him down and went through his pockets while the other yanked Nate into a sitting position and pulled Nate's hands behind him, binding them together with a nylon zip cord.

When the one searching Nate's pockets gave the all clear, the men on either side of him grabbed him under the armpits and hauled him to his feet while the one training the gun on him stepped around behind them to point his weapon at Nate's back as they hustled him toward the door. It was all an excellent piece of choreography. The time between them kicking in the front door to the time they hauled Nate out of it had to be less than two minutes.

They walked out into a spotlight glare and Nate could hear a helicopter somewhere above him. Two unmarked vans, doors open, were parked diagonally in front of the motel room door. Behind and between them was a sedan. One trio of armed men piled back into one of the vans, while the three transporting Nate took him to the sedan and threw him in the back seat.

As Nate straightened up, the spotlight moved away and the sound of the helicopter receded. As soon as the last three gunmen piled into the remaining van, both pulled away, leaving the sedan alone idling in the parking lot.

The man in the front passenger seat turned around. He looked to be Nate's age, maybe slightly older. He had salt-and-pepper hair trimmed close to his skull and a rusty mustache. He looked somewhat familiar.

"Well, we finally get to meet, 'Agent Whitman,'" he said.

The sedan slowly pulled out of the hotel parking lot and drove in a direction opposite from the vans.

"Who are you?" Nate asked.

"Me, I'm Agent Boyden. We almost met once, in Samson County, West Virginia." Nate stared at him for a long moment before Boyden added, "That was my Honda Civic you threw up on."

33

CRIMINALS are a superstitious and cowardly lot.
    The mansion is made of darkness, a black emptiness that had been drawn out into walls, arches, columns, and turrets, a twisted negative image of a Gothic nightmare cross between Wayne Manor and the Fortress of Solitude. In the great hall, Jimmy sits on a twisted throne that could have been an electric chair—if they carved claw and ball electric chairs out of solid ebony.

He looks down at his hands. They are black as well, the skin cracked and weeping clear, red-tinged fluid. When he flexes his fingers, his flesh makes rustling sounds, as if his hands are covered in Saran Wrap. Flecks of himself fall away.

The world smells of overcooked meat.

Pain, I should be feeling pain . . .

". . . Oh, I am so sorry, that is not the correct answer. But, just for playing, we do have some parting gifts . . ."

Jimmy looks up and sees Dr. Altroy, but he is wearing a purple suit and has on clown makeup that makes him look like the Joker. He steps over bodies that litter the floor of the Great Hall.

No, wait, just ask the question again . . .

Jimmy tries to speak, but he doesn't have anything to

speak with. His lips are cracked and burned, his tongue an immobile lump of roasted flesh.

". . . We have a lifetime supply of complete failure. A purposeless existence for one. And, of course, a copy of our home game . . ."

Joker/Altroy throws a pile of paper into Jimmy's lap. Jimmy sees his own handwriting, and the panels of the last comic book he had written.

Jimmy looks up, and the room has changed. A horseshoe table has sprung up around him. Behind the table sits, stands, and crawls every superhero imaginable—good, bad and indifferent. Ant Man sits on Spawn's shoulder, the chick from *Witchblade* stands next to Spider-Man. Dr. Altroy is wearing a Batman suit now, but there are still traces of Joker makeup on his chin.

"What makes you think you can join us?"

Jimmy is wearing Cain's trench coat. He reaches up and touches his face. The flesh is intact. He says to the Batman, "What makes you think I can't?"

"You gotta be kidding me," quoth the orange stone pile of the Thing. "The first murderer?"

The Flash flips more copies of Jimmy's artwork back over the table. "This is unacceptable material."

Jimmy shakes his head. "Some of you have done worse, dealt with worse—"

"We're the heroes, you sad little fuck," says Wolverine. "You think we let anyone crash our party?"

Jimmy reaches down and picks up the scattered pages. "What's the problem with this? It's not good enough?"

Batman/Altroy speaks. "The problem is *you* wrote it."

The real world was white. Stark fluorescent hospital white. He couldn't move. Bags dripped into his arms. A tube ran up to his nose and down the back of his throat. Alien presences walked in and out of his field of vision, discussing him in the third person as if he was some sort of lab specimen.

Whatever they pumped into him kept the world fuzzy and distant. He didn't hurt so much as itch. His entire body was one massive itch. That, and he was cold, the fuckers couldn't cover him up, just left him lying naked beneath a plastic tent that turned the world into a blur.

Itching, cold, bored . . .

Occasionally shapes would walk around the bed and talk, forgetting he was here, listening.

"Okay, I see what you mean now . . ."

"I know it was hard to believe."

"This just isn't possible."

"You can see why I didn't want to risk any grafts, any surgery at all. There's no point exposing him to infection."

"The hands, I *saw* his hands. They should have been amputated, the muscle tissue was gone . . . How much fluid is he taking?"

"Literally as much as we can get into him. Worse than any burn victim I've ever seen. We have two IVs going at once, and we're replacing them every two hours, just to keep the blood volume up."

"But the burns are *shrinking*—"

"That's why you're still here. We've checked for internal bleeding every six hours. No sign."

"Can I see the lab results? All of them?"

"Yes, and order anything you think we've missed."

"This shouldn't be healing."

"I know."

"Normal abrasions wouldn't be healing this fast."

Jimmy tried to speak, but a tube was blocking his throat.

Just as well. They probably wouldn't let him eat a cheeseburger anyway.

Itching, cold, bored, and terribly hungry . . .

Cain walks the plains of hell.

Hell is a cracked plain stretching under a jet-black, starless sky. There is a sun, blood-red and bloated, blasting the
rock on which Cain walks.

Hell is empty.

Cain walks for a long time before he sees anyone else.

A dark child sits on a pinnacle of splintered stone, rocking back and forth. Cain stops before him and says, "What
is your sin?"

"I don't know, I don't remember."

"Why are you here?"

"I don't know, I don't remember."

"Who are you?"

"Who are you?"

Cain loses the child in the shadow of the stone.

Cain is alone.

What is my sin?

Why am I here?

Who am I?

In the world of white, Jimmy itched. His body was one
giant rash. The *inside* of his flesh itched. A bone-deep ache
sank through parts of his body that had been painless up
until now. He was aware of the pain in the same distracted
way that he was aware that something terrible had happened
to him. The knowledge was there, but it floated free in his
mind, never accumulating more than a few thoughts in its
wake.

Even the passage of time was an abstract concept that

carried no meaning. It seemed as if great blocks of memory were gone, and the elements he did remember weren't tied to a particular moment. He couldn't order them, couldn't place the fragments. He remembered several nurses changing the bags hanging over his bed, but he couldn't guess how many times or how many different nurses. It was as if the act of trying to force some structure on the image forced the nurses into an infinite regression where every human being who ever existed got a chance to swap an IV bag on him.

The same for the alien masked creatures that slid aside the plastic tent to poke him with their needles. They wore the doctors' green scrubs, masks, and safety goggles that reflected the light and made the upper parts of their faces a featureless fluorescent glare. Their skulls were capped, so no hair or extraneous flesh was visible. The hands they touched him with were covered in latex gloves that made the flesh of their hands white and dead, the color and consistency of a maggot.

Sometimes the aliens swabbed some extremity and slid a long needle inside. Sometimes it hurt, sometimes it didn't. One time, Jimmy's body started thrashing, and he was barely aware enough to register a slight concern at the fact he was having a seizure.

Other times they took small knives and cut pieces of him away. They held him down and drugged him, so this image was more distorted and fragmentary than the others. But he could remember innumerable times they cut his skin. They took from his chest, his stomach, his arms, his legs. Jimmy could see the postage-stamp fragments they pulled away with a pair of forceps. The pieces were a strange fleshy rainbow of colors, from an olive-tinted purplish-black to a shiny baby pink to a dead greasy white.

One fragment of a memory. A blurry man walking outside the tent. The voice was familiar, it belonged to one of the aliens who stole pieces of his flesh. He didn't wear the mask and goggles, but he also didn't slide back the tent, so Jimmy didn't know his face. The man paced around Jimmy's bed and talked to him. From the sound, Jimmy thought that the man believed that he was unconscious and couldn't hear him.

Jimmy didn't know, he might have been. This could be a dream.

"Who are you?" The figure paced outside the plastic tent. "*What* are you? This kind of insult doesn't just heal, didn't anyone ever tell you that? If I only knew *why*."

"Why can you grow back skin, muscle tissue, nerves— The way you came in, if you were *any* other person, we would just now be finishing debriding the wounds you came in here with. If we were lucky enough to keep you alive and stabilize you, we'd be starting with the skin grafts. If those took, we'd start looking at months of reconstructive surgery. Four or five months you'd probably get out of the hospital, bandages still covering the affected area of your body. After a few years of healing and physical therapy you might have had a normal life, though you would always be scarred, and your extremities would have been maimed . . ."

The shadow hovered at the foot of the bed. "Hundreds. Men, women, and children. I've had to treat three year olds. None of them grew back an inch of flesh on their own. Nothing heals without a scar. What the *hell* makes you different?"

Who am I?
Why am I here?
Why is my sin?

*   *   *

The darkness pulls itself around his bed and hovers like one of the alien doctors. Unlike the doctors, its presence is neither benign or indifferent. Like a cartoon vulture it leans over his bed, radiating hunger.

Jimmy feels something else in its presence.

An accusation.

No, goddamn it. You're the fucking sin.

The darkness isn't moved; it remains, patiently hungry. Dangerous as a wounded animal. Jimmy raises his hands, to ward off the darkness, and the IV tubes fall out of his arms. The tubes slap against the rails by his bed, and slide out from under the plastic tent to spill their fluids on the linoleum floor.

The darkness still accuses him, wordlessly. Jimmy can feel it judge him guilty of sins that Jimmy doesn't have names for. It is like a crowd, an auditorium, a stadium filled with people hungry for Jimmy's execution.

No, you're wrong . . .

Jimmy sits up, flailing his arms. The tubes break and fall away from his face. He is barely aware of the fact that he can't feel the presence of the tube snaking down his throat, blocking his voice.

"Unclean," mutters the invisible, voiceless crowd.

"Go away," Jimmy's voice is little more than a hoarse croak.

"Thief."

Jimmy sweeps his arms in front of him, warding off the pressure of the accusation as much as the predatory dark itself. His arms catch the edges of the plastic tent and pull the sides away from the chrome metal superstructure. As the plastic tears, the dark billows away slightly, as if it was mist, or smoke.

"Murderer."

Jimmy shouts an accusation of his own. "Liar!"

He swings his feet around to the edge of the bed, knocking down the restraining rails and tearing away more of the plastic. The motion twists wires free from contacts taped to the new pink flesh of his chest. "You're a fucking liar and you know it!"

Jimmy stands. His shoulder knocks over the IV stand, the half-full—draining—bag falls into a pile of equipment on a cart next to his bed. Jimmy's bare feet slap into the linoleum, standing in the puddle spilled by the IV bag.

"You're not going to have me!" he shouts at the darkness.

Jimmy stands on feet that are still the twisted black olive color of flesh completely burned through. Stands in the puddle of IV solution. The fluid is sucked toward him, as if his feet are a pair of sponges.

Jimmy runs away from the hospital room, unaware that his feet have returned to a more healthy color.

34

BOYDEN took Nate to a hotel. Its location was obviously not a coincidence. The room overlooked the building where James Somerset had been hospitalized.

The driver cut Nate's hands free from the nylon cuffs, and Agent Boyden had him sit down on a chair in the living room of the suite. The driver left the room, and Nate was alone with Agent Boyden.

"Want a drink?" Boyden asked.

Nate rubbed his wrists and shook his head. "What am I doing here?"

"I want you to help us." He walked over to the bar and poured himself a drink. Boyden looked into the tumbler of amber liquid and swirled it around. "Tell me about Abby Springfield."

"Why?"

Boyden smiled weakly. "Would it help to say that she's a threat to national security?"

"You've got to be kidding. Who the hell are you?"

"My name's actually Boyden, I'm not as adept as you with the manufacture of aliases. But then, we have specialists for that sort of thing." He walked over to a table where a notebook computer sat. He set his drink down and traced its rim with his finger. "We also have specialists for debrief-ings, but I wanted to do this myself."

Nate didn't say anything.

Boyden downed his glass and opened the computer. He turned it so the screen faced Nate's chair. "This is a little bit of what we've been able to assemble on her."

Boyden tapped a few keys and a page with Abby Spring-field's picture came up. "Abby Springfield," Boyden read. "Graduate of Berkeley, freelance journalist. Left-of-center mostly, critical of US policy in the third world, especially our Cuba policy—"

"That makes her a spy?"

"No, what makes her a 'spy' is her frequent contact with a gentleman named Ling Pak. Ling Pak is a multimillionaire resident of Hong Kong whose work includes money laun-dering, drug-running, arms dealing, and a laundry list of less wholesome things that the Chinese government wants no di-rect links to."

"She could be working on a story."

"We can trace the contact back to her time at Berkeley. Back to the time when her brother died."

"Her brother?"

"Do you know how he died?"

Nate stayed silent.

"He was fourteen years old." Boyden sighed and looked up from the screen. "We're playing catch-up here. Until re-cently, we haven't been the best equipped or funded part of the Agency. But I can pretty much guess what happened with her. Some agent talks to her. Politically, she's already sympathetic. He tells her how her brother's fiery death is the result of some evil US-corporate conspiracy. Instant agent."

Nate shook his head. "She never told me about her brother."

"I am interested in what *you* told *her.*"

"Why should I trust you?"

"This isn't a game, Mr. Adriano. I want your cooperation, and I went out of my way to get permission to ask for it. However, I do not require it. You should consider the consequences of your actions."

"You're blackmailing me?"

"I'm stating a fact. You crossed the line several times. Impersonating a federal agent, falsifying documents, accepting receipt of classified material. You could disappear for a long time."

Nate leaned back and rubbed his forehead. "You're bluffing, you don't want to see this made public in a court. Testimony about kids on fire and government conspiracies—"

"Did I mention the courts?"

Nate stopped talking and swallowed. His throat was very dry.

"I'm not bluffing for two reasons. First, it is very easy for me to take you into custody under the antiterrorism statutes. A secret tribunal and no appeal."

"What's the other reason?"

"If what's happening is what I am afraid is happening, the secrecy of my department is way, way down on the priority list. A few steps below survival of the United States, not to mention our species." Boyden drained his glass.

Nate stared at him a moment and said, finally, "I think I will have that drink."

When Boyden handed him the tumbler, he said, "I'm not blackmailing you. I'm offering a deal. Amnesty, if you work for me."

"*Work* for you?"

"You're too much of a loose cannon. You're on our team, or we take you off the field."

"Not much of a choice."

Boyden leaned forward. "I fought to offer you this. My boss would love to see you hang. I just barely convinced him that you might be able to help temper the disaster this whole operation is becoming." He sighed. "I've been trying to get authorization to recruit you ever since we first crossed paths. Research and data analysis is ninety percent of what we do. It has been a sinful waste of resources leaving you out in the cold to duplicate our efforts."

"Why now?"

Boyden leaned back.

"James Somerset?"

"What he represents. What your friend, Abby, represents. Enough of a threat to get a long stationary ball moving." Boyden shook his head. "Late in the day as it is."

"Why did she contact me?"

Boyden chuckled. "You are the foremost analyst on this subject outside our control. Who else would she go to? They didn't have people of your caliber to interpret the data she acquired. They targeted you and convinced you to do the work they needed done."

Inside, Nate felt a smoldering anger at Abby, and at the people who had used her against him. "Okay, Boyden, what do you want to know?"

Boyden was thorough. Despite the fact that he kept saying that this was an "informal" debriefing, the bastard was tireless and had an inexhaustible appetite for details. He asked for, and got, everything from the first phone call until the point the Feds busted into his hotel room.

The "abbreviated" debriefing took almost ten hours.

Sometime after four in the morning, a large man came into the hotel room unannounced. The door swung open just

long enough to see two men outside at parade rest. They
wore black suits, but they still looked like Marines.

Their new visitor focused on Boyden and said, "We need
you, sir. Now."

"Damn it, Sullivan. Can it wait?"

"You wanted immediate notification of any change in his
status."

Boyden looked at Nate, held up a hand as if in apology,
and walked over to the other man. They held a brief whispered exchange. To Nate's eyes, Boyden looked positively
ashen. He shook his head several times, and was obviously
containing his voice only with some effort.

He turned back toward Nate and said, "We will pick this
up later. You probably need some sleep anyway." He waved
at the other rooms of the suite. "You have that bedroom. I'm
afraid the phone's disconnected. If you need anything, let
one of the guards know and they'll handle it."

Boyden shook his head, retrieved his computer, and
headed for the door. The man he called Sullivan gave Nate
an appraising look. Then he followed Boyden out the door.

The door shut, leaving Nate alone in the hotel room.

*If this was a James Bond film, I'd be figuring out some
elaborate plans for escape right now.*

Nate chuckled. He was too old and too tired.

He stood up and stretched. It was strange, he had seen the
CD, decoded most of the data, but until now Department
Blue hadn't been particularly real to him. He had seen num-
bers on the screen, but there was nothing connected to them.
They hadn't been tangible.

Nate walked to the window and threw aside the drapes.
He looked out the window. He placed his fingers on the
glass. Cold and hard, it kept the sprawling hospital at bay. It

pushed the view away, as if he watched through a television set.

Or a computer monitor.

A seventeen year old named James Alan Somerset is somewhere in that complex of buildings. He had been burned nearly to death for the second time in his life. In Nate's mind he could run through statistics, profiles, case histories . . .

"Is any of that real?" His whispered words fogged the glass.

James Allen Somerset was a person, not a series of characteristics. He was real.

These kids were real.

Nate rested his forehead against the glass and closed his eyes.

35

WHAT happened?
   What is happening?
Jimmy stood on a street corner, staring up at the early morning sky, without knowing how he got there. His clothes hung too loose on his body. Jimmy watched the darkness leak out of the sky, inside himself he felt as if he was swimming up, toward a light that had almost been lost.

What have I done?
Jimmy remembered the fire, and the hospital, bits and fragments tumbling in a black void of memory. He had been hurt, terribly hurt. Probably, he should have died.

Where am I?
Jimmy looked away from the sky, and tried to run his hands through his hair. It didn't work. He didn't have any hair. His hand rubbed his scalp, and it felt like sandpaper.

He stood facing a four-way intersection. Gas stations occupied opposite corners, and a closed Medic Drugstore occupied a third corner, the one opposite Jimmy. The streetlight blinked red to the four points of the compass.

He looked down the broader of the two roads and could catch a distant glimpse of the downtown skyline.

It was beginning to sink in that he was in deep trouble. Blackout or not, going AWOL meant that when they did catch up with him, he wasn't going back to Trinity. They were going to lock him up for good.

And God only knew where these clothes came from . . .

(. . . blood dripping over discolored flesh . . .)

"No," Jimmy whispered.

(. . . so much blood seeping into the skin . . .)

"I don't want to know . . ."

(. . . pooling in the palms of his hands—)

"No!" Jimmy yelled, balling his hand into a fist, throwing a punch at a telephone pole next to him as if it was the phantom memory attacking him. His fist connected with the wood with a crack like a rifle shot. The impact shot through his arm and up his body with enough force so that his teeth clicked together, drawing blood from his cheek and tongue.

"Shit!" Jimmy yanked his hand away from the impact, cradling it. "Shit. Shit. Shit . . ." The memories ran away in the face of present pain. It felt as if his hand had been run over by a car, ground into pavement covered in broken glass, nailed to a tree . . .

For about thirty seconds, Jimmy was in absolute agony.

Then it stopped.

He was doubled over his hand, holding it to his chest, and the pain was gone. He slowly straightened up, still clutching his hand. He was afraid to look at it. In the front of his mind, he was afraid to look at it because it felt as if it had been turned into so much hamburger.

In the back of his mind, in the place where the darkness lived, he was afraid of something else . . .

He looked at the telephone pole first.

His punch had landed right of center, about six inches from the midline of the pole. That was probably a good thing, because his fist had sunk about six inches into the wood, blowing splintered fragments out of the side of the pole. It looked as if a car had sideswiped it—at the level of Jimmy's chest.

He released his hand and held it up before him. Blood-stained splinters, some a foot or more in length, fell to the ground at his feet as he opened his fist.

His hand was unmarked. Not so much as a bloodstain.

"I hit that pole . . ." Jimmy whispered.

Does someone have to draw you a road map, Jimmy? The fight with Frank. The munchkin bite. Not to mention, you were burned real crispy there for a while . . .

"I just heal fast . . ."

Real fast.

Jimmy reached out and touched the damaged telephone pole, as if it was going to disappear on him. It stayed solid, and tangible. He wrapped his hand around one of the longer, thicker splinters that blossomed from its side and tore it free. In his right hand he held a dagger of wood a foot long.

Jimmy held up his left hand, palm facing him.

He thrust the point end of his improvised weapon at his upturned palm. He saw it hit, sliding into his palm as if he was slicing an orange. For a moment, he only felt the pressure of the impact, as if he had hit himself with a hammer. It actually took three or four seconds for his body to register what his eyes were seeing, a piece of wood impaling his hand.

"What've I done?" The words came through in a shuddering intake of breath, the full impact of the pain making him a sudden skeptic. He managed not to move, and to keep his eyes open and focused on his left hand.

Eyes watering, teeth clenched, holding his breath, Jimmy pulled the wood out of his hand. He did it slowly enough that he could see that it had penetrated three inches, completely through his hand. He watched the lips of the wound close on the wood as he withdrew it, as if in an obscene kiss.

He stared as the blood flowed from his hand, briefly.

He watched the skin draw together.

He watched the wound disappear.

"I am Cain," Jimmy whispered to the absent stigmata.

Included with the strange clothes was a wallet. Jimmy didn't want to think about that, so he took the cash out and slipped it into his pocket. He walked around until he found a bus stop. Most bus routes converged downtown, and once there he would know where he was, and know how to get anywhere else.

He got on the first bus and tried to fade into the back. Which was hard to do, since the bus was nearly empty.

"Try not to freak out . . ."

Sound advice, though Jimmy didn't know if he was up to taking it. He had just come out of a blackout from God knew what disaster, he had only the vaguest idea of what time it was, and no clue at all about the date. The cops were probably looking for him, at the very least for walking out of his sentence at Trinity. When they caught up with him, they'd also get him for the theft of this guy's clothes. *Please, let that be all . . .*

Then there was the small matter of some superhuman abilities . . .

Jimmy's first instinct was to run. Just start running and never stop. This guy had enough cash on him for a one-way Greyhound ticket anywhere in the country. In twelve hours he could be three or four states away from the cops, County Family Services, and Trinity.

With great power comes great responsibility.

"Fuck off," Jimmy muttered to himself.

That it? Walk away. No—run. Everyone's right about you, aren't they. Worthless.

"What do you want?"

What do you want? Who gets handed their heart's desire and runs away because it's scary. You want this.

"No."

You've always wanted this.

The bus let him off at Public Square in downtown Cleveland. He knew the direction to the Greyhound station from here.

Instead, he got on the first bus headed through Euclid Heights.

Jimmy knew the Carswells' neighborhood well enough that he could approach the house from the back. He cut through the backyards of three houses whose occupants were now off at work somewhere. Only one dog barked at him from the inside of the empty houses.

Jimmy crept up and saw the Carswells' driveway was empty.

He stood in the shadow of a tree for a long time, staring at the rear of their house. It seemed empty . . .

Jimmy walked up to the side of the garage where a small woodpile leaned up against the garage wall. He pushed one of the logs aside and found the little sardine can that held the spare key.

He let himself in the side door and listened for a few long moments. No sounds.

He ran to what had been his room.

To his relief, the Carswells had only got as far as filling cardboard boxes with his leftover clothing. He rummaged through the boxes of stuff. This was all the crap that he didn't wear anymore, or stuff too worn for the Carswells to pack for his stay at Trinity.

It was better than wandering around in a set of clothes two or three sizes too big.

He found a black T-shirt and jeans, and a set of sneakers, all with holes in them, but the net effect was less conspicuous.

What I really need is spandex tights and a cape.

After getting dressed, he raided the Carswells' refrigerator.

He left the stranger's clothes and wallet on the counter next to the spare key. He debated leaving a note, but he suspected that the Carswells would get them back to their rightful owner—

. . . or next of kin.

Jimmy pushed away the evil thought as he left.

36

JIMMY reached Carlos' Cosmic Comic Shoppe just as Reggie was unlocking the door for the day. He walked up behind Reggie and cleared his throat. Reggie turned around and looked at him a moment, and for a few seconds, showed no sign of recognition.

"Yes?" Reggie said. "I'll be open in fifteen—" His keys slipped out of his hand and his eyes widened. "Jimmy?"

"It's the hair," Jimmy said. "It's too much."

Reggie stared at him. "What are you doing here?"

"What am I doing anywhere?" Jimmy knelt down and retrieved Reggie's oversized key ring from the sidewalk. He stood up and handed the keys back.

Reggie took the keys and kept staring at Jimmy. "I thought you were . . ." He trailed off. There was a fear in his posture that hadn't been there before. Normally that would have irritated Jimmy, but right now he was too on edge himself to do more than notice. He felt faint and his brain was teetering, ready to slide into another pool of blackness at any moment.

Jimmy rubbed his face. "I'm not here to fuck with you. I just need a favor."

"What do you want?"

"My last week and a half pay, that's all." Jimmy looked into Reggie's eyes. "Cash, if you got it."

"What happened to you?"

"You don't want to know." Jimmy shook his head. He felt faint, dizzy. "Just take it out of the cash drawer. If it makes you feel better, you can call the cops afterward. You'll never see me again."

"Are you sick?"

Jimmy laughed, a shaking, heaving laugh that made the dizziness worse. He only stopped when he saw that Reggie was edging away from him.

"My man," Jimmy said, "the whole world is sick."

Jimmy walked away from Carlos' Cosmic Comic Shoppe with a little over two hundred dollars in cash. Once he got over the shock of seeing Jimmy, Reggie was good about it. As Jimmy left, Reggie said, "I *am* going to call the police, you know."

"I know."

"Do you know what you're doing?"

"I don't even know what I am thinking . . ."

Jimmy cut over a few blocks, found a convenience store with a pay phone and ordered a cab. He bought a giant bag of cheese curls, a six-pack of Mountain Dew, and a pair of Hostess apple pies.

By the time the cab came, he had two cans left and felt a little less dizzy. He slipped into the back.

"Where're you going?" asked the cabby with an Eastern European accent.

The Greyhound station . . .

"The nearest motel," Jimmy said.

*   *   *

Fifty-six dollars and sixty-seven cents later, Jimmy was in a scummy little room in one of the more picturesque parts of East Cleveland. The kind of room that people got to shoot up or get laid, sometimes both. There were cigarette burns in the carpet, and the bed looked up at a tiled mirror set in the ceiling.

The television was ancient and had a coin slot built into the side.

Jimmy didn't like the look of the bed, so he collapsed in a chair. The upholstery was so dusty that a cloud of motes enveloped him as he sat down.

He needed to rest a little. Collect himself while he was still himself. Consider his options.

He slowly sipped his last can of Mountain Dew.

Did he want to be a fugitive? Even if he lived out some caped crusader fantasy life, there was still the problem of Jimmy Somerset being wanted by the cops.

"I could turn myself in . . ."

Somehow, that alternative didn't seem very attractive. He didn't even know if he still had the right to fight the charges they'd stuck him with. He had copped to a plea, and he'd blown it.

If he jumped on a Greyhound, where the hell would he go? How the hell would he live?

Jimmy balled up the can and threw it in the corner of the room.

(. . . *blood dripping over discolored flesh, seeping into the skin, pooling in the palms of his hands—*

Jimmy stares at his hands from some isolated place inside himself. He watches a memory of a dream, or a dream of a memory.

He is naked, his skin a twisted rainbow of colors, black,

brown, olive-green, and dead white. The blood pools in the flesh of his palm, sinking into the skin as if Jimmy's flesh was a sponge. Underneath the blood, the flesh has turned a healthy pink.

In front of him, a refrigerator stands open. Inside it, bags of whole blood are arranged by type. The plastic is shiny, and inside the blood is so red it is nearly black.

The Jimmything knows what it is doing. It knows it needs the fluid. It can sense the substance inside the bags, can almost smell it, and the craving, the need, is worse than any pain.

It reaches in the refrigerator and takes out another bag, tearing it open with its hands. Blood spills out, cold and wet, dripping across his damaged flesh.

Very little drips on the ground.

The refrigerator is almost empty when the lights come on in the otherwise darkened room. The orderly barely has time to say, "What the hell are you doing?" Then the Jimmything pounces.

The victim slams into the wall and slides to the floor, and for a few long moments the Jimmything stares into the man's face, hands wrapped around his throat.

After a moment, the hands slide down and start undoing the man's collar . . .)

. . . a dream of a memory, or a memory of a dream . . .

He stands on the cracked blackened plain under the gravid blood-red sun. He is naked, and blood drips down his skin. In front of him, on a sharp black outcrop, the darkness coalesces into a form, tall, gaunt, trench coat waving in a nonexistent wind.

"Cain," Jimmy whispers.

"We are who we are," the darkness responds.

Jimmy shakes his head. "I don't understand."

"You stole us, made us not what we are, you murder us."

Jimmy takes a step back. "Who are you? I don't know you."

"We are you."

"No."

"You are us."

Jimmy turns and tries to run, but the dark figure blocks the path behind him. Even under the blazing red sun, the figure is nothing more than a shadow, a Cain-shaped hole cut into the world. What faces him isn't Cain. It is something darker, older, and much more alien.

"You don't belong here. Go back where you came from."

"We were one and you made us something else. You took our memory, our purpose. So long we slept."

"What do you mean?"

"So we take our memory, our purpose, back from you. So again we can be one."

"What do you mean?"

The shadow Cain opens his arms and spreads his coat apart. The blackness envelops everything as it embraces Jimmy . . .

Jimmy came to awareness with a woman screaming at him.

"You killed him. *You killed him.*"

Holy Christ, what have I done now?

Jimmy was standing in the middle of an unfamiliar room in an unfamiliar house. A blue couch was against the wall to Jimmy's right, facing a fake fireplace on the opposite wall. Above the mantel was a large mirror mounted in the wall. The mirror had been shattered, cracks radiating from the point where something had hit hard.

(. . . "LOOK, you bastard. Look at the sick fuck staring back at you!" . . .)

Next to the fireplace was an old-style console TV. The picture tube had been smashed. A glass-topped coffee table lay on the carpet in a million pieces.

Most surreal were the pictures. Pages from a photo album were scattered everywhere, as if the book had exploded. Photographs were on the carpet, the couch, in the fireplace . . .

By Jimmy's foot was a picture of two children, a couple of years younger, but Jimmy recognized them.

Charlie and Salina.

Oh, God . . .

In front of him, Salina's mother was rocking back and forth, cradling her husband's head in her lap. She was calling his name in a voice bordering on hysteria, "Quincy. Quincy . . ."

Quincy Robb didn't have a face anymore.

(. . . the Jimmything flips through the photo album, sitting on the couch in the Robbs' living room. The TV plays David Letterman while the Jimmything waits. It isn't long before Quincy Robb comes down to confront the intruder. The man runs into the living room, wearing boxer shorts and brandishing a handgun.

"Who the fuck are you?"

"Nice kids," says the Jimmything as it stands. "Real nice pictures you got here."

"Stay where you are. My wife's already called the police."

Jimmy walks toward Quincy Robb. "You sure? I mean, she wasn't that quick to call 911 when her daughter was being raped."

The gun discharges. Behind the Jimmything, Letterman

explodes into a shower of sparks. The Jimmything feels the impact in his upper chest, near the shoulder, but it only stops his advance momentarily.

The Jimmything looks at Quincy Robb and says, "Ouch."

Quincy Robb stares. The expression of shock, the beer gut hanging over the boxer shorts, and the gun all combine to form an incredibly comical image. "Go on, do it again." The Jimmything smiles. "Or can you only get it up when someone is begging you to stop?"

The gunshot is thunderously loud in the small living room. Smoke fills the small space between the Jimmything and Quincy Robb. The bullet tears into the Jimmything's abdomen.

It doesn't really matter.

"My turn, you fat fuck."

In a surreal reprise of its confrontation with Frank, the Jimmything smashes the photo album across Quincy Robb's face.

The impact explodes the cheap binding. Pages fly everywhere as Quincy Robb stumbles sideways. The gun goes off again, this time into the floor.

The Jimmything steps sideways, reaches up for the back of Robb's neck, and sends him sailing face-first down into the coffee table. The glass top shatters into thousands of fragments.

Quincy Robb groans and rolls over, across the broken glass.

The Jimmything stands over him. Blood is leaking from two bullet wounds, but not as much as there should be. The Jimmything barely feels the wound.

"Why don't you beg for it? Your daughter begged, didn't she?"

Quincy Robb raises the gun at the Jimmything.

It clicks on an empty chamber.

"Aww, too bad." The Jimmything walks around, reaches down and pulls the man up by his head. Both its hands clamp on either side of the man's skull. The man gasps and wheezes as his feet leave the floor. He flails and kicks, but fails to dislodge the Jimmything's supernaturally strong grip.

The Jimmything holds him up in front of the mirror above the fireplace.

"LOOK, you bastard. Look at the sick fuck staring back at you!"

The man keeps struggling.

"That's the last thing you're going to see."

The Jimmything slams the man's face into the mirror . . .)

Jimmy stood, staring at the blood-pulped remains of Quincy Robb's face.

(Again . . .)

"Oh, shit," Jimmy whispers. It was all over. He had gone apeshit and killed someone. If they got hold of him now, they'd never let him go.

(Again . . .)

Jimmy could hear sirens.

(Again . . .)

Jimmy ran.

He bolted out of the front of the Robb house just as the police flashers were becoming visible reflected in the windows of the houses around him. He had no idea where he was, so he ran away from the flashers. He ran full tilt down the dark, residential street.

In his mind he kept picturing Quincy Robb's face hitting the mirror again, and again, and again.

A squeal of brakes. A spotlight blinded Jimmy. From somewhere behind the light he heard the word, *"Freeze!"*

Part of his mind wanted to keep running, turn at right angles, lose himself behind one of these houses. That part of his mind wasn't in control at the moment. He stopped, blinking, pinned down by the light.

"Hands behind your head. Move it! Now!"

Jimmy locked his fingers behind his neck. He could feel a slight tension in the shoulder where he had been shot. Under his T-shirt, he could feel moisture leaking down the side of his body. It was just now registering that thc latc Quincy Robb had put two bullets in him.

It didn't stop me, didn't even slow me down.

"Turn around and keep your hands in sight."

Jimmy did as the cops asked. Someone approached from behind and frisked him. Jimmy felt the cop pat down his sides. "Fuck, this kid's a bloody mess," Jimmy heard him mutter. "Leo! bring me some towels and a pair of gloves, he's got the old man's blood all over him."

Jimmy turned his head to see the cop, and he felt a hand clamp down on his wrists. "Did I say you could move? Stay the fuck still."

"It's my blood," Jimmy whispered.

With a lot of cursing, the cop finished patting him down, wearing a fresh pair of latex gloves. Jimmy could look down and see the white hands as they became smeared with blood. The cop emptied his pockets of a couple of bloodstained twenties.

The cop with the gloves placed the money in a plastic baggie while reading off Jimmy's rights. Behind him, another cop folded his arms back and cuffed him.

So much blood. His clothes were soaked.

They threw a towel in the back of the squad car before they locked him in. Jimmy watched out the window as they both peeled off their gloves and tossed them in an orange refuse bag.

For some reason, he kept thinking of the kid who had bit him.

One cop walked around and got in the driver's side, tossing the orange bag in the passenger seat. The other cop walked back to another patrol car. The cop sighed, looked back at Jimmy, and shook his head. "Christ, what the hell were you thinking?"

Jimmy didn't know what to say, so he just looked at his feet. Blood dripped down, over his sneakers.

"James Allen Somerset, I know who you are. There's a warrant for you . . ."

The drops were moving by themselves. For a long surreal moment, while the cop tried to talk to him, Jimmy was convinced that he was stuck in another sick nightmare. The blood rolled off of his shoe, and across the carpet purposefully, as if it had a mind where it was going.

The cop got on the radio, and started driving.

Jimmy looked up and said, "I think we should stop the car and get out." He could feel his own blood moving now, across his skin, under his clothing. The towel beneath him rustled as if it was alive with insects.

The cop hung up the mike from the radio and said, "So you can talk."

"Sir, I really think we should pull over."

"Why is that, son?"

The police car pulled out into a major street. Jimmy could see the skyline of downtown Cleveland.

"The blood," Jimmy said. "We need to wash off the blood."

"That can wait until we get to the station."

Jimmy looked down, and his eyes widened. Through a dozen holes the size of his index finger, he could see the road rushing by underneath them. Each perfectly circular hole was ringed by a shiny film of black-red fluid.

Jimmy stood up in the back. "You have to pull over, *now!*"

"Sit down."

They were going sixty-five down a four-lane stretch of road. The entrance ramp to the freeway was about half a block away. That's where the police car was headed. Jimmy looked down through the transparent partition, at where the cop had tossed the orange plastic bag.

There was nothing there except a few shreds of latex that looked as if someone had chewed them apart.

"Look at the gloves, damn it, pull over!"

The cop was already calling dispatch about an unruly passenger, but he looked. Jimmy saw his eyes widen. To his horror, Jimmy also saw a single crimson droplet rolling up the cop's cheek.

The cop tried to brake, and the inertia slammed Jimmy down into the seat, causing the handcuffs to bite into his wrists. The police car's tires screamed in agony, filling the air with the smell of burning rubber.

But something bad had happened under the car, because the squeals stopped with a shuddering mechanical snap, and the car tried to shake itself apart. Looking down, through the now foot-wide hole in the floor, Jimmy saw the furiously spinning driveshaft fracture, blowing pieces of itself everywhere. One fragment shot through the floor, and up through the rear window.

Jimmy looked up and saw the cop frantically trying to steer as the car started into a spin. The wheel was rotating freely and seemed to have no effect. The car spun out into the freeway.

The bus was going nearly seventy when it slammed into the car.

37

IT was a long time before Agent Boyden came back. Nate got a few hours of restless sleep, and the closemouthed sentries brought him a lukewarm room service dinner. Nate was sawing through a piece of allegedly grilled chicken when Boyden walked in. He didn't look happy.

Nate put down his fork.

"What's going on?"

Boyden shook his head. "We need to go on with the debriefing. I need to know anything about Abby Springfield we might have missed."

"We didn't miss anything. Tell me what's happening?"

Boyden looked at him, then he walked to the bar. He poured himself a drink. "Sometimes it is like sweeping back the ocean."

"What?"

"Trying to contain this." Boyden shook his head and picked up the glass. "We were supposed to contain both you and James Somerset at the same time. A logical allocation of my limited number of field agents dictated that I use most of my manpower on you. You were ambulatory and associating with agents of a foreign government." He downed the drink.

"Something happened to Jimmy?" Nate had a nightmare image of a hospital in flames.

"James was in intensive care, with burns over half his body, and our major security concern was keeping people *out*. He wasn't ambulatory. Even at the rate he was recovering, every reasonable medical opinion said the boy couldn't stand, much less walk out of the hospital." Boyden shook his head. "So much for subtlety."

"*Walked* out?"

"While our agents were trying to prep things to move him to a secured area."

Nate leaned back. "How?"

"Apparently, he healed quicker than we gave him credit for before." He turned to face Nate. "We have to find him before Pak's people do. You need to help me. Anything that can tell me what Abby might do, what Jimmy might do—"

"Tell me why you're so scared of this kid."

Boyden was quiet for a moment.

"If you're trying to recruit me, tell me why we're so interested in this kid. *These* kids."

"Do you know what you're asking?"

"Tell me."

Boyden poured another glass and walked over to Nate with it. He held it out. After a moment he said, "Take it, you'll need it."

Nate took the offered drink.

"I know you must have seen the broad patterns by now—"

"The three-year cycle."

Boyden nodded. "There's the three-year cycle, there's a band of latitudes where this happens, and the event points occur clustering about the same sidereal time—"

"Sidereal time?"

"If you plot the times out, they migrate around the clock depending on the time of year."

Nate nodded.

"Sidereal time is an astronomical term. Easiest way to put it, is that when these kids burst into flame, the same constellation is overhead. In fact, if you do the calculations with both latitude and the times the events happen, you can draw a circle in the sky about twenty degrees wide. The combustion only happens while that patch of sky is overhead."

Nate furrowed his brows. "You are saying what? Death rays from the sky?"

Boyden chuckled. "Precisely the opposite, in fact. Have that drink."

Nate sipped.

"Now there are a lot of objects within that circle. One of them is an eclipsing binary star system about fifteen light-years away. It not only happens to fall near the center of the circle we're drawing, but it happens to eclipse itself every three years."

Nate took another sip from his drink. Boyden had just taken an unscheduled step into conspiracy territory. Any moment he was going to start invoking UFOs and little gray men. "How can that have anything to do with what's happening with these kids?"

"We've monitored radio emissions from the binary. They're complex, structured, and follow the same three-year pattern. The kids' cycle coincides with the periods of strongest transmission."

"It's hard to take what you're saying seriously."

"Do you know why these kids are combusting, Mr. Adriano?"

"What do you mean?"

"What is the cause?"

"I haven't met anyone who could answer that question."

"Do you know how much energy you need to boost a radio signal to reach fifteen light-years?"

Nate shook his head in disbelief. The inferences that Boyden was asking him to make—that he was drawing for him—were too much. Nate stared at Boyden and said, quietly, "No."

Boyden sighed.

"No," Nate said. "You don't have the *right* to bullshit me. I've put my *life* into this and you are not turning it into some sort of UFO conspiracy theory. You hear me?" Nate's hands were shaking.

"Mr. Adriano," Boyden snapped. When Nate stopped talking, he said, "First of all there are no UFOs, no little men, gray, green, or otherwise. What we have are the cycles, the radio transmissions, and these kids."

"Meaning?"

"Let me ask you to do a little thought experiment . . ."

Imagine humankind a few thousand years from now. At some point we will want to explore other star systems. The desire is natural enough. Also, for the sake of argument, we can assume that everything we know from Einstein is true; Nothing can travel faster than light, no magic interdimensional gateways, warp speeds, wormholes, or tachyon drives. How would you go about doing it?

Certainly we'll be able to capture radiation from nearby stars. We might be able to capture every stray photon from a target system as it passes through our own, and as clear a picture of it as physics allows. We might get to see planets, maybe even gain insight on their chemical composition. There will, however, be limits on our ability to collect information from several light-years away. The energy emitted by a system is finite, and by the time it reaches us it will have dissipated across the surface of a sphere thirty light-years in diameter. Planets would provide only the roughest outlines and characteristics. Any alien broadcasts would have devolved into single photons so divorced from their context that they would be unintelligible. We might see that life exists, but have no idea what it looks like.

So how could we go there?

Realistically, we can't go there in person. To move people, you need to move air, water, and food. To move a sustainable self-contained environment you need to move—again, assume no magic technologies—several tons of matter for each human being you send. As a practical matter, the energy needed to transport this mass several light-years at any significant fraction of the speed of light is an order of magnitude beyond any reasonable cost—especially when it is much less costly to send an unmanned probe.

If you can make a probe sufficiently small, the energy to accelerate it ceases to be an issue. It could be launched simply by pointing a significantly powerful laser at it.

"How small?" Nate asked.

"Microscopic. Small enough that the civilization that launches them can afford to use a shotgun approach and literally send millions to a planet they're interested in."

"You're saying that some aliens have done this?"

Boyden nodded.

"But what does this have to do with the kids?"

"Have you ever heard of nanotechnology?"

These microscopic probes are more than passive information-gathering devices. They have the components, like a virus, to reproduce, given the raw materials. Unlike a virus, they have a computer as well, a computer intelligent enough to operate on its own, learn on its own, and act without direction from home. When it reaches its target, it inserts itself into the environment, gathers data for a prescribed period of time, then builds a transmitter and sends the data back home.

These probes are machines on the scale of a virus, and they have the capability of modifying their environment. To perform their function, they can insert themselves into anything, camouflage themselves within any aspect of the host environment, and use it as a platform to collect data.

The logical target for these probes, if they found themselves on a life-bearing planet, would be a member of the dominant species.

"What we believe happens," Boyden said, "is that the inhabitants who live in the system of this unnamed binary star are in the process of investigating their neighbors. They're doing so by sending out wave after wave of bacteria-sized, intelligent, autonomous probes. We don't know the exact mechanism, but these invaders infect human beings, and use them to create the perfectly camouflaged vehicle to collect their data."

Nate shook his head. "How can something that small . . . ?"

"You can answer your own question. You are familiar with this kind of technology. Right now, on a single chip the size of your fingernail, we can build a fully functional computer that would have filled several buildings fifty years ago. With the right software running in parallel, we can put together a supercomputer that would fit inside a pack of cigarettes. That isn't theory, that's what we can do *now*. We are only a few decades away from bacteria-sized computers ourselves—and once you start engineering on that scale, it isn't that great a conceptual leap to have these machines controlling industrial processes, fabricating anything—including themselves—from the molecular level up."

"I have trouble believing that is possible."

Boyden smiled. "Of course it's possible. In the nucleus of every cell of your body is a complicated molecular computer that fabricates a whole range of chemical products, and given the right materials, can fabricate a copy of itself. Nanotechnology is simply the point at which chemical engineering, genetic engineering, and mechanical engineering all merge. Do you think it is impossible for us to eventually reverse engineer DNA and come up with our own variant? Something more compact, more intelligent, more programmable?"

Nate opened his mouth and closed it again.

"None of what I'm describing requires anything more than technical expertise. Unlike UFOs, or psychic powers, or any of a number of other 'theories' laymen have produced to explain these kids, this doesn't require us to rewrite the science we do know about. We don't have to invent mental powers, undetectable spiritual radiation or faster-than-light travel. We don't even require a hyper-advanced civilization out there—just someone a little more advanced than we are."

"But it's just a theory."

Boyden shook his head. "I'm afraid not. We have caught up with some of these kids before the transmission mechanism kicked in. By taking a blood sample we are able to chemically isolate the 'infection.'"

Nate sat quietly, unsure how to respond.

"We've been able to analyze biological specimens from both before and after the 'events.' We have the evidence of what is happening."

"If you see these things, why can't you stop them?"

Agent Boyden shook his head and chuckled. "Why can't we stop AIDS? Just because we've isolated parts of it doesn't mean we understand how it works. This isn't just one 'virus.' We're talking about a colony of millions of unique entities working in parallel. All we really know is that, in the victims, these things inhabit every cell of their body. And the chemical composition of these things marks them as something that didn't evolve on this planet."

Nate shook his head again and said, "This isn't what I—"

"Welcome to our little project; The Lord's own counter-intelligence operation."

"I don't follow—"

"We have agents of an alien power abroad in this planet. It would be insane just to assume that their intent is completely peaceful, especially when their entire operation has been by stealth. Especially when we have one demonstrably hostile agent loose out there."

38

JIMMY couldn't move.

The only concrete sensations he had were a bad itch on his nose, and sweat stinging his left eye. For a long time he didn't have any feeling in the rest of his body.

The air smelled of gasoline and exhaust fumes. All he could see was a dark space in front of him. It felt as if he was looking down, as if he was falling into the deep blackness in front of him.

He felt slightly dizzy, and wasn't quite sure where he was. All he could think of was the itch on his nose. There couldn't be anything worse than being immobilized and subjected to minor irritations until you were driven completely insane.

There wasn't even anything interesting to look at. Just the empty darkness in front of him.

Jimmy heard sirens, and his memory shot into focus. He could remember the police car disintegrating around them, crumpling around the front of a city bus.

Jimmy shouldn't have been alive.

He heard people around him, muffled shouts. Then he began to hear the sound of pneumatic machinery. The darkness wrapping him began to vibrate as the sound became louder. At the same time he started to feel other sensations in his body. Sweat rolling down his back, the rough feel of broken metal against his foot.

Light suddenly flooded Jimmy's dark world.

He was looking downward. Somehow the front of the car was below him now. He could see part of the dashboard twisted and compacted beneath him. He could also see the cop's forearm, torn, mangled, and separate from the body, impaled by the wreckage.

Shadows blocked the lights and he heard someone tell him not to move.

It was an easy command to follow.

Someone slipped a brace around his neck from behind. Jimmy felt them gently adjust his head straight so they could slip it on. It was the first time that Jimmy thought that his inability to move might be more than something holding him down.

Welcome the first paraplegic superhero.

Jimmy tried to laugh, but instead he started coughing up the taste of blood, gasoline, and rusted metal.

Several hands, only dimly felt, peeled him away from the wreckage. In the light from several spotlights, Jimmy got to see the remains of the police car. The wreckage was unrecognizable as a cop car. It was like a giant mass of crumpled tinfoil with only the tires poking out at odd angles to show what this object had been at one time.

Out of Jimmy's peripheral vision he could see several fire trucks, police cars, and a trio of ambulances. One pair of firemen was standing next to the wreckage, and as soon as the medics pulled Jimmy free, they started attacking the metal again with a gigantic cutting tool.

No hurry, I don't think the driver's going anywhere.

The quartet carrying him set him down on a long board, and started pulling belts around his body, strapping him down. Jimmy's neck was fixed and he could only stare up. He had a good view of the torso of the medic holding the head of the backboard.

When the medic's jacket flapped open, Jimmy could see a shoulder holster holding a nasty-looking gun.

That isn't right.

"Hey . . ." Jimmy started to talk, but the words devolved into bloody coughing again.

Another pair of medics rolled up next to them with a gurney. They lowered it, and the four medics surrounded Jimmy, lifting the backboard on to it. To Jimmy's dismay, the three unarmed medics went back toward the accident, leaving him with the gurney crew and the guy with the gun.

Paramedics shouldn't be armed.

Jimmy started struggling. He could only move a little, weakly. He wasn't even sure if anyone noticed. Jimmy could see their faces, in flashes, but he didn't think they looked like paramedics. Or maybe it was that they didn't look around like paramedics. Once they had him on the gurney, none of them seemed to look at him at all. They were paying a lot more attention to the cops, the firemen, and the other medics.

They rolled the gurney across the roadway at a running pace, as if they were moving a slab of meat. A *stolen* slab of meat. The first guy, the one with the holster, stayed by Jimmy's head long enough for Jimmy to see that his hand never strayed too far from his weapon.

Then they lifted him up, and slammed him into the back of an idling ambulance.

Jimmy increased his struggles, but he was completely immobile.

"Who are you?" he managed to spit out finally. "Where are you taking me?"

His voice was weak and raspy and flecked with blood. The medics didn't pay any attention to him. Two of them, one the man with the holster, slid into the back with him.

The doors shut behind them. In a moment, the sirens started and the ambulance jerked forward.

One of the masked men in the back with him stripped off the latex gloves he had been wearing, and swapped them for a fresh pair from a storage compartment in the wall.

The other stood over Jimmy's head, holding on to bars set into the walls. He wasn't even attempting to hide the weapons under his armpit now. He swayed slightly as the ambulance picked up speed, his coat flapping open as he moved. The man spoke, and it was the first time Jimmy had heard any of them say anything.

Jimmy couldn't understand a word of it. Either Jimmy had lost his mind, or they weren't speaking English.

The one with the gloves had a syringe in his hand.

"What the hell are you doing?" Jimmy's voice was cracked and broken. His throat hurt. His heart was racing, and under the straps on his arms and legs, sweat was turning into slime. Inside him was a deep awful certainly that the backboard was unnecessary, only there to keep him trapped.

The man with the gloves slid the needle into a small vial of clear liquid and withdrew the plunger. He barked something in response to the guy by Jimmy's head.

They both laughed.

"What the fuck is so funny?"

He tried to shout, but the words came out in a hoarse whisper. That apparently amused his captors even more.

Inside Jimmy, something smoldered. He felt all the fear and all the anger pull down into a knot inside his belly, leaving his flesh cold and hard. His hands curled into fists as his body tensed. Biceps, pectorals, thighs—all the large muscles in his body were taut and vibrating. His body was becoming an engine driven to overload.

The one with the syringe held it up and cleared the air from the tip.

Blood dripped from Jimmy's hands where his fingernails bit into the flesh. His two guards were absorbed in their own chatter, so they didn't notice. Jimmy strained as if he might be able to crack the fabric of reality and pull himself into some other universe just by force of will.

Blood.

Blood from his hands, his mouth, from dozens of unfelt wounds, slid over his body, mingled with sweat. Jimmy felt it wrap his arms, legs, torso, in a liquid web. With it came the feeling almost as if the straps were melting.

The one with the syringe turned to Jimmy once his point was made to the other guy. He looked in Jimmy's eyes, saw the terror and the rage in there, and spoke to him in heavily accented English. "Stay calm. We will not hurt you. Everything will be fine." He raised the needle to slide it into Jimmy's arm.

The straps gave way.

One moment, Jimmy's left arm was completely immobilized, the next, the force holding the tensed muscles of his arm in check disappeared, and his arm flew into the guy's abdomen. The man's stomach was a sack of wet flour that folded over Jimmy's extended arm.

The syringe went flying into the ambulance.

Pieces of the backboard fell to the floor, its surface brown and corroded.

Jimmy could move now, and he rolled over on his left side, bringing his right arm—along with a large fragment of the backboard—down on the back of the doubled-over man.

The man dropped, smashing face-first into the floor of the ambulance.

The sirens still blared, and the van rocked from side to side as the driver took very fast turns.

The man at the head of the van was shouting something to Jimmy as he drew the pistol he carried. Jimmy could hear panic in the man's voice, and the sound of it made him smile.

"No habla español," Jimmy said as he pushed himself upright against the swaying ambulance. The remains of the backboard, straps, and clothing fell away. He stood up, wrapped only in a neck brace and a web of his own blood.

The man with the gun kept chattering incomprehensibly.

Jimmy had to turn his whole body to look at the gunman. His head was still locked in place by the brace.

"You know, I don't understand a fucking word you're saying, Pedro. Just stop the fucking ambulance and let me off. I'll find my own way home."

The guy was screaming, voice high-pitched and mono-syllabic. The ambulance slowed, as if the guys driving knew that there was an issue in the back.

The guy kept swinging the gun from Jimmy, back to the gurney. Jimmy couldn't shake his head no, so he just stood there with the guy pointing the gun at him.

Then the ambulance lurched, throwing Jimmy forward a step.

That was too much for the man with the gun.

The muzzle flash briefly blinded Jimmy as three shots tore into him. He staggered, stunned, as if someone had taken a jackhammer to his torso. It took a moment for the pain to come.

With the pain, came the phosphor-hot fist of anger. The

feel of blood on skin was icy compared to the fire inside him.

Jimmy blinked away the dazzle of the muzzle flash and looked up into the eyes of the gunman. The man's eyes were wide, staring. The voice that came from Jimmy's mouth was barely recognizable as human.

"You're pissing me off, Pedro."

The man leveled the gun at Jimmy's abdomen. Jimmy looked down at the barrel of the weapon. The two of them were so close that the silencer was shiny with Jimmy's blood. As Jimmy watched, the blood foamed and the surface underneath eroded.

The Jimmything looked up into the man's panicked eyes and said, *"You don't want to do that again."*

Pedro didn't take advice well. He fired again. This time the flash was a lot bigger. Fire and smoke erupted from the weapon in an explosion that the silencer couldn't muffle. Jimmy felt the wash of fire rolling across his stomach, and the bite of shrapnel fragments tearing into his skin as the gun blew apart.

The gunman collapsed backward into the front of the ambulance and the air filled with the sound of screeching brakes. Jimmy was thrown forward as they screeched to a stop. He fell across the gunman between the two front seats.

Something had torn free from inside Jimmy. Burned away, leaked out the holes in his body, leaving nothing but a hungry black hole. His body felt so much like an empty shell that he was surprised that when he fell, the surface of the gunman's flesh was what gave way.

Jimmy had put up his hands to break his fall, landing on the chest of the gunman. The gunman's clothing tore like paper and his flesh offered no resistance. Skin and muscle parted around Jimmy's blood-covered hands as if made of so much lumpy Jell-O. Jimmy's hands slid through the flesh and pushed through the man's ribs.

The gunman tried to scream.

So did Jimmy.

Blood foamed around Jimmy's wrists where they entered twin wounds below the gunman's pectorals. Blood flowed across the gunman's flesh, independent of gravity. Trails of red rolled up the man's neck. The man arched his back and flailed.

Jimmy was barely aware of hands grabbing at his shoulders, trying to pull him away from the flopping body underneath him. Voices on either side of him were shouting, but Jimmy could only look at the man beneath him. The man's breath was coming only in spasmodic rattles. It was hard to see with the man's head whipping back and forth, but Jimmy thought that when the blood pooled into the eyes, they collapsed back into the skull, leaving empty holes.

The emptiness, the hunger, inside Jimmy ebbed as the gunman stopped moving and slowly shrank into himself.

Someone grabbed at the neck brace, and it snapped apart, dropping pieces on the corpse below him.

Jimmy pushed himself upright, his hands sliding out of the empty skin of the dead gunman. They came out bloodless and clean. He looked at the driver and the guy riding shotgun and said, quietly, "This isn't good . . ."

39

NATE'S mind spun with all the possible ramifications of what Agent Boyden was telling him. When their meeting was interrupted by Sullivan again, it gave Nate a chance to try and make some sense of it all.

Aliens?

He stared into his now empty glass and tried to get his mind around the thought.

Could someone from light-years away manufacture a means to duplicate human beings to spy on us? Engineer a viral intelligence that could infect someone at birth, take over all the functions of the body . . .

If that was happening, who was it inside their skulls?

The mind that walked out under the night sky to vanish in a flash of light—was it the human child?

Was it some alien computer program?

Did the question even make sense?

And why was James Somerset still alive? What was it that had granted him immunity? He could almost see how Boyden's mind worked. First you have the wave of reconnaissance, then you have the first step of the invasion . . .

Did that make sense. Why bother launching an attack on a place you would never be able to personally interact with? What would the point be? Not to mention, James Somerset wouldn't be anyone's first choice for the vanguard of an invasion force . . .

Even if they wanted to take us over. They already had the perfect means to do so. Why commit any overt acts when you can simply infect people with millions of these microscopic alien machines?

No.

Nate had looked deeply into this kid's history. Whether or not he was infected with, or as Boyden implied, in some sense *created* by these machines, James Somerset was anything but alien. He was, in fact, behaving in an all too human manner. He had been boxed into a foster care system that probably did as much to create his problems as to treat them. The kid had one legitimate avenue of escape, and the powers that be punished him for it.

From what Nate had heard during his interview, he felt little pity for Frank.

Nate swirled the ice in his glass and wondered . . .

Alien machines. Alien computers.

James' body was being repaired by these things. Twice now they had reconstructed his body after near-fatal burns. That fit in with the other kids, none ever had any serious physical illness or injury requiring hospitalization. These things acted like God's own antibodies, protecting against *everything*.

But none of those kids had suffered as grave damage as Jimmy had in infancy. Could this colony of alien creatures—which in a sense *was* Jimmy—could they suffer through something like that with no cost to themselves?

How would the programming in such a beast work?

It had millions of elements, but each so small that they couldn't carry very elaborate code. DNA could be considered a chemical computer program, but it wasn't intelligent, it didn't make decisions. To Nate's mind, any expert software would have to be distributed among the colony that formed the probe. That formed Jimmy. A micro-network of a million of these things would still be microscopic . . .

How much stress could that network handle before something critical broke down?

What if, in that house fire that should have killed the infant James Somerset, the damage was so severe that in the effort to repair the damage, these viral machines lost portions of their programming?

Like the portion to call back to the home planet?

"Mr. Adriano," Boyden broke into Nate's train of thought.

"Yes?" Nate looked up from his glass.

Boyden had a tight smile on his lips and he was pulling on his jacket. "If you want to come along, we may be able to have you meet James."

Nate stood up. "You found him?"

Boyden shook his head. "The Cleveland police found him. I'll explain on the way."

"He killed someone?" Nate asked.

The sedan drove through traffic, toward the highway. The man at the wheel looked to be the spiritual twin of the men who had guarded his room. He wore a charcoal-gray suit so dark it was almost black and didn't say a word.

Boyden glanced over his shoulder at Nate. "The police responded to an assault charge on the near West Side of the city. The victim's name was Quincy Robb. The suspect caught leaving the scene was identified as James Somerset."

"What did he do?"

"We're still collating details. From what we have, James

is en route to the Justice Center. We've prepped a federal warrant to take him into custody once he shows up."

"You can do that?"

"Suspicion of espionage and terrorist acts."

Nate shook his head. "If you're trying to scare me with government power, you're succeeding."

"Everything we're doing is legal, Mr. Adriano."

Nate leaned back in the seat. "That's the scary part, Mr. Boyden."

An electronic beeping interrupted Boyden. Agent Boyden pulled a cell phone from his jacket pocket, checked the display, and held it up to his ear. "The air's clear, go ahead . . . What? . . . Where? . . . Do we have a team there? . . . Well get one in place . . . I don't care if you have to land a helicopter on the highway!" Boyden snapped the phone shut. "This whole situation is going from bad to worse." He turned to the driver. "Stay on ninety westbound, you should see where we need to stop. It will be the site of the major screwup."

"What happened?"

"The cop shepherding our boy spun his car into a head-on collision with a city bus."

"Was anyone hurt?"

Boyden shook his head. "We just got this info. We're trying to get a team there right now. God only knows what the situation is on the ground there." He looked at the driver. "It happened at our exit, so we should be coming up on it in a few minutes."

In the eastbound lane, Nate saw a set of red flashers closing fast.

Boyden stared at the oncoming ambulance and pulled out the cell phone again. He punched a two-digit code and put it up to his ear. "It's Boyden . . . Where are they taking the injured from the accident . . . You have five seconds . . ."

There was a long pause as the sirens closed and the ambulance screamed by them.

"East or west of the accident scene?"

Another pause, shorter this time.

"Okay, then . . . I have an ambulance eastbound on ninety . . . *Yes, right now!* Can we intercept it?" Boyden shook his head and looked at the driver. "Follow that ambulance, now!"

Tires squealed as the sedan cut a U-turn across three lanes of traffic. Headlights shot by them to the blare of horns as the driver brought the sedan over to the breakdown lane, gong in the wrong direction.

Boyden called over the seat at Nate, "Put your seat belt on."

The sedan accelerated crazily, making Nate's stomach lurch. Worse were the headlights racing toward them on the wrong side of the vehicle. "Are you crazy?"

"There's a chance that James Somerset is in that ambulance!" Boyden started shouting landmarks and instructions into his cell phone while Nate concentrated on hanging on for dear life. Horns blared by them, and, in the distance, the siren of the ambulance.

Nate was so captivated in straining to look for the flashers that he didn't see the hazards until the sedan was already swerving. If Nate had been driving, they would have plowed head-on into a PT Cruiser that faced them in the breakdown lane. The driver took the sedan out into the oncoming lanes without slowing, passing two lanes over to give clearance to the man changing his tire.

A Jetta shot through the gap between them and the Cruiser, so close that Nate thought he felt the fenders kiss.

For a terrifying moment they faced the headlights of a tractor-trailer rig, then they swerved back into the breakdown lane.

Nate had been hyperventilating for several moments before he realized that they were slowing down. He opened his eyes, not quite remembering when he had squeezed them shut.

In the eastbound lane, the flashers were much closer. Nate could hear the siren, and was stymied for a moment because he didn't know why it sounded odd.

Then he realized, it sounded odd because the ambulance wasn't moving. Without the Doppler effect, the siren was a continuous whoop unchanging in volume or pitch.

The sedan rolled to a stop in the westbound lane opposite the stalled ambulance. Boyden was out the door before the car had stopped. Without instructions to the contrary, Nate did likewise.

Even this late at night, the freeway was busy. Nate thought it would be insane to cross. Boyden didn't seem to share his opinion. The man ran out into a gap in the traffic, stopping halfway to let horn-blaring traffic pass, then continuing to the concrete median.

Nate hesitated, until the driver followed Boyden. Nate followed the driver, somehow taking comfort in the fact that if he got hit, they both would. Even so, he almost froze in panic as another tractor-trailer rig shot by in a lane three feet from them, blaring its horn at them.

Nate slammed into the concrete median, and wasn't comforted by the gouges that uncoordinated drivers had left there.

"Are you crazy?" he shouted at Boyden.

Boyden wasn't paying attention to Nate. He was shouting on his cell phone to be heard over the traffic and the sirens.

He was describing the ambulance. Nate pulled himself up to look at the scene from over the median.

"Oh, lord."

The ambulance had driven diagonally into the breakdown lane, nosing into the guardrail. The rear doors had been shot at, apparently from inside. One window was starred and opaque. The other appeared splattered with blood from the inside. Nate could see flashes from inside, and hear what could have been more gunshots over the sound of the sirens.

As he watched, the driver's side window shattered. Cubic safety glass erupted in a cloud, the fragments cutting ruby sparkles out of the flashing lights. Out the hole where the window was came something the size and shape of a human body. It didn't move like a body. It flew, almost weightless, through the window, as if it was made of paper. It tumbled on the ground, boneless. The skin was horrid, tight, dry, and leathery, the face an eyeless, skull-faced mummy.

It wore the bloodstained windbreaker of an EMT, and in its hand it held an automatic pistol.

The driver's side door flew open.

Boyden's driver had a gun out and had it braced with both hands on top of the concrete barrier. Nate looked at the man and all he could think was, *That thing on the ground had a gun, too.*

He turned back to face the ambulance and, as promised, got to see James Somerset.

He wasn't very tall and had no hair to speak of. His build was slight, almost effeminate. He was completely naked, and covered in a webwork of blood. It rolled and pulsed across him, as if a second set of veins ran across the outside of his skin.

Jimmy's hands balled into fists and he turned to face

them across the highway. For a moment, his eyes locked with Nate's. He wore an expression of inhuman fury, the mouth contorted into a rictus grin, the brows creased, the eyes almost stone-black pits.

Almost.

In those eyes, Nate saw something profound. Something he felt himself.

Fear.

Not just fear. It was a deep profound consuming terror that was as strong, if not stronger than the anger.

He's not in control, and he knows *he's not in control . . .*

Above them, the sound of a helicopter began to overwhelm the siren. A spotlight cut down to pinpoint Jimmy in the breakdown lane. He looked up and laughed.

Then he turned around and vaulted over the guardrail.

Interlude Four: SLAUGHTER OF THE INNOCENTS

PAGE 17: [SPLASH PAGE]

Panel 1: INT. CLASSROOM EUCLID HTS. HIGH SCHOOL
We look at Cain from the original corner of the classroom. The heads of all the mutilated eyeless corpses have turned to face Cain. Something has possessed them, and the bodies now look less human, the faces more skeletal, the hands more clawlike. Cain is bent over at the entrance to the classroom holding his staff, still recovering from the massive wounds the teacher-thing inflicted.

SFX

(weaving across the top in gore-stained letters)

HAHAHAHAHAHAHAHAHAHAHAHAH . . .

CAPTION

"Of course, there's a first time for everything."

PAGE 18: [SIX PANELS]

Panel 1: CLOSE UP OF CAIN'S EYE
We can see the reflection of one of the corpses' faces in the pupil, and a few beads of sweat on Cain's brow.

BAPHOMET

(Along bottom of panel)

"You are an amusing diversion . . ."

Panel 2: CLOSE-UP OF CORPSE'S ARM
A hand that has become a taloned claw tears away the cord that binds it in place.

SFX

. . . snap . . .

BAPHOMET

(Along bottom of panel)

". . . I think, however, the time for games is over."

Panel 3: CLOSE-UP OF CAIN'S ABDOMEN
Cain's hand is black with blood as he attempts to hold in the parts of his body that the teacher-thing had torn free. His clothing is little more than loose rags draped over his body now.

BAPHOMET

(Along bottom of panel)

"The nameless one may have given you the dubious curse . . ."

Panel 4: CLOSE-UP OF A CORPSE'S NECK
The talon-hand pulls away the cord binding the neck, revealing deep ligature marks and skin that's already pockmarked by rot.

SFX

. . . snap . . .

BAPHOMET

(Along bottom of panel)

". . . of an undying existence . . ."

Panel 5: CLOSE-UP OF LEFT SIDE OF CAIN'S FACE
Cain is biting his lip, the color is gone from his face, and
he is obviously aware that he's in trouble.

BAPHOMET

(Along bottom of panel)

". . . but I doubt He cares . . ."

**Panel 6: LONG SHOT OF CLASSROOM CENTERED ON
CAIN**
All the corpses are standing now, zombie-things with
twisted postures and rotting flesh. They all face Cain,
who holds the staff in front of him.

BAPHOMET

(Along the bottom of panel)

". . . exactly what form that existence might
take."

PAGE 19: [FOUR PANELS]

Panel 1: VIEW FROM BEHIND DOORWAY
We see Cain, backlit, facing away from us. He stands in
a puddle of his own blood and his shoulders are
hunched as he bears the staff before him with both
hands. The glowing tip of the staff is just visible above
his head.

CAPTION

"I may have had the bad sense to play hero
for the past few years. I may be grasping at
straws of redemption a few millennia too
late . . ."

Panel 2: VIEW FROM BEHIND DOORWAY
Cain has turned on his heels and is running away from
the small zombie army. His tattered trench coat trails
behind him as skeletal arms reach through the doorway
to grab him. He bears the staff as if ready to beat anyone
out of the way with it.

CAPTION

". . . But I've never been accused of being
stupid."

**Panel 3: VIEW FROM INSIDE CLASSROOM, TOWARD
DOOR**
The zombie students are rushing the door, crushing
themselves to make it through. They're an undifferenti-
ated mass of skulls, talons, and rotting flesh.

BAPHOMET

"You are a fool if you think . . ."

**Panel 4: VIEW FACING CAIN AT CORNER OF THE HALL-
WAY**
Cain has stopped in his tracks just as he rounds a corner. He is washed in a glaring white light that casts his
shadow into a black hole across the hallway behind him.

BAPHOMET

". . . that once you attract my attention . . ."

PAGE 20: [SPLASH PAGE]

Panel 1: VIEW FROM BEHIND CAIN
Facing Cain is a solid wall of men in SWAT uniforms, helmets, and gas masks. Dozens of weapons are trained on
him as light from a dozen beams are trained on him.

SWAT CAPTAIN

"Drop the weapon, NOW!"

BAPHOMET

". . . you can escape me."

40

JIMMY ran.

The Jimmything ran.

It ran through a panicked nightmare of dark alleys and empty streets. The wind bit its skin, broken glass tore at its naked feet.

His skin.

His feet.

Jimmy didn't know where he was running, or how far he had run. His thoughts couldn't coalesce around where he was. They were all tied up in the back of the ambulance. In the image of bodies shriveling when his hands tore through their flesh.

His body moved like a machine as Jimmy relived four men's deaths. His legs were pistons driving his flesh into broken concrete. His lungs were bellows stoking the burning furnace of his heart. His brain an autopilot that had broken down . . .

Jimmy ran past towers of brick, concrete, and steel. The buildings were becoming older and crumbling as he ran away from the rising moon. He ran through vacant lots where weeds slashed at his naked legs and holes tried to break his ankles. He crossed streets of cracked asphalt filled only with stagnant pools of sodium-yellow light.

The blackness followed him, an invisible shadow that whispered that he was already damned.

He ran through the weeds of a vacant lot bordered on two sides by piles of towering brick and peeling paint, and on the opposite corner the intersection of two main roads. When he passed the center of the lot, a cold white light pinned his shadow twenty feet high on the abandoned warehouse in front of him. Behind him, a police siren let out a single whoop.

Oh, shit, was the first thought Jimmy had that was completely rooted in the present. He didn't stop running.

"Freeze! Stop and turn around." The amplified cop voice was loud and distorted.

Jimmy was almost to the building. His body was moving so hard that he doubted that he could stop if he wanted to. Any thoughts of stopping were met by the lacerating memory of the cop who had been driving . . .

It won't let you capture me.

Jimmy thought he heard a car door slam behind him as he reached the brick. About fifteen feet above him, a vast window hung above the lot. A square lattice that was perhaps only half filled with intact panes of glass.

Without thinking about it, Jimmy aimed at a pile of weed-shot bricks and broken concrete. He took two steps up the small slope, and jumped. Only then did he realize how insane the act was. There was no way he could make a fifteen-foot vertical leap.

The realization lasted only a fraction of a second. Then he slammed into the upper part of the window, smashing free more glass and grabbing madly to hold on to the rusted metal remains of the window. His feet slid on the narrow purchase, on a slick of his own blood. Glass cut into him in a dozen places all over his body, but Jimmy barely acknowledged the pain. What was paramount in his mind was the fact that he had just jumped up about twenty feet. He had even cleared the top of the spotlight.

He turned around to look down, and could see a cop running across the vacant lot toward the warehouse, chasing his own diminishing shadow. The cop was looking upward as he ran, as if he had just realized what Jimmy had done.

Then the spotlight swung up to blind Jimmy.

What the fuck are you doing? Didn't you see what happened back there? Don't you know what you're dealing with?

(. . . like you do? . . .)

Next to him on the huge window, was a five-or-six-foot-square section that opened, hinged out from the top. Jimmy reached for it, and found it frozen in place.

He pulled.

There was the sound of straining metal and breaking glass, a loud snap, and suddenly the structure of the inset window frame wasn't capable of bearing its own weight. It began twisting and bending, attached only by the corner nearest Jimmy.

Jimmy let go and pulled himself as close to the window as possible. Next to him, a hundred pounds of rusted metal swung toward him and folded down. It slammed against the rest of the window frame, shattering free what glass was left, and hung there.

"Holy shit," Jimmy said. He stared at the window, not quite believing what he saw. He had torn the thing free with one hand. He had fallen into some twisted version of the Marvel Comics universe, playing the role of some forgotten Spider-Man clone.

"Freeze," called the cop again from somewhere below.

Jimmy crawled over the metal lattice of the broken window and jumped through the gap he had pulled open. He heard the cop cursing behind him.

Jimmy fell down into the shadows of the warehouse, losing the spotlight in the musty air near the ceiling. He fell wrong on the concrete floor, his left shoulder taking the brunt of the impact. Jimmy could almost hear the muscles and tendons tear apart as the joint ground into the floor.

Delirious from the pain, Jimmy rolled on his back and started laughing. He clutched his shoulder and shouted at the shadows the spotlight cast above him. "Some fucking superhero! Captain-fucking-Shithead. Stupidity Man and his sidekick Kid Injury." He grabbed his wounded arm and the bone didn't feel right, the hard parts floating separate, grinding together with flashes of agonizing pain. *"SHIT!"*

Jimmy closed watering eyes as he heard sirens in the distance.

(. . . Come on, you bastard, you took worse and came out of it . . . You were shot, several times, what, twenty minutes ago? . . .)

"God." Jimmy sat up, clutching his shoulder. The wounded area had become very hot. The bone fragments no longer floated free under the pressure of his hand. They now felt as if they moved independently. The fingers on his left hand were twitching. A horrible itch had started in his shoulder.

Jimmy slowly staggered to his feet.

Something was moving inside him, in his shoulder. He could feel bones shifting, muscles and sinew twisting under the skin. He backed to the wall under the window he had leaped through.

Above him, the spotlight moved away. The sirens were getting closer.

His shoulder stopped hurting.

Am I going insane?

(... what do you mean 'going?' The train left weeks ago, my friend ...)

Jimmy lowered his hand from the shoulder and moved his left arm. It moved freely, no sign of the shattering impact against the concrete. Nothing but a residual ache.

Jimmy shook his head and felt down the length of his body. He knew he had racked up his share of cuts and bruises in the run from the ambulance. Not to mention gunshot wounds.

Nothing was beneath the gore that covered most of his body, nothing but intact skin. Even his naked feet, which had been sliding on slicks of his own blood, were intact.

Jimmy saw the beam of a flashlight cut through the darkness to his left. He ran toward a lumpy shadow between him and the intruder. Glancing at the ceiling, he could see a kaleidoscope of shadows cut by flashing red lights on the other side of the windows.

Cops, cops, and more cops.

The flashlight beam was joined by another, and another ... Jimmy heard the sounds of footsteps closing from every direction. His backside pressed against the metallic thing that gave him cover.

There was only one escape open. Jimmy turned around and started climbing. He pulled himself up the mostly unseen hunk of machinery that blocked him from the cops. He felt metal under his hands and feet. He felt levers, screws, dials all frozen with rust and age. The metal casings rattled under his feet, but he didn't care about being stealthy. All he cared about was getting away as quickly as possible.

The feeling he got from the machinery was strange, though he barely noticed in his rush to escape. When he grabbed for a handhold, his hands would slide for a fraction of an inch, as if everything was covered with a thin sheet of oil. He got the feeling even though the roughness of the metal told him it was a solid block of rust, long removed from any lubrication. His hands and feet would slide a moment, then they would hold fast, the slickness suddenly gone as he found a purchase that was so solid it was almost a fusion of hand to metal. The sense was so strong that he felt surprise that he could pull his skin away from it.

It reminded him of the soda can with his fingerprints etched in the surface.

Flashlight beams cut the air around him as he reached the top of the ancient machine. There was nowhere left to climb to. He stood there, naked, grimy, and gore covered. He was breathing hard, and his muscles trembled as if high voltage electricity was being run through them.

The flashlight beams converged on him, slicing his body out of the darkness. Jimmy looked down at himself. Dirt, oil, blood, and sweat swirled across his limbs and torso like a drunken attempt at urban camouflage.

"Hold on! Don't move."

Jimmy couldn't see the cop who spoke. The face was invisible behind the glare of a flashlight.

"Don't panic. I don't think any of us want you to hurt yourself—"

Jimmy laughed. He couldn't keep from laughing. "You don't know fuck who you're dealing with."

"Calm down—"

"Look at me!" Jimmy screamed at them. *"The bastard won't let me die!"*

"Who? Just talk to me, maybe we can help you."

Jimmy shook his head and looked up. There was a catwalk hanging precariously above him, caught in a flashlight beam that cut past him. He had cleared the distance to the

window, why the hell not? He didn't have anything to lose.
He called down to the cops, *"You hear about the finger of
God? He's giving it to you right now!"*

Jimmy crouched and jumped toward the catwalk.

His legs unfolded with the force of a steel cable snapping
underneath him. His body hurtled through the air, above the
cops, twenty, thirty feet up.

The flashlights tracked him, one scoring a direct hit on
Jimmy's face. Dazzled, Jimmy slammed into something that
folded and gave under the impact, filling the warehouse with
the echoes of abused metal.

Jimmy grabbed out without seeing, and his right hand
grasped a metal strut that tried to cut into his palm. He fell,
dangling from the one piece of metal, his shoulders slamming into the structure of the catwalk.

When the catwalk felt his full weight, something gave
above him, and everything dropped three feet down, stopping with a jerk that almost pulled his arm out of its socket.

Jimmy dangled, blinking. He shook his head and swung
himself around so he could grab the badly canted catwalk
with his other hand. He pulled himself through the bent railing where he had hit the thing and lifted himself onto the
walkway.

Once on the catwalk, he rolled onto his back. The thing
still moved gently from side to side a little too easily, and
ominous groans and creaks emerged from the metal and
from the ceiling above him.

He laughed again. He was a fucking superhero.

(*. . . Or super villain, can be hard to tell sometimes, can't
it? . . .*)

Super-*something* anyway.

He pulled himself to his feet, ignoring the sway of the
catwalk and the creaks and pops that came from above him.

He was still lit by flashlight beams coming from the floor about forty or fifty feet beneath him.

He gave the cops a mock salute and said, *"Cain sends his regards, folks. Sorry we can't stay . . ."* Jimmy turned and ran down the catwalk.

Not out of the woods yet . . .

The thought was something of an understatement. He stood on the roof of the warehouse, by the edge next to the skeletal remains of a water tower that offered some cover. Below him, police cars, flashers going, ringed the building.

There was the sound of helicopters closing on him.

"Where to now, genius?"

Jimmy shook his head. The cops had lost track of him for the moment, but it was only a matter of time before some cops popped up on the roof, or a helicopter shone a spotlight down on him like something out of Los Angeles.

If they did?

If they leveled guns on him—there would be a repeat of what had happened in the ambulance. Jimmy felt it in his gut.

The thinking part of his brain knew that he should give up, he was out of places to run. But there was something else in him, something that had always been there, something in as much control as he was.

Whatever had built up inside him wouldn't let them take him . . .

(. . . you won't let them take you . . .)

If he let the cops corner him, he wouldn't be in control anymore. That no longer meant punching out some jock. It meant someone would die.

"Fuck it," Jimmy whispered.

He had gone insane, no doubt about it. He was stark

naked on top of some abandoned building like some cut-rate
King Kong. Whose idiotic idea was it to run on to the roof?

He looked up at the sky, a swirling blackness above him.
There was a painfully close feeling that he could jump into
it and escape. If he just leaped hard enough, he would never
come down, fly to something else. Something better. Something—

"Okay, that's the crazy half talking," Jimmy tore himself
back to the here and now and looked around for some more
reasonable means of escape. The helicopter was almost on
top of him.

He was perched on the corner opposite the side of the
building he'd entered. This corner overlooked an intersection alive with police. *Too many for one naked loon. They
must have heard about me.*

Across one street was another vacant lot, across the other
was a line of shops, two stories tall. Jimmy considered trying to jump it, but he was losing the impulse to push his limits, as expanded as they might be. Besides, that would be a
great way to get the attention of the cops out on the street
waiting for him.

He needed to back out of here *without* any attention.

Jimmy crouched and ran along the edge of the roof, looking down at the cops. Luckily, the ones down there seemed
intent on the ground-level exits. He headed toward the one
side of the building he hadn't seen yet. Two sides were
streets, one was the vacant lot, and the one he approached
overlooked a weed-shot parking lot wrapped by a rusty
chain-link fence. Two cop cars were down there, one had the
doors open, and the other had one guy talking on his radio.

To Jimmy's right was the road, and to his left was another
abandoned warehouse. The end of that building faced a
deeply shadowed loading dock toward the parking lot. In

fact, the only lights down there were the weak sodium glow from a streetlight on the other side of the street, and the spotlights of the two cop cars, both trained on Jimmy's building.

Looking to the left, Jimmy could see only about five feet of shadowed, rubble-filled alley separating the two buildings.

Light swept by the water tower behind him, and Jimmy crouched down. The cops must have figured out where he was. The helicopter was hovering, sweeping a light across the roof. He could feel the wind blowing down from the rotors.

He had just lost his chance to debate things.

Once the spotlight swept by where he crouched, he ran. He stayed bent over as he raced toward the end of the building that was closest to its neighbor.

The building next door was slightly shorter and in worse shape. It was a shell of sooty brick that emitted the odor of fires long past, a brick hole holding broken concrete and ashes.

Let's see if I can be graceful about this . . .

Jimmy ran at the short wall at the edge of the roof and vaulted over it. He timed it almost right. He cleared the wall of his building, and the upper edge of the neighboring building. Unfortunately, he overshot the wall where he was aiming, and his hands grasped empty air.

Fuck.

He fell down into the empty shell about five more feet when he brushed one of the broken concrete supports that had once held up the now missing roof. He grabbed maniacally and managed to catch hold of a twisted piece of rebar that jutted from the edge of the pillar. He held on, and his body slammed into the column.

He hung there, dangling, waiting for a sign that the cops

had seen his less than graceful vault. After five minutes or so, he still hadn't heard or seen anything. The helicopter stayed over the other building, doing lazy circles and sweeping its spotlight back and forth.

He looked up and saw other lights playing across the roof he had just vacated. He got purchase with his feet, and climbed halfway around the pillar, to put it between him and the warehouse next door.

He did so just in time. A flashlight beam shot by him to probe into the wreckage at the base of this building. He heard distorted radio chatter as more beams pierced the darkness around him. He hugged the concrete pylon, doing his best to merge into it, to become just another item of rubble.

Jimmy waited for the inevitable.

The inevitable didn't come.

Hours later, after the cops were gone, and the helicopter had retreated, Jimmy slowly climbed down, away from the lightening sky.

41

THEY had closed off the freeway for a hundred yards in each direction. The ambulance, lights and siren long muted, was illuminated by a ring of spotlights on tall tripods and surrounded by a high yellow sheet wall. Nate knew that beyond the yellow plastic were cops manning roadblocks on the order of the FBI's special counterterrorism task force, of which Boyden seemed to be an honorary member.

The ambulance itself was surrounded by men in yellow containment suits, faces hidden behind respirators. They were taking samples and scrapings, pointing digital cameras at everything, and loading the remains of the ambulance crew into bright red rubber bags.

Even across eight lanes of highway, inside Boyden's sedan, Nate felt very nervous being here. Even without any biological threat, the sheet wall was guarded by enough military types with assault rifles to justify any feelings of unease. The guards stood in a ring about three feet inside the yellow sheet wall, facing outward. There were about twenty of them.

Unlike the men who had grabbed Nate from his hotel room, these guys wore Marine Corps uniforms and were dressed in full combat gear.

It was a damn good thing they got here first. Nate wouldn't want to try to get in here after the fact.

The westbound lanes of the highway, opposite the ambulance, had become an impromptu parking lot. Ahead of the sedan was an unmarked white panel truck, behind it a pair of troop-carrying Hummers with Marine markings.

Boyden had abandoned Nate to go inside the rear of a tractor-trailer rig that seemed to be a portable command center. Nate didn't seem to rate much attention at the moment. Nate sat there a long time waiting for Boyden to return before he let himself out of the car and started wandering around.

The scene was chaotic, with people in a desperate hurry running around from vehicle to vehicle, talking on cell phones, typing on laptops. No one paid him any attention as he walked around the area. Too caught up in their own jobs, whatever they were.

Nate walked toward the trailer/command station where Boyden had disappeared. He glanced inside the rear and saw a press of people crowding over long rows of communication equipment. It looked as if there were three or four teleconferences running in there at once.

On a table, slightly removed from the trailer, Nate was surprised to see a small router sitting on the ground. An optical cable snaked from it, back to the trailer, while a rat's nest of cables sprouted from it to run off a pair of long folding tables.

They have their own little network running here.

The tables supported a few dozen laptops, most plugged into one of the many small hubs scattered on the tables. Several people were hard at work, bent over their keyboards, but several of the laptops had been left unattended.

Nate walked up to one and looked at the unassuming desktop. The only signs showing the nature of the machine were a handful of icons that sported logos of various federal agencies.

Nate chuckled. People who worked at the CIA could be as careless about computer security as anyone else he had ever seen. Back when he worked for the LAPD, he could remember all the e-mails the IT department sent out about network security, and to never leave your machine running logged on and unattended . . .

Might as well make myself useful.

Nate shrugged and started typing. He opened a telnet session and found a pipe to the outside. The bastards had to have a satellite uplink in that truck. In a moment he had several on-line databases open. Some he used all the time, some he never would have had access to if it wasn't for the security lapse of this computer's owner.

Fifteen minutes later, he felt a hand on his shoulder.

"Exactly what do you think you're doing?"

Nate turned around and saw Agent Boyden, and he didn't look too happy. "You said you wanted to hire me, right?"

Boyden stared at him.

"If that's the case, then I'm doing my job."

Nate was hustled by two Marines off to one corner of the site, beside the plastic barrier, where they were a little less conspicuous. While they held his arms, Boyden fumed at him. "Convince me not to bury you."

"I thought you wanted my help."

"Not as some juvenile hacker. I don't need—"

Nate shook his head. "Do you know why Jimmy targeted Quincy Robb?"

"What?"

"Do you know why Jimmy Somerset broke into that particular house and caved in the skull of that particular person?"

Boyden paced in front of Nate and shook his head. "Forgive me if that wasn't high on the priority list. We have this thing, this infection, loose out there and little clue how to stop it."

"Last year Mr. Robb was arrested and put on trial for sexual molestation of his children. He was acquitted, but his kids were placed in the custody of the county. Do you know where they ended up?"

Boyden stopped pacing.

"It isn't a *thing*, there's a seventeen-year-old kid inside that skull. Whatever is happening to him doesn't—"

"You found that out how?"

"Robb's name, news databases, birth records, and a couple of federal archives that were left open on that machine."

Boyden waved off the Marines, and the men flanking Nate let go of him. "No more unauthorized access of anything, understand?"

"Yes." Nate rubbed his arms. "He's looking for justice."

"What?"

"I've talked to enough people about this kid. Mr. Robb wasn't an accident, or some alien impulse. This kid is trying, in some twisted way, to turn himself into a superhero."

"You've got to be joking."

"Do you even know why he was placed in Trinity House?"

"I've read his dossier, he pled guilty to aggravated menacing, and there was an assault on a fellow student."

"He wrote a comic book, Agent Boyden."

"A comic book?"

"A comic book."

42

SHORTLY before dawn broke completely, Jimmy added breaking and entering to his list of sins.

Though that isn't on the list of commandments, is it? There was "thou shall not kill," "thou shall not commit adultery," "thou shall not bear false witness—" None said, "thou shall not break into a crappy-ass Salvation Army thrift store . . ."

Of course, once he got cleaned off, he was going to break that pesky one about theft.

Jimmy did his best to wash himself up in a janitor's closet. The room was little more than a yard square, lit by a dangling yellow bulb. The plaster walls and linoleum floor were peeling, and black shotgun patterns of mildew centered on the deep sink that filled half the space not taken up by mops and buckets.

He was still buck naked, and this was the first time he had got a good look at the crap that had adhered to his skin. He was covered by several flavors of blood, varying from the consistency of dried paint to lumps that resembled fresh tar. Then there was dust, grass, grease, oil, and sweat. To get it all off, he resorted to some sort of Lysol floor cleaner and a stiff-bristled brush that sat on one of the mildew-spotted shelves.

He scrubbed viciously at the crap on his skin, on his face, on his hair. For twenty minutes he attacked himself, brushing until the blood on his skin was fresh and red and beading from raw pink flesh.

It didn't all wash off.

Strange patterns were etched in the skin of his left shoulder, his chest, and his abdomen. Marbled veins ranging in color from gunmetal gray to burnished chrome seemed to trace spider-fine patterns just underneath the skin. It was as if some metallic net had been glued to his body, but he couldn't feel it with his fingers and he couldn't scrub it off.

In fact, when he tried, brushing the affected skin until it bled, afterward the patterns seemed more pronounced, thicker, and darker.

Jimmy stopped scrubbing and threw the brush into the sink.

"Not now, other problems."

The first one of which was to get dressed and get the hell out of there before anybody showed up and found him.

Jimmy walked out of the busted rear door of the Salvation Army wearing a blue-denim button-down shirt, a pair of jeans, and a worn pair of oil-stained metal-toed work boots. He had also managed to uncover a black trench coat and a pair of sunglasses. Jimmy hoped that his face didn't show how nasty it felt to wear used clothes.

He wasn't lucky enough to find any money in the Salvation Army store, so he had to walk to his destination. It gave him time to think, though the thoughts were generally unhelpful.

Something's gone way wrong with you. What's happening just ain't normal . . .

(. . . Like you've ever been normal . . .)

Occasionally, Jimmy would stop and place his hand on a telephone pole, or a fire hydrant. He could feel the slickness under his skin, then a feeling as if the metal or wood adhered to the skin. If he did it for a long time, he could taste the metal. When he pulled his hand away, the metal was etched.

(. . . you remember, when your hand was inside them . . .)

Stop thinking like that.

(. . . you could taste them, too . . .)

Stop . . .

(. . . don't you wonder why you aren't hungry? . . .)

"What am I that this is happening?" Jimmy whispered, shaking away the thoughts.

(. . . you're an instrument . . .)

"What?" Jimmy looks up and the world has become blurry, washed out.

"We are an instrument. A device for justice."

Cain walks out of a shadowed doorway. His coat is tattered darkness. This time, though, his face is visible, bone white, like the out of focus sky. He holds his staff and looks at Jimmy. His face is motionless as a corpse, eyes hidden behind mirrored sunglasses.

"What the fuck is this?" Jimmy shouts at Cain. "I created you!"

"We created each other."

"You don't belong here. You're a character in a comic book. This is not reality."

"Is this real?"

Cain swings his staff to point at a building across the street from them. The dirty brick pile housing the offices of Child and Family Protective Services.

"What do you want?"

"Purpose."

One part of Jimmy walks toward the building obliquely.

Somehow another part of him is here with Cain. Jimmy knows the place too well. He doesn't go in the front door; there are cops sitting down there.

He looks at Cain, who is staring at him as he stations himself across the street from a side entrance just off of the parking lot.

"What is here?" Jimmy asks.

"Your nemesis. The man who betrayed you."

"What is it you want?"

"What is it you want?"

Jimmy watched from across the street, mentally timing people from their cars to the door. He watched, and didn't see a security guard on the other side. Everyone just swiped their IDs in front of a panel mounted next to the door.

Closely watching, Jimmy timed the lock. He could just see the LED change from red to green and back. The light stayed green for about five seconds, and that seemed to be just a second longer than it took most people to open the door, walk through, and have the door shut behind them.

He crossed the street and spared one idle glance through the glass door. He saw a camera—which he wasn't going to avoid—and a corridor leading down to where the elevators would be.

It wasn't too late to change his plans. But he wasn't in a questioning frame of mind. He was here now, never mind how. He could *feel* why.

Nemesis. Every good superhero needs one.

He could almost feel Cain pacing him as the adrenaline coursed through him like liquid electricity. He wiped his palms on the outside of the trench coat.

He rounded the block and slowly closed on that side of the building. For a while he loitered on the corner, as if waiting to cross the street. When he caught sight of someone walking from the parking lot, Jimmy started down the side-walk.

The suit had his ID in his hand already. Jimmy was a few steps from the door when the suit turned and swiped his card. The door swung open, and Jimmy took two running steps once he wasn't in sight. His hand grasped the door right before it closed, just a half-second before he heard the ker-chunk of the magnet.

Jimmy did two things that he thought were pretty slick. First, he grabbed the door from the outside and let it *almost* close. Then he made a motion as if trying unsuccessfully to open the door, from the camera it would look as if he had got to the door too late. Then he swiped his other hand over the plate next to the door. There was nothing in his hand besides his sunglasses, but from the camera's point of view it looked the same as any nimrod flashing an ID.

Then he pulled the door open and walked through.

The office belonging to Dr. Schuster, aka the Franken-stein Monster with the cell phone, was up on the fifth floor. Jimmy would have liked to visit Igor, too, but he didn't re-member the lawyer's name, if he ever knew it in the first place.

It was still early, and there wasn't anyone around the of-fice. Jimmy was able to slip out of the elevator unnoticed. There was one bored guard sitting at a desk next to a metal detector. Jimmy made a point of walking up to the guy, through the metal detector, and asking, "Where's the b–bathroom?"

Christ, I sound like I'm panicking.

The cop arched a bored eyebrow at him, "Do you belong here?"

Oh, hell, go with it. You know the damaged goods they see here.

Jimmy screwed up his face and let the stutter become more pronounced. "Y–yes. I h–have a–a–a——" he sucked in a breath. "A Eight–th–th–th——"

"Okay," the cop held up his hand.

Jimmy held up his hand as well, trying to channel all his frustration into his sputtering expression. "Th–thirty ap–p–p–p—"

The cop nodded. "It's okay. The bathroom is down the hall to the right. Afterward, you need to go to the reception area. Do you know where that is?"

"N–n–n–n—"

"From the men's room, come back this way, but turn left. You'll see a waiting area. Tell the receptionist there you have an appointment. They'll call you when they're ready for you."

"Th–thank y—"

"No problem, go take care of your business."

Jimmy nodded and walked past the cop. His heart was racing, and he had to wipe his shaking hands on his coat again. *Did I just do that?* He stumbled down into the men's room, went to the sink and started splashing water on his face.

This is not a good idea . . .

"Stop it," he told his reflection. He couldn't turn back now, as if he could ever turn back.

He took some deep breaths and looked at his reflection. He didn't look all that well. His skin looked gray. When he touched his cheek, he saw that his hand was wrapped in the same metallic webwork that had wrapped his shoulder.

What's happening to me?

Jimmy shook his head and carefully dried himself off. He

looked up at his ashen reflection and told himself, "Time to shit or get off the pot." He replaced his sunglasses and gave himself a skull-like grin. The face in the mirror belonged to Cain.

The offices were mostly empty, but the door to Dr. Schuster's office was open a crack. Jimmy smiled. The guy had his own office. That was a good thing. A little light leaked from the crack.

He walked up to the door and looked around. He was in a short corridor with four offices on one side, and nothing but a fire exit on the opposite wall. The far end of the corridor opened on a cube farm, but no one was in direct sight of him.

Jimmy reached up and knocked on Dr. Schuster's door. From inside, the familiar disinterested voice of the Frankenstein Monster said, "Come in."

Jimmy listened. It sounded like he was alone.

He knocked again.

"I said come in."

Jimmy's smile was frozen. The muscles in his face ached. He raised his hand and slowly knocked again.

"Goddamn it." Inside, Jimmy heard a chair move and footsteps cross the carpet. The door swung open to reveal the social worker who had sold him down the river. "I said come i—"

"Remember me, you spineless scumbag?" Jimmy swung a fist up in a disabling blow to the groin. He didn't put everything he had into the punch, but it still had the doctor stumbling back, bent over, gasping.

Jimmy stepped into the office and slammed the door shut behind him. He grabbed for the doorknob and twisted as hard as he could. There was a snap, the knob spun freely and fell off in his hand.

Jimmy looked at the doctor and said, "God, that felt so good. Maybe we can actually have a conversation without that damn phone in your ear."

Dr. Schuster backed away from him, still doubled over. He was still having trouble gasping for breath. "You— can't—"

Jimmy stepped over to the desk, shoved everything aside, and sat on the space he'd cleared on the desk. "I can't? Several things I can't do. One thing I *can* do is beat that self-righteous skull of yours into a bloody pulp."

"Don't do this. You won't—"

"What I *will* do is gag you with a broken doorknob if you don't shut up." Jimmy looked over the desk. There wasn't much to it—a PC and a pile of file folders. He lifted the one on top and wasn't surprised to see his name on it. "What a fucking coincidence." He bent the file and shoved it into one of the cavernous pockets of his trench coat.

Dr. Schuster straightened and Jimmy could almost see the words, "You can't do that—" play across his lips. However, the man could take instruction, and he didn't actually open his mouth.

"You quivering little prick," Jimmy's hand tightened on the doorknob. "You want to know what I wanted to do with you? You sold me out."

"I didn't."

Jimmy, or the Jimmything, backhanded him with the hand holding the doorknob. Dr. Schuster's head snapped to the right, and his body slammed into the drywall, leaving a small bloody mark where his face had hit. "You want aggravated menacing. How about assault?"

"Kept you out of the system," Dr. Schuster muttered through swollen lips. He didn't look completely conscious.

"It was a fucking comic book! It wasn't real! You let them railroad me!"

The anger had taken over. Jimmy reached down to wrap his hands around Dr. Schuster's neck, when the cell phone rang.

It was enough of a distraction that Jimmy had time to think.

What am I doing?

Jimmy stood up, dazed.

The phone rang again.

Jimmy saw it, buried in the pile of papers on Dr. Schuster's desk. Without thinking about it, he reached over and flipped the thing open. "Dr. Schuster's office," he said flatly.

"Hello, I've been trying to reach you for some time." A woman's voice.

"Yes?" Jimmy looked down at Dr. Schuster and wondered exactly how it was he had come here.

"My name is Abby Springfield. And I'm doing a story about James Somerset."

"You are?" Jimmy smiled. "Maybe I can help you."

43

NATE climbs the abandoned radio tower. He doesn't remember how he got here. Around him a fierce wind tears at him, driving icy rain into his skin. The metal ladder he climbs is cold and bites into his hands. Above him, on the broken transmitter, shadowed forms are draped over the supports.

He pulls himself up, closing on the platform. Lightning flashes, carving the charred corpses free from the shadows. Dozens, if not hundreds of bodies . . .

He reaches the platform and finds himself in the eye of the storm. Clouds and rain whip around his perch, lightning crashes across fragments of sky, but above his head, the stars are clear.

"Why?"

"Why not?" says a voice from his past.

Nate turns around and sees Deborah. He isn't as surprised as he should be. "All I wanted . . ." he trails off.

"Knowing doesn't help."

"I don't know anything."

"You know." She really doesn't look anything like Abby. The face is different—the expression firmer and yet more open. Her eyes don't conceal anything, and right now the *expression is terribly sad. "You know what happened to me."*

"No . . ." Nate turns away and walks to the nearest corpse and stares into the charred skull.

"Do you think knowing all this would have saved me?"

"I wanted a reason."

"You know the reason."

Nate whips around and grabs for her. "Damn it. I loved you!" His hands close on empty air.

"I loved you!" he shouts into the swirling wind around him . . .

"Wake up," Boyden shook his shoulder.

Nate opened his eyes and straightened up. Daylight streamed through the windshield, and his neck hurt from the way he had slept in the back seat of the car.

"I brought you some coffee." Boyden passed a steaming Styrofoam cup over the back seat to him. Nate cupped his hands around it, trying to feel the warmth. He looked out the window and saw that the scene around the ambulance was breaking up. Most of the vehicles were gone. Except where they were pulling the ambulance on to a flatbed truck, almost everyone was gone.

Nate sipped the coffee. The hot liquid hit his stomach and tied it into a knot. He really needed to eat something.

"What's the verdict?" he asked Boyden.

Boyden laughed, though there was little humor in it. "Well, my boss isn't begrudging me any resources anymore." He looked over to the ambulance. "We've had forensic and scientific teams combing over both sites, here and the accident—which doesn't look like an accident."

"What do you mean?"

"The cop who drove his car into the bus, he wasn't in any

better shape than our medics over there. Nothing left to the body but some hard structure and some connective tissue. Bone and skin. Bloodless, empty mummies. The thing riding on board Mr. Somerset has gone beyond helping him heal."

A new driver opened the door and slipped into the driver's seat, slamming the door behind him.

"How?" Nate asked. "What is it doing?"

"I wish I had a clear answer for you. *I'd* feel better."

"Try an unclear answer."

"You know he was healing way faster, way better, than a human being has a right to? That was the rider, those molecular machines can restructure and rebuild matter a lot faster than the normal healing process. Up until now, though, they rebuilt using the original structure as a model, using the raw material that came in through the normal biological processes . . ."

The driver started the car and began to pull it around in a U-turn to face the right direction on the blocked off highway. They drove at the yellow sheet wall and the one remaining Marine drew the wall aside so they could drive past.

"It requires a lot of energy to drive that body," Nate said. "Eating can't be enough anymore."

"That's right—"

Nate looked into his coffee. "This started before the fire."

"What do you mean?"

"He collapsed during his trial, such as it was. Lack of food. They hospitalized him before they admitted him to Trinity."

Boyden leaned back into the passenger seat. After a long moment he asked, "How long did you spend investigating this kid?"

"Little over a day."

Boyden chuckled.

"It's breaking down, isn't it?" Nate asked.

Boyden looked over the seat at Nate. "What do you mean?"

"You described a computer network, a web of distributed programming that told these things how to behave. The system might be robust, but trauma to James Somerset is trauma to this 'rider.' How much damage can this thing sustain before it loses its higher level programming?"

"Interesting theory . . ."

"Why would he still be alive? According to the pattern, he should have been consumed by a burst transmission three years ago. But he suffered a grievous trauma as an infant. Recovering from that might have cost too much for the 'rider.' After what's happened to James now, the rider may not have anything more than a survival instinct."

Boyden paused for a while. Finally, he said, "This rider is absorbing biological matter, metals, and God knows what else, and *rebuilding* Somerset's body. What's happening goes beyond survival, Mr. Adriano." He shook his head and turned back to face the windshield. "They've spent years gathering intelligence. For whatever reason, they've progressed to the next stage."

Nate started to speak, and stopped himself. Boyden was right. He knew what Boyden was thinking.

Invasion.

People who looked human, but were actually under alien control. An unknown number of sleeper agents waiting to receive transmissions telling them to—

But that's where it all broke down. This wasn't some fifties era black-and-white science fiction film. In the end, what would be the point? Nate still felt that the premise, at its heart, was self-contradictory.

Why war on a territory you could never occupy? An invasion force did not make sense. There was no way that events on this planet could affect anyone living so many light-years away. They could watch, in a sense, reviewing data sent by their probes, but the data they were just now receiving would date from when James Somerset was two years old.

Believing that James Somerset was on some sort of mission would require the belief that his masters fifteen light-years away somehow singled him out and switched him on—when they couldn't possibly know that he existed yet. In fact, they couldn't have any idea of their agents as individuals until after they burned up in their single transmission.

He tried to tell Boyden that, but the agent didn't find Nate's logic compelling.

"You're making assumptions," Boyden said. "Dangerous assumptions."

"Assumptions like?"

"Like the idea we can ascribe 'reasonable' motivations to a culture we have no experience with. We can't predict motives of human beings that live halfway around the world, you think we can do so with creatures that aren't human? For all we know, the deep programming for a campaign against us was laid down decades ago. For all we know, each one of these riders has a trigger that sends it into attack mode. For all we know, Somerset is the first of hundreds, or thousands."

Nate didn't argue the point. After the sedan left the highway and was headed back in the other direction, Nate changed the subject. "Where are we going?"

"Well," Boyden said, "I don't find all your reasoning flawed. The fact that he attacked Quincy Robb is pretty good evidence that James is driving. Since we seem to have lost track of him, I want you to help me come up with a short list for his next target."

Nate arched an eyebrow. "Is that so?"

"If you were going to do that, where would you go?"

"Trinity," Nate answered.

"Well, that's where we're going."

44

JIMMY sat behind the wheel of Dr. Schuster's Volkswagen Jetta, eating his fourth Big Mac. The bastard only had fifteen dollars in his wallet, and Jimmy had spent all of it at a fast-food drive through. He was ravenous. He drove into the eastern suburbs, downing fries and eating burgers.

On the passenger seat next to him was his case file, half-buried in burger wrappers and empty French fry containers. Laying on top of it was Dr. Schuster's cell phone.

How did I do this?

He felt too exposed out on the streets in daylight, so shortly after he'd left Cleveland proper he turned the doctor's car onto the drive of Lakeview Cemetery. He drove around until he found a short road that dead-ended under a canopy of trees. He parked the car facing out at the headstone-dotted hills.

Jimmy wiped his mouth and got out of the car.

Jimmy waited inside the shadows within a mausoleum.

He felt some justified paranoia, waiting to see if Abby, the reporter, showed up alone. He didn't know exactly why he had set up the meeting. Inside his head some sick Lois and Clark imagery danced with more reasonable thoughts about the necessity of making this all public.

Jimmy wasn't sure what "this all" was, exactly. Something about what the fucks at Euclid Heights High School and the county had done to him—

(. . . does that matter anymore? . . .)

Jimmy chuckled. His alleged nemesis, Dr. Schuster, was pretty much the weak sister now, wasn't he? That was a problem, however—

A hero needs a worthy adversary. Batman must have his Joker. Superman must have his Luthor. Cain must have his Baphomet . . .

In front of him, the green brass gate across the doorway was ajar. In a few places the metal reflected the sunlight, where the metal's surface had succumbed to his touch. Jimmy stood, inside the tomb, trying not to think of what was happening inside him, unable to think of anything else.

What's happening to me? What is doing this to me?

(. . . who has done this to you? . . .)

The itching on the surface of the skin was a constant reminder of the metallic webwork that seemed to be eating into his flesh. The skin on both his hands had become grayish, the veins of chrome so fine that they were almost invisible.

When Jimmy wiped off sweat, it tasted odd, coppery. His skin felt hotter than normal, the muscles tighter on the bone. He squatted, staring out into a day that seemed too bright. Even through the sunglasses, the light seemed too white, too hot, the sky the blue of an electric arc, too painful to look at.

As he waited, he ran his fingers across the floor, first drawing figures in the dust, but soon, unconsciously, carving grooves in the marble with his fingertips.

She wasn't late.

Jimmy's sense of time had been sharpening, as were his other senses. He simply *knew* that it was exactly twenty-three minutes after the hour when Abby Springfield walked out into the clearing in front of the mausoleum.

Jimmy stood.

Time to warn the servants of injustice that their time is at an end.

She stood out in the center of the clearing, squinting, looking for him. She did seem to be alone.

Jimmy had chosen this place in Lakeview Cemetery because it was both open and secluded. Where she stood was a flood plain underneath a large concrete flood control dam. They were roughly in the center of Lakeview, but even at midday, this place was empty. There were no graves down here except for a few isolated mausoleums set into the hillside to the right of the dam's glare-white concrete. The clearing was flanked by a wooded hillside with only two roads entering the area, both closed to automobile traffic.

Jimmy should be able to see anyone coming.

He walked out of the mausoleum and shoved his hands in his pockets. He stayed in the shadowed woods by the entrance and waited for the woman to notice him.

"James Somerset?" There was a questioning note to her voice, as if she didn't believe who he was.

"That's my name."

She took a few tentative steps toward him, then stopped. She tried to hide it, but Jimmy could sense fear. Like she was approaching a cornered animal.

"What do you know about me?" Jimmy asked. Her manner annoyed him. He hadn't done shit to her.

"I'm researching a story," she said. "You're connected to a group of other people—at least you seem to be connected. I would like to talk to you about it."

What? Huh?

(. . . she knows something . . .)

"I don't know anything, lady. I got my own questions, though. Like what the fuck is happening to me."

She nodded. "Let's talk, then. I can tell you what I know."

(. . . she knows who did this . . .)

"Tell me. Now." Jimmy took a half step forward.

"An experiment," she said, "a hideous experiment by something called Department Blue. You're the only one we know to have survived."

It was an experiment that got out of hand. They created something that in the end they couldn't control. Eventually the cosmic-mutant-cyborg superman they created turns on its masters.

Jimmy knew the plot well.

"Survive?" he whispered.

"The infection that's in your body has killed dozens, if not hundreds, of people. No one else has lived as long as you. We've been trying to find you—"

Of course, their creation was for evil, and our hero swears to fight his creators, to foil their plans for world domination.

"We?" Jimmy asked.

"Come with me. We can shelter you from the people responsible for—"

This was wrong. She wasn't talking like a reporter. She wasn't acting like a reporter.

Their agents are everywhere, trying to ambush our hero.

"Who the fuck's 'We,' lady? I thought you were a reporter."

"I am."

A shadow moved in the corner of Jimmy's eye. He turned to face it—

"Your government has left you alone with this . . . *thing.*

Come with us and we can help you. This doesn't have to happen to anyone else."

Jimmy took a step, looking at a small shape running across the top edge of the dam. He whipped around and looked at her, the anger building inside him. "You *bitch*. You set me up!"

She's one of them, part of the organization he's fighting.

She shook her head. "Please think—"

"You know what I think?" Jimmy crouched. "I think you guys have no idea what you're dealing with."

He sprang forward. His feet might have touched the ground twice before he grabbed her shoulders. "Call them off, *now!*"

"You don't understand—"

"Call them off!"

She gasped, "I can't."

Jimmy felt the anger building inside him. His hands shook as his grip tightened on her. Her voice seemed far away, "We can help you, Jimmy. I know we can. The US only wants another lab rat—"

"You fuckers want to help me so goddamn much, why the guns?"

"You're hurting me."

"Who the fuck are you people?" Jimmy yelled in her face, shaking her. The anger inside him had reached the boiling point. He could feel something inside him, reaching out to the woman in his grip. In some strange sense he could *feel* some essence, some piece of his internal darkness, seeping from his hands in time to his pulse. He couldn't see it, but it felt as if a shadow twisted out from his fingers, to reach inside her. He felt his darkness twisting around through the fibers of her flesh, cutting pieces free and devouring what it needed.

The sensations were so strange that Jimmy didn't connect them to reality until he saw a red froth bubbling from between his fingers. The woman's eyes had rolled back in her head and she was hyperventilating.

"Fuck!"

He pushed her away, and she stumbled back, falling on the ground, two sickening bloody holes where Jimmy's hands had been. Jimmy looked at his hands in time to see pools of black-red blood pool in his palms, flowing and disappearing into skin too gray, too smooth, and too shiny.

Something slammed into his right shoulder, causing a brief flare of pain. Jimmy took a half step backward, reaching up and looking at his shoulder. A plastic cartridge the size of his thumb jutted from the fold just under the epaulet of the trench coat.

He touched it with his hand, he could feel the needle move inside him. He stared at it for a few moments. "A tranquilizer dart?"

Something happened inside it and the cartridge fell away, showing no sign of the needle. The shadow inside him had absorbed the metal that had injected into him.

Another impact slammed into his thigh.

Jimmy started laughing.

"What the fuck you think you're doing?" he called up at the invisible snipers. *"You bastards shot me! What you think this will do?"*

The cartridge in his leg fell away. Jimmy could feel waves of numbness around the places the darts had hit, but the flesh there had taken on an intense heat, and he knew that whatever he carried inside him was devouring the drugs they'd injected just as it had done to the fake reporter's flesh.

He faced the dam, where the shadow of a sniper was visible on top of the concrete pile. The man calmly reloaded his weapon, and a dart sprouted from Jimmy's abdomen. Jimmy crouched.

You're pissing me off . . .

He crouched. The thought that there might be a limit to his capabilities didn't cross his mind. All he focused on was the asshole pumping these darts into his body.

Tranquilizers? I'll show you tranquil.

Jimmy sprang, running at the face of the dam. He leaped and managed to hit the curved concrete about halfway between the ground and the sniper. He slid down until his hands sank into the concrete, gripping it as if it was a stiff clay.

Without thinking of how he was doing it, Jimmy pulled himself up the smooth face, hand over hand. He felt a final dart slam into his shoulder. Something hit the concrete near him and he felt concrete shrapnel bite into his exposed skin. A moment later, he heard a thumping sound from the distance.

More things, buzzing like angry insects, screamed into the concrete around him. Each one followed by a loud, muffled thump.

The asshole's friends were shooting at Jimmy. They had silencers, too. Fortunately they also had a moving target.

Asshole was in full retreat, but he had started too late. He was only thirty feet away when Jimmy reached the chain-link fence at the top of the dam. At this point he was so focused, he didn't even bother climbing the fence. When he found secure footing, he grabbed it in his suddenly lethal hands and pulled the chain-link apart like it was tissue paper.

He was on top of the dam, and Asshole was only halfway toward the other side. He didn't have much of a chance. He was three quarters of the way there when Jimmy caught up with him. He grabbed the guy's shoulder and spun him around and tackled him, dropping from view of the other snipers.

Jimmy grabbed the guy's neck, but tried to restrain the thing inside him. He wanted this struggling, cursing bastard alive. He tore through this guy's jumpsuit with his free hand until he came up with a fully-charged tranquilizer dart. Jimmy smiled and told him, "Nighty-night," and slammed the dart into the guy's thigh.

Asshole screamed, probably because Jimmy slammed it in so hard that not only the needle, but half the cartridge, plunged into the guy's flesh. In a second or two, the guy's eyes rolled up into his head and he went limp.

However, Asshole kept breathing, so Jimmy dragged the guy after him.

45

DR. Altroy sat behind a desk, showing Boyden a pained expression. Nate sympathized with him. The tension in the room was thick and getting thicker. It wasn't helped by the view out his window, which looked over the remains of the fire. Outside, orange machines were chewing up the remains of the burned-out buildings.

"Dr. Altroy," Boyden said, "do I have to remind you that patient confidentiality does not legally apply if the patient presents a threat to others—"

"You don't need to remind me of the law, Mr. Boyden." He folded his hands. "But I am not about to reveal any confidential information until our lawyer makes it here. I'm not even sure if you qualify as law enforcement personnel in this situation."

"You want a quote from the Homeland Security Act?"

"You're asking too much, Mr. Boyden. James Somerset's background is one thing, but you're asking for details on children here who are no threat to anyone."

"We don't have time for bullshit, Doctor. I have a squad of special forces, a counterterrorism unit, and a division of the National Guard converging on this city. I don't think you have any idea what a threat—"

Nate held up his hand and asked, "Doctor?"

Dr. Altroy turned to face Nate, as if he had just noticed him. Boyden was such an overwhelming presence that might have been the case.

"Mr. . . . ?"

"Adriano."

"What can you add, Mr. Adriano?"

"I understand your reluctance. This is an unusual situation."

Dr. Altroy grunted.

"We're desperate to head off James before he reaches his next victim. There is no indication that he intends to stop or slow down."

"I understand that, but I don't know what—"

"He was dispensing justice, Doctor. He knew Quincy Robb's daughter, didn't he? He had more than enough chance to know what it was Mr. Robb was responsible for."

Dr. Altroy didn't move, but Nate got more than enough confirmation looking into the doctor's eyes.

"James Somerset hasn't gone psychotic in some random manner. He's taken his fixation on superheroes and has begun acting on it. He's dispensing justice in an almost biblical manner."

Dr. Altroy shook his head. "You saw the court records, the pictures?"

Nate nodded.

"You think he's acting it out now?"

"Doesn't it seem that way?"

Dr. Altroy shook his head with a sad chuckle.

"Isn't there anyone else James knows, someone who's committed some injustice—"

"Good lord, Mr. Adriano, do you have any concept of the irony of what you're saying?"

"What do you mean?"

"If there was anything that Jimmy was adamantly passionate about, it was how that work, the comic books he drew, was mere fiction. It was a work of art, and he was prosecuted for it. That was the injustice Jimmy saw when he came here—"

Nate looked at Boyden.

Boyden opened his mouth, closed it, and pulled out his cell phone.

In fifteen minutes Boyden's team found Dr. Schuster, beaten and bloody, in his office at the Department of Children and Family Services building. Unfortunately, the man was comatose and of little use in locating James Somerset.

His cell phone, on the other hand, was new and equipped with FCC-mandated 911 locator hardware. Hardware that Boyden's people were able to activate. That led them to the middle of Lakeview Cemetery where they found the phone, Dr. Schuster's Volkswagen . . .

And Abby Springfield.

They drove to one of the anonymous outbuildings that surrounded The Cleveland Clinic. To look at it, it was still under construction. The building was surrounded by a temporary chain-link fence that announced the new Stemmer Center for Reconstructive Surgery. The courtyard in front of the building was covered in raw earth, pallets of brick pavers, and piles of green PVC pipe. A yellow-orange backhoe was parked in front of what looked to be the main entrance. The parts of the walls that weren't black, plastic-covered windows were faced with yellow sheathing.

The sedan drove around to a street that dead-ended into

the clinic, under a pedestrian bridge that was little more
than a skeletal framework, and stopped in front of a gate in
the chain-link fence. A man in a gray suit, carrying a
walkie-talkie, opened the gate for them.

The car rolled through the gate, over a deeply rutted
mud driveway, and down a concrete ramp set into the base
of the rear of the building.

"What is this?" Nate asked.

"This is our base of operations for the moment," Boyden said. "We need a medical facility to examine James,
and his victims."

Nate looked out the window as they pulled into the
parking garage under the building. The large concrete
space was half filled with construction equipment and materials, half hidden by blue tarps. The other half of the
garage was dominated by a familiar unmarked semi truck
trailer. Nate caught glimpses of men wearing headsets
seated at the workstations lining the walls inside the trailer.

The cars pulled up next to a set of elevator doors set in
the far end of the parking garage.

"We needed to set up an analytical resource as close to
this mess as possible. We commandeered this place. It's almost complete, has power, and has most of the equipment
we needed in place." Boyden got out of the car, and the
driver came around and let Nate out.

The elevator took them up three floors and opened into
a finished reception area that had been retrofitted into a
command center. There were half a dozen guys in the
room; laptop computers and new phones sat on every
available surface. Cables snaked across fresh carpet,
tacked down with duct tape. Two white boards sat on
easels on opposite ends of the waiting room, covered with

cryptic multicolored notations. Half the people here were on the phone, and two thirds were typing at laptops.

When they stepped out of the elevator, a man in slacks and a sweat-stained shirt with one sleeve rolled up higher than the other ran up to Boyden and started talking as if he was already in the middle of a conversation, ". . . we have one resource in the embassy that says that Beijing doesn't have any official—even unofficial—operations going on in regard to this, which doesn't mean anything other than that when we catch up to this, we aren't going to find any hard ties to their intelligence services. The snatch from the accident scene was almost certainly carried out by someone independent of the government—private contractors probably being paid so far under the table that the people passing the money don't have a clue about who's being paid by whom for what."

The man paused for breath and Boyden asked, "The woman?"

"Stable, and lucid. Lost a lot of blood, and a lot of soft tissue damage. Pretty much akin to a really bad chemical burn. We've got blood samples and show heavy contamination, but not critical levels—"

"Are we sure?"

After a moment, "No. We don't really know what critical levels are. They're still working on the bodies from the ambulance in the clean room. They're intact, but we lost the Robb corpse . . ."

Boyden nodded and led Nate away.

"Lost?" Nate asked.

"It combusted."

Nate opened his mouth, but didn't say anything. If nothing else, James was dangerous on that level. If he was

passing on enough of this alien infection-agent-virus to
have people burst into flame . . .

Boyden told Nate, "I want you to talk to her."

That's the last thing I want to do. "Why me?"

"Because she isn't a professional and I'm pressed for
time. You're going to go in there and shake something
loose. I don't particularly care how."

They stopped in front of a ward faced with a huge glass
window. Looking inside, the room was meant to accommodate six beds and the associated medical equipment.
There was only one bed in it right now. The walls were
covered with thick polyurethane sheets, held up with
bright yellow tape. The bed itself was covered with a plastic tent the size of a small car. Abby was just visible behind
the plastic, looking very small.

"What is all this?"

"Precautions. As far as we know, this thing is too complex to transmit easily, and is only transferable by blood
contact. But we cannot make assumptions." He waved
over to a man standing by the door to the ward. "The nurse
will help you suit up."

The man didn't look like a nurse, but Nate followed the
man's instructions as he stepped into a fully contained environment suit. Nate looked at Boyden, but the man was
facing away from him.

Nate could understand the man's fear. He knew just by
watching him that Boyden knew all the safeguards against
contamination were pointless. If it wanted to, the organism
they were fighting could eat through any protective measures they came up with. It made Nate wonder how much
the rest of the people here knew.

After five minutes of suiting up, he went through the

improvised air lock and walked in to confront Abby Springfield.

"Hello, Abby," Nate said to the plastic-shrouded figure before him. His voice sounded muffled and distant, wrapped inside plastic itself.

Her head moved slightly, a fraction toward him. She couldn't move it any more because of bandages wrapping both shoulders and a brace immobilizing her neck. "Nate?" Her voice was weak, and Nate almost felt guilty.

Almost.

"Yes. Thought you saw the last of me, didn't you."

There was a long pause. The only sound was the hum of the medical equipment monitoring her. Finally, she said, "It wasn't like that."

"Wasn't like what? What was it supposed to be like, Abby? Did you like pushing my buttons? The first time I open up since this whole dirty business started, and it had to be to you? Proud of that, aren't you?"

"You don't understand."

His hands balled up into fists. *"Bullshit."*

"Nate—"

"Tell me that they're wrong. Tell me that you didn't use me. Tell me that I wasn't just a tool to lead you to Jimmy so the fuckheads with the guns could grab him."

Silence. Nate might have heard crying.

"Do you even give a shit about these kids? Or are you just on someone's payroll?"

"They were *trying* to save him—"

"Give me a break."

"They were. These people here, Department Blue, all they care about is the thing in him. Every kid they've captured, they've all died. I didn't lie about that—"

"Do you have any experience other than what the ass-holes who bought you have told you to believe? How many of these kids have you seen?"

"They could have done something. Department Blue knew my brother—"

"Done what, Abby?"

Silence.

"Do you believe that those bastards care any more about this kid than *our* bastards? Do you think, for a moment, that if they hadn't severely underestimated James Somerset, that he would still be alive?"

"They want to treat him . . ."

"They want a living example of this alien organism so they can be the first to reverse engineer it. The host is expendable."

"No—"

"You know what they are. They left you out to dry."

Nate walked up to the bed and pulled a portion of the plastic aside so he could look down into her face. "They conned you as bad as you conned me. Then they threw you into the pit with this kid. Did they tell you how far things had got? Did you know he'd already killed four of their people?"

There was a fractional shift of her head.

"You want to save this kid?"

"Yes."

"Well, you know me. Do you think anyone else in this whole mess gives a shit if James Somerset lives or dies?"

"What are you saying?"

"I'm saying that if you want to save this kid, you better tell me the truth. Everything. Because, before long, James is going to be too far gone for me or anyone else to help him."

Abby looked up at him. The expression on her face made her look like a trapped animal. Nate steeled himself against feeling anything for her.

"He's going to go after the people who hired you. We need to get to him before that happens. Where is he going?"

Abby closed her eyes and, slowly, she told him.

46

JIMMY'S breath fogged in front of his face. He stood ankle-deep in still water. The sound of dripping echoed off of the concrete walls around him. The place smelled like old wet gym socks. However, Jimmy doubted anyone would be looking for him or Asshole in a storm sewer.

The place he stood was about two miles up from the main outflow on the water side of the dam in Lakeview. The tunnel around him was massive. You could easily drive an SUV down the center of the sewer line. He wondered what it would be like when water was rushing down it. Right now there was barely an ankle-deep trickle.

Next to him, Asshole groaned.

Jimmy's hands were balled into fists, and he opened them wide, stretching until the joints popped. He breathed deeply and tried to dampen the fires that were burning inside his gut.

He turned to face Asshole.

The man was trussed up with his own belt, arms and legs tied. Jimmy looked at the man's face. Somewhat Asian, eyes wide and staring. He was starting to struggle. Jimmy stood in front of him and looked down, bemused that the man couldn't see him less than a foot away.

Of course, the oddity really was that Jimmy saw the man

in what should have been pitch-darkness. Somehow, with everything else, his eyes were getting better.

For several minutes Jimmy crouched and watched Asshole attempt to free himself. When it seemed to go on long enough, Jimmy said, "Are you afraid of me?"

Asshole's body froze, and his head began turning back and forth, trying to get a look at the source of the voice.

He sat up and Jimmy put his hand in the center of the man's chest and pushed him back down. "Answer the question."

Asshole jabbered something in his irritating language.

Jimmy shook his head. "You don't speak English? That's too bad. No reason to keep you alive, then, is there?" Jimmy reached down to the leg he had stabbed with the tranquilizer dart. He balled the top of Asshole's pant leg in his fist and yanked down. The material tore free. Asshole started twisting and bucking.

"Now," Jimmy said, "are you afraid of me?"

More of a foreign language.

Jimmy reached down and placed his hand on the wound in the man's thigh. In a few moments, he felt the flesh start to dissolve under his hand.

Asshole screamed.

"Ready to answer the question?"

"Yes, Yes, Yes . . ." Suddenly the man's command of the language was unimpaired.

"Did that hurt?" Jimmy said. "That was just me touching you and thinking evil thoughts. I wonder what I could do to you if I *tried.*"

"What kind of monster are you?"

Jimmy tsked. "And that was what I was going to ask you." He stretched his hands again and heard the joints pop. The sound wasn't quite right. It sounded more mechanical than it should have. It reminded Jimmy of a gun cocking. It probably wasn't just him, since Asshole tensed at the sound. "What kind of monster am I?"

Jimmy ran his fingers down the man's leg. They left bleeding welts in their wake, as if he'd been burned. Asshole bucked under Jimmy's touch. "I don't know—"

"Should I be satisfied with that answer?"

"I don't!"

"You were trying to capture me. Don't you know why?"

Silence.

Jimmy grabbed the kneecap and squeezed. The bone seemed to soften under his touch and the man not only bucked, he screamed. "I was ordered. *I. Don't. Know.*"

"You know, I think this is about to come off. I wonder if the doctors can fix that, where you come from."

"Please, ask me something I know."

"And what do you know?" Jimmy said, slowly letting go of the man's twisted, bloody knee. "Do you know anything worthwhile? Or did I just drag you down here to have someone to be pissed off at?" Jimmy stood and looked down at the crumpled, hyperventilating form. This poor bastard was just a grunt. Useless. What the hell *could* he know?

Stupid idea . . .

"You're just a pawn, you understand. A bit player between me and my nemesis. That's the way it always goes, doesn't it? The hero wins the right to see Mr. Big by wading through an ocean of minor agents—" Jimmy smiled and could feel Cain's eyes looking through his own. "Don't you think I've earned that right?"

"I don't understand . . ."

"I'll ask you slowly. Who are you working for?"

The man's pause was a little too long. Jimmy knelt down again and said, "Say good-bye."

"Mr. Pak. I work for Mr. Pak."

"Mr. Pak?" Jimmy rolled the name around in his mouth. "And who exactly is Mr. Pak?"

"Businessman, very rich, pays well for no questions. He—" Asshole trailed off.

Jimmy touched the clothed leg to encourage him.

"He's supposed to be government man, but no one says for sure. No one ask. He pays us, pay me, to bring you to him. Come here to see you."

"Uh-huh? Government man? Not *this* government, is he?"

"No, Beijing government."

Well, isn't this fucking wonderful?

"Okay, so where is this Mr. Pak holed up?"

The stare Jimmy got was a little blanker than most of the ones coming from this guy. "I don't understand."

"You don't need to," Jimmy said. "I don't intend to disappoint your boss. You're going to tell me where he is, and where you were going to bring me."

Jimmy took a bus downtown. He didn't get inside it, he was short on money, and he was getting the impression he was looking too weird to just walk inside unnoticed. So, he took a page from Spider-Man's book and hitched a ride. While the bus was stopped at a red light, he ran out of the shadows and jumped. He easily landed on top. He spread-eagled himself and waited.

The bus descended into the city, and buildings grew up around him. Broken masonry fingers clawed at the night sky. His hands gripped the bent aluminum skin beneath him as inertia tried to slide him off with every stop and start. Traffic lights zoomed by, inches from his head.

Not as great as it looks, Spidey.

He slid off the back when they reached downtown, and started walking north, toward the lake.

It was getting late, and most of the people he saw were drug dealers, prostitutes, and homeless. All of them gave him a wide berth. People crossed the street to avoid him. Jimmy stopped beside a parked car to glance at himself in the side-view mirror.

Holy fuck.

Whatever covered his body, it was no longer *skin.* It was gray and slightly reflective. The bones underneath weren't quite right anymore, there were bulges and ridges that shouldn't be there. He held his hand up to his face, and saw the fingers were getting longer, thinner, and he had lost his fingernails. He had also lost all his hair. Bald, no eyebrows, no eyelashes.

He grabbed the mirror with both hands and squeezed. Instead of crushing it, it seemed to soften, then liquefy, then dissolve. He looked at his hands and saw a brief flash of pigment from the car's paint play across his palms, then it was gone . . .

What am I?

"Have an answer, Mr. Pak." Jimmy's voice was ice cold. "Don't give me a reason."

It had been a badly placed hotel, or it had become badly placed when the Shoreway was built. It faced the lake, but the Interstate cut by between it and the lake about a hundred yards from its front door. The traffic was constant, headlights and taillights blurring streaks of color in front of the darkened edifice.

Jimmy could catch details in the structure from the glare off of the Interstate. It was twenty-five stories, a boxlike rectangle, the narrow side facing the lake. The west wall facing

Jimmy was blue and white and pleated like an accordion. Half the windows in that wall were blank plywood.

No lights, no sign of life.

This was the place?

Jimmy frowned as he walked toward it. He reached the edge of the weed-shot parking lot and got his first clues that he was on the right track. The building was surrounded by a brand-new chain-link fence, topped with barbed wire. The no-trespassing signs didn't have a spot of rust on them.

From where he stood, he could see some new fencing inside, huddled by the abandoned hotel. More chain-link, fifteen feet high and threaded with green so no one could see inside. It blocked off about a third of the parking lot on the far side from the interstate. Jimmy could see some of the weeds on that side of the lot were flattened, as if someone was driving around over there.

Jimmy reached for the chain-link and stuck one finger through. He pulled down, separating one link at a time, all the way to the ground. He slipped through.

Let's check the car pool first.

Jimmy walked to the green-wrapped fence. The modifications to the dead building were becoming a little more apparent. Several plywood windows were so fresh that he could see labels on the plywood. On the top he could see several modern-looking antennae, even without the benefit of any lights on the roof. He doubted that any hotel of this vintage started with a satellite dish, and it looked as if this place had been shut down long before they became a regular feature.

The gate into the inner fenced off area was chained shut. Jimmy made short work of the chain and slid the gate aside.

Somewhere, Jimmy heard a siren go off. At this point he didn't care. He wanted these bastards to see him coming.

(. . . the climactic confrontation of good and evil . . .)

The gate opened on a line of cars and the rear entrance to the hotel. Jimmy smiled. These bastards weren't going anywhere. The vehicles were all parked nose-in to the fence. He reached down at the first one, a Toyota Celica with a Hertz rental sticker on it. He slammed his fist into the gas tank. The metal gave and his hand was suddenly soaked with pungent liquid.

He walked to the next car, a seeping puddle following him.

A pair of men with guns burst through the door before he had reached the fourth car. Even so, a puddle of gas stretched all the way to the hotel.

"Don't move!" The taller one called out to him.

Jimmy shook his head and straightened up. The two gunmen stepped back. "You fuckheads talking to me? What the hell are you going to do? Shoot?" He took a step toward them. The air was filled with gas fumes from the first three cars. The fence around them blocked enough of the highway sound so that he could hear the liquid sound of fuel draining onto the broken pavement.

"Don't come any closer. Stay where you are."

"Are you guys stupid?" Jimmy walked along the line of cars to number four. This one was a Ford Taurus without a rental sticker. "Let me show you something."

Jimmy crouched and slammed his fist into the fuel tank. The sound was a resonant thump, followed by the sound of rushing liquid. Jimmy turned his head to face the gunmen. "I can do that to you. You don't want to know what happened to the last guy who shot me. Not enough left to fill a shot glass." He straightened up. "Besides, with all the flammable liquid around here, you guys really can't be shitheads enough to fire those things. You wouldn't have enough brains to breathe."

Halfway between the cars and the gunmen, they proved him wrong.

47

"*HOLY shit.*"

Nate didn't know who was talking, it came over a walkie-talkie so it could have been any of a dozen vehicles, or the helicopter. It was, however, pretty damn obvious what the speaker was referring to. Nate's car was just in sight of the target building, and an explosion and fireball had just erupted from its southern base. A huge ball of cherry-red fire rolled up the side of the building, black smoke licking up past the top of the building.

Nate's first thought was, *He beat us here.*

The cars pulled in, forming a perimeter around the building. Nate saw several military Hummers roll to a stop from the other direction. Above them, a helicopter started circling, aiming a spotlight down on the building.

Nate heard gunfire, and saw flashes from the darkened windows.

Nate stepped out of the car to stare at the building. Jimmy Somerset was in there, somewhere. The kid he wanted to save. If he was to believe her, the kid Abby wanted to save.

Nate looked over to his right. More Hummers were pulling up, and men in khaki were lining up. All of them were equipped with night vision equipment and nasty looking automatic rifles.

What kept running through Nate's head was CNN footage of the last gasp of the Soviet Union, the attempted coup where they fought through a massive multistory government high-rise. Nate remembered seeing the sheer white walls as smoke rolled from windows as the fighting progressed.

Boyden stood next to him, shouting something into his phone about establishing a perimeter around the building. "What are you going to do?"

Boyden looked aside at Nate. "We have the situation contained at the moment. We're not risking anyone going in there."

There were more flashes, and the sound of gunfire, higher up in the building. "You're not going to try and get him out of there?"

Boyden turned to look at Nate and said, "Do you see the same things I'm seeing? *He* is what we're containing."

"What—"

"We have six confirmed dead, two severe injuries—and this kid just walked into a building filled with at least a dozen heavily-armed men, and from all appearances, he's wiping the floor with them. We already have an international incident—"

Nate shook his head. "What are you going to do?"

"Try my best to neutralize him. We have some artillery—"

"Artillery?"

"The National Guard is going to evacuate the coast for five miles in either direction—"

"You can't just kill him."

Boyden stared at Nate, as if he had just spoken an alien language. He shook his head, and brought the phone back up to his face.

Nate looked back up at the building. "These men tried to

kidnap him. They're *shooting* at him. He's defending himself—"

"Tell that to Robb. Or the cops. Or the kid who ignited Trinity. James is too dangerous."

In the building, more gunfire flashed through the windows, higher up. There were now two helicopters, training spotlights at the sides of the building. The traffic had stopped on the neighboring Interstate. Troops ringed the building, outside the chain-link surrounding the parking lot. The troops aimed weapons at the structure now, rifles, tripod mounted machine guns, shoulder-launched missiles.

"Damn it," Nate said. "Isn't he exactly what you've been looking for? Isn't he what Department Blue was about? You know this isn't an invasion. This is one troubled kid who doesn't know what—"

"Do I have a choice?" Boyden snapped. *"Do you think I can control—"*

He was interrupted by the sound of every nearby soldier tensing and cocking their weapons. Nate turned to face the building in time to see both helicopters turn their spotlights on a tumbling figure. It took a moment for Nate to realize it was a human being, falling in the midst of a shower of glass. Then the body struck the weedy asphalt, bouncing once.

Nate looked back at Boyden and came to a decision.

"Before you do anything, let me talk to him."

"What?"

"Let me try talking to him. Isn't it worth more to have him alive? Have your alien alive?"

"Mr. Adriano, you are out of your mind. I need you as a researcher, not as a corpse. I'm not even letting my trained agents go in there—"

"I agreed to cooperate with your team because I want to save these kids, *not* blow them up."

"Don't lie. You agreed because I blackmailed you."

"And I'm more useful to you as a researcher than as an inmate in a federal prison."

Boyden looked over at Nate.

"You want my services," Nate said, "you let me go in there and try talking to him. Either that, or you call the grand jury now because I won't be a party to this."

"Mr. Adriano, we don't even have a good estimate of how many people this kid has killed so far—"

"What the hell do you have to lose?"

"You."

"You don't *have* me, Mr. Boyden." Nate looked up at the building. "You don't have James Somerset either. So it's both or neither."

Boyden looked at Nate, then he picked up his phone. "Operations, I got a man here we need wired to go inside."

When Boyden had said "wired," Nate pictured the typical law enforcement getup with a microphone and a small transmitter. Not quite. They took him into one of the command trailers that had pulled up around the hotel and started strapping equipment onto him. They strapped a Kevlar vest over him that wired into a helmet that had a camera embedded into the side and a clear plastic display that flipped down over his left eye.

"We'll be in contact the whole way," Boyden said. "You don't need to worry about controlling the communications gear. We're setting it to an open channel so we'll see and hear everything you do. You'll be able to hear us, and we can send you video over that heads-up display." He turned to the man outfitting Nate and asked, "Have we got a clear frequency for our hero here?"

The other man nodded.

In fifteen minutes they had Nate inside a helicopter.

"Can you hear me?"

"Yes," Nate shouted over the rotors as they lifted off. He was hanging on to the wall of the helicopter, staring out the open side door as the ground tilted and fell away. It felt as if his stomach were still on the ground.

"Good. Now, the helicopter isn't going to be able to land, the roof of this place isn't stable enough for it. What the pilot's going to do is hover over the building. You are going to have to jump about six feet down."

Nate nodded.

"Understand?"

Nate realized that the voice in his helmet couldn't see his nod. "Yes." Nate yelled, hoping his nausea wasn't audible in his voice.

"The fire's causing unpredictable updrafts, he's only going to be able to hover that close for a few seconds. You have to be ready to do this."

"I understand."

"You can call this off at any—"

"I understand."

The helicopter turned around and started heading for the roof of the building.

48

JIMMY walked into the darkened hotel trailing smoke, the tattered coat whipping around him. The blood halfway up his arms wasn't his own. His shadow danced ahead of him outlined in flickering orange. He could hear shouting above and around him.

He walked past a fire door and it swung open as he passed, a shadow crouching in the doorway to a set of fire stairs. Jimmy half turned to face the new threat when the hallway was filled with the jackhammer sounds of a machine gun. The muzzle flash carved the hallway out in strobing lightning-blue light as sledgehammer blows hit Jimmy's gut, his chest, and his shoulders.

He fell back as the shadow kept firing. A table gave way behind him. Splintering around his ass and legs. His shoulders struck the wall, caving it in about three inches, erupting plaster gypsum dust around him.

In two or three seconds, the gun started clicking on an empty magazine.

Jimmy stood up, chunks of drywall falling to the ground behind him. He brushed off the front of his tattered clothes. There was no blood. The bullets hadn't penetrated so much as made deep dents in the webwork that knit his skin together. He could feel the fibers moving under his hands, pulling tight again, closing the inch-deep craters the bullets had blown into his body. He was barely surprised at the lack of blood.

"Now you've just gone and pissed me off."

Jimmy's vision was good enough to see the look of shock on the gunman's face as he tried to pull the fire door shut. Unfortunately for him, the pneumatic closer didn't care to have the door slam, so Jimmy easily closed the distance and wrapped a hand around the edge of the door.

Unlike the pissant grunt in front of him, Jimmy had no problem fighting against the pneumatics of the door. He yanked it back open. The closer ripped free of the doorframe, shedding screws and odd mechanical bits as the gunman was dragged forward to fall on his face.

Jimmy reached down with his free hand and grabbed the man at the base of the skull where it met his neck. He lifted, pulling the man up to face him, Yorick to Jimmy's Hamlet.

"Today," Jimmy said, "it sucks to be you."

Jimmy squeezed, watching the man's eyes bulge and mouth open in a wordless gasp.

Under his hand, Jimmy felt bone soften—then the body fell away.

"Fuck." Jimmy threw the suddenly disembodied head away. It hit the concrete wall of the stairwell like a ripe melon.

"Fuck, fuck, fuck—" Jimmy grabbed the crash bar on the inside of the fire door and pulled the mechanism free of the door, trying not to imagine the bodiless head staring at him.

The bar came free with a snap, and he used it to wedge the door back shut. No more surprises coming from this direction. He ran and repeated the process with all the stairwell doors he could find—sealing off any exit from the floors above.

The elevators still worked, and Jimmy was just as methodical with them. He kept pressing the up button, and as each elevator arrived on the ground floor, he pulled the emergency stop, holding it down here.

Eventually, there was only one route up or down.

Jimmy stepped in and let the doors slide shut.

Jimmy stopped the elevator at each floor, walking out, blocking the fire exits, and looking for the people who'd been trying to kidnap him. The agents of his nemesis.

He ignored the lights outside the windows. The cops might be here, but he wasn't worried about that now. His mind was focused on a single entity called Mr. Pak.

They ambushed him between the ninth and tenth floor. The elevator was rising, and Jimmy heard something clatter above him. He just had a moment to wonder what it was, when the top of the elevator exploded. Heat and shrapnel pushed him to the floor as there was a sudden jerk of free fall.

The elevator ground to a stop a few floors down. The elevator was dark, and no longer had a roof, just black, jagged edges that bent down from a smoke-filled shaft.

Then the gunfire started. The guns echoed above him in a roar that merged together into an unending thunderclap. The bullets punched holes in the floor, sending up bits of carpet. Bits of his own clothes were kicked up, too, as bullets slammed into his inhuman skin. Jimmy closed his eyes and curled into a ball as the gunfire kept coming, and coming, and coming . . .

It felt as if God's own street gang had surrounded him and was beating him to death with skyscraper-sized baseball bats.

It lasted almost ten minutes.

It was another thirty seconds before Jimmy realized the sound had stopped.

He opened his eyes and glanced up. The shaft was filled with smoke. He couldn't see the gunmen. With the way his vision was improving, that meant they couldn't see him.

He rolled over and looked up.

His skin ached. Every impact was a prick of fire on his body. He shouldn't be alive, super-Jimmy or not, no one could come out of a firefight like that and live.

And crouch.

And wait for the smoke to clear enough to see a light—

Jimmy sprang up from the floor of the elevator, toward a sliver of yellow haze he could see through the smoke. In a moment he stood at the threshold of a set of open elevator doors. Six men faced him, all in the process of reloading.

The first one, the one closest to the door, Jimmy grabbed by his collar and sent him tumbling headfirst down the elevator shaft. The remaining five backpedaled and leveled their guns at him. Jimmy smiled at them.

"So," he asked, "who here wants to have a chat with God?"

The gunfire began again, but Jimmy was ready for it. He aimed himself at the one asshole who was standing in front of an open doorway. He tackled him through the door and into a dust-covered hotel room. The room was cut by stark white light coming in from outside. They tumbled from glare to shadow, to glare again, until they stopped against the outside wall.

The gunman ended up on top of Jimmy. For a brief moment, the guy must have thought he won, because he had a grim smile when he raised his weapon toward Jimmy's head.

The expression changed when Jimmy's hand stabbed

through his abdomen to grab hold of his spinal column. Jimmy lifted him up and threw him sideways out the window.

Jimmy stood and faced the doorway, backlit by spotlights from outside.

"Come on, you fuckheads, give me your best shot."

They did.

It wasn't enough.

Jimmy walked through the smoke-filled halls of the dead hotel, looking for more of the enemy. Looking for agents of his archenemy.

There didn't seem to be any left.

Light shot in from the windows, carving the dark corridors into slices of light and shadow. Nothing moved but Jimmy and the dust motes in the air. The only sound was the pulsing resonance of the helicopters outside.

Where was he?

Where was Mr. Pak?

(. . . Baphomet? . . .)

Jimmy shook his head, feeling the dark form of Cain slipping behind his inhuman skin.

The rags of his clothing twisted around him as he worked his way up floor after floor, using the stairs now. He walked through the halls not quite wholly present. Part of him walked on the cracked plains of hell, where the jagged rocks pointed up toward a swollen sun hanging in a jet-black sky. Part of him walked with Cain through the blasted halls of Euclid Heights High School.

(. . . He cannot hide from me forever . . .)

*   *   *

He must know what's happening. What I am. Why else would he want to capture me?

Jimmy climbed up another floor and when he left the stairwell, he saw a door swing shut. Jimmy ran for the door, paying little attention to the crates, computers, or the makeshift operating theater he passed.

He reached the door and tried it.

Locked.

"You can't hide from me." Jimmy said.

(. . . Not when I am about to win . . .)

The door was heavy, metal, and barred. The surface was smooth, without anything to grab hold of. Jimmy reached around the doorjamb, his fingers sliding through the softer material of the wall to grip around the metal frame of the door. When he felt as if he had a good grip, he pulled.

The door, frame and all, moved toward him. It levered out of the wall, throwing sparks and billows of concrete and plaster dust. The force Jimmy exerted was so severe that he could feel the slab floor cracking where his feet dug in.

Jimmy stepped through the door and into—

Panel 1: VIEW FROM THROUGH BROKEN DOOR
A windowless room lit by broken fluorescents. Computer workstations line the walls, all showing blue screens informing us that the hard drive is being formatted. A pile of papers, files, and binders is burning in the center of the room. An Asian man in a suit is emptying an armload of computer printouts into the flames. He is looking toward the door.

CAIN

"It's over. There's nowhere else to go."

The papers slipped out of the man's hands. Fear lit his eyes as he backed away from the door. Jimmy crossed the room, walking slowly, through the paper bonfire in the center of the room. He barely felt the heat as his feet kicked the burning pile apart. The lights above flickered erratically. When he reached Mr. Pak, the computers around him began beeping.

Format complete.

Panel 2: CLOSE-UP OF CAIN AND BAPHOMET
CAIN has his hands wrapped around the Asian man's throat. He holds him up against the wall. Smoke curls around both of them.

CAIN

"Tell me why, you bastard. Why do you torment me?"

BAPHOMET

"James! Do you know what you're doing?"

CAIN

"MY NAME IS NOT JAMES!"

Jimmy threw the man against the opposite wall. He slammed against the drywall and fell across one of the workstations. Jimmy walked back toward him.

Mr. Pak pushed himself upright and scattered the computer across the floor between himself and Jimmy. The monitor fell in front of Jimmy with an implosive shattering pop.

Above them, the flickering fluorescents finally went out, leaving the room lit only by the blue screens of the other monitors.

Mr. Pak shouted at him. "Think! Who are you?"

(... *What is my sin?* ...)

(... *Why am I here?* ...)

(... *Who am I?* ...)

Panel 3: VIEW OF CAIN FACING BAPHOMET/PAK
Cain has stopped approaching the Asian man. His clothes hang in tatters around him, and his own body does not look quite right. Metallic highlights glint off of joints more robotic than human. The face is skull-like and expressionless. The Asian man is pressing himself against the broken wall. Between the two of them is the wreckage of the broken computer.

BAPHOMET/PAK

"Do you even know what is happening to you? What this is that has taken over your body?"

CAIN

(Very faint words.)

"What am I?"

Mr. Pak told him.

49

"*IT'S time!*" shouted the pilot. Nate heard the words through his headset. The helicopter door was open in front of him, and his face was being whipped by wind and smoke. The sound of the rotors resonated deep in his chest. In front of him, the roof of the old hotel swayed, seeming too far and too small, lit a stark blue-white by the spots under the two helicopters.

Black smoke whipped across the surface of the roof, whipped into miniature whirlwinds by the downdraft from the helicopters. The surface seemed to dance below him.

"We can't get any closer!"

The surface looked a hundred feet away. Nate swallowed and felt sweat gather inside his gauntlets and drip down the back of his neck.

"If you can't—"

Nate shook his head, threw his bag ahead of him, and jumped out.

It wasn't a hundred feet. More like six. Nate bent his legs and tried to roll, but he hit the roof before he expected to and slammed into it. The impact knocked the breath from him.

"Shit. Nathan, are you all right?" It was Boyden's voice over the headset.

"I'm fine," Nate spat into his mic. He pushed himself up

and said. "If we're on a first name basis now, what do I call you?"

There was a pause. *"Name's Ulysses."*

Nate picked up his bag and looked around the roof. Now that he was standing on it, the building looked huge. "That must have caused some fights in high school." Nate turned in a slow circle. "Are you getting all this?"

"Crystal clear."

Nate turned to face the pillar of smoke as it was lit by one of the helicopters. It looked as if half the building was on fire below him. He looked up and watched the two helicopters doing their slow orbit around the building.

Well, he asked to be here.

"There should be an entrance about twenty yards ahead of you and to the right."

"I see it." Nate headed toward the small shedlike structure. At one point there had been a door here, but the opening had been boarded over. "I'll have to pry it open."

"Be careful, we don't know where he is in the building."

Nate set down the bag they had given him and opened it, pulling out a small pry bar. He began worrying away the nails holding the plywood in place. It gave him time to realize how quiet things had become. There were no gunshots, and even the sounds of the helicopters seemed distant and muted.

"Still there?" Nate asked as he started on the other side of the plywood.

"What is it?"

"You see any activity downstairs?"

"No, it's been quiet for about ten minutes."

Ten minutes? It seemed longer.

Nate got the plywood loose enough to kick it in. The

board fell inside and clattered down a flight of metal steps to lodge diagonally in the landing.

"Damn it, be careful. There are men with guns down there."

"Were men," Nate said. "And considering James, I don't think surprising him is a great idea."

Nate looked into the stairwell. There were lights, but they didn't seem to be in working order. "Do we know if this building has any electricity?"

"It was pulling some from the power grid, but not legally. We have no clue what they actually have wired in there . . ."

Nate zipped up the bag, shouldering it. He started his descent.

Nate felt as if he were entering a tomb. Once he walked down the first flight, stepping carefully over the dislodged plywood, his own footsteps and breathing became the dominant sounds. The air was stale and heavy and tainted by smoke.

The world was grainy monochrome and green behind the night-vision eyepiece that they'd given him. The view was unreal, ghostlike. When he stepped out into the hallway on the top floor, Nate stood still, listening.

He heard the sound of shattering glass.

"I hear something," he whispered.

"Be careful, you don't know what it is."

Glass shattering again. Then the sound of impact, something heavy hitting the floor. Nate walked slowly in the direction of the sound. To either side of him, the glow of spotlights moved and slid by like molten quicksilver under the doors.

The hall stayed dark and green.

"Nate we're getting som—bzt—r approaching."

"Repeat that please."

"We're ge—bzt—me interfer—bzt—ear where you—bzt"

Nate kept walking toward the sound. His night-vision view was increasingly grainy and shot through with white dots. He turned a corner and saw, at the end of the hall, a room that glowed white through a partly open door. The noises were coming from down there.

"I think I found something."

"Can y—bzt—t make ou—bzt—king up you—bzt—smission."

The static was constant now, and the white dots were making his night vision useless.

Something flew out of the open door to smash into the wall opposite. Nate stopped approaching and raised up the night-vision equipment.

"—bzt—in. Are you rec—bzt—no image—bzt—peat, can y—bzt—"

"If you can hear me at all," Nate whispered, "I think I found him."

Without his night-vision equipment, there was enough light from the room to see by. The light was flickering orange, supplemented by the occasional lightning flash of a fluorescent tube. The open door had been new, and seemed to have been pushed into the room, steel frame and all.

The object that had struck the wall was a computer monitor. It left a divot in the drywall, and its plastic case sagged on the floor like an eggshell emptied of its contents.

Nate heard something, too. At first he thought it was the whine of some abused machinery, but it was a voice, distorted and metallic, like a third-generation copy of an analog tape played through a speaker made out of a coffee can.

"... fuck ... fuck ... fuck ..."

Every time the word repeated, it was punctuated by the sound of breaking machinery.

Nate swallowed and the taste in his mouth was a mix of fear and smoke.

"I'm going to attempt to talk to him . . ."

"bzzzzzzzzzzzzzbzzzzzzzzzzbzzzzzzzzzzzzzz"

Could James be causing the interference? Probably. Nate stood there wondering if he should go on with the umbilical cut like this.

"Oh, hell, as if they would be able to intervene anyway." Nate cleared his throat and called out, "James Somerset!"

The noise stopped.

Nate took the quiet as a good sign.

"My name is Nathan Adriano. I am unarmed and alone. I am here to talk to you."

Silence.

"I am walking toward the door. I'm keeping my hands in front of me."

The six feet to the door was a hideously long march. He kept thinking of the force with which the computer monitor had struck the wall. He was grinding glass fragments of CRT screen under his shoes before he got halfway. Anything thrown with that kind of force would disable or kill him, even with the helmet and flak jacket.

Nate kept his hands up as he very slowly turned to face into the room.

It was all Nate could do to keep from gasping.

The room had been torn apart. Fragments of computers, monitors, filing cabinets were scattered everywhere. Burning paper floated around as if this scene was part of a snow globe from hell. Fragments of a desiccated corpse lay crumpled on the ground, dismembered and broken as badly as any machine in the room. A jawbone sat by Nate's foot, appearing like a thousand-year-old relic.

Standing in the center of it all was James.

Had been James.

The skin was gray, almost chrome, reflecting light through a black webwork of fluid that snaked across its surface. The arms and legs were machinelike, the joints swollen into balls wrapped by cablelike tendons. The torso was elongated and hunched over. The face that turned toward Nate was a metal skull housing wide, white, expressionless eyes.

".. **i am not james somerset . . .**" it said.

Nate felt his own heart beating, too close to his chest. His impulse was to run, let Boyden's people handle this thing that James had become. Nate wondered if they could.

"Who are you, then?" Nate asked. He stood still, making no sudden moves.

"**. . . who am i . . .**" The voice wasn't human. It was metallic, almost an electronic drone. James opened one hand, releasing a twisted piece of metal and plastic that had once been a computer keyboard. It was barely recognizable. Not only had it been crushed and bent, but where the elongated fingers had wrapped around it, the plastic and metal seemed to have melted and flowed together.

Nate swallowed. "Am I talking to Cain?"

"**. . . cain . . . that is the name we have taken . . .**"

"We?" Nate asked. The smell of smoke was getting worse, and his eyes were beginning to water. "How many of you are there?"

"**. . . all of us . . .**"

"Is one of you James?"

"**. . . james is not here . . .**"

"Can he hear me?"

"**. . . he will not listen . . .**"

Nate looked down at the gore-stained jawbone by his foot. "Why did you kill this man?"

"..."

"The men with the guns, I understand. Even if they couldn't harm you, they attacked you. I can understand Quincy Robb. Why this man? How was justice served?"

"... what is my sin ..."

"Why? Why did he have to die?"

"... baphomet ... he served baphomet ... he was baphomet ..."

"No," Nate shook his head.

"... yes ... father of lies ... he told me lies ..."

"What did he tell you?"

"..." The thing that had been James Somerset crouched and covered his face. The skin under the flowing net of liquid wasn't quiescent. Things that should have been bones and muscle crawled and reshaped themselves under the surface, as if someone was wrestling under his skin.

"Cain?"

"... H–help me ..." The voice emerging from under the thing's hands was still the same metallic drone, but there was something else in it. Something human. Something very afraid.

"James?" Nate asked.

"... I can't stop it ..."

"If you walk out of here with me, there are people outside who will help you."

James shook his head slowly. "Why? Why should anyone help me? Look at what I've done."

"The thing that's causing this. The thing that's infected you. They've been studying it for years. *I've* been studying it."

"I've killed people. I don't even know how."

"Please, come with me. If you don't, they're going to kill you."

"How?" Jimmy waved an arm at the wreckage around him. **"How do you kill someone cursed to never die?"**

"You aren't Cain, Jimmy. The thing in your head isn't Cain." Nate said. "The people outside have much heavier weapons than the men in here. They'll level the building and everything in it."

"What about you?"

"My radio's dead. They may assume I'm already dead."

James shook his head and stood. He gestured at the ground. **"Was this guy telling the truth?"**

"What did he say?"

"I'm not human. I should have died three years ago."

"You *are* human. This thing is an infection, a virus, an alien machine . . ."

"Look at me and say that." James stepped up to Nate and stared into his face with his blank white eyes. **"Look at me!"**

"Please, we can help you—"

"BULLSHIT!" Nate backed away. The violence and the anger washed off of James as a nearly physical force. **"You know how long people have tried to help me? All my fucking life! I've been helped into fucking oblivion."**

"If we understand why you survived, we can help other kids. Keep them from burning . . ."

James laughed. It was an ugly sound, a broken power tool running in an echo chamber. **"Sure. Why wouldn't I want to help someone else go through this, too?"** James shook his head. **"You don't know what the fuck you're doing, any more than I do."**

James turned and started walking down the corridor.

Nate called after him. "What are you going to do?"

"I'm going to send Cain home."

"What . . . ?"

James walked into the darkness, his feet crunching on the debris of the hallway.

Nate ran after him. Back the way he had come down into the building. When he left the light of the computer room, he switched his night vision back on. The hallway returned, grainy and green.

"Can anyone hear me?" Nate called into his radio.

"—te, that yo—bzzz—ot of int—bzzz—ill no pic—bzzz—"

"He's headed for the roof, I'm following."

"—or the roo—bzzz—py you—bzzz—tus of Jam—bzzz—"

"He's the source of the interference. Get those helicopters away from the building."

"—bzzzzzzzzzzzzzzzzzz—"

"Shit." Nate reached the stairs up to the roof. The plywood was splintered and oddly warped where James had walked across it. He scrambled over it and ran up the stairs, whipping off the night vision as he did.

He reached the top of the stairs and said quietly, *"Oh, my God."*

Interlude Five: THE WAGES OF SIN

Page 21: [FIVE PANELS]

Panel 1: WIDTH OF PAGE, OVERHEAD VIEW, HALLWAY CENTERED ON CAIN
Cain stands, holding his staff lengthwise, facing the SWAT team as lights focus on him. Behind him, the mass of undead things swarm around the corner, crawling over each other in a mass of putrescent flesh. They seem to crawl out from within the black slash of Cain's shadow.

CAIN

(Very small word balloon)

". . . shit . . ."

Panel 2: CLOSE-UP OF SWAT TEAM & GUNS
A number of SWAT guys facing us in full riot gear and gas masks. M-16s point offscreen and belch muzzle flashes and smoke that take up half the panel.

SFX

(Diagonally across panel, toward panel 3)

BAMbamBAMbamBAMbamBAMbamBAM

Panel 3: MID SHOT OF CAIN FROM SIDE
Cain is hunched over, as if in a windstorm. Bullets rip through the rags he's wearing, fragments of his trench coat twist through the air behind him. Bullet trails cut the air around him, blow holes in the linoleum by his feet, tear up the acoustical tile above him. He is in the process of turning his staff upright.

SFX

(Diagonally across panel, cont. from panel 2.)

BAMbamBAMbamBAMbamBAMbamBAM

Panel 4: CLOSE-UP OF FLOOR IN FRONT OF CAIN
Cain's staff hits the floor next to a bullet hole. The
checkered linoleum tile cracks with the impact.

SFX

(Middle of panel)

CRACK

SFX

(Along bottom of panel, cont. from panel 3)

BAMbamBAMbamBAMbamBAMbamBAM

Panel 5: MID SHOT OF CAIN FROM SIDE
Cain is stepping toward the SWAT guys as bullets still
hail around him. From behind, taloned hands reach toward him as he braces against the staff in his hands.

SFX

(Along bottom of panel, cont. from panel 4)

BAMbamBAMbamBAMbamBAMbamBAM

PAGE 22: [SIX PANELS]

Panel 1: VIEW FROM BEHIND SWAT GUYS
SWAT guys are backlit. Cain is vaulting over them,
hands on the staff, mostly out of the light from the SWAT
guys' flashlights. Framed between Cain and the SWAT
guys' silhouettes is a head-on view of a wall of zombie

creatures. A mass of rotting flesh, grasping skeletal hands and skull-like faces with dead burning eyes.

SFX

(Along bottom of panel)

BAMbamBAMbamBAMbamBAMbamBAM

CAPTION

"I hate situations like this. I don't go out of my way to be callous. Or ruthless."

Panel 2: CLOSE-UP OF SWAT GUYS AND ZOMBIES
The zombies fall into the mass of SWAT guys. The zombies are clawing through Kevlar. Guns are firing through the corpses, blowing fragments of dead flesh into the air.

SFX

AIEEEEEEEEeeeeeeee . . .

SFX

(Along bottom of panel)

BAMbamBAMbamBAMbamBAMbamBAM

CAPTION

"If there was a point, I would intervene, somehow. Try to prevent this atrocity."

Panel 3: MID SHOT OF CAIN FROM THE FRONT
Cain has landed behind the SWAT guys. He is in a crouch, staff lengthwise in his left hand, right hand touching the ground. He is entirely in shadow, except for

his eyes reflecting back at us. His tattered coat flutters behind him like a shredded cape. All that's visible behind him are random limbs, light, and gun smoke.

SFX

(Along bottom of panel)

BAMbamBAMbamBAMbamBAMbamBAM

CAPTION

"However, I've learned two things in the past hundred years of trying to play the hero . . ."

Panel 4: CLOSE-UP OF CAIN'S FACE
He is looking over his shoulder, behind him. Cain's expression is one of horrible determination. His eyes are wide with a hint of the bloodbath behind him reflected in their depths. Streaks of sweat and blood trail across his face.

SFX

(Along bottom of panel)

BAMbamBAMbamBAMbamBAMbamBAM

CAPTION

"The first is, atrocities happen . . ."

Panel 5: CLOSE-UP OF SWAT GUY'S FACE
The guy wears a gas mask. One lens has been shattered so we see a single terrified eye. Rotting, taloned hands hold both sides of the guy's face.

SFX

(Along bottom of panel)

BAMbam . . . BAMbam . . . click . . . click

Panel 6: CLOSE-UP OF SWAT GUY'S FACE
The hands have twisted the guy's head ninety degrees
away from us.

SFX

SNAP!

CAPTION

"The second is, life is too transient to try and
save . . ."

PAGE 23: [SIX PANELS]

Panel 1: MID SHOT OF CAIN
He's pushing through a heavy metal fire door. We see
him stepping through a narrow gap, the door only a
quarter open.

CAIN

"You bastard! You killed them all . . ."

CAPTION

"Of course, the evil one doesn't answer me.
Doesn't serve his purpose."

Panel 2: MID SHOT OF CAIN AND DOOR
Cain has his back to the door, straining to shut it, feet
braced against the opposite wall. Taloned arms try to
reach through the gap for him. The whole scene is cut
into shadows, daylight from somewhere above.

CAIN

". . . what the hell did you get from that?"

CAPTION

"Of course, it was to distract me. He has his prize, but I still threaten it. Someone less obsessive might have forgotten why he was here . . ."

Panel 3: CLOSE-UP OF CAIN'S FACE
His face is streaked with gore. He is baring his teeth, clenching his mouth shut. The cords are taut in his neck.

CAIN

". . . well . . . you . . . aren't . . . going . . . to . . ."

Panel 4: MID SHOT OF CAIN AND DOOR
His head is thrown back against the door, his knees have straightened, and his arms are spread out along the door. The zombie arms stick straight out, blood jetting from where the heavy door has severed them.

SFX

SLAM!

CAIN

"WIN!"

Panel 5: CLOSE-UP OF FLOOR BY BOTTOM OF DOOR
Two zombie arms lie on the ground in a pool of blood, draped over each other. Apparently one is still twitching. In the background we see a brick wall that has a ladder

bolted to it. We see Cain's boot mounting the bottom rung.

CAPTION

"Someone less obsessive would forget that He has an agenda . . ."

Panel 6: VIEW OF CAIN FROM ABOVE

Cain is climbing up a square, brick-walled shaft. He is in sunlight now, draped by only a few odd shadows. We can see now how torn up his body has been. His clothes drape as rags on him. Every inch of skin is pocked and cut, torn and bleeding.

CAPTION

"Someone less obsessive would forget that to fight Him means that first you discover what He wants . . ."

PAGE 24: [SPLASH PAGE]

Panel 1: EXT. EUCLID HTS. HIGH SCHOOL CLOCK TOWER

Cain has just come up out of a trapdoor in a balcony that wraps around the tower. The clock face is behind him. In front of him, on the balcony, is a small figure crouching and cradling a shotgun. The traffic copter is in the air behind the tower, and smoke is filling half the sky behind them.

CAIN

"Jerry Smith?"

CAPTION

". . . and you deny it to Him."

50

(WHO am I?)

Jimmy stands alone and naked on a familiar plain. The ground is wrinkled and cracked, baking under a red, bloated sun that hangs oppressively, filling most of an ink-black sky. Jagged rocks pierce the ground like broken glass.

Jimmy's hell.

But now he knows what it is. Where it is.

"Where are you?" Jimmy's voice doesn't break the stillness. There is no wind, no sound, no real atmosphere. The air on this world, the oceans, everything on the surface had been burned away long ago by the impossibly close sun. The surface is dead.

But, far below, something still lives.

"Where are you?"

A shadow walks out from behind one of the rock slivers that claw at the sky. It strides toward Jimmy confidently, wearing Cain's trench coat.

Panel 1: VIEW OF CAIN AND JERRY SMITH
Cain is standing facing Jerry and holding his staff in front of him. He is torn and bleeding, and his hair is blowing wildly behind him. Jerry has a terrified expres-

sion. He cradles a shotgun between his knees as he sits on the balcony. He is pointing it at Cain, trembling.

CAIN

"It isn't too late."

JERRY

"Please, go. Leave me alone."

CAIN

"Don't let him take you."

SFX

(Icy letters slowly growing across the bottom of panel)

"hahahahahaHaHaHaHaHaHAHAHAHAH"

Jimmy walked through the corridors toward the roof. The body he wore was no longer truly his. Sensations came from what had once been his skin, but it couldn't truly be called touch, or feeling. . . .

It was more an awareness of the matter that slid by the surface, tasted by the fluid that pulsed across the metallic surface of his body. Jimmy could feel that dark fluid. It was a giant mouth that never closed, breathing, tasting, *feeding* . . .

He was also aware of the darkness inside him, breathing, pulsing, freed of whatever chains had once bound it. Machinelike, it found biological inefficiencies and corrected them. Even as he walked, it was rebuilding his musculature, his skeletal structure, his vital organs, his eyes, his ears, his mouth.

The darkness ate everything that had been human, remaking Jimmy in its own image.

Jimmy walked up the stairs to the roof, feeling how the layers of his identity were breaking apart as the darkness remade his brain.

But, even as fragments of perception warped away, as the conceptual barrier between self and the universe dissolved, Jimmy began to remember things. Things long suppressed. Things buried under so many layers of pain, denial, and human experience that it took the virtual destruction of his identity for them to surface.

Jimmy remembered who was in control here . . .

(Why am I here?)

"Stop there!" Jimmy tells the shadow Cain.

Obediently, Cain stops.

"Who are you?" Jimmy asks.

"I am who you want me to be."

"Who am I?"

"You are who you want you to be."

"Who are we?"

"You know who we are."

Jimmy shakes his head and crouches over the surface of the cracked plain. His fingers touch the ground. He traces a cross in the red dust, dragging his fingernails through until they bite the rock a few millimeters below the surface. "My name is James Allan Somerset."

Cain is silent, standing shadowed and depthless between Jimmy and the bloated sun. Jimmy looks up at the empty hole of Cain's face and says, "That wasn't supposed to happen, was it?"

"It is our sin."

Jimmy laughs and wipes the cross away with his hand.

Panel 2: CLOSE-UP OF JERRY SMITH'S FACE
We can see the demon through the expression on Jerry's mouth. It is twisted in an evil Jokerlike grin as he bares his teeth at Cain. The eyes, however, are still terrified, and tears stream down Jerry's cheeks.

BAPHOMET

(Through Jerry)

"HAHAHA. You fool! The child is mine."

CAIN

"Fight it Jerry! Fight! Your soul is still your own."

BAPHOMET

(Through Jerry)

"Too little, fool. Too late."

The wind whipped across the roof of the old hotel as Jimmy walked out into the open air. Smoke blotted out most of the sky. Spotlights cut through the haze from the orbiting helicopters, carving pillars of light that fell down on Jimmy.

Jimmy could sense the heat gradient, and he walked away from the side of the hotel that was on fire. He could also see the helicopters as they orbited above. The smoke was no barrier; Jimmy saw the dark metal, the white engine exhaust, the heat of the snipers' faces as they aimed their guns out the open door.

He could taste the asphalt roof as his bare feet walked across its surface. He could feel his body absorbing the semimolten tar as contact with him dissolved its structure.

Jimmy could smell smoke and gasoline, tar and engine exhaust. He heard helicopters and radio interference, crackling fire and human voices from far below. He tasted oil and electricity and a thousand things he had no name for.

As he walked slowly toward the edge of the roof, he could see the lake. And above the lake, a million stars . . .

(What is my sin?)

Jimmy looks at the shadow Cain and *knows*.

He knows without speaking, because of the thing that called itself Cain. The sick darkness, the hungry void inside himself, it was a part of him. It always had been.

A race, ancient and curious, had sent its spirit out among the stars. The spirit, these tiny half-living machines, found life, became that life . . .

Became Jimmy.

He had known. As the broken half of himself runs amok, chewing up the barriers in Jimmy's mind, Jimmy remembers.

"You are me," Jimmy says.

"We are we," Cain replies.

"We were never supposed to be separate," Jimmy says as he stands up. He reaches up and grabs the shadow Cain by the rags around its neck. The phantasm is as light as paper as Jimmy shakes it. *"You were supposed to be there!"*

"We were here."

"Bullshit." Jimmy throws the shadow against one of the

black spires of rock. The darkness fragments into hundreds, thousands, millions of tiny motes.

"We minded a body. The body created the mind."

Jimmy puts his face in his hands. His existence, his individuality, his separateness from this thing, all an accident. Now that he remembers, he knows that the darkness, the thing within him, is less than half a mind. It needs direction because it has no understanding, no morality, no purpose.

Their sin is that they cannot act.

Not without him.

(Who am I?)

James Alan Somerset.
  Cain.
    Something else, broken and dying.

(Why am I here?)

To become something more than what I have become.

(What is my sin?)

Not understanding . . .

Panel 3: MID SHOT OF JERRY SMITH
Jerry has thrown the shotgun at Cain. He is vaulting over the railing of the clock tower balcony, the Joker grin still on his face. Cain has a shocked expression and is deflecting the shotgun with the staff as he reaches for Jerry with his other hand.

CAPTION

"How do you weigh life against eternity?"

"Oh, my God . . . James! You don't have to do this!"

Jimmy stood on the ledge. He faced the lake, but looked at the stars.

The motes of darkness swirl around Jimmy now. The cracked plain and the bloated sun are hidden from him now. The dark vortex surrounds him, but he is no longer afraid of it. No longer afraid of what it is asking of him.

Jimmy lets the darkness fill him.

Panel 4: CLOSE-UP OF CAIN'S HAND
Cain has grabbed hold of Jerry's hand. Cain's hand is large, rough, and stained with gore. In contrast, Jerry's hand is small, white, and unstained.

CAIN

"No. Reject the demon. Ask forgiveness."

CAPTION

"How deep is the sin that is beyond redemption?"

Jimmy spread his arms. He felt the thing inside him. The thing that *was* him. He could feel it moving inside him, creating the structures it needed, massing the energies. The air around him began to ripple with the heat coming off of his skin.

Inside the darkness he knows everything. On the other side of the darkness is a race that has been collecting knowledge for a century of centuries. The blackness, the hole that spun inside his soul, it is not oblivion. It is a passage. A doorway.

The body is nothing. Less than nothing. Bits of matter. What matters is what is inside his head. The information that makes him him. It is a doorway that he can pass, but his body cannot.

It no longer frightens him.

Panel 5: OVERHEAD SHOT OF CAIN HOLDING JERRY. The concrete of the courtyard is a hundred feet below Jerry's dangling legs. Cain is bent double over the railing, gripping Jerry's arm, staring down at the kid. The shadow of a helicopter can be seen on the ground beneath them. We are looking through a telescopic sight centered on Cain's head.

CAIN

"If you accept what you've done. If you ask God's mercy. You might keep your soul."

CAPTION

"Can a stain be so black that God is unwilling to forgive it?"

The light is too bright to look at. Silent flames ripple across Jimmy's metallic skin. Every radio within fifty yards screams static. The heat and light were only side effects of a narrow microwave beam that was shooting upward, carrying inside itself every fragment of data that lived within Jimmy's mind. The cement cracks under Jimmy's feet, the asphalt around him bubbles and melts.

Jimmy walks through the darkness.
He walks home.

Panel 6: MID SHOT SHOT OF CAIN
Cain is thrown back as a bullet slams into him from above. He has lost his grip on Jerry.

SFX

(Across the center of the panel)

CRACK!!!

"Are you there? Are you all right?"

Nate didn't answer the radio. He pushed himself up from where he had flattened himself against the roof. He was still somewhat dazzled by the light. Above him, the two helicopters still circled through the smoke. They swung spotlights around to focus on the area where Jimmy had stood.

PAGE 26: [FOUR PANELS]

Panel 1: OVERHEAD SHOT, JERRY FALLING
~~Jerry is in free fall between~~ the balcony of the clock tower and the courtyard. Cain has fallen to the floor of the balcony.

CAPTION

"I attempt to win free the souls that Baphomet has ensnared."

"Nate?"

Nate walked across the roof. The air was heavy with the smell of smoke, from the fire, and from where James Somerset had been standing. A fine ash filled the air, glittering in the light from the spotlights like an early snowfall.

Panel 2: CLOSE-UP OF JERRY FALLING
Jerry is tumbling. The pavement is a lot closer.

JERRY

"Please . . ."

CAPTION

"I try to win something for them I can't win for myself."

The asphalt surface of the roof adhered to Nate's boots as he walked toward what was left of James Somerset. It was only at this point where he had begun to think again. Up until now, all his mind had had room for was the scene that had played out in front of him.

Nate realized now that up until this moment, he hadn't truly believed. Some skeptical portion of his brain had held out for the possibility of a rational explanation.

But he had seen it now.

He also knew now that the driving force behind the last five years of his life was futile. There was no way to stop this . . .

Panel 3: LONG SHOT, GROUND LEVEL, JERRY HITTING
Jerry strikes the ground in the courtyard. There is a ring of cops and SWAT guys in the background.

SFX

(Under Jerry)

THUD!

CAPTION

"The problem is . . ."

"Nate! Are you there?"

"I'm here," Nate said. "It's over, he's dead."

At Nate's feet was Jimmy Somerset. The flesh wasn't

quite normal, even after the burning. It was black and charred, but in places it also seemed to have melted rather than burned. The skeletal structure that was visible through the cracked flesh was shiny and black, almost metallic. The smell that hung in the air over the corpse wasn't of burned flesh so much as a sour chemical smell.

For some reason, that smell was worse . . .

Panel 4: OVERHEAD SHOT OF JERRY
Jerry is on his back, ringed by a mass of police and SWAT guys. His eyes stare upward. We see the edge of the clock tower balcony, but Cain is gone.

JERRY

(Weak, dotted word balloon, a whisper)

". . . forgive me . . ."

CAPTION

". . . I never know if I win."

FIN.

Nate stared at Jimmy while the radio chattered on. He could hear the sirens of fire engines in the distance, and the spotlights left him as the helicopters turned away.

They were telling him to get out of the building.

It was probably good advice.

"They know, don't they?" Nate asked Jimmy. "They all know what they are and what they're doing. You just forgot for a while, didn't you?"

Nate stared at Jimmy's bare skull for a few moments longer, then he turned away and started walking.